A Small Part of Me

NOËLLE HARRISON was born in England and moved to Ireland in 1991. While based in Dublin in the early nineties she wrote and produced plays. She has won awards for her short stories and has written extensively on visual art in Ireland. Her first novel, *Beatrice*, was published in 2004. A new play, *The Good Sister*, premiered in Ireland in 2005. She lives in Oldcastle, County Meath, with her partner and their young son.

'Harrison is an intriguing and sensual writer,
confidently charting out her own distinctive territory'
Sunday Independent

'The search for redemption and the simple
heatbreaking love of a mother for her child imbues
this novel with echoes that you won't forget'
Irish Independent

Also by Noëlle Harrison

Beatrice

Noëlle Harrison

A Small Part of Me

PAN BOOKS

First published 2005 by Tivoli,
an imprint of Gill & Macmillan, Dublin

This paperback edition published 2007 by Pan Books
an imprint of Pan Macmillan Ltd
Pan Macmillan, 20 New Wharf Road, London N1 9RR
Basingstoke and Oxford
Associated companies throughout the world
www.panmacmillan.com

ISBN 978-0-330-46379-9

3 5 7 9 8 6 4

A CIP catalogue record for this book is available from
the British Library.

Printed and bound in the UK by
CPI Mackays, Chatham ME5 8TD

For my brother, Fintan
And for my mother, Claire, a small part of me

She is the song like river.
Her hair flows long, long time to the sea's opening.
She is wide-eyed; open-mouthed; a lonesome heart.

She is the song like river.
Her notes carry far, take me far, and push me down the
mountain.

She is the song which whispers,
'Spring showers patter like a tiny child's heart.'
She is breathless, fleeting, exquisite.

She is the song that started as it ought:
A tiny cluster, a blossom.
The song worked through her, and she let it let her go.
She glides downriver,
She sings from within,
I hear her.

The song remains.

She is the song…

In each moment is a choice.
D.A.

THE STORM

The day her mother left was the same day that the Reed family drowned in the river, all of them.

It is summer, close and sticky. Christina is six years and ten months old – nearly seven. She is wearing a cotton print dress and a blue and yellow sun hat. She has taken off her shoes and is dipping her toes in the stream. She is allowed to play here.

The flies buzz around her head and annoy her. She picks up a stick and bats it about but it makes no difference, and when she looks down she notices that the stick was muddy and her sundress is spotted with little dark dots all down the front. She whines but there's no one to cry in front of. She hates to get dirty.

The stream is another land. In the place where she likes to go, there is a little muddy trail down to the edge and on the other side a lovely big, leafy chestnut tree. It is cooler here and the leaves whisper above her head, playing with the sunlight and teasing her eyes. Christina is hot and she puts both of her feet completely in the water. She begins to go forward, sliding on the mossy stones and staggering across to the other side. The cold stream feels nice. She squeezes her toes, enjoying the soft, soily shore as she gets out on the bank. She squats down then and looks back at the way she has come. The reeds and cow parsley are so high she can only just see above them – a little bit of the lawn, the end of the bridge and their big grey house. The water tinkles in front of her and she spies several large stones, which will be perfect for her plan. She wants to build a bridge.

Christina stands up and starts pulling up a reed. It's sharp and tough and makes her hand sore. She groans with the effort. Finally she has four. She takes a reel of red cotton out of her dress pocket and a small pair of scissors she found in her mammy's room and lays out her four long green reeds.

Christina makes her family: Papa Reed, Mama Reed, Babby Reed and their Angeline. When she has to concentrate hard, Christina sticks out her tongue. Some of the children at school laugh at her when she does this, and once the music teacher made a joke about it and now she refuses to learn the piano. She can't help it. When she's working hard she forgets everything, even herself. This is why she doesn't hear her father calling and is shocked to see him when she looks up, standing on the other bank.

Christina, he says, will you come into the house?

I don't want to, Daddy. Look, look what I've made.

That's lovely, but I want you to come in now.

She looks up at him and squints because the sun is in her face. Why?

Behind him, coming across the lawn, is a figure in brown. She walks very slowly, and Christina believes she could be floating. It is her mother. And now, across the bridge, running, is Angeline, her shiny black hair swinging back and forth. As she reaches her mother, Christina thinks that her mammy looks like a queen and Angeline is her maid, so that means that she must be a princess. Christina twists the thread around Babby Reed one more time, then leans over and pats the earth with her hands.

I want to stay here and play, she says.

You have to come in, he says, and Christina senses something different in his voice, a note of something…urgent, dangerous. She stops what she's doing and stares at him. He leans across to her, his arm stretched out, his hand shaking.

No, leave her, Tomás, her mother says. Please, let's just leave her be.

Her daddy looks at Christina and then at her mother. She is tall today, long and thin, like one of the Reeds. And she smiles at Christina. It's a tiny smile, so you might not notice. Her lips move but her eyes say nothing.

Everything all right?

Angeline stands with her hands on her hips, panting from her run across the grass. She is in a bright yellow dress, like the sun, with green sandals and a green scarf in her hair. Her dark eyes sparkle.

I'm making some people, a family, Christina says.

Let's see.

In one bound, Angeline is across the stream and crouching down beside her. Christina explains.

This is Papa Reed and Mama Reed and Babby Reed. And this is Angeline.

Angeline laughs, and it feels like a tickle running down her side. An Angeline?

Yes, every family should have an Angeline.

It is then, when she looks at her sweet Angeline's face and nuzzles her, that she can see that her parents are gone. And there is a feeling of something left behind. It is the smell of overzealous weeds, their noxious odour on that distant, dream-like August afternoon; it is Christina's first smudge of guilt.

The sun slips behind a cloud, the stream runs dark and all the colours of Angeline fade.

Christina stands, and collecting up the Reeds, she carefully slides them into her pocket. I want to go in, she says.

Angeline frowns. I thought you wanted to make a bridge, she says.

I'm hungry. Christina chews her lip.

Okay, Angeline says, and she takes one big giant step back across the stream.

Are you going to jump it? she asks. She opens her arms wide and looks like a large yellow flower, swaying on the other side.

Christina shakes her head.

Go on, says Angeline, you can do it.

No. Christina twists her foot in the dirt.

Go on, girly, I know you can jump it!

Angeline waves for her to come and the sun darts back out, bouncing off her dress so that she looks like a large light just switched on.

She can catch me if I fall, Christina thinks, so she takes one big leap and she makes it. For one second she's extremely happy, but then she feels her pocket and she knows instantly what is wrong. The Reed family fell in.

The Reeds, she wails, and Angeline wades out into the stream but it's too late. Christina can see them, twirling around and around in the water, flushed downstream.

So they run alongside them then, right to the end of the garden, but it's no use. She has to wave goodbye as she sees them pulled into the big river, and then in a flash they go under, never to come back up again. Angeline puts her arm around her.

Never mind, darling, she says, you can make some more.

How? The Reeds were people. You can't make the same people twice.

Angeline knots their hands together. That's true, she says. Let's imagine they've gone somewhere better then – a miniature cloudland, at the very tippy top of the sky.

What's miniature?

Tiny.

Would it be nice there? Christina sniffs.

Just perfect, Angeline replies, quite beautiful, and imagine they are all together, no one got left behind.

When they go back in the house, it's quiet, just the tick of the clock and the sound of the river outside, two constants that never change. Angeline makes the tea and Christina sits at the big kitchen table cutting out her new paper doll and all her clothes.

Where's Mammy? she asks.

Out, says Angeline.

Where's Daddy?

Out too.

Christina stops her cutting and watches Angeline at the kitchen sink, her hands sheathed in gloves the same colour as her dress, her head bent over the bucket of potatoes as she peels them. The window is in front of her and Christina watches the dark clouds gather. She senses the hum in the air, and it makes her hair itchy.

Is it going to rain? she asks.

Angeline raises her head. Clever girl, she says, I think you're right. And pulling off her gloves, she says, Come on, quick, help me bring in the laundry.

They dash out back across the river, onto the grass, and pull the clothes off the line without even unclipping the pegs. Christina is excited. It's a race, they have to make it back inside before it rains. And they nearly win. She's just outside the back door as she feels the first hot drops on her head.

The sky turns black and the dog runs behind the sofa. Angeline switches on the lights and they stand at the window and wait for each sheet of lightning and then count for the thunder.

The storm is close, Angeline says, and as she speaks the lights go out. Christina giggles nervously.

Angeline opens the bottom press and pulls out some candles. They light more than they need, lace each shelf of the dresser with three candles each, each windowsill with two and four in a line on the kitchen table. Christina is afraid to leave the room. The kitchen is safe, filled with little pools of golden light, warmth, the smell of the food and the heart of the family. But if she went into the hall, the breeze of the storm would pass through her, chill her and make her think of scary stories.

They sit at either end of the kitchen table, Angeline and her, connected in silence, waiting for the storm to end, for someone to come home. Angeline smoothes her hair down with one hand and Christina can see wisps of it lift, like tiny electric charges in the static air. Her eyes are circles of comfort and Christina goes over to her and climbs on her lap. The rain whips against the glass panes, her heart beats fast.

It'll be over soon, Angeline whispers.

It's hard to remember a whole day as a child. Everything we were in that time has been broken up, still in us, but as tiny shards. We get confused. If we go back sometimes our memories are wrong. Things get mixed up.

Christina is sure of this, though. The day her mother left was the day the Reed family drowned. The very same one.

ATLANTIC

CHRISTINA

She drove straight there without thinking. It was habit. The house looked the same, although the garden could do with a tidy, and she noticed that Declan hadn't bothered to open the curtains in any of the bedrooms. That annoyed her.

Christina parked a little further down the lane, almost in a ditch. It would probably have been fine if she'd parked the car right outside the house. Their closest neighbours, the Healys, would be out at this time in the morning, but she didn't want to risk being seen, or worse still, getting caught.

She walked around the house twice. The row of evergreens swished behind her in the early morning breeze, the grass still sparkled with dew and she could hear the cattle lowing. The place had never seemed so nice.

She tried the door, but of course it was locked. It didn't matter because the downstairs bathroom window was open. She stumbled over the loose paving and pulled it back. There was still steam on the mirror and she was tempted to draw a face, but it was important that no one noticed she had been there. She couldn't leave any trace behind.

She slowly went up the stairs and into the bedrooms, each one dark, still holding her children's sleep. She sat on Johnny's bed and stared at all his football posters, rows of men lined up in green, the tribes she had never been able to understand. On his desk were a pile of history books and scribbled notes. He must have an exam today.

She opened his wardrobe and flicked through his clothes, but suddenly she felt sick. She couldn't take anything from here. What if Declan came home for lunch? What if he noticed?

She stood in the landing, swaying, her past and present converging. How had she lived in this house for seventeen years? It felt so empty.

She looked at her bedroom door, at Cian's toddler finger marks on the white gloss which she had never bothered to touch up. It was shut tight and she had no desire to open it, not now. Instead she turned to her right, pushed the door to Cian's room open and was surprised to see how tidy it was. There on the floor was the little wooden train set Santa had brought the Christmas before last, and on the walls hung all of his puppets, their bright smiling faces nodding at her. His bed was still crumpled and she bent over it, smoothing the duvet, lifting up the pillow and pressing it to her face. She could still smell his hair. The crack in her heart deepened. Wounded, she opened his drawers, pulling shorts and T-shirts out from the back, stuffing them into her carrier bag.

Christina tore herself down the landing. She could still hear the echo of her children as they left the house that morning. She stopped then, gripped the top of the banisters and sighed heavily; she could feel the well of her regret deepen. How could she have let this happen?

With one foot on the top stair, she glanced back, and it was only then that a thought occurred to her. She needed some memories to keep her sane. Just a few pictures would do.

Christina pulled down the loft ladder and climbed up into the attic. It didn't take her long to find the photo albums; a pile of them had been stacked in a small green box. She put them in the carrier along with Cian's clothes and was turning to go back down when she saw it.

The sewing box.

It was hers. She had every right to take it.

10

CIAN

Daddy is shaking him. He squeezes his eyes tight, but it's no good.

'Come on, Cian, up you get,' he says.

Cian rolls onto his tummy and then pushes up. He twists his body so he's sitting and looks around. He's in his own bed. When Mammy was there he always went across to her and snuggled in the bed with her. She was so soft.

But now she's gone, and Daddy doesn't like it when he does that. He just carries him across the landing and puts him back in his own bed, which would be cold. So now when he wakes in the night, and he always does, he just hangs onto Paddington and as many of the others that he can feel around him – Ludwig the badger, Aunt Lucy, Batty Barry and Billy Moose.

Cian rubs his eyes and slowly walks out of his room and down the stairs, clutching onto Paddington. The telly is already on – Johnny is watching *Rescue Heroes*. Cool. Cian likes it in the mornings because Johnny lets him watch his cartoons, not boring teenage programmes like after school.

'Hiya bro,' Johnny says, pushing the cereal box over to Cian. He has to pour his own now, and there's only cold milk. Mammy always makes it with warm milk, but he doesn't say anything any more because it makes Daddy and Johnny mad. Sometimes Cian thinks that they both hate her, especially his brother. No one tells him why. And if he asks, no one tells him anything anyway – only his granny said something. Why does my Mammy have to live somewhere else,

11

on her own? he had asked her, and Granny had said, She's not able to look after you properly, Cian.

But why?

His granny wouldn't answer him then, and instead she gave him five euro to spend in Sheila's shop. He hadn't forgotten, though. He wanted to know why.

He said to his daddy that he wanted to live with Mammy, but his daddy told him the judge said no, and you always have to do what the judge says.

Daddy is running around. He's talking on his phone and pulling clothes off the hanger over the stove, smoking at the same time. Like a juggler, Cian thinks. My daddy is like a clown. That's what he wants to be when he grows up. But Daddy's job is very important – he buys and sells horses and he's always on the phone. Everyone has a phone except him. He showed Daddy his new coat, which has a special pocket inside it just for your mobile, and told him he had to have a phone now. But Daddy just laughed at him. It's not fair, Cian had said, Johnny has one. And Daddy said that when he was seventeen and doing his Leaving Cert, he could have one too. That was ages away. He was only six. He wasn't even sure how many years that was.

Johnny is out the door now. He has a lift to school. Daddy shouts out good luck as he gets into the big blue car. Johnny has an exam. Daddy said that if Johnny did well he would buy tickets for them all to go to the next Meath match. Football's boring, but Daddy and Johnny think it's great. Daddy says he has to do the GAA summer camp this year, but he'd rather stay at home, watch telly and play with his toys.

Cian goes back into his room to get dressed. He used to let Daddy do it, but he got so angry and shouted at him if he moved that he does it himself now. Mammy used to dress him while he watched telly. One moment he was in his jammies and the next all ready for school. That was great.

12

How many weeks was it since she had gone? It felt like ages.

Daddy is calling to him. 'Come on, Cian, we'd better go.'

He places Paddington back under the covers – poor Paddington is sick today – and picks up his school bag. Daddy is standing by the back door. His hair is sticking up like a hedgehog and his skin is all prickly on his face.

'What day is it, Daddy?' Cian asks.

'It's Friday.'

'Is that the day before the weekend?'

'Yes.'

'So am I seeing Mammy tonight? Am I staying with her? Does the judge say I can?'

'Yes, you are. And I say you can. It's up to me now.' Daddy sounds cross.

Cian is smiling because he knows that Mammy will be meeting him after school. He tries to hide his face from Daddy. He looks down and sees a little green thing on the road.

'A frog!' he squeals, bending down and picking it up. 'Can I bring it to school? Please, please, please? Can I show my friends? Please, Daddy?'

'Don't be ridiculous, Cian, of course you can't. Come on, throw it away, you're going to be late.'

Throw it away! Mammy wouldn't say that. She wouldn't let him keep it either, but she'd make him find a little leaf somewhere and put him down, gently, very slowly. He looks around, hunting for a leaf.

'For God's sake!' Daddy is in the car, hollering from the window. Cian panics and throws his little friend. He sees the small green thing flying through the air, and says, 'Oh sorry, sorry, sorry!', hoping he doesn't break his bones.

13

CHRISTINA

It was a beautiful article, her mother's sewing box.

Made out of mahogany with little brass handles on each side, the box was a perfect cube. Christina opened the little door. There were four rows of drawers, two drawers to each row, except the bottom one, which was one big drawer. She had never used it. Angeline gave it to her years ago, just after she got married. But she had been so caught up in her new life as a young wife that she had completely forgotten about it and shoved it in the attic. At the time she hadn't wanted to think about her mother or be reminded of her in any way, even if it was only through her sewing box.

The box probably hadn't been opened since her mother had last used it, because Angeline certainly never sewed – she had always sent stuff out to Mae Cassidy, from socks to curtains.

Christina nervously fingered the outside of the box. To think that her mother had probably been the last person to touch its contents. She shook herself angrily.

What did she expect, for her to come popping out?

She impatiently pulled open the first drawer to find several packets of ancient snap fasteners, one of them with *War Time Pack/Guaranteed Rustless* written on the back. The sewing box was older than she thought. It must have belonged to her mother's mother.

In the next drawer was a little doll made out of tiny coloured beads. Mainie. Christina remembered that little doll. Her mother had

14

made it for her. She picked it up and twisted it between her fingers, letting it drop on the floor.

In the third drawer there was a thick plastic needle case with a picture of a yellow rose on it and the lettering *Rose of England Needlecase*. She opened it up and pulled out one long needle.

The fourth, fifth and sixth drawers were full of reels of cotton, some really old wooden reels and some more recent plastic ones. Each drawer was a spectrum of colour, with bits and bobs of elastic, tiny pin cushions and one or two thimbles.

One reel was strange. It was wooden, not plastic, and the biggest by far. Wound around it was hair, not thread – human hair. And it wasn't just from one head. There was a strong black shiny strand like horsehair, a delicate line of red hair and then a soft brown piece. They were all knotted together to make one long multi-coloured thread. Christina pulled it through her fingers. A part of her wanted to snap it off.

There was only one drawer left – the large one at the bottom. Christina opened it. It was empty apart from a round metal box. She pulled it out and flipped up the lid. A hundred buttons came cascading out, none of them matching. She remembered playing with these, the exotic buttons made from shells and pearls, and then the treasure trove ones, small round coins of silver. She fingered each one and then slowly put them back in the box.

That was it then. But as she pushed the button box back into the drawer, she could see something else right at the back: a curl of thick paper.

It was a photograph. Christina pulled it out. It was creased, as if someone had held it many times. Some of the black and white detail was lost in the folds, but the image was still strong. It was a picture of her as a little girl. She was standing next to a large snowman, grinning broadly, with a wool hat on her head and mittens on her hands. And next to her wasn't her father or Angeline – next to her

15

was her mother. She was a tall, thin woman with long ginger hair. She was smiling too. She was holding her hand.

Christina started. A pulse passed through her body and she fell back on her heels, knocking her bag over. She had never seen a photograph of her mother. She turned the picture over.

Greta and Christina, January 1976

It was written in her father's handwriting. She flipped the image over again and stared at the stranger in the snow, her own flesh and blood. She let the picture drop, brushed the tears from her eyes and looked up at the skylight in the attic. The wind was chasing clouds across the sky, hiding the sun. She pulled herself straight, and leaned over in the near-dark. The roof of the attic pressed in on top of her head, the wooden boards pounded in her ears, as she picked the photograph up off the dusty floor. It was then that she noticed the needle sticking out of the top of her middle finger. She had felt nothing. A tiny bead of red dripped onto the white print.

Greta and Christina, January 1976

That was the year she'd left.

GRETA

It's another sparkling winter morning, so bright it almost hurts the eyes, and I'm in conversation with my tree. He's so bare now, hardly a leaf on him. He looks like a big shaggy mound of twigs. I'm sitting huddled beneath him. It's so very chilly here and I shan't stay too long, but I have come to tell him something.

I'm pregnant.

Yes, it's official. I went to Doctor Marsh on Monday and he told me I'm pregnant! At last, after trying for six years, I'm expecting again!

Tomás is very pleased. I haven't seen him this happy in a long time. He didn't have to say anything. It was what he did that told me. He drove me home from the surgery, holding my hand the whole way, one hand on the steering wheel, humming a little song.

We've decided not to tell Christina yet, just in case anything goes wrong, which, please God, it won't. She asked Santa for a baby brother so now, hopefully, her wish will come true. I know Tomás would like to have a son, but as long as the baby is healthy I don't care. Just as long as everything is as it should be.

I can see a red fox darting across the field, a flash of colour against the white sky. Last night I heard her howl, making her love call. I could recognise that desperation, its piercing shrill, the need to create, to be a mother again.

I had begun to think that we would never have another child.

CHRISTINA

Christina stumbled back down the lane. The sewing box was heavy and she had to carry it with both hands, her carrier bag slung on one of her wrists. By the time she shoved the box onto the back seat of the car she was out of breath and her shoulders hurt.

As she drove around the potholes she prayed that no one would be coming the other way. She could see one of the Healy boys on a tractor on the far side of the bog, but he was too far away to mind her. Back on the main road she relaxed a little, then sped up. She went past the old cemetery and small green fields undulated by her, the odd one marked by a fairy hawthorn tree or a single standing stone, each small patch separated by soft grey walls.

She was on the lake road when she suddenly pulled in. She leaned back, stared at the sewing box, then whipped around again as if stung, looking out at the sheer blue lake. The sun had come back out and the light was almost blinding. The sky was white and glaring.

Only last summer – it seemed an age ago now – they'd had a barbeque here. Declan had organised it for her birthday; it had been a surprise. And she *had* been surprised. He had never done anything like that before.

Although it had been July, they had all shivered by the side of the lake as a cold wind whipped about them. Quite a few had turned up, mostly Declan's friends, but still, it had been nice. She remembered that, and feeling vaguely guilty that she wasn't more thrilled, that she didn't talk enough. In the end she had sat on a log,

18

gazing into the fire, drinking beer and listening to all the others singing songs.

She had got drunk.

And when they got home that night, she had laid down on the hall floor sobbing, accusing Declan of letting her drink when he shouldn't have. He had begged her with urgent whispers to get up, be quiet, saying the children would hear her. But she had been unable to move and continued to berate him until in the end he had given up, put a blanket over her and gone to bed. She woke the next morning with her eldest, Johnny, staring down at her, his lips curled in distaste.

It was hot in the car and she suddenly yearned to get into the water. She got out, climbed the gate and walked down the gravel path, passing grazing horses, smelling the crisp morning air.

Down by the water's edge, the flies buzzed around her. The brambles were thick, the gorse yellow and prickly. Light bounced off the lake's surface, dappling a metal water barrel half sunk on the shore. Beside it a large twisted white stick protruded out of the water, looking like a solitary ghost heron. She crouched down behind a large ash tree, took off her dress and sandals, folded it neatly and then, in her underwear, waddled towards the lake over the parched stones.

The water was low. It had been a dry spring. She avoided the sticky shore and followed a path of paving slabs until icy water lapped around her ankles. She let herself fall forwards then, straight in.

The water soothed the ache in her heart, the desperate pull she felt as a mother. She swam in a circle, plunging her head beneath the surface again and again, as if she needed to wake up. When she tried to put her feet down there was nothing solid to stand on, just a swirl of muddy bed and weeds, so she immersed herself in the freezing water and swam further, out by the diving board. She was tempted to go out even further, but knew she couldn't. There were currents out there that could suck you down in an instant.

Losing her children was like drowning. Sometimes she would find herself gagging, as if she was being suffocated, her throat dry right to the back of it. It felt unnatural to be on her own after being a mother for seventeen years. It wasn't right.

Yet her own mother had done it to her. She had only been six when she left one day, not a word to her, just gone.

Christina shivered in the water and slowly turned towards the shore. The stones were smooth and slippery beneath her feet as she tried to keep her balance, stumbling onto the grass verge. She could hear the hum of a distant car, but apart from that there was no one about. A lumpy hill faced her – they called it the Noggin – and she could see a lone cow stuck on its top. The lake was an oval pool of blue, a drop of silence, pure space in the place where she lived, where the hills were so low they could hardly pull you skyward and the small, uneven fields closed in around you. She sighed, shook out her wet hair and walked up the bank a small way, sitting down to let herself drip onto the grass.

She just wanted to come home to herself, even if it meant she would have to go on the longest journey of her life.

GRETA

I remember now how you change when you're pregnant. The dreams that come in the night, like dense fog, so hard to lift the next day that I could sit for hours here, on the windowsill in the landing, staring at the brown river, swollen and churning beneath me, listening to the sound of the water cascade, the rhythm of the mill. I slow down and nothing is urgent any more. I can hardly believe it as I look out at the view: the wooden bridge across the river, the stretch of garden, the ditch with the stream and the fields beyond. Even the woods at the top – all this I am mistress of.

We never owned our own land, not even a house. Daddy thought it was more important to spend money on our education. Maureen always said it was my fault that we were sent away to boarding school. I was father's favourite and she said he always did what I asked. I don't remember asking for that, though. Grateful as I am, I would rather have been at home with my precious father.

Dear Lord, keep my father safe and by your side, and my mother too. Forgive their sins, and let them rest in heaven. Guide me. Show me their souls, two twin stars on a winter's night, watching over me and my family, my unborn child. In the name of the father, the son and the Holy Ghost. Amen.

I like to make up my own prayers. It's my poetry, my way of not feeling lonely.

And it can be lonely here sometimes at The Mill. When I was at school I was surrounded by other girls. There was always someone

21

about to sit and have a talk with. But when you're a wife, there's no time for talking. You have to look after your family, and they are your priority.

Oh, but to be part of a family again! When I lost Mummy and Daddy, I felt so alone. Even though Maureen was there, it didn't make us any closer. I used to spend hours trying to make sense of it all. How could they be taken away so suddenly? But maybe that happens when people are special. And I'm glad they went together, that one wasn't left without the other.

I like the animals here, and I think that Tomás is pleased at the way I look after the chickens. We have good eggs, and always plenty of them. And I can understand him when he talks about the cattle and we discuss whether we should move into pigs, but I told him that I didn't like the idea of that, not at all. It's not just the smell of them, but whenever I see those poor pigs crushed into the lorries on the way to the knacker's yard, I can't help feeling awfully sorry for them. I don't think I could live with such accusation! Tomás says there's money in it, but he listens to me, and for the moment he's not changing anything.

I've learned to make jam. Well, a sticky, runny mess at least. But I do think that my cooking is improving. Tomás scratches his head sometimes and can't work out why it takes me so long to do anything in the house. I suppose, he says, smiling, it's because I've had the fortune to marry one of nature's ladies! You're living in the wrong century, my darling, and should have a couple of servants. I look at him uncertainly then, because I'm worried that this is a criticism, but he always takes me in his arms and touches my hands delicately and says he's sorry about the life I have to live, and how it's making my hands rough. It was your hands I fell in love with first, he says.

He reminds me of that day in the church. My parents were dead just two weeks and I had come to live with Aunt Shirley. It was Saint

22

Blaise's day, the first week in February, and the church was freezing. I didn't know that I was standing next to Tomás, shivering, as the priest went along the line, blessing our throats, two candles in his hands, crossed beneath each chin. I didn't see Tomás, but he saw me, or my hands, that is. Pressed together in prayer and then opening, fluttering with cold, like a tiny white butterfly, he says.

He pursued me, and I was happy for the attention. It distracted me from my grief. My Aunt Shirley was constantly criticising me, calling me a plain Jane, like my mother, she said, which of course upset me, and then Maureen went to America. I didn't want to go with her. What would I be doing in America? But mostly I didn't want to go because someone had to stay behind to look after the graves.

At first I didn't notice Tomás. I was too preoccupied by my loss. But then, sometimes after church, I would see this young man with curly hair that refused to stay down although you could see a gallon of grease on it! He had kind eyes and he was very tall. To me he felt nearly as tall as a tree. And then one week he came up to me and held out his hand to introduce himself – Tomás Comyn, he said. He sounded like a character in a book by Thomas Hardy, and I squirmed with pleasure as Aunt Shirley looked stiffly on. The next week he did the same thing, then on the third week he asked me if I was going out on Friday night, as there was a dinner dance in aid of the hunt. I had said nothing and felt the colour rising in my cheeks. He rephrased his sentence and asked me if I would like to go to the dance with him, and I whispered yes, still looking at the ground.

Aunt Shirley called Tomás an oaf. She was against us but before long we were going steady, and three months later we were engaged. I didn't just do it to spite her, of course. I had fallen in love. I'm still in love with my husband.

Tomás drove me all the way to Boyle twice a month and helped me pull out the weeds on my parents' grave. Then he taught me to

23

drive and let me use his car so that I could go on my own. Tomás told me I was beautiful. He said that I was a true redhead, not like Aunt Shirley, who called me as ginger as the cat. Tomás said I was a pure Celt, with pale skin and green eyes, and he even loved my freckles, begging me not to conceal them any more.

Tomás has saved me from my brooding. The only way to deal with grief is to keep busy. He has filled my life with activity – a farmer's wife always has work to do!

It's only in the woods that I have time for my thoughts. I talk out loud to the trees. If he saw me he might think I was barking mad, but these conversations are precious to me, a tiny oasis of peace in my busy life.

I'm not even sure to whom I'm talking. God? My father? My unborn child?

CHRISTINA

The midday sun gradually crept across the floorboards, yet Christina remained curled up in the foetal position in Helen's old bed, looking at the faded photograph on the pillow beside her. She traced her finger yet again over the tall, ghostly figure of her mother, a silhouette against the snow. Did she look like her?

A blaze of sunlight illuminated the room, distracting her, and Christina looked at the old cobwebs hanging from the ceiling and the dust on the floor. She had never cleaned this place. It was just as Helen had left it. It still smelled faintly of her. Helen used Ponds coconut butter, like Angeline used to. It brought a sense of the familiar to her strange bedroom in the stone cottage two miles down a rutted bog road, five miles west of Oldcastle. This was where she lived now – in her cousin's discarded house.

She slowly clambered out of the bed, naked, and opened the skylight. A warm breeze touched her. It really was quite hot.

She picked up her dress but it was still damp from the lake, so instead she took a giant cardigan from the wardrobe and wrapped it around her.

She glanced at herself in the mirror. Helen had loads of these things – big, men-sized woollies, probably belonging to her husband. Christina liked them and the way they made her feel – tiny and feline. She never wore stuff like this at home. For a start she never slept naked because Cian always got into the bed with her in the middle of the night, and it didn't seem appropriate.

25

Cian.

His name choked her. The last time she'd seen him was Sunday night when she had dropped him home. She pressed her thumb into her palm as if she could conjure up his little hand and its warm trust inside hers as she led him up to the door. He never questioned it now and had stopped asking her why she didn't come home. He was a clever little boy, her boy, and she felt that he could sense her distress.

He still loved her.

But maybe one day he wouldn't. Maybe he might learn to hate her too, like Johnny. Things had never been easy with Johnny, but when he saw her now he looked as if he wanted to spit in her face.

Christina ran her hands through her hair, pulling the curls until they hurt. She could feel her body trembling, the dryness in her throat, the fear.

She walked over to the window and opened it wide. The land spread quietly before her and she couldn't see a single soul. She watched three tiny rabbits as they hopped across the field, each one pausing in relay to sit up like little statues. A fuchsia bush dripped pink and mauve bells, each flower looking extravagant against the dour yard wall. A long-tailed rat dashed into the hedgerow and she could hear the chatter of the birds as it disturbed them. In the distance she could hear a lone car speeding along the main road.

The world kept on turning, and she could hide from it no longer.

GRETA

It snowed last night, and everything was covered by a couple of inches of pure white bliss. This morning Christina and I ran whooping out into the garden, with Tomás running behind us shouting at me to be careful not to slip on the ice. Then the three of us built the most fantastic snowman I've ever seen. It was so good that we took photographs of it. The snowman was nearly twice the height of little Christina. He was, of course, big and round and we dressed him up in an old gardening hat of Jim's, a pair of rubber gloves and a big orange carrot for his nose.

Afterwards we were very cold indeed, so while Tomás stoked up the fire I made hot chocolate and tried to bake some scones; a disaster as usual. Tomás keeps asking me to get a cook or someone to help in the house, but I would feel like I've failed him if we did that. I just have to keep on trying. Poor man, I suppose he's used to my cooking by now. Christina ate up anyway. I let her dip the scones in golden syrup and then she was all sticky like a little munchkin.

Later we took down the Christmas tree, which always makes me a little sad. When you're packing up those decorations Christmas seems so far away again. To think that this time next year there will be a new addition to the family. The baby will be just over three months old then. It's hard to believe. I put my hand on my stomach and I can feel nothing in there. It's so tiny now, little more than a seed. Yet I feel different, in my mind.

Will it change things with Christina? I don't think so. How could it? The baby will bring us all closer together, make us more of a family.

I laid hands on Christina tonight. She said her head ached and her little cheeks were so flushed. It was all the excitement, running in and out of the house in the snow. Tomás doesn't like me to do this because he says that if people knew, well, they'd all be knocking on our door. Tomás is a very private man. My daddy told me I have a gift from God. He said it was because I was born on Good Friday. I don't know where my talent comes from, but when I see my little one in pain, I need to take it away, so if I can, I will.

CHRISTINA

She and Declan had thought they were Romeo and Juliet, so keen were they to flaunt their parents' rulings. As neighbours, Declan's father and Christina's daddy had had a long-standing feud about fences. Declan's father's cattle destroyed them and got onto their land, and then there was the fight over who was responsible for repairs and were they in good order in the first place and so on so that over the years the argument had mushroomed to proportions of complete non-communication between the two families. It was against this background that Declan and Christina had sought each other out in the schoolyard, both of them wilful teenagers. And it was by the lake they would meet, even in winter, where they explored each other's bodies, tucked beneath the gorse bushes so that no one would see them, the pain of a few loose prickles on the skin so worth it. Somehow they kept their clothes on, but one day, before they could stop each other, it had happened. Somehow he had slipped inside her. Was that the day Johnny had been conceived? If not, it hadn't been long after.

Christina sighed. What fools they had been. They had still been at school, just kids. Johnny's age.

Theirs had been a proper shotgun wedding and an uneasy truce between the two families, her father grimacing as he welcomed Declan into the family.

Their wedding day had been a drunken one. The tension in the church and at the reception made everyone drink too much, even

Angeline. She had been against it, the only one of the 'adults' who had advised her not to get married, telling Christina that she was throwing her life away, that she had alternatives.

Christina had been annoyed with her stepmother then, maybe because deep down she knew she was right. But for the moment, she and Declan were delighted with themselves. No more hiding, no more prickly sessions under the gorse bushes, shivering on the damp grass. What did Angeline know of the world anyway? As far as Christina could remember she had always been there, in the house, first as their housekeeper and then later on becoming her stepmother. How could she have helped her, really? She'd had no alternative. And look what they had done – hadn't they brought an end to that ridiculous feud? Wasn't their love going to last forever?

Declan was a hard worker. Those first few months he'd worked morning, noon and night, a lackey for her father. He'd had dreams of his own, but he ignored them and kept on slogging, taking all of her father's impatience and contrariness on board. Declan had wanted the best for her and the baby.

Overnight he became a man.

But he left something behind, his old skin, like a suit of clothes lying on the bank by the lake, a place he had no time to go to any more. The laughing boy full of kisses and surprises was gone. The man who stood before her was different. He had a similar face, but the eyes were lighter blue, more drained, and his chin was hard.

She had still been a child.

She danced around Declan, trying to make him smile, and when he didn't, or wouldn't, or couldn't eat the food she made him because he was too tired, she behaved like a baby, hurling herself on the bed, clutching her hideous bump and crying loudly until he came, sat down beside her and put a limp hand on her shoulder, until she could feel the weight of him, his sadness, his entrapment.

It had terrified her.

She closed her eyes, and for a moment saw Declan as he had been – too thin for his morning suit, like a child in fancy dress, a grin on him like the cat that got the cream. That had been nearly eighteen years ago now. To think they had lasted that long.

'Chrissie?' came a voice outside.

Christina snapped up the blind on the kitchen window. It was well after noon.

'Chrissie, it's me, Padraig. You told me to come.'

She had forgotten. She slowly walked across the kitchen floor, her cold soles peeling off each chill tile, and unlatched the door.

'Jesus, Chrissie, are you not even dressed yet?'

'So what? I've been busy.' She walked over to the counter and flicked on the kettle.

Padraig stood behind her. She could sense him appraising her.

'I always said you had great legs,' he said, 'for someone your age.'

'Jesus, Paddy, I'm only thirty-four!'

'Ah, you should see Dee's – she's them veiny things already.'

'Lovely, Paddy, I really want to know about your wife's legs.'

'Sorry.' He looked crestfallen. He was such an eejit, really, but handsome.

Padraig smiled at her sheepishly. She had always noticed how good his teeth were. He never smoked and his smile benefited from it, with his two rows of perfect white teeth.

'I brought it, so,' he said, throwing down a brown envelope on the kitchen table.

'Thanks, Paddy.' She picked the envelope up and took out some notes.

'It's a grand,' he announced proudly.

'Are you sure that's not too much?' she said, stuffing the money back into the envelope and leaving it on the table.

'Well, I wasn't so sure last week when you asked me. But now that we can move some of the cattle around, things are getting better.'

31

Paddy scratched his head and smiled at her.

'I'll pay you back, every penny.'

She spooned some instant coffee into her mug and took out a fresh one for Paddy.

'What do you need it for, Chrissie?' Padraig asked as she poured boiling water into the mugs.

'I can't tell you.' She handed him his drink, not daring to look him in the eye.

'You're all right, aren't you?' He lifted her chin with his finger, trying to look at her.

She sighed, shaking her head and still not catching his eyes. 'Yeah, I'm okay,' she said, then moving away from him, added, 'I'm just missing my boys.'

'I said it was too harsh. I can't believe you lost them.'

She sat down and smiled sadly, looking at the black and white tiles. 'Ah, Paddy...' He stood tall in front of her. She wished she could be him, so sure of himself. 'You're a good man, Paddy,' she said, sipping her coffee.

He smirked.

'What's so funny?' she asked.

'I can see your nipples poking out through the wool. They're hard.' He bent down and touched one with his fingertip.

She pushed him away, reddening. 'I have to get dressed.'

'Come on, Chrissie, we haven't done it in months.'

'I told you, it's over.' She crossed her legs and wrapped the giant cardigan tighter about her.

'Yeah, but that was because of the case. Now it doesn't matter. Sure, who's going to know?' He grinned at her with his bright, wide smile.

'No, Paddy. I don't want to.'

He looked at her for a second, but she turned away and watched a fat bee banging against the windowpane. He coughed and when she swivelled around again, he was no longer smiling.

'Right so,' he said stiffly, picking up the envelope.

'What are you doing?' Her face dropped in horror.

'Well, if you can't help me out, maybe I can't help you. You know that Dee won't let me touch her any more.'

'Why don't you force yourself on your wife then? It's her duty, not mine.' She spat out the words like a slap.

Padraig came close, his blue eyes steely. 'Jesus, you've been drinking already. It's not long past midday and you're pissed. Look at yourself, Chrissie.'

'No, I'm not.'

'I'll be seeing you.' He made for the door, the envelope in his hand. She needed that money.

'Wait!'

That first time Paddy had actually cried. They had been in his jeep and he had pulled in off the road. They had sex there and then. It had been hot and crazy, fast and passionate, and afterwards Paddy had sobbed on her shoulder, confessing that Dee hadn't let him touch her in two years, begging her not to tell anyone, while a floodgate opened in the small of her back and she felt like a torrent of hurt was released.

It was only a temporary feeling, but completely addictive, and that's why she had continued sleeping with Paddy. To get that hit, to feel that someone cared.

He came over now in one big step, pushed the cardigan off her shoulders and lifted her up. With the other hand he cleared the table. The jar of coffee wobbled on the edge and then crashed onto the tiled floor.

She bit into his neck, trying to summon herself from the past, when just to stand next to him made her feel tight and hot. He was on top of her and the table was hard and unyielding on her back. It was all very uncomfortable.

33

She closed her eyes and made a picture in her head. She could see herself running through a meadow with high, long grass and waving trees in a ring around her. It was a nice feeling, her thoughts; they were more real than the sex.

'Oh, baby,' Paddy said, his voice intruding. When she opened her eyes his face was all squeezed shut, with his chin in the air. She felt sorry for him. He was only lonely too.

He came, lay on her for only a second and then sat up, pulling her with him. He picked up the cardigan and wrapped it around her, kissing her gently on the lips. He tasted of the land, salty and dense.

'Thank you,' he whispered. He handed her the envelope. 'I'll call tomorrow,' he said.

'I've got Cian,' she replied, getting a dustpan from under the sink and bending down to sweep up the broken jar of coffee.

'Sunday then,' he said. 'I'll come Sunday night, after McGintys, on my way home.'

'Okay.' She tipped the broken glass into the bucket.

He ambled to the door and, turning before he went, said, 'You know, Chrissie, I thought I was in love with you once. Last Christmas I think I might have left Dee for you.'

Christina shook her head. 'No you wouldn't have, Paddy.'

'Well, we'll never know now,' he smiled softly. He walked back towards her and reached out his hand to touch her face, but she stepped back. She could smell the bitter scent of coffee.

'Bye, Paddy,' she said and quickly walked out of the kitchen and up the stairs, before he could say something else.

In the bedroom Christina stood still, listening to his jeep drive off. She picked up the picture of Johnny and Cian on her bedside locker. Johnny was fifteen in it, and Cian was four. It had been taken the time they all went to Waterworld, and the two boys were standing in the queue outside. They both had baseball caps on and were grinning broadly.

She remembered that afternoon. It was just after she and Declan had had a terrible row. She didn't even remember why they'd been arguing, just the row itself, the venom, and throwing herself into it, not even caring that the kids were in the car with them, sitting behind them, frozen and tearful. Declan had been driving across a moor and the rain was lashing on the windscreen. He had swerved off the road and skidded to a halt, jumping out of the car and stomping to a reservoir. Then he had just stripped off and dived into the freezing water. The kids had piled out of the car, delighted at the diversion, laughing and roaring at their father.

She picked up the photograph of the children and stared at it, the tears welling.

That was when she should have left. If only she had taken the boys right there and then, everybody would have been on her side.

But instead she let it fester. Her husband no longer wanted her. And it was like her mother walking out on her all over again.

GRETA

I don't know why they call it morning sickness, for me it's all day sickness. It's all I can do to keep a glass of Seven-Up down. Poor Tomás has had to buy up bottles and bottles of it and packets of Tuc biscuits – that's all I want to eat. At least it's not jellied eels or something. We still haven't told Christina, too early yet, or anyone else in the family. We've decided to wait twelve weeks first and then it should be safe enough. Tomás has been so good, treating me like a princess and looking after Christina, making her breakfast and taking her to school. I'm so lucky to have him.

He made Christina a bird table, and every day she and I put out some bread crumbs and a little dish of water. Then we watch them from the kitchen window. The robin is always the first, so cheeky! Christina still believes that he'll tell Santa on her if she isn't good! She's such a dear. Then the tits come, mostly coal tits or great tits, not many of the little ones. Lots of sparrows. They're so bold and come very close to the glass. Sometimes I think they can see us. We hate it when the crows come, because they scare all the little ones away. Christina runs out the back door yelling at them to go away and flapping her arms as if she could take off and chase them. I've told her that we'll get special little nets full of seeds, which the big birds can't get at.

This world is a miracle. It surprises me when other people forget that, or have no time to look at the simple things, like a fat red robin pecking in the ice.

The snowdrops are out. Myself and Christina went for a walk after school and picked some. Today is St Brigid's day, the patron saint of mothers, so in her honour I made a little altar for her. I got Christina to help me. We took out the little coffee table in the corner of the sitting room and we placed my best white linen tea towel on it and the snowdrops and a bowl of milk for St Brigid.

Let the snowdrops purify my heart, and the milk nourish me. As you are a mother, enrich my soul, dear Brigid, and bring me into the fold. Holy Brigid, hear my prayer.

I forgot to take the altar apart and when Tomás came in he looked at me oddly and asked me what I was doing. When I told him he said I was wrong, that a good Christian would never put a bowl of milk out for Brigid. He told me that what I was doing was a pagan tradition.

My mother used to do it.

Still, I poured the milk down the sink because he looked displeased, and I don't like it when he's in that mood.

CHRISTINA

Christina lined up what was left on the kitchen counter – half a loaf of brown soda bread, a small amount of honey, one banana and a bag of dates. That should be fine. Cian liked all those things. Glancing at the clock, she took a knife out of the drawer and made a couple of banana sandwiches using the honey as a spread instead of butter. She was unable to think about herself, all desire to eat gone.

She used to love cooking. Food had been such a big part of her childhood, and she had always watched Angeline when she prepared the meals. She had learned many recipes from her and the way of doing things, not just the ingredients. In time, she understood that for food to taste good it had to be handled with care, prepared with love. That was what she had hoped to nourish her family with.

But Declan liked plain food. In the beginning he tried to eat what she made, but in the end he told her it was all a little too exotic – even garlic tasted strange to him – and so she had given in and made the usual – Irish stew, spuds and cabbage, the Sunday roast. Cooking was no longer creative, but a chore.

She licked her fingers, sticky with honey and crumbs, and caught sight of a small spore of mould on the crust. Without thinking, she gathered up the sandwiches, took them out into the yard and threw them in the bin. The crows rose out of the trees, cawing with excitement.

There had been good times too. Family meals when she had proudly produced something a little different, and Declan had done his best and the children had eaten well. They had all loved spaghetti bolognese. That was something they'd eat on a Saturday night, after they'd got home from shopping in Mullingar. She and Declan would share a bottle of red wine (two as time went on) and they would all squeeze up on the couch and watch the Big, Big Movie on TV. She had been happy then, anaesthetised by the wine, warm and cosy, with Cian curled around her, so tight she could feel the beat of his heart.

Christina paused on the edge of the cool yard, watching the shadows of the crows as they landed and alighted, scavenging for crumbs. She stood as still as a stone pillar, black wings flapping around her, alone in a crowd. She touched her face, her cool cheeks, her dry mouth and quick, hot breaths.

Could she really be about to do this? She wasn't at all sure that it was the right thing to do, but she couldn't stay here, transfixed. The blood rushed to her head and she pressed her hand on her forehead. She had to keep moving. It was impossible to think.

One scraggy crow followed her all the way to the back door. She stamped her foot but he didn't move. He held her with his unflinching shiny black eyes, as if it was a challenge.

GRETA

I can't help feeling a little sad. Nothing is wrong. Oh, I'm just being silly!

I suppose I'm still a little upset with Tomás over Brigid's Day, and then only yesterday he said that he couldn't eat the dinner I gave him. He said the steak was like a piece of rubber. He doesn't realise that when you're pregnant you become a little more sensitive. I was hurt and I answered back, saying that I didn't make the meat like that, it came that way. It was a tough piece of meat. He pushed his knife and fork together on the plate and looked me down, saying, Jesus Christ, woman, you know nothing about food.

He made me cry.

As soon as the first tear fell, he said he was sorry and cradled me in his arms and asked my forgiveness, that he was just a big old fool and what did he know. But I can't forget what he said because he's right. Ever since the day we got married I've been trying to cook decent meals for my family, but it's a constant hit and miss. And I'm pretty hopeless at housework as well. I don't seem to have enough time for all the cleaning. This house is so big, and everything gets dirty very quickly, and I'm so very slow. Thorough, mind you, but slow. Being pregnant is no excuse. All the other women in Tomás's family, his sisters and sisters-in-law, work so hard, right up until they have their babies. Maybe I'm just not made of the same stuff.

Maybe I'm weak?

I'm six weeks gone already, and I was never this ill with Christina.

The slightest thing might set me off. Catching a whiff of one of Jim's cigarettes if I'm in the garden, or the smell of the grease in the pan when I fry bacon, or the dog blanket when I shake it out. It's terrible. I think it must be like being sea sick, permanently.

Tomás can't understand it. None of the Comyn women get sick. It's just my luck. Rita said I should have a packet of rich tea biscuits beside the bed and a flask of hot tea so that first thing in the morning I should take that before my body has a chance to think and decide to be sick! But sometimes I don't even have time to drink a cup of tea. Tomás gets up so early and I like to be up with him, to make his breakfast, have a few moments before he sets off. He can be gone for such a long time.

It would be so nice if we could all go away from here, just for a couple of weeks, a little family holiday. Anywhere would do. We've only been away once. It was our honeymoon, in Paris. That surprised Aunt Shirley! It must have been so expensive because we could only stay a few days, but every part of it was special – getting onto an aeroplane for the first time, riding in the Metro, looking out our hotel window at Notre Dame…what an article of devotion that was! We thought of nothing else but ourselves. We walked hand in hand across the bridges, down the little narrow streets, swinging our arms, taking each step forward together. We were completely in unison.

It would be so nice to go somewhere foreign again, and this time with Christina. But there's no point daydreaming about that now. For a start, when would Tomás get the time to go away? And I'm pregnant; I need to be here.

He (because I believe the baby will be a little boy, curly topped and charming like his daddy) will be born in an Indian summer, when the garden will be overflowing with apples and plums and all the trees will be heavy and green.

Dear Lord, keep my baby safe. Bless my family – my husband, Tomás, my daughter, Christina, my sister, Maureen, my sisters-in-law, Rita,

Margaret and Mae, my brothers-in-law, Martin, Brendan and Raymond, and my father-in-law, John. Please let those who have gone before us rest in peace, in particular my father and mother and my mother-in-law. Forgive me my sins, and fill me with your light. In the name of the father, the son and the Holy Ghost.

Amen.

CHRISTINA

Christina dashed around the cottage with a duster. There really seemed very little point. By the time her cousin, Helen, came back from Australia, the place would be thick with dust again, but it made her feel better to leave the house spotless. It gave her a sense of completion, an end note.

Helen was the only one in the family who'd helped her. Even her father had ended up being on Declan's side. It would never have crossed Christina's mind that Helen might have been on hers. They had never been close as children – in fact, Helen and her sisters used to slightly frighten Christina. They were horsy and had no interest in playing dolls or any of the other sissy stuff that Christina was into.

But things had been tough for her cousin too. She had been trying to have a baby for years only to have a series of miscarriages, and then earlier that year her husband had died in a hunting accident. Helen took it on the chin and announced just one month after the funeral that she was heading off to Australia. At the time Christina had been staying in the Fincourt and running out of money fast. She could have forced her way back into her own home, but she was too ashamed.

It was Helen who came to the rescue. They ran into each other in town, just the day before Helen was leaving. Instead of avoiding her, like everyone else, Helen looked her straight in the eyes.

'So how are ya, Chrissie?'

'Not great, to be honest.'

'No, I'd say not.' Helen wasn't into long chats. She stuck her hands in her pockets and looked behind Christina's head as if she was expecting someone.

'And how are you, Helen? I hear that you're off to Australia,' Christina said uncomfortably.

'Yep,' she said, and taking Christina by surprise she continued, 'you can stay at my place, so. You might as well, it'll be empty.'

Christina moved in two days later. The key had been left for her, above the door.

Helen's cottage was as far off the beaten track as you could get. Even the postman didn't come all the way but left the post in a Quality Street tin at the end of the lane.

To reach the cottage you had to drive down a small twisty country road, then down one tiny lane into another, even smaller, boreen, hardly more than a grass track. The cottage stood on a small rise, overlooking a messy bog of broken reeds. There wasn't another house in sight.

Was it its isolation that made the place so magical? Over the past few weeks, just being there had gradually made Christina feel better. And Cian loved it too. The front yard was framed by a series of mature chestnut trees and Helen had hung a car tyre for any visiting child to swing on under the largest of the trees. Around the back was a spring well and a stream that framed the entire field. Helen let the field out, and usually there were horses there, frisky geldings cantering up and down.

It was a relief to be in Helen's house, away from town and somewhere that wasn't hers, that couldn't remind her of the past.

Nothing fit in. Helen didn't possess one pair of matching cups or plates and none of the furniture or furnishings were co-ordinated, but she liked it. Here were all the strands of one person's life – a rug from Morocco, a teacup from Barcelona, a Chinese lantern hanging over the light, a batik from Indonesia.

In Christina's house everything had matched, and nothing told a story because she had never gone anywhere or seen anything apart from Ireland. Her perfect house had been her mission, and it was never ending. How many years had she worked on it?

Seventeen.

It was her life's work. Apart from her two children, that was her contribution to the world. One perfectly designed, decorated, co-ordinated, executive-style bungalow in north County Meath.

She had been passionate about that house, buying up all those interior design magazines like an addict, watching the do-it-up programmes on the telly. And it was beautiful, a shimmering testament of glimmering steel surfaces in the kitchen and spotless white leather in the sitting room, a bedroom kitted out for Marie Antoinette with fake French furniture that she herself had distressed. It was all gilt and twirling frames, with floral curtains and matching linen.

Declan hated that room, and now he had it all to himself. The image of him lying alone in all that female opulence made her burst out laughing.

But then, maybe he was going to change it, paint out all of her? The thought was sobering and made her angry. All that work.

Once, not long after Johnny had started school, she suggested that she might enrol on the diploma course in art at Cavan College. It was only for a year. Declan couldn't understand why she wanted to do it at all.

'I think it's great that you want to get a qualification,' he had said, 'but why don't you do something useful, like a secretarial course, something you could get a job in?'

'But don't you remember that I always wanted to study art?'

'Sure, I remember you were good at it, but it's not going to bring any money in, is it?' He'd stood firmly in the doorway, still in his wellies, checked shirt buttoned up, his hands leaning against the

45

doorframe, looking at her, right into her.

'Declan, aren't you doing what you always wanted to do now?'

And he was. He had only stuck it with her father and the pigs for a couple of years, and with determination he had made the right contacts, got into horses. It meant he had to go away a lot, travelling. This was what he had to do if he wanted to get on.

'That's different,' he'd said. 'I'm doing a job.'

There was no getting past that. In the end she convinced herself he was right. Who did she think she was anyway? Then she became pregnant with Cian and so there was no need to be thinking about jobs. In the end, it was a relief. She could retreat further and further inside her shell, inside her beautiful house. It became her canvas. Through it Christina was able to pour out all her creative longings, play with colour, texture, watch the light falling through the windows, catching the tone or shadow of her handiwork. She could try to be the perfect homemaker.

And now, it had all been for nothing.

The past month had been so strange for her, living the single life. Suddenly she was free again. She didn't have to organise babysitting or ferry Johnny to the football or take Cian to school or sort out the boys' uniforms any more. Declan was doing all of that now.

Christina felt completely dislocated. Everything that had been her life was taken away, and when all her family was out of the picture, what did she have left?

A big fat nothing.

That was why she had decided to do something.

THE DINNER PARTY

Branches scrape the windows, the boiler hisses and one of the black cats gets up, stretches and slides down to the floor. Christina is in her pyjamas, curled up in the dog basket, watching Angeline cook.

Another gust of wind passes through the house. Christina feels it from under the door. It chills her and she pushes herself further under the dog blanket so that only her toes are sticking out. The door to the hall creaks and she looks up, expecting her father to come in, ordering her to bed, but it's just the shadow of the wind, tricking her.

Angeline is still at the sink. She has paused and stands staring out at the black night, grater in one hand, carrot in the other.

Are you still here? she asks softly.

Christina doesn't reply.

I know you are, you naughty girl. But still Angeline doesn't turn around, just bends back down to her work.

She's trying something new tonight, she told Christina. It will be the first time that Tomás or the other guests have ever eaten Chinese food. It's even new for Angeline. It sounds strange to Christina — lemon-glazed chicken and little deep-fried balls with prawns inside. There will be rice as well, and long ribbons of vegetables fried very fast. Angeline showed her what she was cooking it all in, a black frying pan so big and deep it could be a hat if you turned it the other way up. She called it a wok.

Christina couldn't wait until she was grown up. Then she could go to dinner parties like this one.

Would you lay the table for me, darling?

Christina reluctantly heaves herself out of the basket and goes over to the kitchen drawer.

Six of everything, says Angeline. Knives, spoons, forks. I'll do the glasses, but you can arrange the napkins, can't you? They're over there. She waves towards a stack of white linen cloths, immaculately folded and ironed.

Christina loads up a tray and crosses the hall into the dining room. The fire is lit but there's only one lamp on in the corner. Flames rush up the chimney, fanned by the wind outside. A few sparks land on the rug, but die immediately. The room is dancing with light from the fire, and although there's no one in there, it doesn't feel empty. It feels magical and exciting.

She puts out the placemats and then lays the table. She's an expert at it. This is always her job, every day, that and helping Angeline make the beds.

Shall I put out candles? Christina asks as she comes back into the kitchen.

Just pop them on the table there, I'll do that. Angeline bends over the oven to check the chicken. Will you taste this for me?

Christina comes over dutifully as Angeline dips a teaspoon into the lemon-coloured sauce.

Mmm, it's lovely.

Sure?

Yes, I like it.

Thanks, darling, you're my best taster. Angeline beams at her and Christina thinks how she would like to be like Angeline one day, to be as pretty as her.

Now up to bed with you before your daddy catches us, she says, patting Christina's bottom.

Please can I stay a little longer?

No, no, I already let you stay up late.

Oh, please?

No, the guests will be here soon. She opens a large cake tin and hands Christina a meringue. Go on, you can have one of these. They embrace.

Night, night, sleep tight, don't let the bed bugs bite, because if they do... They say together in unison.

Parcel them up in brown paper and string and send them off to Peru, adds Angeline.

That's a good one, Christina says and skips out of the room, up to bed.

Christina keeps the light on in her bedroom. She hears the people arrive, the low notes of the men's voices, the light chatter of the women. She smells the cigarette smoke as it drifts up the stairs, mixing with the enticing scent of the food. She gets out of bed and creeps along the landing, sitting on the top step, straining her ears, hoping to catch a word or two.

When her mammy had been there, living with them, Christina couldn't remember any dinner parties. But she couldn't cook. Now Daddy was proud of Angeline. She was like an exotic bird everyone wanted to come and see.

GRETA

Something very strange happened today. And it wasn't the sort of day you'd expect anything to happen. A filthy, wet day.

I was on the way to the bank and there was an absolute downpour. My hands were freezing, numb with the cold and the wet. I was just darting in through the door when I heard someone calling my name, calling me Greta Stone. No one calls me that any more.

I turned, and I saw this vision coming towards me. A tall, dark woman with long, black, shiny hair. She was wearing a beautiful pair of purple velvet trousers and a large, hairy Afghan coat. I couldn't believe my eyes, because I instantly recognised her. She looked so different, but it was unmistakably Angeline.

Greta, she cried, flinging her arms around me, remember me? Angeline, Angeline Mahony, we were in the same class at school.

Of course I remember you, I said, pulling back, staring at this transformation. But you look so different.

I suppose I've lost a bit of weight, she said, putting her hands on her hips.

But you're taller as well!

Oh, that's these, she said, lifting up one of her feet and showing me a giant platform boot.

Goodness! I exclaimed, thinking what Tomás would say if I came home in a pair of those.

Well, you haven't changed a bit, she said, reaching out and flicking my hair with her hand. Still the girl with the golden hair!

I nodded, blushing, uncertain what to say. And then, glancing at the clock in the middle of the square, I noticed that I needed to be home soon.

I'd love to chat, I said, but I have to get going. Let me give you my telephone number and maybe you and your husband could come over for dinner sometime. Are you over for long?

Angeline's face changed then. The smile disappeared and she put her hand on my shoulder, as if she was stopping me from walking away.

Thank you, Greta, she said, but I'm divorced now.

I was mortified. Oh.

That was all I could say, oh. Divorced! I didn't know anyone who was divorced.

You probably don't believe in it, right? she said, sounding almost American.

Well, I'm not sure...

I didn't want to lie, but still, I didn't want to insult my old friend.

It wasn't through choice, Greta, she explained. He ran off with another woman, deserted me.

Oh, that's terrible.

Yes, she said, staring straight at me, her eyes direct, her face open, the rain dripping down it as if she didn't care how wet she got. I can't have children and, well, he wanted a family.

I took her hand. It was all I could do; it was wet but warmer than mine.

Could you not have gone for adoption? I asked.

That takes time, she sighed, and he was in a hurry. She gave a little laugh, then dropping my hand, she said, I'm sorry, how rude of me to launch into all of that.

No, it's fine, I asked you.

And then, to my embarrassment, I found myself saying, Angeline,

I've missed you so much. It was a little too dramatic, but she seemed pleased and smiled some more.

Let's go for a cup of tea, out of the rain, she said, linking her arm through mine. I want to hear all about your life, and your family.

That had been it. Something pulled inside me, a part of myself so completely smothered that it made my lips dry.

Okay, I said, knowing I didn't have time, knowing that I had to get to the butchers and the green grocers and back before school was over, otherwise Tomás would have nothing for the tea. But all that flew out of my head, was washed away in the rain. In that very moment all I desired was to talk, and the only person I wanted to talk to was her, my smiling dark friend.

CHRISTINA

In the kitchen Christina turned slowly, her eyes half closed, and stopped at the window. The hours she had spent staring at the field, listening for the latch to drop, for Angeline to walk in, to come and help her...but she had never called round, not once. She seemed so distant to her now, her advice flat, without resonance. Instead there was a hum inside Christina's head, a thought which refused to go away – what about her real mother? What about Greta?

Christina opened her hand and looked at the old photograph curled up on her palm. The dim, vague shadow of her mother reached up, appealing to her. It was hard for her to draw the distinction between the point at which her mother ended and Angeline began.

She looked out the window. The land was one big empty green sweep, rising and falling like the ocean. Clusters of sheep pricked the view. Spots of white, they appeared motionless, as if frozen in time and the only movement, sudden and grand, was a single black crow diving out of the clear blue sky to land on the bins.

She shook herself, rinsed out the dirty mugs and put them away. Her hands were trembling as she locked the door and slipped the key in behind the brick on the lintel. She felt breathless already, nervous.

She paused outside the house and a warm breeze pushed into her, lifting her shirt. Flies buzzed around her and the air tasted dry. The reed bed was cracked and broken, though the reeds had somehow still found moisture and were an alarming shade of red. She watched a tiny blue damselfly hover, then gradually drift off. She could hide here forever.

But she wasn't going to give up. It was no longer a matter of choice.

The pressure of her loss was bursting out of her, something so physical and real that it could happen at the strangest moments, a sensation that she was dying, that her heart might give out.

The first time she was just walking down the street, on the way to the video shop, when she started to cough as if there was something stuck in her throat, and then her breath came shorter and shorter. She could feel her heart pounding, her chest tightening and she started to sweat. She staggered back to her car and sat inside it, hands shaking on the steering wheel, for at least half an hour. At the time she had been terrified. But then, with everything going on, she had forgotten about it, putting it down as a one-off.

Weeks later, right after the case, it came back. She had been in the supermarket trying to get some food for Cian for the weekend when she felt the prickle of fear inside her, like a bad taste in her mouth. It was Friday and the place was packed. She held onto the edge of the freezers, staring down at packets of peas and spinach, beans and sweetcorn, and everything merged into a sea of green. She tried to breathe in but all she could do was gasp desperately, trying to get enough air. The pain in her heart was excruciating. She thought she was having a heart attack.

That time people had noticed. A boy packing shelves had seen her and made her sit down in the back of the shop. Someone else brought her a cup of tea. She was in a circle of pity.

Doctor Marsh told her she was depressed. He frowned at her, and she felt like he was telling her off when he said that there was absolutely nothing wrong with her heart. He asked her if she smoked or drank a lot. She said no. Then he told her to cut down on coffee and gave her some pills – Prozac. She had been embarrassed when she had found out what was really the matter.

She didn't take the Prozac, because if she did it would be like before when she couldn't feel anything, and that was worse, and that was why things had gone wrong in the first place. So she put them in her bedside locker. Still, she couldn't stop taking them out, spilling them onto the bed and playing with them on the eiderdown, tempting herself.

She had made pictures with them. Taking some of Cian's paper and his art box, she had sat on the bedroom floor and methodically stuck all the pills onto the paper in little geometric patterns. Then she had painted around them in strong, bold colours, dabbed each one with a spot of glue and sprinkled glitter on them, and finally cut out strips of tin foil and stuck them around the pills. She made little pill icons.

It was all a conspiracy, Christina had told herself. They just wanted to make sure that she stayed in line. All those colours and circles and brushstrokes had had so much energy, the pictures just kept moving in front of her eyes. They were dancing in the dusty afternoon and hypnotising her. She had sat staring at them until dark.

GRETA

I have a plan.

The day after Angeline and I had tea in town, she telephoned me and invited me over to her parents' house. She said that her mother and father were both out for the day, and it would be a chance for us to continue our conversation from the previous afternoon. I'd had to dash off to collect Christina from school in the middle of her telling me all about her life in England. It had been so fascinating.

So I asked Tomás if he minded and he said of course not as long as I didn't forget his dinner again. But he was smiling when he said it so I knew he didn't really mind. I was still feeling sick but I was so excited about seeing Angeline that I managed to keep it down!

Angeline lives the far side of Mountnugent, just off the Cavan road. It's a long, straight bog road to her house. I like driving it because you go up and down, up and down, and it's like being on the sea. It reminds me of when Daddy took me out on a boat in Galway, many years ago now.

When I arrived Angeline was opening up all of the windows. Isn't it a beautiful spring day? she called down to me as I got out of my car.

And she was right. The birds were twittering away and I felt far too warm in my woollen coat and hat. There were dozens of snowdrops scattered all around the house and crocuses sprouting up everywhere.

Look, she said, coming out of the front door in a splendid-looking dress, all twirls and swirls and circles of red, orange and yellow, like flames. There's the first primrose!

I crouched down with her and examined the tiny bud. She made me feel excited over something as little as a flower.

Come on in. She took my hand and pulled me up. We strode into the house, arms linked, like in the old days. Now you sit here, she said, pointing to the big carver at the head of the table.

Isn't that your daddy's chair? I asked.

I don't see his name on it! It's just a chair, sit, sit. You need to rest in your condition.

I was stunned. We've only told close family. How did you know?

To me, it's as plain as day, she said. The colour of you, and the way you're moving even.

But I'm not even showing yet.

Well, if you notice the little things, like me, you can just tell. Now what would you like – tea, coffee or my spectacular cocoa?

Oh, I have to try your cocoa.

I felt awkward then that there I was, pregnant right in front of her, and she couldn't have a child. But Angeline didn't seem to mind and she continued what she was doing, cool as a cucumber, taking out a pot and putting it on the stove.

This is a special recipe my mother learned from her mother and so on and so on. You know that my grandmother was half French and half Algerian?

Goodness, how exotic!

That's where my name comes from. Angeline Cassar was my grandmother. She grew up in Algeria and that's where she learned this very special chocolate drink recipe. She handed me a giant cup of steaming chocolate. Now try a slice of this.

Sitting down opposite me she placed a honey-coloured cake in front of us. It looked plain enough, a small round circle glazed with syrup on the top.

57

But oh, mother divine, for the next twenty minutes I was in heaven! I have never drunk or eaten anything quite so delicious in my entire life. The drinking chocolate was like pure melted chocolate but with something else – something sweet but not too sweet, something creamy but not sickening. The effect was pure contentment. And the cake…although she only gave me a small slice, it was enough. The sponge was dense yet soft, and slightly almondy. It melted in my mouth, instantly, so that the syrup could slide across my tongue, leaving a lovely honey taste behind.

Oh my goodness, Angeline, you didn't learn to cook like this at school!

She smiled proudly. You like it?

I don't know which is better, the drink or the cake. I could just carry on like this all day.

I've worked at my cooking, she said. It was part of our livelihood, you see.

She continued, clearing the table as she spoke. When Jack and I moved to England, he decided that he'd like to work on one of those grand estates as a gamekeeper or something like that. He'd had plenty of experience here with the Synotts. So when we were looking for work we noticed that it would be better if I had a skill too. That's when my mother unearthed all of Granny's old recipe books and sent them to me. Well, Greta, I found my calling, so to speak. From the first day I picked up a mixing bowl and a wooden spoon, I loved it. It became a passion. In the end we became quite a sought-after pair.

It was then that I had an idea, that I formed this plan. I was looking at my old friend and eating her excellent food that was making me feel so well, better than I had done in weeks, and she was gazing down at the table looking sad and lonely. And I thought, We need each other. It could all be so simple.

Surely she'd be happy of the company, to be with me and my little

58

girl as well, rather than living on her parents' charity?

Surely she'd feel better having an occupation rather than being the deserted wife, all alone? And I needed a cook. It was time to face the truth – I would never be able to create things like this. I couldn't even imagine Tomás minding, because you know what they say – the way to a man's heart is through his stomach! If I could make sure he had good food, then he would be happier with me. Wouldn't he?

CHRISTINA

It was time to leave Helen's house. Christina could hear a tractor and saw it crawling up a hillock in the field next door. She had a perfect three hundred and sixty degree view. The land rolled across from her, the fields broken up by unkempt dry-stone walls, the odd patch of bog a deeper, richer shade of green, clumps of razor-sharp grass encircling them. It felt like the West.

She couldn't see one other house, apart from a derelict farm two fields away. She had walked there one day, fascinated that there had been no road, not even a track to its front door. The place was deserted, but not that long empty. She had noticed light switches and a septic tank. Whoever had lived there had loved their garden. The place had been jammed with bluebells. Spread before her feet had been a carpet of blue tinged with purple and deep green stems. The aroma of the flowers had made her feel slightly light-headed. They reminded her of the woods at home.

It had always been her favourite time of year, to go walking ankle deep in a blanket of violet, and to pick away at the bluebells but never see them diminish. When she was a little girl, Angeline would go with her. Maybe her mother had too, but Christina couldn't remember an occasion. Angeline had a special basket – Christina called it her Little Red Riding Hood basket – and together the two of them would fill it with the limp bluebell bodies and charge home to resurrect them in legions of jam jars placed all over the house.

May. The month of our Lady, the time Angeline called Bealtaine.

Not until Christina was in her late teens did she explain what it meant. They had been arranging the bluebells at the time, filling up the kitchen sill with their posies, when Christina asked Angeline.

It's a pagan festival, when May represented a month of fertility and sexual fun, she'd told her. It amuses me to think about these two extremes. There's our Lady, divine symbol of virginity, and on the other hand there's the May Queen, a sexy young maiden wanting to mate. In the olden days, Angeline whispered, young people would use Bealtaine as an excuse to go out into the fields and have sex. It was the time of year for it.

Had Angeline sensed that Christina already knew about these things? Did she pick it up in her guilty glance at the floor, her reaction not to giggle but let the slow flame of red pass across her cheeks? It must have been obvious.

Angeline had been more than a mother. She had been like a sister too. There had always been something conspiratorial about their relationship, little things they shared that Daddy didn't know about. Angeline knew everything, too much. It was she who told her she wasn't able to mind Johnny and Cian any more. It was she who convinced her to give them up.

Angeline betrayed her.

Christina got into the car, taking care to put her case in the boot first. She had to stay focused.

Friday. It was busy in town. There were cars parked on yellow lines, delivery trucks right out in the middle of the road. She squeezed her car in next to the vegetable stall. Getting out, she tucked her chin to her chest, kept her head down and tried not to look about her. The last thing she needed was to meet somebody now. She ran across the road to the chemist, only to discover it was closed for lunch. She glanced at her watch.

'Christina!'

She ignored the voice, and instead of turning around, walked briskly into Kraft Kaffee.

The place was packed, with just one free table in the corner. She walked over and slid in. She was hot now. She knew her cheeks were red, and it wasn't just because of the heat outside. Her sense of shame felt like a brand.

The radio was playing in the background, and the one o'clock news came on. She picked at her nails, waiting for her coffee to arrive, her heart pounding already at the idea of what she was about to do. Should she do it? Was it the right thing to do, really?

She leaned back against the large glass windowpanes of the café and looked up at the board and the lunch menu, but she wasn't hungry for food.

She had sat in this café so many times on her own, pretending to read the newspaper or a magazine on her way home from shopping, trying so desperately to be normal, like all the other mothers. She knew this place so well, yet it felt different today. It was hotter, the midsummer heat blasting in from outside. The French windows were open, and Kathleen, the owner, was busy bringing drinks outside. Christina tried not to catch her eye, the need to confide was so strong. There was a new picture on the wall, a bright and colourful landscape, with energetic slaps of yellow and green paint.

She could have done better than that, although she had long since stopped trying. That had always been her problem – she had been afraid. All she had ever wanted to do was paint, and she had been too much of a coward to even do that. She had never followed anything through.

Christina gripped the tall steaming glass of coffee tightly.

Now she was going to.

GRETA

I watched Tomás's face as he ate. Oh, it was a picture! If you could actually measure contentment, then I would say that his was ten out of ten.

Angeline made us a stew, but one like no other I've ever eaten. She called it her winter stew for cold days. Very apt for today, because it's been bitterly cold all week, with hard, icy rain, even hailstorms, and a nasty east wind whipping around the house. We lit the fire in the dining room after Mass, and then all we had to do was wait. My husband and I sat on either side of the fire, sipping sherry. He was reading the paper and I was dreaming. I could hear Christina in her room above, hopping up and down and chattering to her dolls. We were the picture of bliss.

I had tried to go into the kitchen to help, but Angeline had just shooed me away, joking about her secret recipes. What I smelled was making my mouth water and my stomach groan. All sensations of morning sickness are completely gone!

We started with paté. She said that she had made it yesterday at her parents' house. I've never been a fan of anything too meaty, but this was delicious. The pork was blended to a soft texture and dotted with little peppercorns, herbs and garlic. She served it with a kind of French bread, which was flavoured with oil and herbs. I was studying Tomás's face as he tried it. He seemed hesitant at first, but then, do you know what he said?

Greta, isn't this just like some of the food we had in Paris?

63

Oh yes, I thought, this is where Angeline's cooking takes me, back to the romance at the beginning of our marriage, all the way to our honeymoon. It's doing it for him too, it's reminding him.

Then came the stew. She carried in an ancient earthenware pot like a baby and carefully placed it on the sideboard.

I didn't know we had that pot, I said.

Oh, it's mine, said Angeline. It belonged to my grandmother. It's all the way from France.

It's beautiful.

It's also crucial to the composition of the stew. Angeline took off the lid and a sweet aroma rose through the steam. There's years and years of flavour soaked into this pot, she continued, the souls of a thousand different stews, rich gravies and sweet onions, ancient herbs.

Tomás raised his eyes to the ceiling and made me giggle. He thinks the way Angeline talks is very funny. He calls her a hippy.

I thought Angeline looked wonderful, though, ladling out that stew. She had tied her jet-black hair back with a purple ribbon and was wearing a long purple velvet dress, with long, long sleeves, which she skilfully managed not to dip into the stew. She had a pendant on – I've never seen anything like it. It was silver and shaped like a little bottle, with coloured beads hanging off it.

We had all dressed up for the occasion. I could hardly fit into my dress, but Christina looked sweet, of course. I put her in pink. It's her favourite colour and I think it suits her complexion.

Back to the stew. I have to admit I was a little nervous when she told me what was in it – ham hocks, white beans and root vegetables – but it was just delicious. She had put all sorts of herbs in it to bring out the flavours of the meat, and the carrots and parsnips were soft and sweet. Christina ate all hers up and asked for more.

Make sure you leave room for pudding, Angeline warned.

Baked figs with orange and red wine.

I've never eaten figs, I said.

But that's crazy, Angeline exclaimed, pushing a strand of black hair behind her ear. You've a fig tree by the back door.

We do?

She laughed, shaking her head. Although these are from home, dried from last year. I baked them slowly in the Aga until they plumped up into wine-loaded bundles.

Absolutely delicious, Angeline, Tomás said, spooning thick, frothy cream on top of them.

The cream is my father's as well, Angeline said proudly.

Well, Tomás said, sitting back and stroking his chin, you're a wonderful cook, Angeline. And then, leaning forward, he suddenly said, with absolutely no prompting whatsoever from me, We really would be delighted if you'd come and work for us.

And live with us, as our friend, I added.

She didn't hesitate at all. I'd love that, she said, licking the fig syrup off her lips.

Oh, goody! cried Christina, clapping her hands.

CHRISTINA

The door of the café opened, letting in a gust of air and light. Angeline.

Christina dropped her head, but it was too late, she had seen her. She walked steadily towards her, a small red bag tucked underneath her arm, her shopping basket in the other hand. Her hair was still long and black, her skin smooth and glowing. She didn't look a day over forty.

'Christina, pet, let me join you.'

'If you want.'

Kathleen came over and she ordered a pot of tea. 'How are you?' Angeline asked as she settled into her seat.

Christina drained her coffee. 'Okay.' She didn't want to tell her anything. She no longer trusted her.

'Good, good. Have you been keeping your appointments, darling?' Angeline smiled at her and reached out her hand to touch her.

'Yes,' Christina lied. 'I'm fine.' Christina drew back and tucked her hands in her pockets.

'You're not drinking then?'

'No. Not that it's any of your business,' Christina glared. Angeline looked shocked.

'What do you mean? Of course it's my business, I'm your mother.'

'No, you're not. At least, you don't act like one.'

A cloud passed across Angeline's face. She spoke so low Christina could hardly hear her. 'How can you say that, Christina?'

'Forget it.' Christina shook her head. She didn't want to argue with her, not here.

There were things she didn't understand, like why her father had been so angry with her. She had gone back to The Mill first and asked if she could stay there, but he had refused her, said it was about time she stood on her own two feet. He was furious that day; she had never seen him like that.

'Just look at yourself, Christina,' he had raged. 'You're thirty-four years of age and look at yourself – the state you got yourself into, and no house, no money, no husband. You're not fit to look after your own children, let alone think about getting a job. I'd think that you'd be hard pressed even to serve someone a drink.'

She had thought that Angeline would stand up for her, but she had said nothing.

'It's probably better if you don't stay here,' she had said later on when Christina was leaving. She had given her stepmother a searching look, but she let her hair fall across her face so that Christina couldn't see her eyes. 'You should have done what I said, Christina,' she sighed. 'If only you had, things might be all right.'

'But I couldn't,' Christina struggled. She wanted to tell Angeline everything, why it had happened, how she had felt, but her stepmother stopped her, putting out her hand as if to keep her back.

'You should have thought of your children,' she said.

Christina didn't understand why she was so angry with Angeline now. Nothing had been her fault.

Angeline had always listened to her, and when she saw how unhappy Christina had become she had helped her, hadn't she? And yet why did she feel so let down by her stepmother, more than her father, more than Declan?

They sat in silence. Angeline's tea arrived. She poured it into her cup, blew over it and took a sip, all the time looking at her. Christina tried not to catch her eyes, but suddenly her stepmother leaned across the table and forced her to look at her.

'I love you, Christina. You have always been my girl,' she said gently.

'I'm not your girl. I'm not your daughter,' Christina said hotly. She felt herself blushing, the tears welling.

Angeline sighed, and her radiance dimmed. Suddenly she looked tired, almost her age. 'I can only feel about you the way a mother feels about her child,' she said sadly.

'You have no idea what it feels like to be a real mother,' Christina spat back. 'Have you any idea what it's like for me at the moment? To be without my children?'

'It's for the best, darling. Just for the time being.'

'But for how much longer?' Christina groaned, putting her head in her hands as she leaned over the table.

Angeline took Christina's hands and brought them down, gripping them so tightly that her knuckles hurt. 'Be strong,' she hissed, 'it will be all right.'

Christina pulled away. 'How can you tell me that? You, of all people, because nothing in our family has ever been all right.' She got up clumsily, knocking her glass over.

'Christina—' Angeline started to say, but Christina didn't stay to listen.

After her mother had walked out, Christina had been afraid to leave Angeline's side. She had been her shadow, like Mary's little lamb. And Angeline had let her be so. She had nurtured Christina, and in turn Christina adored her, even when she was a teenager. She remembered the day Angeline and her father had finally got married. She had been so happy because then they had become a proper family. She asked Angeline how they could marry again, and she told her that Tomás's marriage had been annulled, they had got special permission from Rome, and that she was now widowed. (Angeline never spoke about her first husband, but her father had told her he was a wicked man.) The whole community had accepted Angeline. Everyone thought she was a blessing for poor Tomás Comyn and his deserted child.

Things had changed a little when Christina got married.

'Are you sure this is what you want?' Angeline had asked her.

'Yes,' Christina had replied petulantly, 'I love him.'

'But darling, he's your first boyfriend. You're so young.'

'What else am I supposed to do?'

Angeline had licked her lips. 'Your father doesn't know about the pregnancy. It's still early yet. I can help you, Christina. We can go over to England and—'

'No!' She had been terrified of the idea of an abortion. It was more frightening than the thought of having the baby, which was vague and distant and still unreal.

'Darling, you have your whole life ahead of you. Please don't throw it away.'

But, uncharacteristically, Christina had held her ground. Angeline had given up then, comforting her sobbing stepdaughter and promising that she would always be there for her.

And she had been at the beginning.

But as the years went by, she could see her stepmother becoming irritated by her whining about Declan, and Christina had had to listen to her say on a number of occasions that hadn't she told her so? Hadn't she known that Declan wasn't the man for her? She told Christina to think of the children. And she had tried. But when her void became so large that she had to fill it with something else, she hid that from Angeline. She had been too ashamed.

The sun was blasting off the pavement, and the light blinded her momentarily. She caught a glimpse of Angeline inside Kraft Kaffee, paying Kathleen, and looked away. She tried not to think about her and her father. She concentrated on each step to her car, entering each moment clean and clear. She wasn't going to bring any of that baggage with her.

THE IRONING PILE MONSTER

A noise wakes her. Christina's room is completely dark. Angeline must have turned her night light out after she fell asleep. She whimpers, cries a little louder.

Mammy!

It slips out. But Mammy is gone. Mammy has been gone a long time now. She shakes her head with frustration, the tears falling harder, her fragile heart aching.

Angeline! she calls, holding her breath in the darkness, but there's no quick step, no light turned on.

Angeline!

She sits up. Her bedroom door is ajar and she can see shadows in the corridor outside. She's able to make out the outline of the large oak chest, and on top the pile of laundry to be ironed, which never appeared to shrink. She knows it's just sheets and shirts and tea towels, but in the darkness she can see it moving, she's sure of it. Maybe there's someone or something underneath?

Angeline! she calls again, louder this time, but the words echo down the hall, making her feel more alone.

She shivers and climbs slowly out of bed. She has to get her daddy, because where is Angeline? Did the ironing pile monster get her?

The house creaks around her and she jumps nervously. The building feels alive, she can sense it heaving, breathing, changing shape. She runs down the corridor as fast as she can past the laundry pile, and now she's out on the landing and the moon is shining through the windows. The curtains aren't drawn and she can see the garden is silver. Everything, even the roof of the shed, is shiny and bright. The clock ticks behind her, but louder is the sound of the river, the water falling out of the mill, its rhythm making her feel sleepy, and all she wants to do is to get into bed with Daddy, be safe and warm.

She puts her hand on the door, pushes it open.

It's only a second, but what she sees, that one tiny fragment, is permanently lodged in her mind.

There's a gap in the curtains and the moon shines a light on the bed. Christina can see clearly. The sheets and blankets are up on her daddy's back, and he's a mountain. He's making a strange noise, like one of the grunting pigs, and he's going up and down, up and down. It looks funny, but when she sees Angeline underneath him, she's frightened. Is he hurting her? Her eyes are shut tight and her mouth is wide open. She looks like she's dying.

Daddy!

The light from the hall spills in behind her, and the two shocked adults sit up at once.

Get out of here this instant! her father bellows.

She hesitates, and looks over at Angeline. She doesn't look happy at all, although she can see now that she isn't hurt.

Christina, she says sharply, go back to your room, now!

Go on, get out! her father shouts again.

Christina turns on her heels, runs back down the corridor and falls onto her bed.

What did she do wrong? Why were they angry with her? What had happened to her daddy? And why did Angeline stay in there with him?

She hugs herself, crying silently in the dark. She looks out into the black landing and now she can see clearly that the ironing pile is only a stupid old heap of crumpled clothes.

There are other things to be more afraid of.

GRETA

Suddenly our long winter is over. We're astounded — only yesterday icy sleet had battered the land. Now it's warm and the fields are shouting for joy. We can see little primroses bursting out of the hedgerows, birds twittering on their barbs and baby lambs stumbling around in the fields.

Angeline and I walked to the woods. Imagine the pale green colour of new leaves as they emerge from the ground, she said. Close your eyes and smell them, the aroma of spring after a long, damp winter.

I shut my eyes, inhaled deeply and immediately tumbled into a ditch, skidding on a cowpat. Yuck!

We laughed then till our bellies ached and we had to sit down.

We had only walked the length of two fields, but we no longer had a view of the house and the river. We were adrift in all this new, fresh greenness. I felt wonderful.

Ever since Angeline has come to live with us I haven't been sick once. She makes me special little treats — for the baby, she says. She's so attentive and kind and absolutely brilliant with Christina. My daughter adores her as much as I do, and I think Tomás likes her, for all her 'hippy' talk.

At first he was a little confused that Angeline didn't go to Mass, but she told me that she doesn't believe in God any more. Maybe if she'd stayed in Ireland she'd still believe in God. I think it's because she was in London for a long time, and then what happened to her

– her dreadful husband breaking their wedding vows, and then having to get a divorce.

She told me that she meditates. Once, at night, I heard a humming sound coming from her room. At first I thought it was the pipes until I realised it was actually her – it was so low, the hum, under the tail end of sound.

If you go into her room, it smells lovely and she burns these perfumed sticks called incense, which Tomás doesn't like at all, but she's such a good cook that he says nothing. I like the smell – I find it relaxing.

Angeline picked some leaves off a small tree and placed one on her tongue, then handed one to me.

Go on, she said, taking her leaf out. Put it on your tongue.

What if it's poisonous?

Don't be silly. It's a bay leaf.

I placed the leaf on my tongue. What did it taste like? Bitter, but sweet, alive.

Angeline told me a story as we walked, and I picked little yellow buds from the gorse and sprinkled them on her hair so that they looked like bright stars on a dark night.

There was a time of chaos, she said, a churning black river, swollen and violent, which swept all in its path. The river wouldn't permit any to sail on it, even the birds that lived along its course. It wouldn't allow the fish to pass through it without tossing them up and out of it so that they were dizzy and lost. The river took over. It burst its banks and flooded the land. All the fields were submerged and the creatures climbed the trees. But out of this confusion, under clouds, which lashed rain, was one dry hilltop. And it was on this first hilltop, on the first day, that came the first sunrise.

What happened then?

The sun shone down, and fed a tiny seed of hope. It was the beginning of our world.

74

CIAN

Cian forgot to eat his lunch again. There never was enough time. Today he and Corey went into the trees at the edge of the schoolyard and played monsters. Sometimes it gets so dark in there he could be inside a tomb. Sometimes he really does get frightened.

Teacher tells them to line up like a crocodile, and they walk out of class. Nearly all the boys run, but Cian doesn't like to do that. He likes to walk slowly. That's cool, more like a cowboy.

There she is, standing behind some of the other mothers. She steps forward, but he doesn't run, just slowly goes through the gates. They say nothing. He just takes her hand and they walk to the car.

'I'm starving,' he says as he plugs in his seatbelt.

'Did you not eat your lunch?'

'No, I forgot. I was playing.'

She sighs and he can see her eyes in the mirror. 'So what do you have in there?'

'Sandwich and two bars.'

'No fruit?'

'No.'

She sounds cross now. 'I told your father that you must always have a piece of fruit.'

'He does most times,' Cian says quickly. He doesn't mean to lie, but he doesn't want her to be cross.

Cian opens up the box. The sandwich is okay. His lunches never taste as good when his daddy does them.

'Are we going to your cottage?' Cian asks.

'No,' she hesitates. 'We're going somewhere else. It's a surprise, but first we're going to see if Johnny wants to come with us.'

'Oh, I don't think so, Mammy, he won't go anywhere with you.'

Her voice sounds shaky. 'Why not? I'm his mammy.'

They drive into town and Mammy parks outside Johnny's school, the big school. Cian peers out at the shiny white walls and long buildings. A heap of big kids start to pile out of the gates.

'Wait here, I won't be long,' she says and gets out of the car.

Cian watches her and at the same time sees his brother, in a group of big boys, coming out of the school. Johnny sees Mammy and he doesn't look happy.

Oh no, I hope they don't have a row, Cian thinks.

Cian watches. His mammy is flinging her arms this way and that, and talking, talking. Johnny is just standing there, not moving, and his arms are crossed.

Johnny does that to him sometimes, just stands and stares at him, as if he hates him. And sometimes he gives him a wallop on the back, and if Cian tells Daddy, he says toughen up and don't be such a tell-tale tit. Mammy always tells Johnny off. Once when Cian was a toddler she made Johnny stay in his room all day because he kicked Cian with his football boots on and Mammy said that was dangerous. She said that Johnny could have given him brain damage.

Now it's just the three of them, Daddy, Johnny and him. Daddy and Johnny have each other, but who does he have? So he has a make-believe friend and he calls him Jake, and he's nearly as good fun as Corey is at school.

Cian looks up again. All the boys with Johnny are just staring at Mammy, and some of them are whispering. He can see them hiding their mouths behind their hands. What are they saying?

Mammy stops talking now. She takes Johnny's hand, but he pulls

76

it away. It's no good, it's no good, thinks Cian. He can see she has given up. But it's odd then because he can see Johnny nodding. It looks like he's saying all right.

Still, he doesn't come.

Johnny is very good at football and he's clever too. Daddy says he can be anything he wants to be. Cian thinks he might be a superhero. That would be cool. Imagine if your brother was a superhero! He kneels up in the car, then dives down onto the seat. Whooh! He's flying up in the sky, on a superhero mission!

Mammy gets into the car and starts it up. She says nothing. Cian turns around and looks out the back window. He can see Johnny moving away from his friends, walking on his own, kicking a stone up the street.

Johnny looks up and sees Cian in the car. He waves. It's a big wave, like a really big goodbye. Cian waves back, and then they turn the corner.

CHRISTINA

She couldn't leave without trying.

The last time Christina had seen Johnny was a flash of his back as he walked out of the sitting room and into the kitchen, two weeks ago on the Sunday night when she had dropped Cian home. Even his back had said it all – stiff and hurt and determined not to turn around and acknowledge her.

What had she done to him?

She had tortured herself all the way home.

It was this guilt that had made her give up so easily, to relinquish custody in court. It would have been a hard fight, her solicitor told her, after what had happened, and with Johnny insisting he never wanted to set eyes on her again.

He was seventeen, and she had just blasted him out of adolescence into the adult world. There was no room for compassion in Johnny's eyes, just anger and confusion.

Johnny had cat's eyes, almond shaped and blue like Declan's. His lashes were dark and his cheekbones high. His blond hair was thicker than his father's and flopped around on top of his head, refusing to be tamed.

She remembered a time when Johnny had been happy to let her hold him, when he had needed her. He had been a nervous little boy and she remembered his first day at school, the way he had clung to her, refusing to let her out of his sight so that she had to sit down the back of the class all morning, waiting for an opportunity to sneak off.

There had been lots of times when it had been just her and Johnny, before Cian was born and when Declan was away with work. He used to like to bake, and they would destroy the kitchen trying out Granny Angel's cake recipes. The fun they would have! And then afterwards, cuddling up on the couch together, using the dog as a hearth rug and eating hot doughy cake until their bellies ached.

Oh, God! she thought. How things had changed.

'Johnny…' she hesitated, glancing at a smudge of blue ink on her son's bottom lip. He looked tired, older. She could see the beginnings of the man he would become.

'What are you doing here?' His eyes narrowed and he flicked his hair with his hand, only for it to fall immediately back over his face.

'Your hair's got very long,' she said, reaching over to push it out of his eyes.

'Get off me,' he said, brusquely stepping back. 'Go away. Can't you see how embarrassing this is for me?' he hissed through clenched lips. There were other kids around, but she didn't see them. They were just a sea of navy uniforms holding her son. All she could see was Johnny, and his tight anger.

'Just leave me alone.'

His voice was raw, his eyes filled with hurt.

Even before all of this, Johnny had been a sad child. He cried a lot as a baby, never seemed content. Unlike Cian, a happy baby, always a sunny disposition. Maybe it was her. Maybe while Johnny was in her womb he had picked up on all her fears, her growing sense of entrapment.

'I just need to see you, darling, please.'

'How could you do this to me, turn up here, in front of all my friends, during the exams?'

'Well, come with me now, we'll discuss it in the car.'

'No, I don't want to. Just go away.' He turned away from her, pulling his bag up his shoulder.

'Please, Johnny.' She reached out to him and tried to take hold of the bag. 'We're going somewhere and I want you to come too.'

'What do you mean?' He pushed her hand off the bag and stepped back again.

'Just a little break, for a few days. I really want you to come with me.'

'Does Dad know?' He looked at her strangely, his eyes black slits.

'No, and I'd rather he didn't,' she said nervously, glancing down at the ground. 'I just want it to be the three of us, you, me and Cian.'

'I can't, I've football. Besides, I don't want to be anywhere near you ever again.' He hurled the words out and they hit her like sharp stones.

'Johnny, I'm sorry. How many times do I have to try to explain?'

'There's no bloody explanation for what you did. Did you ever think how it made me feel?'

'Don't swear, please.'

'Fuck off.' His lips curled up in a snarl and he reminded her of a dog defending its territory, all bark and no bite.

'Okay, okay, I'm going. The exams—'

'They're okay,' he interrupted.

'Are you finished now?'

'Yeah. Listen, will you just go?'

She stared at him. He was scarlet. Her son was ashamed of her. A wave of nausea flooded her mouth.

'Right,' she nodded, turning. 'Please don't tell your dad about this, will you?' He said nothing. 'Johnny?'

'All right, just go away.'

She had felt that he wanted to hit her, just flick her away because her presence hurt too much.

Keep him safe, she whispered, her fingers gripping the steering wheel, please protect him. She didn't know who she was asking – she just pushed the thought out, hoping it would remain like a blanket around him after she was gone.

She had taken a risk telling him that they were going away for the weekend, although she didn't say where. Johnny could ring Declan now on his mobile and she could be stopped. But Johnny had promised that he wouldn't tell.

She wasn't sure when she would see him again.

The thought made her feel sick once more. How could she leave him? But this was her only way out, this one tiny opening. She glanced in the rear view mirror. Cian was looking out of the window, talking to himself, oblivious to her turmoil.

Had she lost him forever? Her Johnny boy?

You deserve to lose him.

It didn't matter what she deserved. Whatever it was about Johnny, she was sure that Cian was happier with her. It had always been that way, the family split down the middle.

Johnny had been Declan's, for as long as she could remember. As soon as her husband had introduced Johnny to Gaelic, it had been love at first sight. Every spare moment was either spent playing football and hurling or going to see matches. Christina had always felt that the two of them were in collusion, talking about their precious GAA. Johnny was able to command Declan's full attention, something she had never been able to achieve.

She did try for a while. She went along to the matches, cheered, tried to understand the scoring, but it wasn't in her, this passion, and they knew she was just pretending. So she gave up. Before Cian came along, her life had been very lonely.

With Cian there was a bond, an understanding, which she had never shared with her eldest son. It broke her heart.

Had Johnny always known this? Had he detected a part of his mother he could never reach, a part his little brother was master of?

They say that you love all your children the same way. It just wasn't true.

Declan and Christina had brought out the worst in each other. She could see that now. And when their young love quickly died, smothered by domestic chores and the demands of the real world, they were both too afraid to do anything about it but clung on to what little they had in the hope that some day the old magic might return. She couldn't blame Declan. There were times when he had tried. But as she saw Johnny grow up, she saw that Declan was capable of such immense love, such tenderness. It was a side of him she rarely saw but was there, laid out at her son's feet. She couldn't help a slight feeling of resentment, then shame. What kind of mother was jealous of her own son?

It was around that time she had started drinking during the day. A glass of wine at lunchtime helped her cope with the demands of a cranky pre-school child. And then another glass or two before dinner, a little ritual she enjoyed while she was cooking.

She hadn't been addicted. She gave up when she was pregnant with Cian and didn't drink for a whole year after he was born.

What had made her start again?

She remembered now. It had been her birthday, but Declan had insisted on taking Johnny to a match. She had been so mad, and jealous, especially when they got back from Dublin and Johnny told her that Declan had taken him to the cinema as well. She remembered the two of them, compatriots, almost laughing at her anger while the baby cried upstairs. She had felt so excluded.

Christina hit the main road. It was hot and she opened the sunroof. Although it was the same old road as always, it looked different. She was driving into a dream, or a film. She was watching herself speeding along with Cian in the back, winding down the windows. A delicious breeze passed through the car and Christina's nerves began to dissipate. Finally, she was doing something.

GRETA

I was walking in the woods today, and what struck me was how still everything was. The sky was bright blue and you could still see the moon in the sky. There was no wind, no dampness, an early morning chill, but the sun became a little stronger, the birds sang a little louder. It was a perfect spring day.

I wrapped up and my breath crystalised in the air. It was so quiet that any movement was amplified a thousand times over.

A hawk took off from the top of the hill, and I could hear its wings beating through the sky. It made my heart race. I could hear the conversation of the birds, the dimension of it, the shape of their sounds, flattened now and again by a distant car.

As I walked deeper into the wood, I felt I was coming closer to the heart of it. All this stillness, the peace. I fell on a tree root, but my landing was cushioned by the soft mounds of completely dry earth.

I went into the centre.

And at the top of the wood, the mud was still tipped with white and the puddles were frozen over. I looked at the ice patterns and the water trapped in ice, its flow arrested. I think it was the most beautiful thing I have ever seen.

My walk was one moment in my life. And this one moment was eternal.

And then I saw it. One tiny primrose, come too soon. The air was so clean I knew it would freeze again tonight. That little flower had no chance. I touched it but didn't pick it.

Aren't you brave? I said.

83

CHRISTINA

Christina parked the car in the long-term zone and took the shuttle bus to the main terminal. Cian jigged up and down on the seat beside her.

'We're going on an aeroplane! We're going on an aeroplane!'

Other passengers looked at him and smiled over at her. She smiled stiffly back.

She was rigid with apprehension, her earlier confidence short lived. She opened her bag yet again, checking the tickets and her and Cian's passports. She even had Johnny's passport, which she'd slipped into her bag the day she left home. Even then she'd had an inkling of what she might have to do.

Unless Johnny had said something to Declan, there was no possible reason why they would be stopped. As far as Declan was concerned, Cian was spending the weekend in Helen's cottage.

She pressed the palms of her hands together. They were hot and sticky. Was she doing the right thing? Was this what was best for Cian? Was she able to do this? It was too late now. She had set things in motion and it was as if her instincts had taken over.

Christina pulled the photograph of Greta, the snowman and herself out of her bag. Cian lit upon it.

'Who's that, Mammy?'

'That's me, when I was a little girl.'

'That's a very big snowman.'

'It is, isn't it?'

'And who's that, Mammy?'

'It's my mammy.'

'She doesn't look like Granny Angel,' Cian said, glancing away and looking at a plane taking off.

Christina said nothing. There was time to explain things later.

What was she looking for? A small part of herself that had walked out the door arm in arm with her mother the day she left?

She was looking for sanctuary.

The bus pulled up outside Departures and everyone tumbled out. Inside the airport was busy and she scanned the screens looking for their check-in area. Cian was running about, skidding on the shiny floor.

'Cian, come here please!' She called him several times and eventually he came over, hanging his head, his soft sandy hair stuck to his red cheeks.

'Why do I have to stand still?' he moaned.

'Because you could get lost,' she said. 'Because someone could steal you.'

'Steal me?' His eyes opened wide. 'Why?'

'Some people do nasty things like that.'

He stood close to her and took her hand. 'Where are we going?' he asked.

'America.'

'Are Daddy and Johnny coming?'

'No.'

'Why not?'

'Because they're busy. They have to go to a match.'

'And I don't have to go with them? Great!' He paused for a moment and scratched his head. 'Do you think we can get a real cowboy hat?' He squeezed her hand.

'I'm sure we'll find something,' she replied.

'Great!' He was beaming. She stopped walking, put down her case and bent down so she was on a level with him.

'Are you excited about going on an aeroplane for the first time?'

'Yeah, yeah, yeah!' he grinned, rubbing his hands, pushing his damp face close to hers.

'Me too.'

They rubbed noses and she hugged him as he wrapped his arms around her waist. She kissed his forehead and smelled his sweetness. She felt heady to have him back and she squeezed him tighter.

'I can't wait to get on the plane,' Cian said, pulling away. Suddenly he frowned. 'But Mammy, we forgot Paddington! We can't go without Paddington.'

'We can't go back now, pet, we'll miss the plane.'

His lip wobbled and his eyes screwed up. 'But Paddington!' he wailed.

'I'll get you a new teddy in the shop,' she said hastily, taking the case up in one hand and dragging Cian along with the other. 'I'm sure you'll meet a new member of the family somewhere in the airport.'

They checked in and then made their way over to some shops, but there were no teddy bears.

'Let's go through the gate over there, there'll be more shops,' Christina said. She was feeling jumpy. She wanted to get away from the main concourse.

They went through security. On the other side was a row of fancy shops with lines of people walking up and down. After the isolation of Helen's cottage, Christina felt exposed, as if she was thrust under a spotlight. There were so many people pushing into her, so much noise. Why couldn't they give her some space?

She looked up at the departures screen and brought her hand up to push her hair out of eyes. She could see it was shaking. 'Okay,' she said with mock bravado. 'We've got plenty of time.'

'I'm hungry,' Cian said.

There only seemed to be a swanky chocolate shop cum café, so they sat down there. Cian chose a hot chocolate and two large chocolate cookies. Not exactly what she had intended. Her coffee was a bad idea. The sharp, bitter taste of the strong drink made her feel even more tense.

Her mobile rang and she jumped. She took it out of her bag. Declan.

If she didn't answer he might get suspicious, but if she did he might guess something was up anyway. She couldn't risk him turning up at the cottage and discovering they weren't there.

'Christina, it's Declan.'

'Yes, I know.'

'What were you doing at Johnny's school today?'

She froze, her mind racing.

'I…I wanted to see if he'd come to me for the weekend.'

'But why did you have to go and do that right outside his school, in front of all his friends when he's in the middle of exams? Have you no consideration for how it made him feel?'

'I just wanted to see if he had forgiven me.'

'Me, me, me. Why don't you think of your children for a change?'

'That's not fair, Declan. You know that's not true.' She took a breath. It was no use arguing. 'I can't talk, Cian's with me.'

'Just leave Johnny alone. He doesn't want to know at the moment. Besides, we've a match on Sunday.'

'Oh, yes, of course,' she said hazily.

'That's why I'm calling as well. I want to collect Cian on Sunday morning so I can bring him to the game, with me and Johnny.'

'You can't,' she answered quickly.

'Don't give me that old one, that he doesn't like Gaelic. It's part of the family and it's about time he got involved a bit,' he said, misreading her reaction.

'I've something planned on Sunday. He can't go.' She bent her

87

head down and stared at the dregs of her coffee.

'What?' But before she could think of an answer, he added, 'What's all that noise? Where are you, Christina? It sounds like you're in a train station or something.'

'We're just in that café in the Navan shopping centre.'

Cian stopped eating and stared at her. She looked up and smiled at him.

'Put Cian on to me, will you?' Declan said. 'I want to talk to him.'

'I can't, he's eating. Look, my battery is about to go, I'll ring you later.'

'Okay,' Declan said and hung up.

He had guessed. He was ringing the Guards this very moment. She turned her phone off and slung it back into her bag. It was better to ignore him now, at this stage.

'Mammy, who was that?' Cian's head was on one side, like a little bird.

'It was Daddy.'

'Why did you lie to him?' His eyes were like two black beads.

'What do you mean?'

'Why did you say we were in the Navan shopping centre?'

'Because this trip is a secret, sweetie, just between you and me.'

'Like in Danny the Champion of the World? His daddy has a secret too, and only Danny knows.' He smiled, a chocolate ring around his mouth.

'Yes, that's right,' she said, leaning over and wiping his face with a napkin.

'I wonder what Daddy's secret is. Because every grown-up has a secret.' His eyes sparkled, and then he started whispering to himself. This was a habit of Cian's. Sometimes Christina tried to hear what he was saying but she could only catch one or two words and strange sound effects, like whooshing noises and little squeaks. Once she asked him what he was talking about. He looked at her oddly, as if woken from a dream, surprised she was still there, and said, 'It's private.'

They wandered around the shops. The coffee sat in the pit of her stomach like acid and her mouth tasted sour. She was so tired.

'Oh, look, look,' Cian said excitedly. 'Can I have one of those?' It was a small teddy bear with a T-shirt on that said 'Aer Rianta'.

'Okay, sure,' Christina answered distractedly.

'I'm going to call him Walter,' Cian said.

'Why Walter?'

'Because it suits him,' Cian said with conviction.

At last she heard their flight being announced. As they walked down the tunnel into the plane, everything felt surreal. It was as if they were walking in slow motion, the silver walls twisting this way and that, the floor beneath them slippery and black, the *thud, thud, thud* of their feet in the silver foil tube which was pulling them along. They turned the corner and suddenly the plane was there. A hostess was standing at its entrance, welcoming them. Christina watched Cian as he skipped aboard the plane, charming the cabin crew.

She would never give him up.

GRETA

I watch my body change. In the bath I look at the bloom of my stomach and my breasts, large and full. I always had a tiny little chest, but now I'm positively buxom! When I was pregnant with Christina I didn't grow to such an extent. It's odd how each time can be different.

Tomás is fascinated by my new body. At night he touches my breasts gingerly, feeling his way around them. It doesn't take him long to get excited. I thought that I might go off all of that now I'm pregnant again, because that's what happened before. But this time it's exactly the opposite, as if we have just got married all over again.

Maybe it's all that good food Angeline is cooking. Certainly things between us have been so much better since she came, and there was I, worried that she might get in the way – not in a bad way, just make us feel self-conscious. I was concerned Tomás might think the food was too foreign, but he loves it. He says it reminds him of the meals we ate in France when we were on honeymoon and Christina was conceived. At night, in bed, he tells me it's the food of love.

Angeline's room is on the far side of the house and she goes up there every night to meditate. I can't believe she does it every day – she's like a nun! Once she's gone upstairs, myself and Tomás start teasing each other. It'll start with a silly game, like tickling or blowing in my ear while we're watching the television, and then we start kissing and Tomás becomes all hot and bothered and he has to take me upstairs.

Let me tell you a secret. I never really enjoyed sex until I got pregnant this time. Now I feel voluptuous. I wish I could be pregnant forever! Last night, for instance, Tomás spent ages just kissing my breasts and stroking my stomach – cradling the tiny, tiny bump with his big strong hands – and he makes love to me with such devotion. I close my eyes and let go. It's wonderful being a wife. I feel so safe and protected and cherished.

Afterwards we snuggle up to each other and sleep like two little animals in the wild. I imagine us curled up in the sheets, two feral things.

CHRISTINA

As they took off, they held hands.

'It's like we're in a rocket going to the moon,' Cian said. 'Look, look at the cars and the houses! Look, they're tiny!'

They were silent for a few minutes, watching civilisation disappear, rising up through the clouds. Christina's thoughts scattered as she looked out the tiny window over her son's head. The plane was above the clouds now and they were dazzled by brilliant sunshine.

'Why are we going on holidays without Daddy and Johnny?' Cian scratched his head and pressed his lips together. He looked very serious.

'Well, we're not actually going on holidays. We're going to visit someone.'

'Really?' Cian looked surprised. 'But who do we know who lives in America?'

'Your granny.'

He paused and fiddled with his seatbelt. 'But Mammy, you're wrong, both my grannies live in Ireland.'

'This is a new granny, one you haven't met before.'

Cian knotted his brows together. 'What do you mean? I already have two grannies, how can I have three?'

'Sometimes you can.' Cian looked up at her expectantly. Christina gripped the armrest and continued, 'You have Granny McDonagh, and she's Daddy's mammy, and Granny Angel, who is married to Grandpa, but she's not actually my mother. Granny Angel is my stepmother, so you see, I have another mammy.'

Cian beamed up at her. 'And that makes granny number three?'

'That's right.'

Cian scratched his head. 'But why haven't I met her?'

'Because she lives in America.' She could see Cian thinking. She wanted him to stop asking questions. She quickly picked up his book. 'Shall I read to you, darling?'

'No, I want to look out the window.' He sat back into his seat, squeezing Walter in under his seatbelt.

Christina stared straight ahead, breathed in and watched all the other people reading their books, putting on the headsets and settling in for the long haul. One of the cabin crew walked past, showering her with a bright smile. No one knew who she was, and by the time she met her mother, she could be someone else completely. She could reinvent herself.

Cian was silent and still, looking out of the window, impressed by the magic of what he saw. Everything was new and edged with meaning. A field of clouds looked so pure, untainted Cian said he was looking for angels – and so inside herself, something new began. She was emerging, into uncharted territory.

GRETA

Poor Angeline! It must be so awful to be alone.

If anything happened to Tomás I don't know what I'd do. In fact, just thinking it makes me shake with fear. I think I would have to throw myself on top of his grave like one of the ancient Romans. The only way I could stay alive was for Christina and the baby.

Christina is a big girl now. She's doing very well in school. Who does she look like? A little like Mammy, I think. She has curly hair as well.

This morning she came downstairs very excited because it's St Patrick's Day. Angeline had dressed her completely in green clothes. She looked like a little pixie – she even had green tights on, I don't know where Angeline found those! Then Angeline came into the kitchen and she looked just wonderful – like St Anne! She was wearing an exquisite green dress made of layers and layers of silk that flowed down to the ground. Her hair was loose and she had tied twirls of green ribbon throughout it. She had done the same to Christina's hair, but being longer and jet black, Angeline's looked even more dramatic. She even painted her fingernails green! And she was wearing big green discs on her ears and a huge clump of shamrocks pinned onto her left breast.

Good Lord! Tomás exclaimed. You look like the Emerald Isle itself, Angeline!

I was embarrassed by my husband's forthrightness.

You're beautiful, I said.

And look at the two of you, she teased, not a touch of green to be seen on either of you. She produced a mound of shamrocks and, shaping them into two little bundles, pinned one on each of us.

There, she said, ready for the parade.

Tomás ruffled Christina's hair. I'll see you ladies later, he said, going out into the back hall to put on his boots.

When is the parade starting? Christina ran around the room, a flash of green.

Not for a couple of hours, said Angeline, and taking out the weighing scales, she announced, Let's do some baking!

Christina jumped up and down.

Can I join in too? I asked. I'd love you to teach me some things.

Angeline hesitated then. I don't know why, maybe she thinks that I'm such a bad cook I'm consigned to be a hopeless case.

Of course, she answered a little stiffly.

I may as well have not bothered because I couldn't retain any of her instructions as it was. She said that she was going to make a special Patrick's Day cake and the recipe was extremely complicated. I was ordered to cream the butter and sugar for what seemed an eternity. My arm was heavy and sore by the time she accepted the mixture. The cake was a strange concoction. There were many different kinds of chocolate and toffees and cream all mixed up together.

When it was ready, after Angeline had covered it in a special peppermint icing with Christina helping, and in keeping with the green theme, of course, we went to the parade. It was very cold. The wind whipped right through us and I was ready for a hot port in O'Hagans after it was all over.

It seemed to go on forever, brass bands followed by trucks with loudspeakers and children dressed in green leaning out of trailers and waving. It was the usual St Patrick's Day hilarity all around, especially

95

when Joe Mackey's black pig broke free and ran squealing around the square. At least that made us move a little and warm ourselves up.

By the time we got to O'Hagans, Christina's hands were freezing and I made her stand by the fire. Tomás was inside already with Liam Flanagan and Sam White. He looked very rosy there, up at the bar with his pint and his pals. Angeline and I bought two hot ports and cosied down together by the fire. The place was packed and it was hard to hear each other.

Jack used to love Paddy's Day, Angeline said. He used to always buy a piece of green ribbon with a cut-out gold harp stuck on it and pin it to his jacket and wear it all day long. He'd just be waiting for all the Brits to ask, what's that then? He was never ashamed to be Irish, even after that dreadful bomb in Guildford went off.

You must miss him a lot, I said.

She sat quietly for a couple of seconds, and then to my utter amazement said, No. I'm glad he left me.

I was stunned. I didn't know what to say or do, and luckily she began to talk again because I was speechless. I just couldn't think of a word to say in reply.

That must sound strange, she half-smiled, then looked into the fire and, pulling Christina back from the sparks, she continued. But we were never compatible. We fought terribly, and he used to hit me, more than once, quite a lot. Jack was a very jealous man. If I so much as looked at someone else he would be accusing me of dreadful things. It was a terrible strain. In our last job he was convinced that I was having an affair with our employer. It was very upsetting. And then when we found we couldn't have children, he blamed me. He said that I must have done something awful in the past, he said I must have ruined myself.

That's dreadful, Angeline.

I should have left him, but I kept on hoping for a child. I couldn't face the truth. She turned to me, her black eyes fierce.

You wouldn't have recognised me then, Greta. It was before all of this. She passed her hand over her dress. Before I became conscious.

It's hard to understand Angeline when she starts to talk like this. It's to do with the incense and meditation, this 'consciousness'. From what I can gather it's not that different from our faith, not in the greater scheme of things.

She sighed, sipping her hot port. The funny thing is that it was Jack who was conducting the affair all along. He ran away with the gardener's daughter in our last position.

That's appalling.

He got what he wanted. They already have two children. Poor as church mice, but breeding.

She cradled her steaming glass in her hands.

I just hope he isn't hitting her too.

I looked at her then, surprised, but there was no touch of irony in her tone. She did mean it. She was able to wish this woman, who stole her husband, absolutely no ill will.

Aren't you angry with him? Don't you hate her? I prodded.

Of course I was angry, and hurt, but then I went to live in London and everything changed. I came into contact with Buddhism and it made me understand why this had happened to me, that myself and Jack had been karmically tied.

What does that mean?

It means that I had created that situation and I had to live through it.

But how could your husband having an affair be your fault?

No, I didn't mean it was my fault, but that I could learn from what had happened. I couldn't blame anyone – not his new wife, not even Jack.

I rocked back on my stool, chewing my fingernail. I couldn't be like that, I said with certainty. I'd want revenge.

Believe me, you wouldn't, because the only person you would destroy would be yourself.

I nodded, not knowing what to say, so I took her hand. She had a big ring on her middle finger, a bright green stone stuck in its centre. I stared at the ring and its different states of green.

It's been hard for you, Angeline. I hope you're happier now, with us.

Oh, I am. She squeezed my fingers. You saved my life!

We went home soon afterwards, just us girls, and ate a feast. Angeline made a delicious Italian soup with little pieces of pasta shaped like bows, or as Christina insists, butterflies, and chunks of clove-flavoured ham and fresh peas, tomatoes and basil leaves. Afterwards we had huge slices of her St Patrick's Day cake – an oozing, fudgy, chocolate concoction served with a bowl of whipped cream. The rich, deep chocolate was offset perfectly by the peppermint icing. It was so filling we could only manage one slice each. But when Tomás came in, and very merry he was from O'Hagans, he ate the rest up. The whole thing, just like that!

When he had finished he was sporting a huge chocolate grin like a big child. He made us all laugh so much, and then he chased Christina around the house pretending he was a giant chocolate bear.

CHRISTINA

The lights went out. An occasional shaft illuminated the heads of lone readers, but there was a new peace in the cabin. Most slept. The cabin crew had disappeared and a hush spread through the plane. With all these strangers she shared something so personal – the world of dreams.

She looked over at Cian. His head was resting on the small white pillow and the blue and green blanket was pulled up to his chin. She felt safe when she watched him sleep because his perfection was so clear to her then, and life became simple.

They were speeding through the thick black night, yet in this machine time stood still. The minutes crawled and she had the sensation of time turning backwards, running upstream. Was it possible to start again?

They hit some turbulence and the seatbelt lights blinked orange. Cian stirred in his sleep, but he was too far in to wake. She pulled down her little table and spread her hands on it. They were very small, like a child's. She looked at her wedding ring, the only adornment, fingered it and then began to pull it off. It stuck on the knuckle. It was impossible to get it free and in the end she gave up.

The veins on the back of her hand were raised, like a map of blue lines. Her blood was the river that ran through her and its source could never be denied. That's why she was here. She didn't want anything off her mother, not even an explanation, not now. She just wanted to see her face, survey the flesh, the blood, the breath of this woman she was a part of. Here I am, she would say. I just needed to meet you.

That would be enough for Christina.

THE SLURRY PIT

Christina doesn't want to go, but her daddy tells her she must. He says that her cousins have come over especially for the day to play with her, and besides, Angeline is too busy making lunch to look after her.

But I can help her, she says, I can lay the table.

No, says her daddy, you'll get in the way. It'll do you good, get a bit of colour into your cheeks.

Reluctantly Christina puts on her coat and wellies and goes out into the yard. It's raining a bit and the day is grey and damp. She wants to be inside, in the warm golden hub of the kitchen, dancing to the radio while Angeline cooks. The icy rain bites her cheeks and she blinks, looking across the filthy yard at her three cousins, who seemed completely unaware of the weather. Their jackets are open, hats and gloves off and their hair down, strung around their faces in wet, tangled strands. They're the image of each other.

Helen, Sue and Annie are playing chase but Christina can't make out who's It. They keep shoving each other and Annie falls over in the muck, but she just laughs. She doesn't seem to care that her jeans are streaked with mud and her face spattered and dirty. They're so rough. Christina tucks herself behind her daddy, a tiny shadow, hoping not to be noticed.

Christina!

Helen comes bounding towards her. She's a real tomboy, and today she's wearing a cowboy outfit, a black hat with a marshal's

101

silver star on it and a holster with two guns.

Draw! she yells, and takes them out, firing at Christina. Ah, you didn't draw, she moans.

I don't have a gun, Christina says quietly, ducking just in time before Annie and Sue land fistfuls of muddy gravel on them.

Ow! Helen shouts, turning around. I'll have the pair of ye! She runs off after her two younger sisters.

Come on, you lot!

It's her Uncle Raymond. The men are getting into the Range Rover.

Where are we going? Helen asks as the three sisters clamber into the back, squeezing Christina into a corner. They feel wet and clammy next to her and Sue keeps sneezing.

Up to the pigs, says her daddy.

But the girls aren't listening any more, busy instead squeezing each other.

Dad, Annie's pinching me.

No I'm not.

The men ignore them. Uncle Raymond lights up a cigarette and her daddy turns on the radio. It's Irish music, what Angeline calls diddly-i music, but her daddy likes it and whenever they're in the Range Rover on their own, he puts it on. Pressed up against the window, Christina makes a small hole in the condensation and looks at the wet fields. Notes from the music fill her head, making her heart spin faster, and she pulls her fingers down the side of the pane, making damp patterns. The rain is heavier now, lashing the sides of the jeep, and against the slate sky the grass looks shockingly bright green. It's a lovely colour.

They have turned off the lane and are driving down a boreen. Her cousins giggle as they bounce around in the back of the jeep. Suddenly Sue, the youngest, leans across Helen and pulls on Christina's sleeve. Christina, where's your mammy gone?

102

Helen pushes Sue back into her seat. Don't ask her that, silly.

Sue looks at her sister defiantly, and then, leaning across her again, she pokes Christina. Is Auntie Greta coming back?

Helen pushes Sue right off the seat and she lands with a thud on floor. Ow!

Serves you right, Helen says. I told you not to ask.

Annie is sitting behind them. She leans forward and rests her elbows on the back of the seat. She presses in close to Christina and whispers, Did she run away?

Helen's eyes narrow. What did you say to her? Do you not remember? Mammy said we were to say nothing about Auntie Greta! I'll tell on ye both now, so I will!

Helen glances over at Christina, but she's turned away, her nose pressed up to the window, letting the steam from her breath make clouds. She sees a brown horse cantering in a field alongside the jeep and she's outside too now, cantering beside it. She's not there any more. She doesn't hear what her cousins are saying.

By the time they get to the farm it has stopped raining. The smell is awful when they get out of the Range Rover. Christina puts her hand over her nose but her cousins don't seem to notice and run towards the sheds.

Come on, Christina, says her daddy.

They are standing on the other side of the slurry pit. Her daddy and Uncle Raymond step over it with ease. Helen is across in one bound and Annie follows her easily.

Christina stands nervously beside Sue.

You're next, Christina, says her daddy, but she shakes her head.

You have to go over it, he says. It's the only way through here at the moment.

No, she says quietly.

Helen and Annie stare at her. It's not big, Helen says.

It's easy, Annie says.

Come on, Christina, you're holding everyone up.

It smells.

Ah Jaysus, come on then, Sue, you go first, says her Uncle Raymond.

Okay, Sue trills out happily, but as she steps towards the pit she slips on the concrete and Christina watches, horrified, as she sees her cousin fall into the foul pit. She's screaming. She can see Sue's blond head going under, being sucked down.

Christ, quick, Tomás! Uncle Raymond shouts.

He's over the pit in one swift movement, leans in and pulls out his daughter while her daddy runs to get a bucket of water. They throw it over Sue's face as she coughs and splutters and howls.

They all run back to the jeep then, the men yelling at the other girls to hurry and get in for Christ's sake before their sister gets pneumonia.

Sue is in the front, wrapped in her father's coat on his lap while her daddy speeds out the gate and down the boreen. Helen, Annie and Christina sit quietly in the back. Her cousins are pale and tearful, no longer fidgeting, suddenly meek. Christina can't stop shaking. She clutches her hands together, but her teeth begin to chatter.

There's a terrible smell in the Rover. It makes Annie throw up, but no one notices. The thick, putrid odour of pig shit is filling their pores.

When they get back to the house, Angeline goes up to the bathroom with Sue and the other children are herded into the sitting room, given long glasses of purple Ribena and told to behave. Her daddy and her Uncle Raymond disappear. It's still raining outside, and the room is dark without any lights on.

She's such a silly Sue, says Annie, the whites of her eyes gleaming in the half light as she begins to roam around the room, picking up ornaments and putting them down.

At least she gave it a go, says Helen, bouncing up and down on

104

the sofa. Her cousins look over at her and Christina cringes.

It was too big, she says quietly.

No it wasn't, Sue just slipped, Helen says.

Were you afraid? Annie asks.

Christina wishes they would go home now. She wants to go upstairs and play with her dolls.

Annie picks up a picture of Angeline and Christina the day of her First Communion.

Is Angeline your mammy now? she asks, smiling, a purple moustache from the Ribena framing her mouth.

Shut up about that, will ye? Helen yells and runs across the room, lighting on Annie. The two of them begin to roll around on the floor, pulling each other's hair and biting.

Stop, says Christina, just stop, will you? Please, please!

She begins to sob, the fear and the shame of the last hour drowning her. Her two cousins sit up, a fuzzy, tangled heap.

Why are *you* crying? asks Helen.

GRETA

If the baby's a boy we'll call him Matthew, after my father, and if it's a girl, then she'll be called Lily, after my mother, because we called Christina after Tomás's mother. This way it's fair.

I'm fingering my favourite tree, touching its gnarled trunk and the brittle sticks which shield its base. It's a tree growing within a tree, like the two hearts which beat in my body now.

Winter has stripped it of its glory, although today I can see little red buds on its skinny twig-branches. They're so dense that cobwebs hang between them, and old leaves caught there from last autumn.

As I'm touching the tree, a feeling comes over me like a wave. It makes me sleepy. It's as if a spirit brushes my forehead, clears all my fears away and holds me then, like a father holding his child.

A twig snaps, the wood stirs and suddenly the mood is gone.

I turn around. Angeline is behind me.

Are you following me? I ask her. It just comes out this way because it feels like she is.

And she says, Of course not, I always walk up here.

She comes towards me and today she is all in red. A huge woollen shawl is draped about her shoulders, and she has a big woolly red hat on and gloves. Her cheeks are glowing, and she exhales steam.

It's still very cold, isn't it? she says, standing next to me and looking out of a clearing in the trees towards the hills.

Yes, but it's so beautiful when it's like this. The light plays tricks and everything looks hazy. I point. Look at the gleam on the fields.

106

Yes, she agrees, it's dreamlike, and then pauses before she asks me, Are you all right?

I tell her I'm a little sad because it's my father's birthday. She puts her arm through mine and gives me a squeeze. What are you doing here? I ask.

Oh, I have a headache and I thought the fresh air would do me good.

Let me see if I can make it better, I say.

She smiles at me then as if I'm a fool, but takes her hat off all the same.

I slip my gloves off and rub my hands. Then I touch her gently on the shoulders, and slowly work from her arms up to her neck, her jaw and the crown of her head. When I finish she's completely silent. She stands with her back to me, staring at the fields. And then she says, in a hush, You have a gift.

I know, I say, but don't tell anyone, otherwise they'll all be round.

What do you mean?

Tomás told me not to do it. He's worried I'll turn into a faith healer or something.

She laughs, and I laugh too because it seems like such a ridiculous idea. Then she pulls me forward and says, Come on, let's go and have some tea, I've made a brack.

I groan, No more food, there will be no room for the baby soon.

CHRISTINA

Christina had known for years. She had chanced upon her mother's address quite by accident, when she was only ten years old. It was her father's birthday and Christina had been in his bedroom, searching through his large mahogany bureau, looking for Sellotape. She had been trying to wrap a present.

The envelope was torn open and stuck to her fingertips. She shook it off, and as she did she noticed the name scrawled on the back.

Greta Comyn.

Christina had started. Her mother never came into her daily life. She hadn't thought about her for years. It had been almost as if she were dead.

Trembling suddenly, Christina picked up the envelope. It was empty. She flipped it around. It was addressed to her father. She felt her cheeks suddenly flushed, and bit her lips. Why had her mother not written to her?

Christina turned the envelope over again and read the back:

Greta Comyn, 1274 Chilberg Avenue, La Conner, Washington, USA

She heard her father outside and instinctively shoved the envelope into her back pocket. When he came in she didn't ask him about it. For some reason, she felt it would be disloyal.

Christina had always looked after that old envelope. She took it out from time to time and wondered whether she should write. But something always stopped her – pride, or was it fear? Even now she had decided to just go. She hadn't written first, or phoned. She had been so afraid of rejection that she wanted to turn up there in the flesh so that it would be literally impossible to close the door in her face.

Christina had never really believed that one day they would actually meet. Yet here she was in Seattle, in a hotel room, with Cian tucked into bed. She opened the state map she'd bought when they landed and looked at the pattern of little white islands and peninsulas which seemed to cling to the coast of America. Across a strait of blue sea there was one large island, coloured pale yellow and blank because this map was American. It was Vancouver Island.

She had known for years where Washington state was, in the upper north-western corner of America, yet this map fascinated her. She had spent all her life tucked away from the sea, and now she was heading towards the widest of them all, the Pacific. It was exciting. In between all the confusion and fear there was at least one positive thing. She was finally living her life, and no one was telling her what to do.

Christina got up from the bed and looked out of the window. It was completely dark now, with just the faintest tinge of purple in the sky. She looked down at Seattle, at the lights of the cars swishing by, the street lamps and the neon signs on the building opposite. From the plane she'd been able to see a huge mountain looming in the distance. It had looked like a volcano, like something from the Orient. It had been completely white, pure, with sheer slopes.

This was a completely new world.

She had seen Seattle from above, its tall, sheer buildings sparkling in the sunlight, and behind it a deep blue line, nothing beyond. She imagined all the people like her, passing through on a journey, looking for someone or something.

Christina glanced at her clock on the table. It was nearly midnight and Cian was fast asleep, Walter pushed up onto the pillow beside him so that they looked like brothers.

It was the twenty-first of June, the longest day of the year. It also felt like the longest day of her life.

THE WEDDING DRESS

Angeline wants Christina to come with her. It means a day off school, so her father takes a little persuading but Angeline insists, saying that she needs Christina's advice.

What does a thirteen-year-old know about wedding dresses? her father asks, exasperated.

I want her to be involved, Tom, Angeline says, sidling up to him and giving him a kiss. Besides, she'll need to be fitted for her bridesmaid outfit.

Well, I suppose it does make sense, he gives in grudgingly.

Christina spends ages choosing an outfit for their shopping expedition. They're going to Sligo, to an old school friend of Angeline's who's a dressmaker. It's going to take over two hours to get there, so they have to leave early in the morning. Christina lays everything out on top of her chest of drawers, ready for the next day. In the end she chooses a blue and white striped polo neck sweater and a new pair of jeans that have embroidery flowers down the side.

It's a bright sunny day, warm for March. Angeline drives fast. There's a stereo in the Range Rover and Angeline asks her to choose a tape.

I brought some Abba, Christina says.

Great! Stick it on.

They sing along to 'Name of the Game', 'Knowing Me, Knowing You', 'Dancing Queen'.

I'm very impressed, says Angeline, you know all the words!

Christina looks out the window, continuing to sing 'Take a Chance on Me'. The day feels different and special. It's exciting to be on the road with Angeline, to be going to Sligo, somewhere new.

They go straight to the dressmaker's house, which is up a hill on the way out of town. There's a view of the sea and the square-shaped Ben Bulben. It's windy and colder than back home.

Mary, the dressmaker, takes them into the front room and brings out a folder full of pictures of dresses.

So many different designs! sighs Angeline.

Well, you'll look gorgeous in all of them, Angeline, you've a perfect figure.

I don't want to look like a meringue though!

In the end they pick something Mary calls classic, with a bias cut, very 1930s, in ivory. Seeing as it's not your first, Mary adds. For Christina they choose a pale lavender dress with a soft A-line skirt, no flounces, but simple and flattering.

By the time they're finished it's past two. They spill back out onto the blustery road as Mary promises the dresses will be finished in plenty of time.

It's a May wedding, isn't it?

Yes, Angeline says, the fifteenth of May.

Christina opens the car door. She can hear Mary whispering something to Angeline.

No, she's gone years, she hears Angeline reply. He got an annulment.

Christina turns around. She can see that Angeline is flushed and that Mary is looking at Christina in an odd way, as if she feels sorry for her.

Let's get some lunch, Angeline says as they drive back down the hill. I'm starving.

They go to Wimpy and Angeline buys Christina a hamburger and chips as well as a Coke. The drink is flat and warm, the burger limp and the bap soggy with grease, but Christina doesn't care. It's great to eat out for a change.

We went to school here, you know, Angeline says.

We?

Yes, your mother and I.

Christina stops eating and stares at Angeline, who's looking away from her, out the door at the cars flashing down the high street.

You never ask about her, she says softly.

Christina swallows her mouthful of bap and squirms uncomfortably in her plastic seat. It squeaks.

Angeline turns to look at her. She looks like an Indian. Her dark hair and skin are soft and silky, her long black lashes flutter and her brow is fine and narrow. She sits straight and wraps her scarf around her shoulders.

Don't you want to know about her? she asks.

No, Christina says quickly, her cheeks burning. Her head begins to ache.

Are you sure, darling? Angeline asks.

No, I don't want to know anything about her, she snaps.

Okay, I'm sorry. I don't want to upset you. I won't mention her again.

Christina continues to eat, shovelling down the chips, gulping the Coke, chewing away. She doesn't want to talk about it, not ever.

Angeline gets up. I'm just going to pay, she says, sashaying up to the counter.

Christina watches her. She has never seen such a beautiful woman, and she is hers. Soon she will be her stepmother, and then it will be as it should be. Christina can't imagine anyone else but Angeline. She is her real mother now, and she's perfect. And yet, there's something...

But it's too late to ask now; the moment has passed.

113

It's just one small thing – she wonders if her mother has ever sent her a birthday card.

She doesn't think she has, but when she was very little maybe she did. Christina can't remember. It would have been nice to know. That maybe she's thought of, sometimes.

CHRISTINA

In Christina's dream she was looking for soap. Not a bar of it, but a large dispenser of frothy white soap. She needed to clean herself. And Declan was one step behind, his anger pushing her forwards, making her afraid to turn around. He forced her to the edge of the cliff, and she was frightened because she knew he wanted her to jump, and then she would be gone forever, spinning in the abyss.

She dug her heels in and squatted on the hard, gravelly earth. She ran her hands through it and it was like red dust. She was somewhere like the Grand Canyon, somewhere awesome and intense. I will not let him push me, she thought, and when she turned he was gone and she was sitting on her own.

She went right to the edge then, hanging her legs over into the sky, letting them dangle there. The wind lifted her hair off her face, and she could hear a sound, like a wind chime.

She felt a presence behind her, and suddenly her shoulders were shadowed, the sun blocked out. Two strong arms wrapped around her. When she looked down at her chest she saw that no hands clasped her waist, but two giant wings, crossed over her breast. A large tawny feather fluttered across the gorge.

This was some kind of man behind her. She could feel his body pressed against her back. He cupped her. She wanted now to see what it was like, to feel him slip inside. She wanted to dip into his light.

But she woke then, surprised to be alone. It was raining outside.

She could hear the wet road, see the grey light seeping in through the thin blinds. The air conditioning switched on, and she shivered under her thin blanket. She closed her eyes again and tried to recreate the feeling of company.

GRETA

I'm a little cross with Angeline.

It's silly of me because she was only trying to help and always has the best of intentions, but sometimes I think she's a little too familiar with Tomás. At the end of the day, she's our employee and sometimes she seems to forget this fact.

Isn't that mean of me to think that?

I feel ashamed now, especially when I see how happy she is compared to a few weeks ago, and she's always saying how wonderful it is to work here and not be told what to do all the time. I do leave it completely up to her. Since she's organising all of the shopping I let Tomás give her the housekeeping money directly – there seems to be no point in it going through me. We both trust her implicitly

Angeline and Tomás are quite alike in a funny way. They both have very firm ideas about the meaning of life. For instance, Tomás is a strong Catholic. I too am a Catholic, though I'm also very interested in other religions. But Tomás thinks that our way is the only one, whereas I believe that there are many different paths to the one place. We're all going in the same direction.

What was I saying?

Oh yes. You see, Angeline is quite like Tomás because she has strong opinions on religion as well – though completely different. She hasn't spoken about them in front of Tomás because that would cause trouble. But she tells me. It's all very interesting. Buddha sounds a bit like Jesus because he said that no one is better than anyone else.

We can all become 'enlightened'. When I asked Angeline what enlightenment meant she said it meant that you could have heaven on Earth. She does this chanting business, which she learned in London – it's all in Japanese, and it sounds beautiful. She showed me her little prayer book and her beads, which she twists into a figure of eight and rubs between her hands when she chants, and then she took out this scroll all written in Japanese which she had hidden in a box on a little table by her bed. She called it a *Gohonzon* and she said that it was the mirror of her soul, so that when she was chanting she was chanting to herself.

So it's like praying to yourself rather than God?

I suppose so, she said. It's possible to answer your own prayers.

I thought about that a lot.

And I like the way her religion has the symbol of the lotus flower rather than the cross. That's much softer, more feminine. Angeline says that the lotus flower represents karma, which means that everything you do has a consequence, which is quite like Catholicism, although in a way it's harder because there's no forgiveness – once the deed is done, you pay for it.

So sometimes I feel that Angeline and Tomás are two big boulders of rock, solid and unflinching, and I'm the water flowing between them, going this way and that, oscillating. Maybe I don't have a mind of my own, because when Tomás talks about God, I agree with him completely, but then Angeline talks about Buddha and that seems to make a lot of sense as well.

But I was telling you why I'm a little cross with Angeline. Well, first of all she spoke about how I can heal with my hands to Tomás, and I told her specifically not to do that.

Tomás had a headache – sometimes he has terrible ones – and he was going to take some pills when Angeline asked him why he didn't get me to massage his head. He just stared at her stony-faced and said, How do you know about that?

And do you know what she did? I'm still a little shocked, really I am. In front of me (I suppose that's better than behind my back) she goes over and touches my husband on the arm. She actually stroked his arm from shoulder to elbow, and said, she helped me one day. I had a dreadful headache and she got it to go away in a matter of minutes. It's a gift, Tomás, and you should let her use it.

He didn't brush her off and he didn't tell her off, he just looked down at the ground and mumbled that he supposed she was right. So she made him sit down in the big kitchen chair and she beckoned for me to come over, and my hands were shaking because I was so cross. So then, of course, it was hard to make it work, and Tomás made me nervous. Angeline told me to relax, and I don't know whether she was talking to me or Tomás, but almost immediately I could feel my fingers warm up and I began to touch my husband's head.

She turned her back on us then and made a saucepan of creamy hot chocolate, and I felt that I couldn't be angry any more.

Last night I kissed Tomás all over and he asked me what was wrong, and I said nothing, couldn't I kiss my husband, and then he made love to me, but it was a little different. Oh, that's all silliness, and I'm only thinking these things because I have too much time on my hands, sitting around and brooding. It's hard to watch Angeline, so slim and beautiful, whereas I feel like I'm turning into a round thing. I feel useless. Angeline has taken over everything – the cooking and cleaning and the money, even Christina to a certain extent, and what am I left to do? So from tomorrow I'm going to take out my sewing box again and begin to make things for the baby, and for Christina and Tomás. She may be the better cook, but no one can compete with me when it comes to the needle!

CHRISTINA

She had hoped being somewhere different would make her feel stronger, but Christina was the same person she ever was. And now the concrete path, the whispering buildings, threatened her as much as the dark woods at home. She was afraid in the city, adrift among all these strangers: the street signs, the bars, the shops and hotels, all these foreign symbols felt like a threat. Everywhere Christina looked there were people, and everyone she met had been friendly, sure, but nobody *really* cared. She was alone.

They took a taxi back to the airport. It had stopped raining and Seattle was bathed in bright sunshine. It was getting hot. Out on the forecourt it was all concrete and noise, with buses taking off every few seconds. Christina circled the area twice before she could find the bus for La Conner. The driver was loading up luggage. Other buses flew past, making the air thick with exhaust fumes. She went over and he insisted on writing their names down on a clipboard before asking for fifty dollars. Christina's fingers stuck to the notes as she peeled them out of her purse. The money was running out fast.

The bus headed out of the airport and shot down the interstate. The driver began talking, giving them a running commentary on the history of Seattle, but Christina wasn't listening. She looked at the five lanes of traffic all flying by and twisting past Seattle in one big curve. This city reminded her of Oz – it was tall and shining and looked like it was full of promise. Cian was glued to the window, whispering to himself, and Christina strained to hear him, but she was too tired to pick anything up. Already the motion of the vehicle was wearing her out, and her eyelids began to drop.

She flickered between consciousness and memory. Shards of the recent past splintered her, these fragments and moments all sad. Like the last time she slept with Declan, and how she had tried to touch him and he had shrugged her off. She had cried silently, because by that stage he was immune to her tears. In fact, if he saw her cry it would make him more distant, less compassionate.

There she was, white moon face on the pillow, her hair fanning out, the tears sliding down the side of her face onto the cotton slip. Her hands were placed on her belly, and she kneaded them. She was an ordinary woman living an ordinary life, yet her pain felt so extraordinary.

She floated above the bed, and she could see Declan, cocooned. He was lying in the foetal position, covered in thread. His whole body was bound, around and around, with strands of white thread. He looked like a spider's egg sac. He was trapped too.

Her heart jumped, and she sat bolt upright. Her breath came short and she could feel the familiar tightness in her chest. She opened her bag and pulled out the bottle of water, taking a giant gulp. She had to maintain control, but all she wanted now was to get off the bus. She looked out the window, but everything was blurred.

'Cian.' He was talking to himself again. 'Cian. Cian!'

'What?'

'I need to get off the bus.'

'Why, Mammy? What's wrong?' His little face looked suddenly worried.

'It's all right,' she said slowly, trying to hold on. 'I just feel a little car sick. Can you ask the driver to stop for me?'

'Okay.' He looked at her uncertainly, then walked up to the top of the bus. A few minutes later, he came back, full of the importance of being the messenger.

'We'll be stopping in a minute. He says we have to change buses.'

Christina started to pant. Her body was too small for her, her heart was going to explode. She couldn't faint. What about Cian? They might take him away, they might find out.

The bus jolted to a halt. Christina jumped up, grabbing Cian's hand. Over the rush in her ears, she could just about hear the driver speaking to her, but she ignored him. She dashed down the stairs and pushed the door.

'Okay, lady, just take it easy.' The doors sprang open and she tumbled out, banging into a man who was right in front of her on the tarmac.

'Hey!' he said, jumping back.

She was unable to speak or look at him or focus on anything else but getting inside the hotel where they'd stopped. She could hear Cian beside her, calling 'sorry' to the man. She ran into the foyer, looking for the toilets.

Sometimes this worked – she counted slowly to ten, taking a deep breath in and pushing it out on each number. She undid her bra and took it off, shoving it into her handbag. She took out some Rescue Remedy and put some on her tongue. She needed a drink, but she couldn't let the bus go without them. Shakily, she flushed the toilet and opened the cubicle door. Cian was washing his hands. He turned and stared at her.

'Are you sick?' he asked.

'No, I'm okay.'

'Good, because I don't want to go home yet, we just got here.'

They went back out into the dusky sunshine. The driver was chatting away to another man. They were both wearing dark glasses.

'Excuse me,' she asked, 'but which bus is the one for La Conner?'

'Are you okay? You seemed in pretty much of a rush back there,' the driver said, and the other man stepped back and stared at her. She could feel the blood rush to her face.

'I know, I'm sorry. I just felt a little sick.'

'It must have been bad, you just about knocked me down,' said the stranger.

'Oh, that was you? I'm sorry.'

'It's that little shuttle bus over there, that's the one you want, leaving in a minute,' the driver said.

The men turned their backs on her and continued to talk. She walked over to the bus, still shaky and tremulous. Cian clambered in first and chose a seat right at the front. She settled in beside him and stared out the front windscreen. She could see the stranger chatting away to the driver. She couldn't see his face, but he was tall and long in denim jeans and shirt. In fact, everyone in America looked how she'd imagined them, all jeans or shorts, with baseball caps on their heads.

'Mammy, can I get a cowboy hat?' Cian asked her again. 'A real one?'

'We'll see,' she said. She felt exhausted now, depleted from the effort of controlling her fear. All she wanted to do was hide in bed, back in Helen's cottage. But she had nowhere to retreat, thrust as she was into a foreign environment, and it terrified her

GRETA

Angeline has been trying to convert me! Seriously, though, I'm very interested in her beliefs. We were walking with Christina in the woods the other day, collecting some early spring blooms, and I asked her how long she meditates for every day.

I chant for about an hour and a half, she said.

So you don't believe in God?

No, she smiled. I never really believed, not even when I was a child.

I was astonished.

It all seemed a load of twoddle to me, she said, picking a little wildflower out of the weeds.

But you never said anything at school? I asked her.

Oh, well, I knew better than to question the nuns! She spun the flower between her fingers, then handed it to Christina, who ran ahead up the path.

What do you believe then?

She stopped and looked at me. Against the perfectly blue sky her eyes were the same colour as her special chocolate drink. She scratched the bark of my tree with a twig and continued to walk on.

We're in control of our own destinies, not some faceless God. It's up to us to make good something we might have done which is wrong. There's no such thing as sin or confession. She spoke with conviction.

I thought about this, and I couldn't say that it didn't make sense.

She started pulling back some branches which blocked our way, and said, It's hard, though. We all have negative impulses. Sometimes it's hard to know what's right.

What do you mean?

I looked around for Christina and could see her ahead, bobbing up and down the path in her emerald green coat.

Well, society, and especially the Church in Ireland, dictate that we should behave in a certain way. For instance, we're told that once you're married, that's it – you have to stay together no matter what. But what if your husband beats you? Or if you just fall out of love? Surely it's better to be true to your heart?

This made me uneasy, because I think that marriage should be forever. I think that you make that commitment for life.

But today I tried a little bit of the chanting with Angeline. Tomás was meeting some of the men in town to discuss farming matters over a few drinks in O'Hagans, and so since he was out, Angeline asked me if I would like to try it. I thought why not, though I sent a little prayer up to heaven to forgive me if it was a sin!

We began by chanting a Japanese phrase – Nam Myoho Renge Kyo – and Angeline explained to me what it meant.

Nam means devotion or dedication, Myoho means two opposites together, like light and dark or enlightenment and ignorance. Angeline says it's the Mystic Law – life in its entirety. Renge means lotus flower, which represents cause and effect at the same time, because in the lotus the flower and seed pod appear at the same time. Kyo has two meanings – the first is teaching or sound, and then the second meaning is thread in cloth, meaning the flow of past, present and future. It's such a pretty image. I especially love the meaning of the word kyo. Maybe it appeals to the seamstress in me, but I love the idea that life is like thread woven in cloth, and a sound which never stops.

We took our shoes off and Angeline bent down and lit some

125

incense, then she rang a small bell and bowed to her little bedside table with the scroll on it in the box. She rubbed her beads together and began to chant *Nam Myoho Renge Kyo*. At first I just listened, but then I found myself opening my mouth and the words coming out, and as we went faster and faster, it was like the sound separated from me. I was hardly aware of my mouth moving or my throat pushing the words out. I could feel my whole being lift. It was a little scary at first, but then I think I liked it because it made me feel open and at peace and all floaty, like how I feel sometimes when I'm by my tree.

I don't know how long we chanted for, but then she slowed down and gradually we ground to a halt. She turned and smiled then, all sleepy looking, and I felt sleepy too. And then she kissed me on the forehead.

You have a beautiful soul, Greta, she said.

I blushed and didn't know what to say.

CHRISTINA

It was late by the time the bus pulled into the Red House Inn in La Conner. The rooms weren't particularly cheap, but Christina was too tired to find anything else. They went upstairs and threw themselves onto the beds. Christina emptied out her handbag. There were two packets of crisps, a Hershey bar, a couple of muffins and two apples.

'I'm hungry.' Cian sat on the bed, hunched and pale. He had purple shadows under his eyes and looked exhausted.

'Here, have an apple.'

'I want something hot,' he whined.

'It's too late now. Come on, we'll have a midnight feast. Let's get into our pyjamas.'

Cian perked up, and she helped him get undressed. Soon they were sitting on the end of his bed with their modest feast laid out in front of them. Cian tucked into a chocolate muffin. Tiny crumbs were dropping everywhere, but Christina didn't care.

'Mammy, do trees die?'

'Yes, eventually, but they can live for hundreds of years.'

'So everything has to die? Everything ends sometime?'

'Well, yes.'

He looked at her, his little head suddenly serious. 'Like you and Daddy?' he asked.

'I suppose,' she answered awkwardly.

'When are we going home?' he asked suddenly.

'Not yet. Remember, we have to find my mammy.'

127

'Oh yeah,' he smiled. 'What's her name?'

'Greta.'

'Granny Greta! What does she look like?'

Christina bent down, opened her bag and took out the photograph. 'This is very old, but it's what she looked like when I was your age.'

Cian took the photo. 'You showed me this before,' he said. 'I thought that was Granny Angel.' He put the picture back down. 'Granny Greta is very tall,' he announced, skipping around the room.

'Come on, into bed with you.' Christina lifted him up – he was still so light – and flopped him onto the covers. He crawled inside. 'Can I have a story?'

'No, it's too late.'

'Please, just a little one?' He grabbed onto Walter, holding him fiercely to his chest.

'Just one page.' She picked up the copy of *The Cat in the Hat* that she had got in the airport. Cian yawned.

'Mammy, why is Granny Greta living in America? Why isn't she living in Ireland with us?'

'I don't know, sweetie.'

'Does she not want to know you?'

'Of course not,' she said tightly and picked up the book again.

He lay down in the bed, staring up at the ceiling, quiet and pensive.

'Mammy, what would you do if you were a blank piece of paper?' he asked her, yawning.

'What kind of a question is that?'

'But what would you do?'

'You're a nutter.' He giggled and she leaned down and squeezed him, brushing her lips against his cheek. 'I refuse to answer such a ridiculous question.' She smoothed his hair off his forehead and opened up the book. 'Now come on, let's get settled, otherwise I

128

won't read to you.'

She read for moments, Cian falling asleep before she even got past the second page. It was eleven, and her head felt so heavy, but she had to do something else before she slept. It was seven in the morning at home, and she had to ring Declan. Cian snored softly and rolled over, holding Walter tightly. Looking at her son gave her courage. She picked up the hotel phone and followed the instructions for an international call.

It only rang once, snatched up in an instant.

'Yes?'

'It's Christina'

'Thank God! Where are you? I'm going mental here! Where's Cian, is he with you?'

'Yes, of course he's with me.'

'What the hell do you think you're doing, Christina? You're not supposed to do this. It says it in the court order, apart from being completely irresponsible and selfish.'

'I don't want to row, Declan.'

'Are you mad? But yes, of course you are, because that's why this has all happened anyway. That's why you fucked everything up in the first place, without a thought for me or the kids.'

'Just listen, will you? I'm ringing to let you know that Cian is fine and everything is okay, but I had to do this, Declan. Cian needed me.'

'Bollocks. He needs you like he needs a hole in the head. You'll just fuck him up, like you've done with Johnny.'

'I'm going now, Declan.'

'What? But where are you?' She could hear him breathing deeply, trying to control his temper. 'I'm sorry, okay? I've just been up all night ringing people trying to find out where you are. I've been so worried.'

'I'm sorry. I felt like I had no choice.'

'Christina, please come back now. I'll take the day off work, we'll sort something out, we'll talk.'

'I can't, Declan. I've left. I'm not in Ireland any more.'

There was silence, then he hissed, 'You bitch!' She could hear him spitting down the phone. 'Jesus! What are you telling me here – are you telling me that you've abducted my son?'

'He's my son too.'

'Yes, but you're an unfit mother, Christina. You have no custody rights to Cian any more.'

She was crying now, and angry. She knew she should get off the phone, but she had to fight back.

'Where were you the day your precious son was born? When I was screaming in pain, Declan, and your child turned blue and he nearly died? Where were you then?' She couldn't stop herself from flinging the words out. 'Oh yes, I remember, off on one of your precious jobs. You loved your horses more than you loved me.'

Seconds ticked by. 'Just come back, Christina, and I won't say anything and you'll still have access and maybe we can sort something else out,' he said quietly, his voice icy cold. 'But if you don't, then I'll find you and you'll lose again, and this time you'll never see them again. I won't let you.'

She slammed the phone down, shaking.

You'll never see them again…I won't let you…you'll never see them again…I won't let you…

She glanced at Cian; he was still fast asleep. She crept out of the room and walked down the motel corridor. The pile carpets softened her thud so that she could hear her heart all the louder. She got into the lift and went down to the bar. It was empty. She slumped into a bar stool and ordered a beer. No, she needed something stronger.

'Can you change that to a whiskey, with ice?' she asked the bartender.

The door of the bar opened and a tall man came in. He sat at the

130

other side of the counter and stared across at her. He had longish dark hair and a wide face. She looked away. The last thing she needed was someone talking to her. But he didn't speak, just kept looking at her. Then he took up his glass and drank a pint of clear liquid in three large gulps. He got up and went as suddenly as he had come.

I hope that wasn't vodka.

The thought brought a smile to her face, if only for a second.

She sipped the whiskey. It burned her mouth but gave her courage. She had pushed things right to the edge. There was no going back now. She picked up a bar mat and shredded it slowly. The small white squares of card reminded her of confetti.

She ordered another drink. She was sitting up on high, looking down at the story of her marriage. It replayed again and again like a cheap video, and she wondered how it had come to this, for what feelings were left between her and Declan were now utterly destroyed, little more than a pile of torn paper.

PANCAKES

All the lights were blazing in the house when Christina got home. She tumbled out of the car and went to look at the boot. Not bad, not too bad at all. There was no need for any fuss. Christina fumbled in her bag for the door keys. What was she thinking? They were all home anyway.

She tripped up the stairs and went in. She felt like she should be tiptoeing. She could hear the *thump, thump, thump* of music from Johnny's room. Where was Cian? What time was it anyway?

'Christina!'

She turned slowly. Declan was standing behind her, a dark silhouette against the hall light.

'Where have you been?'

'Just out for a drive,' she replied softly, hanging up her coat.

He walked towards her. 'You've been drinking, haven't you?'

She looked at him. His blond hair was going silver. It shined in the hall light, a bright line curving above his head. His blue eyes were brittle and stern.

'Just a little,' she mumbled.

'Christ!' He moved so suddenly it made her jump. He grabbed her hand, holding her there. 'What the fuck do you think you're doing? You left Cian here all afternoon on his own.'

'No I didn't, Johnny was with him.' She pulled her hand away from him. He let her go.

132

'Johnny had to go to practice.' He was staring at her, right into her. She shifted uncomfortably, rubbing her wrist.

'He shouldn't have gone,' she said uneasily. 'He should have stayed with Cian.'

'He thought you'd be back. He had no idea you'd be this long.' He was shaking his head at her. 'It's not his fault, Christina.'

She sat down heavily on the stairs. 'Is Cian all right? Where is he?'

'He's asleep, and yes, he's okay now.'

Christina put her head in her hands. 'Was he very upset?' She couldn't bear to look at Declan. She heard him move, step towards her.

'He'll be okay.' Declan's voice was softer. He paused. She could feel the tension between them as he lit a cigarette. 'What's going on, Christina?'

This was the moment she had been waiting for. At last, he had asked her.

But it was too late. How could she explain everything now? How could he possibly understand?

Christina was stuck inside a vicious circle, going around and around. It was all she could do in the morning to get up, keep on going. She stumbled through the day, fulfilling her function as a mother – cleaning, cooking, shopping, driving her children around, trying as hard as possible to blot out the ache inside her. That's why it helped to drink a little. When she was in bed at night, she willed sleep to swallow her up, take her away from her pain, but at those times she found it impossible to sleep. She would sit at the window looking out at the deserted land, the cloud-covered skies, dark and foreboding, the rustle of the trees whispering to her, telling her that she was nothing. At those times she would creep down the stairs and phone Paddy on his mobile. Once or twice she had crept out of the house and met him down a nearby laneway. There had been no time for words, only sex. She used it like a salve and desired to be pushed so far that it almost hurt. She wanted her meetings with Paddy to take her outside of herself, and maybe just for a second she was able to do that, get lost in the passion.

How could she possibly tell Declan all of this?

Yet she wanted him to know. She wanted to tell Declan that she had been thirsting for love for years. She had been unable to turn Paddy down, aroused by how he saw her as someone attractive, someone worthwhile. She was under no illusions; she had never felt the way about Paddy that she had about Declan. This was different. It was Declan's fault she had looked for comfort elsewhere, and she was going to tell him that.

Christina looked up. Her husband was standing with his back to her, smoking, looking out the porch doors.

She needed to know if he loved her any more. She didn't think so, but she needed to hear it from his lips. She couldn't live like this, in a hiatus, invisible.

'Declan—'

'Christ, what happened to the car?' he interrupted her, spinning around, his eyes flashing, smoke streaming from his nostrils.

'It's just a little bump.'

'It's more than a little bump! Did someone go into the back of you?'

'Not exactly...'

'Did she not tell you, Dad?'

It was Johnny coming down the stairs. She twisted around so she could see him. He was standing above her in tracksuit bottoms and bare feet.

'Johnny, I'm sorry about today, I—'

But before she could finish, her son talked over her, passing her by on the staircase.

'She crashed into the school gates, pissed as a fart!'

'Johnny! Don't talk like that.'

He continued to ignore her. 'It would have been funny if she hadn't got out and made such a bloody scene. Everyone saw it, her screaming at the head…God!'

'Johnny, it wasn't my fault! There was a van in the way, I couldn't see. And your principal, well, he was so rude to me—'

'Shut up, Christina!' Declan snapped. He was white now, rigid with anger. But she didn't care. It was Johnny she wanted to talk to, to make him understand. She raised her voice.

'Don't walk out on me! Come back here, I need to explain.' But he had gone off into the kitchen and she was left with Declan, looking down at her.

'I've had enough,' he said coldly.

'What do you mean?'

'Of you, the drinking, the way you treat the boys. And us. It's dead between us. I've had it, Christina.'

She shook her head, the tears welling. 'Please, Declan, I'm sorry. I just feel so lost.'

'That's the problem. That's always been the problem with you. You've never grown up, Christina. You've always behaved like this spoiled little girl. Well, I can't do it any more. I don't want to take care of you any more.'

She couldn't believe him. He didn't really mean it, because where would he go?

She closed her eyes. She felt so unspeakably tired and worn out.

'It's no use talking about it now,' he said. 'You're drunk. We'll try to sort something out in the morning.'

'I'll stop,' she whispered. 'I'll change.'

'I don't know, Christina.'

'What about the children?'

'I just don't know.'

The next day she woke early. Declan was still asleep, with Cian tucked between them. She stared at them both. Declan looked as innocent as his child. She listened to their breath – Cian's so quiet you could barely hear him, just watch his chest rise and fall, and Declan, a deep murmur released from his lips, softly snoring.

She pulled back the curtains an inch. It was a bright day, warm for February. She felt better already. The land seemed to sparkle before her, the birds were busy pecking at the earth and she noticed a whole new patch of snowdrops, which seemed to have sprung up overnight. She looked at the calendar. It was Shrove Tuesday. She was going to make pancakes for their breakfast.

Christina got dressed and stood outside Johnny's door for a moment. Should she go in and talk to him? She couldn't hear a sound, and Johnny wasn't at his best first thing in the morning. She would be asking for a row. She wanted to start the day right.

She opened the fridge in the kitchen to get out the milk and eggs and saw half a bottle of white wine in the door. She paused. She stared at it, then taking the bottle out, she pulled out the cork and poured it down the sink before she had time to think. Pleased with herself, she slung the bottle in a box out the back. It was full of bottles, and she winced when she saw them. What had she become?

She beat the pancake mixture with a fork, then covered it and put it in the fridge to let it chill. Cian appeared in his pyjamas, got up on a high stool and shivered.

'Are you cold, darling?' He nodded, so she went and got him a blanket and wrapped it around his shoulders. 'I'm sorry about yesterday, sweetie.'

She could see him thinking for a second, and then he remembered. 'Where were you?' he demanded.

'I'm making pancakes,' she said, changing the subject. 'It's Pancake Day!'

Cian grinned. 'Great!' he said. He loved pancakes.

The family sat around the table eating pancakes for breakfast. There was a tiny shred of harmony in the house. Christina imagined how they looked, like a family on TV. Even Johnny was eating them, saying nothing, but at least eating.

And Declan was so pleased he touched her, ruffled her hair. Nothing was said about the night before. He wasn't going to leave her.

As soon as they had all gone, she rang Angeline. She would know what to do. Angeline said the first thing was to go to the doctor. If she was feeling depressed, the best way to deal with it was with medication, not drink. Christina was nervous, scared about the idea of that, but she had to face the truth. There was something wrong with her, and if she didn't do something about it fast, she was going to lose her husband and destroy her children.

She waited a couple of hours until she had the courage to ring Paddy and tell him it was over. He was shocked. 'What's wrong?' he asked. 'Only yesterday we were together, making love like there was no tomorrow.'

'That's the problem, Paddy. I want a tomorrow.'

He didn't give too much of a fight. He was a realist too. They were both married, for God's sake. It was never going to last forever.

'If you ever need me,' he said, 'you know I'm here, Christina.' He laughed. 'For sex, that is!'

She'd hung up then, smiling, feeling resolute. She licked maple syrup off her fingers and washed up with more enthusiasm than she had done in ages. It was a new beginning. She was going to be okay.

GRETA

Christina calls it the cotton reel song, although there are no words. She likes listening to me use the machine while she sits in her pyjamas, drinking her night-time cocoa and looking at the fire. She loves the sound when I have to transfer the thread from the spool to the bobbin and to watch it spinning from one reel to the next. I like it too, as I turn the handle and watch the coloured thread fly. There's great satisfaction when you see the bobbin all neat and spun, and sometimes the reel is empty.

Last night I found a beautiful old wooden spool in the back of my sewing box and I had an idea. I thought I would make some kind of memento, so I cut a long strand of my hair and then I cut a strand of Christina's hair, and Angeline was in the room, reading, so I asked her if I could cut a piece of hers as well. She looked amused but she said all right. Tomás was having none of it, so I decided that what I was doing would be about just women and I explained to Christina that one day she could add on the hair of her daughters too. So I knotted together Angeline's thick black strand to my red, and then Christina's delicate mousy thread, which I was afraid would snap, and then I wound it around the large wooden spool.

There, I said, this is better than a photograph because it's something physical from us, of now.

You've made a metaphor, Angeline said, putting down her book.

What's a metaphor? Christina asked.

It's a comparison between two things. For instance, that cotton reel with our hair could be a metaphor for life. The thread represents us, as we spin around the reel, which is our destiny.

So what happens when you transport the thread onto the bobbin? I teased.

Well, then you're changing your destiny, aren't you?

She laughed then, and Tomás shook his head. I don't understand one word you females are jabbering on about, he said.

Oh, don't mind us, I laughed, we're just talking about life and destiny, nothing too serious!

I'd feel more comfortable if you were talking about fashion than the meaning of life. Tomás flicked on the television and Angeline winked at me.

CHRISTINA

Christina woke up. The pillow was wet next to her head, and strands of her hair were stuck to her face. She sat up, shocked, and touched her cheeks. She had been crying in her sleep. She wiped her eyes with her sleeve and glanced at Cian. He was up and watching telly quietly, transfixed by cartoons.

She was beginning to remember her mother. A moment in the firelight, her mother looking down at her, the sound of the cotton reel song. She had blue eyes with long dark lashes and very faint eyebrows, and her hair was a colour in between gold and orange. It was clipped back in a butterfly slide, and a few wisps were loose and fluttering off her face.

She remembered the day they built the snowman. Why had she always thought she had done that with Angeline?

But what came back to her in Technicolor was a picture of her mother sitting on the windowsill, looking at the snow. She approached her in slow motion, as if in a dream, and she could see the cotton reel in her lap as her mother twisted the hair around her fingertips. This day her hair was loose and unkempt and looked dark against the white sky. She was dressed in black clothes, a silhouette against the bright window. Her mother, playing with the cotton reel, paused and looked at the sky, pushing her hair behind her ears. Christina saw her chewing her lips. The tip of her nose was red, her eyelids flickering as she watched the falling snow. She was right next to her, looking at her skin. It was nearly as pale as the snow outside.

She could see fine blond hairs and it was as soft as the pink underside of her tabby kitten's paw.

She reached out to touch it.

But her hand passed through the picture and slapped against the cold glass.

Christina pushed the covers off the bed and got up.

'Have you a hug for me?' she asked Cian and he spun around, opening his arms wide. She folded herself around him. They were cheek to cheek, swaying back and forth. Out of the corner of her eye, she could see his sparkling blue irises. His skin was warm and soft.

'I love you, Cian,' she whispered. She squeezed him tighter, feeling his little chest pressed into hers. 'Do you love me?' she asked.

He pulled back and looked shyly at the floor. 'Yep,' he said.

GRETA

Angeline and I had a row, and then Tomás and I argued. And it was all over such silliness, really.

Angeline took Christina shopping in Mullingar and bought her a dress for Easter Sunday.

I was upset for three reasons. Firstly, because she didn't tell me she was going. She said she didn't want to disturb me because I was having a nap, and she was only going to be gone a couple of hours, but she must never take Christina out of this house without either myself or Tomás being informed first. Secondly, she bought Christina a dress, which I know was generous of her, but I had planned to make a dress for Christina. I have the material – primrose yellow, with a print of little pink buds on it and tiny shell buttons to go down the back. It was going to be a surprise so Angeline didn't know what I was planning, but still, she should have asked my permission. And in the third place, when they arrived home Christina was singing *Nam Myoho Renge Kyo* at the top of her voice, and that was awful because it's one thing if I try the chanting, but Christina is a Catholic child and her First Communion is next year and goodness knows what the priest would say if he heard her singing that, let alone Tomás.

All these things compounded and they made me angry.

I told Christina not to be saying those Japanese words, and she said, Why? She said it sounded pretty.

I told her not to be cheeky and to stop it immediately, but she

142

kept on doing it, and even Angeline told her to do as her mother said, and still Christina wouldn't be quiet, so I went over and smacked her, and she burst into tears and hid behind Angeline. It was awful. I don't know why I snapped. Angeline looked a bit shocked and said, That was a bit harsh, Greta. It's my fault she's doing it, don't take it out on her.

I was livid.

How dare you brainwash my child with your heathen chants! I shouted. How dare you take her out and behave like this is your house! It's mine! And how dare you buy her a dress without asking me!

I was panting, and hot, and Christina was staring at me like I was a monster. Angeline stayed completely still.

I'm sorry, she said calmly, if my presence threatens you.

That made me even more furious.

What do you mean? I screamed. How could you threaten me? I don't want to be you, I'd hate to be you!

It was an awful thing to say, I know. Dreadful. But in my anger, I saw something inside her, a flicker of something, and suddenly it seemed clear to me – she covets what I have – and that frightened me, so I lashed out.

Now all that reasoning seems insane and I feel ashamed, especially after what happened next.

Tomás came into the kitchen and asked what all the commotion was, and Christina ran over to him and clung to him, and said, Mammy is angry at Angeline because she bought me a dress.

I was panting now because I was so furious. My heart was pounding, my cheeks burning and I probably looked like a mad woman, so Tomás turned to Angeline and asked her what was going on.

Why don't you ask me? I roared. I'm your wife.

He just stared at me. What are you doing, Greta, in front of the child?

But I had lost all my dignity by then. I said, She's trying to take over. She's trying to take Christina from me, and you as well. Suddenly all my anger was gone, and I felt as weak as a puppy and I began to cry.

Tomás asked Angeline to take Christina upstairs and then he came over to me and put his arms around me.

What's wrong with you, Greta? Why are you suddenly so jealous of Angeline? I thought she was your friend.

But she's better than me — at cooking and running the house, and she's so pretty as well.

Just stop there, you silly moo. It's you I love. You're my wife, and you're having my son.

We don't know it's a boy.

Tomás took me upstairs and made me lie on the bed. He turned out the light and told me to rest.

While I lay there I tried to take all those nasty thoughts out of my head about Angeline. I prayed to Jesus to forgive me.

But I could hear whispering, outside in the corridor.

It was Angeline and Tomás.

Is she all right?

Yes. I think it's because she's pregnant. I'm very sorry, Angeline, I do hope you weren't too offended.

No, it's fine. I know she didn't mean it, but maybe I should leave.

That's ridiculous. This is just one of Greta's silly turns. She'll be so sorry tomorrow, I'm sure. Please don't go, Angeline, I don't think we could do without you now.

There was silence and for a moment I thought they were gone, but no.

Thank you, I could hear Angeline whisper ever so quietly. That means so much to me.

CHRISTINA

'I'm starving!' Cian announced.

Christina sat up on her bed and pointed across the room. 'Go and look in my bag. I think there might be a bar in there.'

'Before breakfast? Am I allowed to eat chocolate before my cereal?' Cian was grinning.

'Yes, just this once,' she smiled back.

'Great!' Cian rolled out of the bed and bounded across the room. Christina looked at the clock on the locker. It was half six. She groaned.

Cian sat on the end of the bed, gobbling the chocolate. 'You're lazy!' he said. 'I want to get up.'

'It's not even proper morning yet. Why don't you go back to bed and turn off the telly?'

'But it's light.'

'I know, darling, it's just that I'm so tired from the jet lag. Our body clocks are all over the place.'

'What's your body clock?'

'It's when your body thinks it's a certain time. When you've been travelling it gets confused because your body thinks it's still in Ireland where right now it's three in the afternoon, whereas here it's only seven in the morning, and not even time to get ready for school.'

'Am I going to school here?'

'No, we're on holidays, remember?'

'Oh yeah.' He was quiet for a second. 'So what are we going to do today?'

'We have to go and find Granny. We're like two detectives, so we are, on a case.'

That pleased him, and he turned back to his cartoons.

Her mouth was dry and she felt pretty ropey. She crawled out of the bed and staggered across the room, switching on the coffeepot on her way into the bathroom. She leaned on the basin and looked into the mirror.

I see my face, but I can't see who I am.

I look normal, she thought as she splashed her face with water, not this messed-up failure. A woman who can't keep her husband, can't keep her kids and can't even get her own mother to want her.

I wish there was a mirror for the soul.

She watched the water trickle down her face like a veil of tears.

Then I could really see the whole of me, and that would help because that would be a place to start.

What would be reflected in that mirror? What does fear look like? And anger, and shame?

And what does it look like when all one lonely soul wants is to be loved, and not the way a child loves a mother or a mother loves a child, but in a way that makes me feel as if there's treasure inside me? What does the unloved heart look like?

Christina went back into the bedroom and put on a tracksuit. She looked at Cian, engrossed in cartoons, his eyes hypnotised by the TV screen. She took one of the blankets off his bed and wrapped it around his shoulders. Then she made herself a coffee, took the photograph of her mother out of her bag and got back into bed. It was too dark, so she got out again and pulled the curtains back an inch.

They were in the middle of nowhere. Where was this town, La Conner?

All she could see was one straight road, and on the other side of it, flat fields stretching into a pale blue horizon, a large white mountain looming above. There was a big red barn just across the road with a white picket fence and a sign. She squinted.

Strawberries, Blueberries, Huckleberries

Fresh Farm Produce For Sale

What were huckleberries? Was this place for real? The barn reminded her of the toy farmyard she had had as a little girl. This was a child's place.

Behind this quaint image, in the distance was the relentless swish of traffic shooting down the interstate. It paralleled the beat of her heart as she looked at the photograph again, tracing her mother's face with her finger, circling their hands, where they held each other, tight.

GRETA

I'm feeling sick again, and I can't seem to keep anything down. Angeline brought me breakfast in bed and I apologised and she said that it was all right, she knew I didn't mean it, but there's a little distance between us now. Maybe that's not such a bad thing. I am her employer.

I ate some fish boiled in milk and a couple of slices of toast, but I felt nauseous the whole time. All my bones are aching, my back especially.

By lunchtime I had stomach cramps so Tomás called Doctor Marsh and he took my temperature and told me I was fine. He said that it was probably a virus so to stay in bed and keep drinking water.

Christina came up in tears this morning because a fox had got one of the kittens in the night. She wanted to get her daddy to try to shoot the fiend, but I told her that this was nature, a fox will kill. But she's not convinced. She thinks the fox is evil.

Later we played draughts and I told her how sorry I was about yesterday. She gave me a big hug and said, Don't worry, Mammy, I'll wear your dress if you want me to, but I said that it was just as well that Angeline had bought her a dress because now I don't feel well enough to sew.

And now I watch the night swallow up the land. I leave my curtains open and watch the cattle slope off to the other side of the field. The house is silent. Christina is in bed, and I don't know where the others are. Maybe Angeline is in her room, chanting, and Tomás is doing the books. It's that time of year, when he gets out all the old red ledgers, takes over the kitchen table and chews several pencils down to their stumps.

I would like to get up now, but my body won't obey me. It's as if it has filled itself with lead. And where has the baby gone? He has retreated right into the heart of me.

149

CHRISTINA

Christina settled up in reception. She winced as she handed over her last hundred dollar bill. On the counter was a framed photograph of fields filled with red and yellow tulips against the backdrop of a blue mountain, with a snowy capped peak..

'Isn't it gorgeous?' the receptionist asked, following her gaze. 'You should see it in the spring. We're just blooming. We get visitors from all over the world just to see the flowers.'

'That's La Conner?' Christina asked, thinking of the flat green fields she had been looking at that morning.

'Sure. Here, take one of these.' The woman handed her a leaflet entitled *La Conner, The Elements for a Perfect Getaway*.

Christina opened it and the first page was split into four – Earth (a picture of the tulips), Water (boats in a harbour at sunset) History (a view of clapboard houses and a large white building) and Art (a close-up of an old house with a large veranda and a small turret). There was a little street map inside the leaflet, and tracing her fingers along the streets, Christina found Chilberg Avenue.

'So where are we now?' Christina asked. 'Where is the town centre?'

'Oh, it's just down the road. Here we are, just off Highway Twenty. It'll just take a few minutes to drive into town.'

'Are there any buses?'

The woman looked astonished. 'Don't you have a car?'

'No. I just want to get to here, to Chilberg Avenue.'

150

'Sure. That's the other side of the reservation. Okay, let me see if I can order you a cab.' The woman took a good look at Christina, then picked up the phone.

Christina sat down on a couch, looking out the front doors at the sun smacking off the tarmac car park. Cian had found a few nickels and was spinning them along the tiled floor.

Why had her mother come here? She felt a glow of resentment inside her. Had she had to go so far away? It seemed as if her mother had gone as far west as she could, right to the edge, as if she wanted to put as much distance as possible between herself and her family.

Christina opened the La Conner leaflet and scanned it.

Inspired by the magnificence and proximity of mountains and forests, river and sea and soothed by the cadence of the seasons, artists in the late thirties first sought refuge – a place and pace to nourish their creativity...

She could already see why artists would want to live here. It was so far away from anything, and looking at the leaflet there seemed to be so many places you could get lost in. Mountains the size of which she had never encountered in her life, and proper forests, not like the woods at home, but great green colonies of cedar and fir trees, where wild animals hid. The last picture in the leaflet showed the sea, and she felt excited now, like the time she went to the Gaeltacht and caught her first sight of the Atlantic on the horizon. They'd had a glimpse of the ocean in the plane, but today she was going to be able to show Cian the Pacific. They might even be able to dip their toes in it. There was something liberating about being right by the sea, something which gave her a little courage.

GRETA

It happened in the middle of the night.

I woke with stomach cramps, like the curse, so I went to the toilet. I was dizzy and confused and I knew something was wrong. And then, when I looked into the toilet...I was screaming and there was blood on my nightie and on my hands. The first person I saw was Angeline. She flung open the bathroom door and ran to me, and when she saw what I could see I could hear her, like an echo resonating around me...

Oh my God, oh my God, oh my God...

I turned, saw her white face, and knew the truth. Then the black and white tiles came up to greet my face.

I woke later in blackness. My head was throbbing, and I could taste blood in my mouth. Doctor Marsh was there, and Tomás's face loomed above mine. He was holding my hand and there were tears in his eyes. I was astonished. I've never seen my husband cry, not even when his mother died. I knew it was bad then, and I croaked, The baby...and he just let the tears slide down his face, and then I knew it was true and I knew it hadn't just been a nightmare, and I was afraid to touch myself, to feel the empty shell I now was.

CHRISTINA

They drove down a long straight road, with the flat fields stretching all the way to the bottom of that large blue mountain. It hypnotised her. Every time she looked at the hazy blue form, it made her want to fall on her knees. She found it hard to peel her eyes away from it.

They passed the odd wooden house or barn. They looked so sweet and old-fashioned. This wasn't how she'd expected America to look. The cab turned right into the main street, and it was even more like a film set. Pretty little clapboard houses and shops stood side by side. The town was bustling with people eating ice creams and wandering in and out of speciality shops, with window displays of crystals and crafts, sculpture and paintings. Everything was shiny and bright.

They left town and drove down a couple of quiet residential streets. Even here the houses were picturesque. She could see water, and the car turned up a slight incline and went across a bridge. Cian pointed out the window. 'Look, Mammy, boats! Is that the sea?'

'I think it's a little river.'

'It's the Swinomish Channel,' said the cab driver, turning slightly. 'Where you going again?'

'1274 Chilberg Avenue.'

'All righty, nearly there.'

Christina's stomach tightened. She found her water bottle and took a huge swig.

'Look, Mammy!'

Where were they now? Suddenly the road had widened and they were driving through a street of run-down houses, some no better than shacks. There was rubbish piled up outside and litter on the road, with scraps of cars here and barrels and bits from bikes there. The picture-postcard image was shattered.

'Sorry about this,' the driver apologised. 'It's just not important to them to keep their houses nice, you know. It's a shame.'

'Where are we?' Christina asked.

'This is the reservation.'

Once she looked past the chaos, she could see pieces of sculpture outside nearly every house. They passed one porch with a huge totem beside the door and another place with a wooden eagle on its gable. There were lots of people about here – children running across the street and women sitting on rusty garden furniture outside the houses, chatting and looking serene amid all the debris. On one side of the street was a hut with FIREWORKS FOR SALE written on the side.

The driver read her thoughts. 'That's for July Fourth,' he explained. 'We're not allowed to sell fireworks, so you can only buy them on the reservation. You should see it down here on the night, it's crazy!'

Once they were out of the reservation the houses became more spaced out, with dark green woods fringing either side of the road.

'Chilberg Avenue!' the driver announced.

The car veered to the left, and they were travelling down a road alongside a scraggy beach with piles of white driftwood and a stretch of blue water. There was land on the other side, an island, not the vast expanse of ocean Christina had expected. To her right were more houses, all different and all equally attractive. There were no people about any more, just beautifully manicured lawns and verandas decorated with spinning wind chimes. The car pulled in to the left outside a dark brown wooden house with glass all along its front.

'Here we are.'

Christina slid stiffly out of her seat, with Cian following her. She licked her lips. Her mouth tasted of dread but she had to do this now. There was nowhere else to go.

'Is this Granny's house?' Cian asked.

'I hope so,' Christina said, paying the cab and taking her case out. There was no one around. Just one truck passed by on the road and pulled into the beach a short distance ahead. But she could see a car parked in the garage of the house. There was someone home.

She walked up to the front door, Cian skipping ahead. There was no knocker, just a hanging chime. Christina tapped it with a metal stick hanging next to it. It tinkled into the distance.

They waited.

GRETA

It's still April, and it's snowing. The world is grieving, like me – all the buds, the new life, has been tricked, shivering and shocked in this unexpected cold spell. I sit at the window on the top landing and stare at the snow. Up I look at the white nothing sky, and down I follow the whirling blizzard. Large flat flakes melt as soon as they land. Some cling onto the grass, but the yard is wet and black, touches of white making it look even dirtier.

Christina comes now and sees the snow, and she starts to jump up and down. Snow, snow, snow, she trills. It's beautiful! Mammy, Mammy, can we go out and play with it?

It's melting, Christina, it won't stick.

But there's enough for snowballs, please, please, she pleads, and her baby blue eyes open so wide that I can't look at her, it hurts too much, so I say, Ask Angeline, and she goes away.

I'm looking at snow falling on snow. The fragile flakes are tiny souls fluttering to the ground, like my baby, like all of our lives. I gaze at the white blank of the sky, and in that instant I lose my faith. It's like a torch that has been pulled out of my grasp, and now I'm groping in the darkness. Everyone becomes shadows – Tomás, Christina, Angeline. I'd like to step into the wall and let them all pass me by.

CHRISTINA

They heard footsteps and a woman opened the door. She was tall, with wavy grey hair and thin lips. Christina looked at her. She thought she'd know, but she was completely unsure whether this could be her mother or not.

'Hello,' she began nervously, speaking slowly so that she could catch her breath 'I'm looking for Greta Comyn.'

There was no recognition in the woman's face. Christina's heart plummeted, her pulse slowing down.

'I'm sorry, I never heard of her,' she said, but just as the woman was about to close the door in Christina's face, she paused. 'Oh, wait! Maybe it's Grettie you're looking for.'

'Grettie?' Christina repeated.

'Yeah, Grettie, my husband's ex. I'll ask him.' She turned and called out, 'Bill!', and then turning back said, 'Who are you anyway?'

Christina paused. 'I'm her daughter,' she stuttered.

'And I'm her grandson,' Cian spoke up confidently.

The woman stiffened and took a step back. She was obviously shocked.

'I'll get my husband. Just wait there.' She didn't invite them in. Her eyes were hard, the colour of flint.

They stood for a few minutes and Christina could feel Cian getting bored next to her. He began fidgeting and then started to kick a large white stone which was on their veranda.

'Stop that, Cian, it could be precious.'

'It's only an old rock.'

'I said stop it.'

An old man appeared. He looked about seventy, with long straggles of grey hair and a cowboy hat on his head. He was wearing a pair of faded jeans, so old they were practically white, and a sweatshirt covered in spatters of paint. His hands were large and bony and covered in paint as well. He looked at Christina suspiciously.

'You looking for Greta Comyn?'

'Yes. She's my mother.'

'She never told me she had a daughter.' He continued to stare at her.

Christina coughed. 'Well, she left when I was very little. I haven't seen her for a long time. I'm from Ireland,' she added.

'I know,' he said. 'I recognise your accent.'

Cian kicked the rock into a small plant pot, knocking it over and spilling earth onto the decking.

'Oh, I'm so sorry,' Christina said, scrambling onto her knees and trying to scrape the earth back in. 'Cian, I told you to stop doing that,' she snapped.

'It was an accident,' Cian whined nervously, staring at his feet.

'It's okay,' said the man. 'Come in, will you?'

The woman had disappeared, so they followed the man into a room overlooking the sea. The walls were covered in drawings and paintings — giant canvases covered in abstract splashes of blue and white paint. He motioned to a large brown couch and Christina and Cian sat down. Then he went over to a small bureau by the window, opened a drawer and pulled out a framed photograph. He passed it to Christina.

'There she is, my wife for a year. Grettie from the Emerald Isle.'

Christina looked at the woman in the photograph. She was in her mid-twenties, with waist-length ginger hair. She took her own picture of her mother out of her handbag and compared them. There

158

was no doubt that this was the same woman. In this photograph she was grinning broadly, holding the hand of a man with long black hair streaked with grey. Christina looked up again at the old man.

'Yep, that's me. Our wedding day would be twenty-five years ago now. 1978,' he nodded. 'I was just starting out as a painter then. We were so broke.'

The couple had bare feet and were dressed in scruffy old jeans. Greta was wearing a cheesecloth shirt and he had on a pink T-shirt. There was a big dog sitting behind them, staring cynically at the camera.

'Is that a wolf?' Cian asked, looking over Christina's shoulder.

'No son, that's a coydog.'

'What's a coydog?'

'It's a cross between a coyote and a domestic dog. We called him Tiger, cos he was wild!' The man sighed and looked straight into Christina's eyes. 'That woman had so many secrets. I'm not surprised she has a daughter. It's funny she never told me though. I've got a daughter too. She lives in Seattle with her little boy now.' He smiled at Cian. 'He loves reading all about wolves and coyotes. Here,' he said, handing Cian a book with a picture of a howling coyote on the cover, 'I got this for him. Would you like to look at it?'

'Thanks,' Cian said, taking the book and slumping onto the floor with it.

The man held his hand out to Christina. 'I'm Bill, by the way,' he said. 'Bill Prynn.'

'Christina McDonagh.'

'I'm sorry if you've come a long way, because I don't know where Grettie is now. We have no contact at all.'

So this was it, the end of the line.

'What about Henry?' said a voice from behind her; it was the woman. Christina hadn't seen her come back in the room.

'Who, Martha?'

'Remember Henry? That Canadian fella? That's who Grettie went off with.' Bill looked confused. Martha walked into the centre of the room.

'Bill's memory is a bit hazy nowadays,' she explained to Christina. 'Grettie was a lot younger than Bill. I could tell she wasn't going to stick around. She went off with Henry, remember, Bill?'

'Oh, God.' The old man's face had gone even paler and he flopped down on to the couch. 'I had forgotten.'

He looked completely shaken. Martha turned to Christina and said in a loud voice, 'So your mother ran off on you, did she? That doesn't surprise me. She did the same to poor Bill here and I had to pick up the pieces. She took off with some drifter from Vancouver, Henry…what was his last name?' she murmured.

'Kittle,' Bill said faintly.

'That's right, Kittle. I think he went to work up on the west coast of Vancouver Island, place called Tofino.'

'Thanks, that's great,' Christina said uneasily.

'Well, I wouldn't be too hopeful. I'd say she's long gone by now. That was years ago.'

'Twenty-four years,' whispered Bill.

'I'm sorry—' Christina started to say.

'Oh, don't mind him,' Martha interrupted harshly. 'He gets real upset when he can't remember important stuff like that.'

All Christina wanted to do was leave. 'Well, thank you, and I guess we'll be going,' she said quickly.

'Stay,' Bill said lamely. 'Have some coffee.'

'No, really, we have to go.' Christina grabbed Cian and hauled him off the floor. She handed the book back to Bill.

'Wait a minute,' he said, and getting up shakily he went into another room. Christina stood awkwardly. She could feel the familiar quickening of her pulse. She had to get out of there fast. Martha was squinting at her.

'I can see Grettie in you,' she said.

'Did you know her well?' Christina asked.

'She used to work in my bookstore in town,' is all Martha said, but the expression on her face told Christina that the women hadn't been friends.

Bill came back in and handed Christina a small dusty canvas. Thick crusts of blue, black and white paint converged in the centre of the picture – it looked like a sea storm.

'I called that one Grettie,' he said. 'I think it describes the essence of her, don't you think?'

'I don't know,' Christina said. 'I never really got to know her.'

GRETA

The snow is long gone. It's sunny and bright. Everything is new and fresh, the lambs and the calves. Everything is full of life, apart from me.

Angeline told me that it's May Day tomorrow. She said I should try to eat something. I know she means well, but food doesn't interest me. I'm trying. I go to Christina's room and watch her play dolls and try to find myself again in her happy little singsongs, and I tell myself my daughter should be reason enough to live.

It was a boy. They could tell me that. Matthew.

Doctor Marsh said that this happens to scores of women and I was only fifteen weeks gone so that it's not so bad, it could be worse. How exactly? I asked him. And then he huffed a bit and said nothing and left Tomás pills, which he called anti-depressants, and said I should take them if I didn't feel any better soon.

Tomás said that we could try for another as soon as I feel strong enough and I just stared at him like he was mad, and I said I never, never wanted to go through this ever again. He looked quite shocked then and said to just give it time, but I said to him no, I don't want another child. I wanted this child and if I can't have him then it's over, all over. He looked frightened then and left me alone.

So he slept in the spare room, but after a few days he came back into our bed. He thought I was better. And when he tried to touch me I just jumped right out of the bed.

He asked me to get into bed and tell him what the matter was,

162

and I said I didn't want him to touch me because I was scared of getting pregnant again, and he said it was okay, he wouldn't touch me, he'd wait, but I said never, never. I don't think he believed me.

A couple of days later he asked me to take the pills because he said that they would make me feel better. And I took them because I didn't care. They made me feel miles away from everyone, like I was bound and gagged and the pain was numbed, but it was still there at the back of it all, waiting for me.

I walked around the garden with Angeline and I told her how the pills made me feel and she said maybe for the moment I should give them a try until I feel a little better and then get rid of them. But I said they made me feel worse. So she told me to stop taking them.

I threw the pills away, and now the pain is sharp again and I'm grieving. This makes Tomás cross. He wants me to smother my suffering. I see him going to talk to Angeline about what to do and I no longer care. They talk about me as if I'm a child.

And Angeline said maybe we should chant together and that might make me feel better, and I said no, I don't want to believe in anything.

CIAN

Cian likes the picture of the coyote puppies. They look just like fox cubs. He saw fox babies once at home, in a den, before they were shot. The two coyote puppies are leaning their heads on a log, and one is asleep and the second one looks all dreamy. Maybe he could bring a coyote home with him, and then if it had puppies with Whiskey, their dog at home, he would have a coydog too. Cool.

He's thinking this when suddenly Mammy yanks the book out of his hand and drags him up. That hurts. But he says nothing because they're in a strange place and there's something wrong. The old man is sitting on the couch looking very sad, and the old woman is staring at him. She looks like a witch.

They are outside now, and Mammy is walking too fast.

'Mammy!'

Maybe she's frightened of the witch too. He is running, but still she's too far ahead. He's scared and wants her to stop walking. He wants her to take his hand. He wants to go home now.

She goes on the beach and he follows her. Normally this would be great because he loves the beach and they could make a sandcastle and all the big piles of wood would be brilliant to make a den. But he runs after Mammy because he's worried she'll forget him.

'Mammy! Mammy!'

She drops down onto the sand next to a pile of wood, and it's like she can't breathe. She looks strange, white, and Cian thinks maybe she's dying.

This is an emergency but he doesn't have a phone, and maybe in America you don't dial 999. He looks around him. He could go back to that house, but the woman is a witch and maybe she made Mammy sick in the first place. Then he sees a big jeep parked right by the side of the beach, and there's a man in it, and he's looking at him. So Cian jumps up and down, and waves his hands.

'Help! Help!' he shouts.

The man gets out of the jeep and stares at him.

'Help,' Cian yells, so the man starts to run across the sand towards him. He runs like a dog.

Now the man has reached him. He's very tall. Cian looks up at him and the sun is in his eyes so he can't see his face.

'My Mammy is dying,' he sobs.

The man turns and looks at Mammy. She's standing up now and holding onto the pile of wood.

'Are you okay?' asks the man.

'Yes,' she gasps, but then she falls down.

She's dead.

Cian screams, a short, sharp peal of fear. The man bends over Mammy. 'It's okay,' he says, 'she's just fainted.'

'Is she dead?' His voice wobbles.

'No, she'll be fine. Let's just sit her up.'

He puts Mammy up against the wood and fans her face with his hat. Cian can see that he has very big hands. Mammy begins to wake up and she whispers, 'Cian.' He goes over to her and holds her hand. The man squats beside them and Cian can see his face now.

He has orange eyes, like a coyote.

165

GRETA

I woke early today – it was just after dawn. I got dressed and went down to the river. I crossed the bridge and took big, long steps down the length of the lawn. At the tip of the garden, I stopped to look at minnows in the stream, see them rush out into the estuary. I could hear a horse neigh in the distance and the birds all around me, competing. I felt part of it all then. It was as if I could look through the mirror that is this world.

How can I explain it? It was like nature was reflecting back to me the beginning and the end of it all in one moment, and if I could see through this reflection, like Alice going through the looking glass, I could be in another world, with my baby. I could go backwards and forwards. And this pleased me. And if it hadn't been for Christina, I would have got into the river, in the deep part, and pushed my head right under and gone on through to Matthew, but instead I held onto this world. I felt lighter then, quite elated, and I listened to the cotton reel song in my head.

When the land felt a little warmer under my feet I decided to go and visit my tree because I haven't been there in a long time. So I walked through the stream and crawled under the barbed wire fence into the field, cutting across the high grass and ignoring the path.

My tree was there for me. Fuller than before, its dark green shadow spreading, blocking out the sunlight and billowing all around me.

Father… I tried to compose a prayer but nothing came. All those words – forgive me, bless me, sin, mercy, love – they all meant nothing to me.

And then I heard a voice.

Greta.

My name sounded like rain falling on a tin roof.

It was Angeline. She came to stand beside me, dressed still in her nightdress, in Wellingtons and with an old cardigan about her shoulders.

She said to me, What would you like to do this very moment?

And I replied, Dance. I would like to dance.

And she smiled, skinny black plaits framing her olive-ripe face.

Let's do that then.

I hesitated but she took my hand and began to spin me. We were on high ground, at the top of the woods, under my ancient lime tree. I could smell bluebells, a carpet of them at my feet. She spun me and we looked into each others' eyes. She had me fixed. And in a moment we weren't in Ireland any more but somewhere hot and Mediterranean, somewhere ancient. The trees around us were columns of marble, and the gentle earth was silvery sand.

She took her clothes off then. It seemed right. So I undressed as well.

I took my shoes off first and rolled down my tights, peeling them away like a chrysalis. Then I unbuttoned my blouse and slid out of my skirt. I took everything off, even my underwear.

She was laughing, dancing in the sunlight. I lost all sense of myself. How could I be Greta? The girl who undressed in the dark so that her husband didn't see her naked? How could I be her?

Angeline was smiling, inviting me to laugh. Why shouldn't I?

I dived into the breeze, screaming as I did so. I swung my arms from side to side like a lunatic contemporary dancer. I kicked my legs, my feet at angles, awkward and graceful all at once. Then I felt myself rise, higher and higher, a mere speck, a particle fluttering this way and that, held tight by the world and then released.

I was laughing so much that I was crying. Angeline became serious then and stopped dancing. She came and put her arms around me. It hurts so much, I wept. Shush, shush, she whispered, stroking my hair. We sat beneath my tree, our skin touching. She was smooth, and brown, and warm.

I dreamed.

That everything was all right. And in the light I was dancing with my children, both of them. I had never been so close to the other world.

Suddenly a rush of cold air hit me, my eyes opened and I was wrenched from the ground.

Hard hands bit into my flesh and a blanket was thrown over my head. Dark, deep black and down, down I went. I started screaming and I grasped the grass, wishing I could go back in time. I kicked and I flailed.

I heard my husband's voice. She's hysterical, quick, get her to the house.

And then Angeline — I'll run ahead and call the doctor.

When they took the blanket off I was at home, with a sheet covering my body. They had brought me into the front room and forced me to sit on the sofa. I saw Tomás there, and the gardener, Jim, and Angeline in a long green dress, with her head on one side. Tomás was shaking me, saying Greta, Greta.

But now I was mute. I stared at Angeline. There were little red circles printed on her dress. I looked up into her black eyes. I felt dead.

Tomás, she was saying, she needs help.

Had she tried to trap me? Or did she share the ecstasy when we danced? Why was she lying? Or did I imagine it all – her dancing, naked in the woods with me? Was it all a figment of my imagination?

At least she's stopped screaming now, Tomás was saying. Jim was looking at me, and his eyes were wet.

Poor wee thing, he was saying, she looks half dead, God bless her.

Doctor Marsh arrived. He looked sternly at me through his big thick spectacles and put me out. But just before, as he was leaning over me, I caught Angeline's eye.

And I fixed her.

And in a moment I knew what she was doing and why.

PACIFIC

LUKE

Luke comes down from the mountain on Sunday.

And he knows what he has to do.

He heads back into town and stops at the first store he comes to. He buys a large regular coffee and a muffin, then sits in his truck with the window wound down, staring up at the North Cascades and thinking about his descent. The coffee warms his fingertips, but it doesn't taste so good. It tastes metallic. After a week on his own, away from people, he feels assaulted by sensations. The scent of the coffee is different from the stuff he brewed up on the mountain, and the cologne of the sales clerk nearly knocked him down. Everything stinks down here.

And the noise. He isn't even on a main road, but the sound of the cars on the hard tarmac hurts him. Everything seems brittle and harsh. Having been among trees, he feels exposed and blinded. It's like he has woken from a long dream, yet this reality is even more surreal.

He spends nearly all his time on the road, with strangers coming in and out of his life every day. These sorts of things never bothered him normally.

But then, that was before he ended up spending the week on his own.

He hadn't planned it that way. He was supposed to take Sam with him, but at the last minute Teri had said that their son was sick. He called round to see Sam then, though he was only allowed in for five minutes. The poor kid looked green. He was so disappointed. Luke had promised him that they would go later on in the summer if he could get more time off work. But he had seen the look on Teri's face – fat chance, it said. He wouldn't be surprised if she'd fed the kid rotten food just so that he'd get sick and couldn't go. He didn't put it past her. That was how bad she could be.

He had gone camping all the same. He went to the campground at Colonial Creek, where they had planned to go. He had spent a couple of days there, hiking along the Thunder Creek Trail. He had enjoyed the walking, but going back to the campsite at night was hard. There were too many families around, and he felt out of place. So he took off on his own. He followed the rules, getting a backcountry permit first, and then leaving his truck behind, he set off. He had a map, enough food and no real purpose. He just wanted to get away from everyone.

It was all about water up there in the Cascades. Your vision was constantly pulled skyward up to the snowy peaks and the hundreds of glaciers. He liked this icy landscape and longed to go right to the top. Of course, he didn't have the right equipment; it would be a fool's venture. But the jagged peaks, the ridges and slopes mesmerised him. This really was the wilderness, and it made him aware of his hunger. Without everyday distractions, he began to feel that something was missing in his life, and he had to find it.

The more time he spent with his son, the more it reminded him of how he had been when he was a kid. If he could go back to himself he'd say to that little Luke, Well, what do you think of this, you're living in America and you're driving a bus every day, collecting people at the airport and driving all the way up the Washington state coast, you nearly make it back into Canada, but then just a few miles from the border, what do you do? You turn around and come all the way back down the interstate. So you taunt yourself every day, up and down, up and down. And all the people see is a guy who drives a bus, nice and friendly. Who cares, really? As long as he doesn't get stuck in traffic and as long as he drives safe and shuts up with that stupid commentary the company makes him do.

Little Luke would be real surprised. And he might say, But why? Why don't you just go home?

Before the holiday, Sam and Luke had read about grey wolves returning to the North Cascades, but even though tracks had been found, no one had seen one for over ten years. Luke had promised Sam that they would go looking for wolves. And then, of course, there was Big Foot. They had found a website all about the hairy monster, with pictures and sightings and loads of detail, and Sam had been convinced that they would find him. It delighted Luke to see his child so fearless.

The first few days he was on his own, he felt an appetite that couldn't be sated, a yearning for something which nothing could distract him from. He went skinny dipping in a freezing glacier pool, walked until even his strong legs ached and stayed up nearly the whole night smoking joints and staring at the star-puckered sky, imagining he could hear one of those lost wolves howl. By the end of the week he came to understand that what he craved was a calling, to find his own path.

He knew then that he would have to go back. He knew this with the same certainty that he would wake the next day breathing, and the cycle of life would continue around him.

Luke finishes his coffee, throwing the empty cup into the back of his truck. He checks his map, tracing his finger along the knobbly coast until he finds La Conner. All he has to do is follow the road back into Burlington, then cross over the interstate.

The sun bounces off the windscreen as he pulls his baseball cap low and puts on his shades. He starts up and pulls out. He grips his fingers around the steering wheel and glances down at his hands. He has big hands. Too soft, he thinks with disgust, I have city hands. His week in the mountains is just a veneer over the life he has chosen and the world he's denied.

He leans over and turns on the stereo.

Cold, cold water surrounds me now...

He loves this song. He picked up the album in the Experimental Music Project in Seattle. Damien Rice, an Irish guy. He had never heard of him before but he liked the case, and then he had listened to it on headphones in the store. Luke couldn't put it into words, but these songs just got to him.

And all I've got is your hand...

He remembers that day. He had taken Sam to the EMP for brunch and then they had hung around in the store for ages looking and listening to music. There was a whole kids section with all sorts of musical instruments. He had bought Sam a little drum. Teri had almost hurled it back at him at the door. Not in my house, no sir, I don't want that racket, she had said. Sam had spoken up quickly, saying, It's okay, Dad, you look after it for me. We'll bring it camping.

This music reminded him of the pain of that day – being alone with his small son and wishing that he had a family to be part of. It was just the two of them, and it was so lonely. When he had picked up the Damien Rice CD and played it, he loved the way it was all mixed up. There were angry songs, grand songs with an orchestra and soulful guitar pieces. But always the words, this man's voice transported him far away from his confined life. The lyrics filled his head with stories, and pictures, lots of pictures. And then there was this girl's voice – it wove in and out of the music and seduced him. It made him think of another type of woman, all soft and misty, with no hard edges like Teri.

He turns the music up as he goes onto the interstate and heads towards Mt Vernon. He's not ready for La Conner yet.

The sky is big and the land sweeps away around him, flat and cultivated. The odd barn springs up, painted merry red, with signs for

176

strawberries and huckleberries outside. He keeps on going.

Cold, cold water surrounds me now
And all I've got is your hand
Lord, can you hear me now?
Lord, can you hear me now?
Lord, can you hear me now?
Or am I lost?

That's how he had felt when he had been with Teri. Things weren't much better now, but at least he was surviving and he was doing something about it.

He had felt completely adrift during the last five years with Teri – half of their marriage. Each time he thought she might be reaching out to him, she was actually pushing him away. And then he got colder and colder. She had no idea who he really was. She didn't want to know about his family or where he was from. She just wanted to be with someone as fucked up as she was so that there was someone else to blame, someone other than herself.

Where the hell had she come from? All her anger.

He had to know. He hated it that his boy was with her now, that she had control over his son's life. He hated it, but he was powerless. There was nothing he could do about it.

GRETA

When Greta wakes she is still in the dream.

She's back inside, looking out a window. It's a view she'll never forget – shapes of roofs, all piled on top of each other, different angles and tones of grey, all banging together. There's moss on the slates and there are large metal pipes crawling all over them, like sinister snakes. To her right is one large glass roof on top of a building with tiny little windows across, and behind that is the incinerator tower. All these buildings block out the light.

She is standing in the stairwell and has to go up.

The smell of the place is in her nostrils – a heavy odour of greasy food wafting up from the ground floor, turning her stomach as she places her foot on the linoleum stairs as she slowly sidles up, her hand touching the two-tone walls.

She doesn't want to go up.

The door. It's huge, a grand entrance, with an eastern arch above it. It's painted orange, which seems sickly and cruel to her eyes. She goes in and can hear it lock behind her.

From this side out she can imagine how she looks.

If you were outside and walking along the road by the pretty green fields or driving into town to do a spot of shopping, your eyes would pull you towards this magnificent building. How could you ignore it? A huge grey stone edifice, solid down to its core, it's the essence of a fortress – dozens of tall chimneys and narrow slits of windows. It's impregnable.

Who was it built to protect? Those inside, or those out here?

If you look carefully from the road you might see Greta waving to you. Look, she's right at the top, standing in that little window, sixth in from the left. She's in a long white nightie.

They won't let her get dressed.

Her hair is dark and lank because they won't let her wash it and her face is as white as a cloud because she hasn't been outside in a long time, and her eyes are big opaque moons because of the drugs. You'll probably want to look away.

But she is mouthing something to you. What is she saying?

LUKE

He pulls into the car park of the Cottontree Inn, his daily pit stop with the shuttle bus. A desire to be somewhere familiar brought him here. Inside the bar is cool, dark and deserted.

'Hi, Luke.' It's Julie. 'What you doing here? Thought you were off this week?'

'I am. I was in the neighbourhood, so I thought I may as well stop by and have a coffee in peace without having to hop on the bus.'

'I hear ya,' she says.

He sits drinking for a while and then pulls a thin book out of his back pocket.

The trouble with him was that he was without imagination. He was quick and alert in the things of life, but only in the things, and not in the significances.

Luke pauses and thinks about this. He reads the cover again, *To Build Fire*, by Jack London. It's his second time reading the book. He discovered Jack London when he read *Call of the Wild* to Sam last year and then they moved on to *White Fang*. Both father and son adored the stories of the dog turned wolf and wolf turned tame, the harshness of the landscape and the adventures of men and animals in this place of extremity. Both those books had had happy endings, but this story is different. It's about failure, a man who isn't up to the challenge. It's slow and relentless and cruel. The story fascinates Luke.

He reads for a short while, but it's hard to concentrate. He feels like he's waiting for something or someone. He glances at his watch.

The bus is due. He gets up, stretches and walks out into the sunshine just as he sees it pulling in to the parking lot. Mack is driving. He signals to him and Mack waves back.

The door flips open and a woman with a small child careers into him.

'Hey!' he says, jumping back. But she says nothing, just ignores him and ploughs on into the hotel, her little boy turning, saying sorry with a sad face.

He can sense the heat off her; it's like she's blazed a trail.

What's wrong with all these women? Why are they all so angry?

Mack is laughing as he gets off the bus. 'She musta been in urgent need!'

'She looks a bit sick to me.'

'Thank Christ she didn't throw on my bus.' Mack offers him some gum; he shakes his head. 'So what the hell are you doing here?' he asks. 'Can't stay away from the place? You're welcome to take over!'

'You must be kidding. No, I'm on my way somewhere, just thought I'd stop by.'

'Well, that sure is nice,' Mack grins, 'Heading home, are you?'

'Home?'

'Back to Canada? That's where you're from, ain't it? Vancouver Island, if I remember right. All you people have so much family, you're like the Italians or the Irish, with the aunties and uncles and grandmas and grandpas!'

'That's right.'

Mack misses his sour tone and continues, 'So are your folks still up there as well?'

'They're dead.'

'Both of them?'

'Yep.'

'I'm sorry.'

'It's okay, it was a long time ago.'

181

'Never been to Canada,' Mack says, changing the subject.

'That's crazy, it's only a few kilometres away.'

'I know, it's just you know how it is when you're driving every day the last thing you want to do is drive on your vacation. Suits me just to be at home with Jen and the kids.'

'Excuse me, but which bus is the one for La Conner?' Mack and Luke look over. It's the woman who knocked into him. She looks at Mack and her hair is flopping over her face. She's very pale, like paper. The little boy stands tucked in behind her, holding a stuffed bear tightly and staring up at him.

'Are you okay?' Mack asks. 'You seemed in pretty much of a rush back there.'

Luke takes a step back and looks at her. Is she shivering?

'I know, I'm sorry. I just felt a little sick.'

'It must have been bad,' Luke says. 'You just about knocked me down.'

She turns to him and suddenly lifts up her eyes to meet his, but he's wearing shades. He has never seen anyone look so sad.

'Oh, that was you? I'm sorry,' she stammers.

He watches as colour spreads across her cheeks, but he says nothing.

'It's that little shuttle bus over there,' Mack pipes up. 'That's the one you want, leaving in a minute.'

'Thanks.'

Mack turns his back on her. Luke can see her hesitate and then walk slowly over to the bus with her boy. They walk in step, connected.

'Hey!' Mack says. 'Gone dumb, have you?'

'Sorry, what'd you say?'

'I asked whether you and Teri were going to Dean's party?'

'No…we broke up.'

'Christ. I keep putting my damn foot in it today.'

182

'Mack, it's no sweat. How were you supposed to know?'

'How long?'

'A while now.'

'Any chance you'll get back together?'

'No chance.'

Mack shuffles his feet. 'Well…' he begins.

'What kind of accent was that?' Luke asks him suddenly. Mack looks confused. 'That woman – where was she from?'

'Sounded Irish to me.'

Luke watches as the shuttle bus pulls out of the car park. The woman is sitting up front. She stares out of the windscreen. Her eyes pierce his body as she looks through him. He glances then at the little boy, who is chatting away to his mother. He's all movement and light, while his mother sits as rigid as a poker.

'Well, I'll see you,' Mack says, moving off into the hotel.

'Sure thing. Say, when's Dean's party? I just might come anyway.'

'July fourth, of course!' Mack slaps him on the back and heads off. Luke begins to walk back to his truck.

Something has happened to him.

That woman.

No, it's something else. He feels flooded with certainty.

He heads back into Mt Vernon to get something to eat, stopping off at the Co-op and picking up some groceries for the journey. He's going to be on the road for a couple of days, and he doesn't want to have to stop too much, not after La Conner. He might even sleep in the truck. He flicks down the rear view mirror, and taking off his glasses, looks at himself. He has a week's worth of growth on his chin and his face is darker than usual. He grins. I look different already, he thinks, I don't look so damn tired. It's true – the dark circles that usually rim his eyes are fading away. That's the outside life for you, he says to himself, starting up the truck. If only Sam could have come.

It's late now, light leaking out of the sky, shadows travelling fast across the land. He thinks about Teri.

What he had liked the most about her had driven him away in the end. She was assertive to the point of aggression. At the beginning that had been fine. He had never thought that anyone would want to marry him, and he had been amazed when she asked him out. It was so rare that two people like them would mix.

Teri was fun. Maybe a little loud, but always up for a good night out. They drank then, a lot. And that's what led to the fights. But they still got married, because didn't everyone in love fight?

That was the last time he had been in La Conner. On their wedding day, standing on her parents' lawn, looking across the Puget Sound at a bald-headed eagle diving into the ocean. It had seemed perfect.

Teri had always looked out for him. She had even fought battles for him, marching into his boss's office six months pregnant and demanding he get a raise, finding their house and badgering the realtor to get them a good deal, even supporting him when he put the phone down on his family, helping him turn his back on them, bitching about them for him.

She was so highly charged, she was like a missile – you just wound her up, aimed and fired. Even pregnancy didn't slow her down. She charged around even right up to the end, drinking, smoking, partying, rowing and loving, all in one exhilarating heap. He loved her for taking command, for giving him excuses, for letting him hide.

After Sam was born, things changed. She didn't calm down – far from it – but it was like she'd lost her sense of humour, and all that energy became progressively vindictive. Suddenly she wasn't on his side any more. He became her target. She wanted a bigger house, more money, a better life for her and Sam. How could he ever possibly give her that?

Luke was lazy, dumb, pathetic, a drunk. The last insult stung so much he stopped drinking, and when he did that there was no going back. He realised that their passion hadn't been real, not at all. This great love of his life had all been alcohol fuelled, and what was left when he took that away? Just a bitter taste in his mouth, that's what, and really seeing things for what they were.

She started off moaning at him, then screaming, and then sometimes, swaying in the kitchen, Sam's bottle in one hand and a beer in the other, she'd spit at him and kick him. From the shins down his legs would be covered in deep, dark bruises.

He had taken it for years. She had pushed him and pushed him, but because of Sam, because he couldn't leave him, he had put up with it. But then, three months ago, something had happened. He still felt sick when he thought about it, and he knew he had to go.

He swings into the car park of the Red House Inn and stops the truck, resting his head on the steering wheel. 'Sam,' he whispers as a deep longing for his son passes through him.

Every day he couldn't see Sam hurt. He sits back now and pulls his picture out of his wallet. It's an old photo, but a favourite. Sam is jumping up and down in the backyard, the hose is on the ground, curled around his feet like a long blue snake, and his son has a blue plastic spade in his hand. They had been gardening that day. Sam is happy and smiling. His eyes beam out at him, and Luke can hear his voice: 'Look, Dad, look, I'm a jolly jumping bean!'

Without thinking, Luke gets out of his truck and heads towards the inn. He hadn't planned to stay here, but he can't go on, not tonight.

GRETA

Greta busies herself, pushes night-time away.

She checks their bags. Have they enough provisions for the week? Chocolate, matches, tortillas, tins of fish and beans, rice. Henry is loading up the truck. She goes outside, a rug wrapped around her shoulders. It's still early, and there's a soft mist rising off the ground. She watches Henry as he ties the kayaks into the back of the pick-up.

'All set?' she asks him.

'Yep,' he says happily.

'Want a coffee before we go?'

'Sure.'

She goes back inside and turns on the coffeepot. The view from her kitchen is of another world. She stands here for hours sometimes, just staring out at the dark blue ocean and the islands, thick with green foliage that's every shade of green imaginable, from emerald to jade. She watches a blue jay land in her garden and sit on a bush. Then it flies past the gladiola, right up to the window and stares in at her.

Henry comes in rubbing his hands. 'I think it's going to be a fine day,' he says.

'Henry,' Greta says carefully, 'how would you feel if I didn't come?'

Henry looks aghast. 'You can't be serious! We've planned this for weeks.'

'I just don't feel right about it. I can't explain.'

'But I can't go on my own, it wouldn't be safe to do that.'

'What about Rick? Or Jim?'

'I can't expect them to drop everything and go at the last minute. I can't believe you're doing this, Greta.' He looks like a small child about to burst into tears.

'I feel like I should stay at home,' she explains.

Henry shakes his head. 'Sometimes I just don't get you, Greta. You know how much I've looked forward to this.' He pushes back the porch doors and goes outside with his coffee. Lofty, their golden retriever, trots up to him and he crouches down beside him, rubbing his tummy.

It's the dream that makes Greta want to stay.

She has never told Henry about her dreams. She has never told him about St Finian's. She has tried her best to forget about it, but then, that would mean forgetting about her little girl too. It's impossible.

She follows Henry outside. He's sitting on the wall now, the dog at his feet, looking at the harbour. A seaplane takes off and there's a spurt of noise before silence falls again.

'I'm sorry, honey,' she says, taking his arm. 'You're right. We'll go, okay?'

He puts his arm around her shoulders. 'I knew you would,' he smiles triumphantly. 'I'll take Lofty over to the Lewis's, you turn on the alarm.'

A short while later they're down at the jetty. The kayaks are loaded up and they're ready to push off. It's been a while since she's been out, a year at least. She wobbles as she slides into her boat.

No one is there to wave them off. It's still early. Henry pushes off and cuts a slice through the smooth water. Instantly Greta feels better. She's glad now to be here, in her boat, with the water, just to stay with this very moment as she launches forward.

Henry is beside her. 'First stop Meares Island?' he suggests.

'Of course, it's our annual pilgrimage,' she teases him.

LUKE

Luke sits on the bed in the dark. The curtains are open and he watches as the moon slowly rises, casting a silver light across the fields, deepening the ridges of the distant mountain. He faces the Cascades and can see the shadow of Mt Baker. He feels like he's saying a prayer. He closes his eyes and presses his palms into his temples. The certainty is still there, and there's a voice inside him now, not his own. It feels like a song running through his veins, guiding him. He can't deny the words any more.

Luke runs his tongue along his lips. He's thirsty. He gets up and leaves the room, walking slowly down the plush corridor and down the stairs, one by one. The reception is empty. A small lamp glows on the desk, illuminating a row of flyers on the town. He can see the glow of the bar through the double doors, the thumping sound of the jukebox. He pushes the doors aside and walks in.

She's there.

They sit across from each other, but she refuses to look up.

He stares at her.

She's narrow, but strong. Her face is long and pale, like a petal. He can't see her eyes, but he remembers them — liquid ether, desperate eyes. She conceals herself in a cloud of dark brown hair that churns around her face, onto her shoulders; wild and outspoken, it courses down her back. He can see her skin. A small triangle is exposed beneath her shirt. He can see the top of her breast, and trace the outline under her clothes. She sits carelessly unaware of herself, her long legs slipping off the stool.

Luke takes all this in. Then he picks up his glass of water, and in three big swallows feels the water course down his throat. He stands up, refreshed, pauses a moment, then leaves. He senses her eyes lift as he walks out the door.

GRETA

They linger on the boardwalk. How foolish we are, she thinks, to deny the trees. Here we are, immersed in the fecundity of the rainforest, and it's obvious that the trees live and breathe. They control our lives. How vain to think that we're in charge. She takes a deep breath, sways on the boardwalk and steadies herself by reaching out and touching one of the giant cedars that loom above like a kindly old relative looking down on a child.

'We originally came from the rainforest,' Henry pipes up.

She smiles. He's repeating himself now; he said this last year.

'If you think about it,' he says enthusiastically, 'our binocular vision and our gripping hands, they evolved over thousands of years, from the necessity of living in the forest.'

'Yes,' she says hazily, looking at the intricately woven roots of an overturned cedar, still desperately clinging onto rocks, sticking to life.

'This is perfection,' Henry says importantly. 'The ideal community. On each level of the forest, different species live and each have their own niche, none damaging the other. If only humans could learn to live in a climax community.'

'And the dead and the living exist side by side,' Greta says.

'Sure,' Henry says, moving on. 'If an organism can no longer survive, then some other organism will cling to it, and take life from it.'

Henry walks through the sunlight. He's tall and wearing khaki, merging into the green. Greta follows him slowly. She watches the

190

light filtering through the branches laden with hemlock and sagging, shaggy moss. It's like everything has let go around her. The boardwalk keeps them on course, while on either side, chaos reigns. We're unable to share it, she thinks, Henry wouldn't want to. He likes to think of himself as anti-authoritarian – that's what he calls it – but he's just as anxious to have a niche. The environmentalist one.

He has stopped and is taking photographs. Always taking pictures. He has one of those new digital cameras now that he attaches to the computer and gets the pictures on the screen. She doesn't really see the point of that. She likes to hold photographs in her hands, to put them in albums. If they're on the computer, you forget about them. Well, she does. Although she's not interested in pictures any more. Henry takes hundreds – studies of flora and fauna – and then sends them all on the Internet to one of his pals, Dick in Calgary. Dick seems just as enthusiastic and sends back reams of himself and obscure geological formations, standing there grinning broadly in a rocky landscape.

The computer doesn't suit her. Henry says she has to get with it, but she resists. Henry laughs at her when she says it, but she really thinks it doesn't agree with her. When they first got it Henry put it in the bedroom, and from then on she couldn't sleep. The screen would blink at her in the corner of the room and she'd stare back, terrified. That was when the flashbacks started, when the dreams came, though she couldn't sleep. A baby's head, soft pink cheeks, a dark matt of hair, fingers which curl and release around her heart, squeezing it tighter and tighter until she'd be gasping and Henry would be awake, shaking her.

That was so long ago. But it will never go away. Every day, as she gets older, it gets closer. She inhales deeply. The benign presence of the cedars comfort her, their scent reminding her that she's in a different family, in another world now. It's a new one, yet more primal – big skies, big ocean and all the space she could possibly desire to lose herself in.

'Greta. Greta,' Henry calls her. 'Come on, we better get back to the kayaks, we've still got a ways to go.'

They walk back down to where they landed.

'It's time to go,' Henry says. 'The tide's receding, don't want to get stuck on the mudflats.'

There's no wind. They glide across the water, leaving Meares Island behind, and weave their way through the harbour islands. She's behind Henry. Tofino starts looking like a tiny toy town in the distance – all the happy little houses, the bobbing boats and the buzzing seaplanes getting smaller and smaller.

Henry points to his left and Greta looks up. She can see eagles at home, minding their nest. Every year they're here. They always look for them. Greta can see two tiny heads poking out of the nest. She thinks it's a miracle the way eagles stay together, year after year, the offspring they rear, the cycle of life. She has a particular fondness for the eagles. All winter she could see them in the distance from her house, huddled together against the storms.

Greta turns her attention to the water again. It's so shallow here that she can see a thousand forms of light and colour, all dancing beneath her. Everywhere there are giant white clam shells, accompanied by moon snails and their egg collars, a trail of grey, rubbery slime. Greta stops paddling for a moment and lets herself float. I'm surrounded in blue, she thinks, cupped beneath the sky, held by the sea. Surely here I can find peace? But her heart continues to thump as she watches an enormous pink sea star drop below. She has been running for so long, and at last – she feels almost relieved by its awfulness – at last she has come to a wall.

This fear started at the beginning of the winter storms. Henry said that he had counted thirteen in a row. She couldn't remember specifics, just that day after day the wind beat the house up and the ocean rose higher and higher in dramatic displays, crashing against the land. It was an onslaught, and it made her uneasy. They tried to stay in most times because the wind made it so uncomfortable, but Henry still went out to his meetings and she still saw clients. She had set up her own consultation room in the house, with an ocean view. It was all lined in cedar and lit by candles and low-burning lights. She played soft mood music while she worked, but this winter it had been hard. The storms had disrupted her consciousness, and she was desperate not to transfer her tension into the bodies of her clients. They didn't seem to notice. They were so wrapped up in themselves. But in the evening when she sat and watched the storms, Greta realised that she wasn't right, that she shouldn't be healing others when she couldn't even heal herself. When she tried to raise the subject with Henry, he just knocked it down.

'But honey,' he'd say, 'nobody's perfect. We've all got issues. That doesn't stop you being a great masseuse. You're helping people, you can't give it up.'

She looks over at Henry now. He's some distance ahead. His arms swing from side to side in a steady rhythm with the paddle. He's starting to cross an open area, heading towards Wickannish Island, to the west of which lies Vargas Island, their destination for the day. He turns and looks shocked to see that she's so far behind.

'Hey, Greta, come on, will you? You know it's not safe to drift too far apart.'

She begins to paddle hard. When they're side by side again, he smiles at her. 'Are you okay, honey?' he asks. 'This isn't too much for you, is it?'

'No, I'm fine. I'm sorry, I was just thinking about things.'

He looks at her. He opens his mouth, is forming the words even, then thinks better of it and shakes his head. 'Onwards we go,' he says positively. 'We need to concentrate now that we're crossing the channel.'

One year Henry had told her that he'd nearly floated out to sea here. But today there's no wind at all, and she can even see the sun breaking out. They glide on.

LUKE

He sleeps well. The bed feels luxurious after his week on the ground. He rises in one swift movement and immediately reaches over for his clothes. What he needs to do now is not think too much. Just go where he has to go without worrying about it or planning what he'll say.

Luke checks out and heads into La Conner. He pulls in outside a coffee shop, but changes his mind and without switching off the engine pulls out again and drives slowly through the town. He can't stop for coffee; he can't stop for anything. He has to do this now. He heads out of town and through the reservation. He remembers this road, although it's over seven years ago now. Loads of kids are already hanging around the firework stand, excited dogs yapping at their heels. The blood rises to his face as he drives by; he feels self-conscious, conspicuous. Are things different now? Are these kids allowed to be who they want to be?

He crawls slowly down Chilberg Avenue. The bay frames his vision. Here it is still and dead, a small estuary trapped from the large expanse of ocean, the other side of the headland. He pulls up outside the house.

They have more things now, Luke thinks as he looks at their home. There is a new red pick-up in the garage and the garden is overflowing with rich shrubbery. Bill's art had been selling well, Teri proudly announced recently. Her father had made something of himself. She hadn't always been that way about her dad. When they first met she had sneered at his work and told Luke how she and her mother had suffered for years with no money for clothes or nice holidays because their father wouldn't get a proper job.

Luke liked Bill. He felt that the man had a kind heart. It was strange that he was surrounded by cold women. Bill's wife, Martha, had never hidden her disapproval of Luke, and Teri had now become her image.

Luke sucks in deeply and chews his lip. If he's going to go back home, this is something he has to do first. He has to do it for Sam. He pulls the keys out of the ignition and goes to open the truck door, but at the same time the door of the house opens. A tall grey-haired woman in a red tracksuit appears. Martha. Luke panics. Clicking the truck door shut again, he starts up and drives on down the road.

He had meant to turn, to go back, but he just kept on driving and now he finds himself in town again.

He parks by the side of the road. It's early still and the streets are empty. He gets out of the truck, leans over by the bumper, breathes in and straightens his back. He can feel the heat already all around him, lifting off the concrete, reflected in the glass and metal from his vehicle. He feels conspicuous in all this brightness, a fool for not being able to face his mother-in-law.

A large modern building faces him. It looks like a museum. He crosses the road and goes inside. He has to get out of the light.

GRETA

Greta lies on the beach, two medallion shells at her feet. Her toes trace the shell's eroded contours and the impression of a small five-petalled shape. The sun is powerful now and she's tired after lugging the boat across the beach to get it as far away from the unpredictable surf as possible. Henry had insisted they do this, so they had gone backwards and forwards carrying the gear and then finally the boats. He was probably right. There was no room for faintheartedness on their expedition. If it was up to her she was bound to make the wrong decision and they'd wake up to wet, battered boats. Henry was always right.

Why did it irritate her sometimes? Would she have preferred more cracks? Like her first husband, in Ireland…

She didn't blame him any more. They were so young.

But when she closes her eyes, all of a sudden there's an image in her head like a sepia-toned photograph – herself and Tomás walking into The Mill, holding hands. Like two ghosts, they're floating through the interior. She picks up every detail – the bright green hall with the hunting prints, the deep, blood red carpet on the stairs and the landing with the large bow window looking out past the river, across the fields. She looks through that window now and can see the cattle, Tomás's herd, the bullocks jousting with each other and smaller creatures, rabbits, a hare lopping across the edge of the field just in front of their garden fence. And in the distance, a dash of orange – the fox, the one she hoped they'd never catch, the one she told no one about, even when it killed the kittens.

Tomás is leading her into their bedroom. She's still in her wedding dress. She remembers now – the guests are downstairs, yes, she can hear them, the hum and buzz and the music from the band coming from the marquee on the front lawn, the relentless rhythm of the mill. She's wearing a long straight dress, empire style with a ribbon under her breasts. Tomás looks so jolly. His cheeks are red from the drink and his curly chestnut hair is tumbling all over the place. They're only eighteen.

Children.

She remembers him closing the curtains and then lifting her up onto the big old bed, with a mattress that sucked you in and was nearly impossible to get out of. He has taken off her dress and she's in her petticoat, and then he undressed too. She remembers her thrill – she's a woman at last, a married woman. And when he enters her, she's looking at her hand and the wedding band sparkling in the dusky light.

Yes, they were very taken with each other. They were fine until she came along. Greta pushes this thought away, and instead she holds in her head the picture of herself, eighteen, in her slip and making love to Tomás.

LUKE

He's never been to a place like this, never sat still and just looked. He lets his eyes wander over the surface of the painting again. It's what they'd call abstract, but he knows what it's about.

It's a journey. He passes his hand over his face and then he can hear the picture, the sounds of the colour. A green root walks like a tall man, its bulb like a large white head bowed over in sorrow. There is a small green circle in front of it and he looks down towards it, to the seed. The whole painting is contained within a wobbly enclosure, embedded in flesh tones, hidden in the soft belly of the oblique. And all the time while he looks at this picture he can hear his grandfather's voice singing one of the songs of prayer.

Luke closes his eyes. He can see little Luke again, sitting beneath his grandfather, listening to him describe *oo-simch*. He curls up like a tiny cat as the elder describes how his own father and grandfather would go with the rest of the family to a secluded spot in the swamp behind the village. First they would bathe in the ocean and then they would scrub their bodies afterwards with tree branches, all the while singing songs of prayer. They would do this every day for eight days, using secret herbs and secret songs, cleansing themselves inside and out.

'Luke, this is how we passed on the secrets of healing.'

When Luke went to school, the teacher had spoken about the baptism of Christ, and in his innocence, Luke had asked him, 'Sir, is that an *oo-simch*?' He had been laughed at for saying that. He had

199

learned to forget everything his grandfather told him. Now, looking at this painting, it was coming back to him.

In the city there was no shortage of Native American imagery, in shops and on the walls of people's apartments. When they had got married, Teri had bought him a large print called *Eagles*. It was made by a native artist and depicted a split eagle with whale heads in the wing joints and a humanoid face in the tail. Teri loved that print. It was up in their bedroom. But it had always disturbed Luke, made him feel slightly uncomfortable. The thick black lines and its rigid geometry made him feel confined. There was always a story in those pictures, and they reminded him of his inadequacy, his failure to live up to anything.

Now this painting, by a white man, meant more to him. It was caught between two worlds. The artist didn't want to tell a story, but the paint itself sang out with no effort at representation. It told Luke something. He could hear the song coming back to him, his grandfather's shaky voice as he sang and stroked his head.

Luke stands up and walks towards the painting. There's a short piece written about the artist underneath it. His name is Morris Graves, and of his pictures he has written, 'I don't want to say anything. I just want them to be.'

GRETA

She's not sure how long she's slept, but when she wakes she's cold. The sun has passed on and is now blocked by a row of trees. She opens her eyes, struggling to remain in the moment, just to let her senses work. Her vision takes in the dappling of the late afternoon and all the blues around, the kind of blue you can only see here, the kind of blue she had never seen in Ireland. Her hands push into the fine white sand and she sniffs the air. Salty, but then she can smell something else. Garlic. Lemon. She stiffens. It's Angeline's scent, the citrus mix with the earthiness of the garlic root. It was singular to her, an aroma that was alien to The Mill before she arrived.

She looks around her. It's ridiculous to think that Angeline might be here. Maybe she was still inside a dream? But Greta can see Henry – he's cooking the supper.

Thinking of Angeline always made her feel uneasy. She didn't deserve this life. She couldn't help wondering if her old friend now viewed Greta as a coward, for she had never returned to claim her child.

But Greta had never felt completely sure of herself. Often she wondered if they were right. Was she really of sound mind? If she took each day as it came, she could survive. In a place so close to nature, with a man who was part of it, she could feel safe. If she went back to Ireland, to her interior world, the part of her that was weak and unstable might resurface. Everything could come tumbling down.

Henry sees her stirring and calls over to her, 'I didn't want to wake you, you looked so at peace.'

He winks at her and she gets up and goes over to him. She kisses him and passes her hand through his crown of silver. She loves Henry for his earnestness. Nothing is hidden. He is what he is. If only this was what she could be.

CHRISTINA

Is she going mad?

A small white hand reaches into the fog and pulls her out. Her legs are stretched out in front of her and she feels like a shot soldier, slumped against the wood. Cian pushes his face against hers and she feels his fingers entwined with her own.

'Cian,' she whispers.

'Give her some air.'

Cian moves back and she looks at the voice. A dark man stands over her and offers her a bottle of water. She shakes her head, terrified to speak.

Where is she?

'You passed out,' the man says. 'Come on, you'd better have some of this.' He forces her to take the water. She sips from the bottle and it dribbles down her chin.

'Mammy, are you all right?'

'She's just fine,' the stranger says. 'Let's give her a chance, hey? Why don't we have a look for some stones and let your mom get up when she can.'

The man moves off with Cian, down the beach. Christina raises an arm. No, this isn't right, but she can't speak, not yet. She watches them and then suddenly feels her breakfast rising in her stomach. She bends over and is sick in the sand.

She remembers everything now.

She has to go home. The thought penetrates her as if she's been

203

hit and she shakes with fear. It's all over now. She's lost control of her life and her son. She'll never get him back.

She gets to her feet, sways, then shakily heads towards Cian and the stranger.

'Mammy, look!' Cian runs towards her, his hands full of white rounds. 'Can we bring them home? Please, please, please?'

'I...I don't know, Cian.'

'Are you okay?' She can see the man properly now. He looks familiar. 'Remember me?' he says. 'We met yesterday when you were riding the shuttle bus. You crashed into me getting off the bus?'

'Yes...I...'

'Small world,' he says, bending down and pushing his hands through the sand. Christina watches as it falls through his fingers.

'What are you doing here?' she asks.

'I could ask you the same question.'

She pulls her hands through her hair. She has a terrible headache. 'I don't know...I...thank you for helping us,' she says, and taking Cian by the hand she begins walking back along the beach towards the road, the two of them sliding across the sand.

When they reach the road she has to take Cian's runners off and empty them out.

'Mammy, will you carry these for me?' He offers up his stones. There must be a least a dozen spread out between his two palms.

'No, Cian, they're too heavy. You can bring one.'

'Only one! But I want them all.'

'Cian, we have to walk back into town. It's a long way.'

'I don't want to walk, my legs are tired.' He plonks down on the ground.

'Cian, we have to walk, there's no other way of getting there. Come on, get up. Come on, please.' She leans over and takes his hand, pulling his arm, but the child is like a dead weight.

'Come on now, I'm getting really, really cross!'

'I want to sit,' Cian says defiantly.

'Hey!' It's that man again. 'Can I give you a ride?'

'No, it's fine, thanks,' she says with her back to him, still pulling at Cian.

'Mammy, why can't we go with him?'

'Because he's a stranger.'

'No he's not, his name is Luke.'

'It looks like you have your hands full there,' he calls from the road.

She can hear the engine stop and the door open. His footsteps approach. Christ, what can she do?

'Are you going into La Conner? It's a long way from here, too far, I'd say, for his little legs.'

She swings around. 'Okay, thanks, we could do with a lift.'

Cian jumps up immediately and runs over to the vehicle.

'Are you okay?' the man asks again. 'You still look pretty shaky.'

'I'm fine,' she says tightly, getting into his truck.

LUKE

He looks over at her. Her pale arms are stretched out, her hands gripping the dash. Her body looks so taut it could snap. Her little boy is sitting between them, silently gazing out at the road. Luke sees an eagle circling above them, following him as he drives into town.

'What kind of bird is that?' asks the child.

'It's a bald-headed eagle,' Luke says.

The little boy rubs his hands together. 'Wow!'

'My name is Luke,' he says.

'I know, and my name is Cian.'

She offers nothing, says nothing.

After he had left the museum he had driven back out of town. He was ready to go inside and talk to Bill. He was going to give it his best shot and try to get Teri's father to understand his side of the story, but when he had got there he had seen her and the little boy getting out of a cab at Bill's house. It was fate that she was there.

He waited.

And when she came out of Bill's house, he watched her running onto the beach, with the little boy following. He had stared at her and then down at his lap, at the notebook in front of him and the swirl of black lines on the paper. The child roused him then, and when he heard him call he had run towards him without thought.

'Where will I drop you off?' he asks.

'Here, just here is fine,' she says quickly.

'But we're not in the centre yet.'

'Oh, well, on the main street then, that will do.'

'Aren't you staying at the Red House Inn? I can leave you there.'
She stares at him. She looks shocked.

'I was in the bar last night,' he explains. 'I saw you.'

She frowns, and staring out of the window, says, 'It's fine, just leave us on the main street.'

Her skin is so pale he can see blue veins on her neck and dark shadows under her eyes. There's a small scar by the side of her left eye. He sees every little detail of her face in a second. Her colour is blue. Her jeans and runners reflect the cloudless sky and her plain white T-shirt adds to her delicacy. She could be pregnant, or sick, very sick.

'Are you sure you're okay?' he asks again. 'Do you want me to take you to a doctor?'

'No!' she snaps, then gently adds, 'Thank you, but I'm all right. It happens to me sometimes. I'm always fine afterwards.'

'Okay.' He pulls into the main street. 'Well, here we are.'

He stops the truck. She pulls her bag over her shoulder and reaches over for the case.

'Here, let me get that.' He climbs out of the truck, walks round and pulls her case out for her. Cian is on the street looking in the window of an ice cream parlour.

'Well, thank you again,' she says awkwardly.

'No problem. You okay then?'

'Yes,' she says emphatically.

'See you around.' He gets back in the truck and drives off. He sees her in his rear view mirror. She stands very still, like a shadow ghost, fading in the bright summer light, almost transparent against the surge of tanned tourists walking up behind her. He turns the corner and parks. He sits thinking for a minute. He drums his fingers on the steering wheel. He hadn't expected this.

Luke picks up the notebook again and rummages in the glove

compartment. He finds what he's looking for – a set of coloured pencils he got Sam the last time they were out. He licks the end of the pencil and then, trying not to think too much, he begins drawing. He pauses, touches the space between his eyes gently with his middle finger, and then, picking up the blue pencil, he continues. He doesn't want to say anything.

GRETA

Greta unzips the tent. Henry is brewing liquorice tea. When she woke from a dreamless night, she sensed the brightness underneath the canvas pressing in on her eyelids, and now when she pokes her head out, she's not disappointed. The sky is spotless blue, not a cloud in sight, with the last quarter moon fading away.

'What a beautiful day!' she breathes, crawling out onto the sand.

'Not bad, not bad,' Henry says, 'though I was listening to the forecast. They're predicting westerlies, building up to fifteen to twenty knots this morning.'

'That should be okay,' she says, taking the mug he offers her.

'Well, twenty knots can be difficult.'

'But look at the sea,' she says, adding soy milk and honey to her drink. 'There's barely a ripple on it.'

'It's calm at the moment,' Henry says with authority, 'As you know, things can change dramatically within just a few seconds.'

'Oh, Henry,' Greta sighs, 'don't be so gloomy.'

'I'm just being a realist,' he replies stoically. 'I'm sure that we can deal with whatever the weather brings. That's what makes this vacation so great. We just have to surrender to nature.'

'Which I must do now,' Greta says, giggling, and jogs across the sand towards some trees fringing the beach. Her mood has changed since yesterday. She feels giddy. Being away from her house and routine makes her feel disconnected from her pain. There's relief.

'I'm not going to run away any more,' she says out loud to a gangly fir, flicking twigs at its base.

An hour later they're on the water.

'Watch out for the boomers!' Henry says as they set off. Greta scans around her. There are a few rocks, but none too close. The swell has increased slightly since they ate breakfast, but not enough to alarm her. I just have to trust in fate, she thinks. It's impossible to determine exactly where all the rocks lie; if a wave is going to crash into her there's really nothing she can do about it. Her heart beats a little faster and she feels flushed and excited.

Henry is paddling beside her now. Although it's early still, there are several fishing boats out already. Henry shakes his head. 'Can't even see the fish jumping any more,' he says sadly.

That's what Henry had done for a while when they first moved to Tofino. He had bought a small trawler and with a tiny crew had made a fair enough living out of fishing wild salmon. Greta had always thought it a bloody business. She had gone out with Henry once and the experience had put her off eating fish for months.

'Don't you get sick of the gore and the stench?' she had asked him.

'I can't think like that,' Henry had said. 'It's our living. And I think it's a good clean one.'

But then things had begun to change. Fish farms sprang up everywhere, causing prices to dwindle, and the wild salmon stock began to decline due to overfishing as well as competition from the American fisheries. Then there were the sport-fishing boats, growing in their numbers, with fat city jackasses, as Henry called them. (Greta had to remind him that he was originally from a city too.) Henry had said that he and the other commercial boats had respected the territorial rights of the Nuu-chah-nulth but the fancy sports guys had just cleaned the place out. Henry got sick of it. Besides, he hardly made any money any more, and he was becoming more and more involved with his environmental work, particularly the anti-logging campaigns. Somehow fishing didn't seem politically correct any more. Greta was relieved. That smell had got everywhere.

They paddle through a series of passageways and tidal pools. As Greta looks across Vargas Island, behind it, in the distance, she can see the Catface range, along with Lone Cone and Mt Colnett. She thinks of the wilderness between them and the absence of people, yet she doesn't feel alone. She feels part of everything. In Ireland the landscape could make you feel so lonely.

Mud. That's what she thinks of now. Churned up tracks in fields and sinking pools in bogs and the boreens, all bumpy and overgrown. Even the woods behind The Mill were a quagmire half the year, when the horses would destroy the track so that you were knee deep in it, struggling to go up the hill. And everywhere you went there was debris. Abandoned cars, plastic bags full of glass and cans next to a heap of ashes where some lads had gathered for a few beers the night before. She imagined what all her Canadian friends would think of that. It's probably different now, she thinks, Ireland's probably like Canada, all cleaned up. But what she liked about this place was that humans hadn't messed it up here yet. Not quite, though as far as Henry was concerned it was an ongoing battle.

Greta looks at green-gold kelp swaying beneath her and the dark red spines of sea urchins glistening against the rocks. An osprey glides above her, looking for fish. Ahead is the Pacific Ocean and an eternity of blue. She feels her body paddling and her soul swimming. It's safe to feel these things here.

Spray off the end of her paddle splashes her face. She's back in her body again. It's time, she thinks.

211

CHRISTINA

His truck is dirty, which is unusual when all the cars around her are gleaming. She watches him drive off and away.

'Mammy, can I have an ice cream?'

Before she can say anything he has shot inside the shop. She follows him. All it serves are ice cream, cakes and fancy sweets tied up in gold ribbons. The room is painted pink and white and the assistant wears a matching hat and apron.

'Well, what can I get you, little man?'

'Mammy, have you ever seen so much ice cream in your life?'

'No, I haven't.'

She's cold in here. Her hands are clammy and she grips them tightly. Cian takes ages to choose, eventually going for double chocolate fudge.

Outside in the sunshine, she finds a bench. Cian sits down next to her, a chocolate beard dripping onto his T-shirt and bare knees. She glances at her watch. Midday. That means it's eight o'clock in the evening in Ireland. She'll have to call Declan. She has under thirty dollars left, not enough for another night in a hotel, barely enough for a meal. She'll have to call him, beg his forgiveness, get him to send money. He'll have to come and rescue them.

She closes her eyes and tries to shut the light out. She hears people chatting as they walk down the street, snatches of conversations, cars rolling by, her son slurping on his ice cream, quiet with concentration. She feels tiny, insignificant. This feeling has always been inside her, since she was Cian's age.

An apology.

It has always been her fault. She remembers now how it used to annoy Declan, the way she was always saying sorry, and sometimes he'd snap and say, 'What for? For God's sake, what are you sorry for now?' He had teased her when they first met and made a bet that she couldn't stop from saying sorry for a week. He had won. She had been so conscious of it then, how easily it had tripped off the edge of her tongue, so that she had begun apologising for other people when they knocked into her, when they didn't hear her, when they were unkind to her.

Of course.

She sees herself now, running through The Mill in her pyjamas. It's early still. The curtains are drawn but the light leaks through onto the landing. She can hear the river running, the birds singing, the cattle bellowing. She goes into her parents' bedroom. The window is open and the curtain blows in gently. She looks at the bed, its faded velvet cover. It's one empty side.

'Where's Mammy?' she asks.

Her daddy sits up in the bed. His face is creased, his smile wobbly, unsure.

'Remember, Christina?' he says gently. 'She's gone away for a while.'

'But when will she be back?'

'Soon, I'm sure.'

She went over to the bed, climbed on it and under the covers. She tucked herself in next to her father and, playing with the frayed tassels on the edge of the spread, she said, 'I'm sorry, Daddy.'

She remembers quite clearly now – she thought it was all to do with her.

'Mammy, what are we doing now?'

She opens her eyes. Cian looks at her. His face, hands, legs, everything is covered in sticky dark chocolate.

'Find a bathroom, I think, and get you cleaned up!'

'And then what?' he says, standing up.

'I'm not sure.'

She has to change his T-shirt and shorts, his last clean pair. She washes her hands three times, inhaling the scent of the soap. It smells of peppermint.

'Okay,' she says. 'First things first. We have to get a phone card.'

'Why?'

'Because I have to ring some people.'

There are phones in the post office. Cian sits on the floor, whizzing Walter up and down it. It's good that he's a little distance from her, she doesn't want him to hear.

The phone rings twice.

'Declan?'

'Christina! Where are you? We've got the police involved now, so wherever you are they'll find you. Just come back, for God's sake. It's better for everyone.'

'Declan, can you understand why I did this?'

'What do you mean? Of course I don't. You've broken the law, you've abducted my son.'

'But Declan, wouldn't you have done the same thing?'

'I would never be in your position, Christina. For a start, I don't drink.'

'It's got nothing to do with drinking.' Her voice is low. 'You know that. Declan, how can you be so harsh? I'm your wife, the mother of your children. Don't you care?'

'But this isn't about you, Christina,' he says emphatically. 'It's about the children.'

'Don't you think I know that?' her voice breaks.

There's a pause. She can hear him inhaling on his cigarette, then he says, 'I don't know who you are any more.' His voice shrinks to a whisper. 'I can't trust you.'

His words feel like a punch. She bends over, presses the receiver into her ear, unable to speak.

How can she ask Declan for his help now? Her husband is the last person in the world who can help her.

'Christina, please tell me where you are. It's better this way. Imagine if you get picked up by the police – what would Cian think? Come on, where are you? England?'

'I can't tell you.'

'But surely you've no money.'

'I have money. Can you put Johnny on?' Her voice is firm; it takes him by surprise. There is a pause, she can hear them whispering, and then she hears Johnny's voice.

'Mam where are you?'

'I can't tell you, darling. I just—'

'Please, come back. Bring Cian back.' Her son's voice is no longer cross; he sounds scared.

'I want to tell you something Johnny, that I love you and that when things settle down we can be together again, okay?'

'But how? You're gone now.'

'I asked you to come with me, remember? But you didn't want to.'

'I didn't know,' he wails. 'Mammy, please come back.'

'Not now. I can't.'

He closes up again. She can hear him sniffing. 'Okay.'

'I have to do this, Johnny. You understand, don't you?'

'No.'

The line goes dead. He's hung up on her.

She holds her sides, closes her eyes and tries to push the lump down in her throat. But she is shaking; she can feel the tears gathering. She wipes her eyes and sends out a prayer for her son. She hopes that somehow it can deflect the damage.

215

When she comes to, everything is carrying on as normal – people standing in queues, Cian playing with his bear. Instinctively she picks up the phone and dials the operator.

'How can I get a number in Canada?'

She's put through to directory enquiries. It's surprisingly simple. Kittle, Tofino. She has a number now.

Nervously she picks up the receiver and dials.

Henry and Greta are unable to take your call right now. We are away until Wednesday, the twenty-fifth of June. If you'd like to leave your name and number after the tone, we'll get back to you as soon as we're back.

It's a man's voice, he sounds old. But he said Greta, so she was still there. She's found her mother…Greta…

'Come on, Cian.'

He runs over, dirty again from playing on the floor. 'I'm hungry,' he says.

'Okay, we'll go get something to eat.'

She has two days. Somehow they'll get there. She doesn't know how, but they will. I'm not being brave, she thinks, I'm doing the only thing I can do. I've no choice.

LUKE

He's eating a large slice of cherry pie with ice cream when they come in the book store cum coffee shop. Cian sees him first. 'Luke!' He runs over to him.

'Well, hi there,' he says, smiling. 'Fancy seeing you here.'

'We're getting something to eat. That looks nice.'

'It is.'

'Mammy, can I have some of that pie?'

She follows her son to his table. She stands on one leg, her head cocked. 'Sorry,' she says. 'I hope he's not bothering you.'

She looks better. There's some colour in her cheeks.

'Would you like a coffee?' she asks.

'Sure,' he says.

'How do you like it?'

'Large regular coffee.'

'How can large be regular?'

'Regular means not decaf, with milk.'

'Oh, okay. I suppose I'm having a large regular one too,' she smiles, just a little, and goes over to order.

Cian squeezes in next to him. He still has a babyish face and although there's only a year between them, Cian seems to be a much younger child than Sam.

'Do you have a dog?' Cian asks.

'No, but I'd like one.'

'I'd like a coydog,' Cian says, rubbing his hands together, his eyes flashing with excitement.

'What about a wolf?'

Cian's eyes open wide. 'Do some people have pet wolves?'

'Sure they do.'

He grips the edge of the table. 'Aren't they scared?'

'No, they're tame wolves.' Luke can feel himself smiling, opening up to this impish little boy.

She comes back with the coffees and Cian's pie. 'Yummy!' he says, tucking in.

'So,' she says, sipping her coffee, raising her eyes yet not quite looking at him, 'we meet again.'

'Yep,' he says. 'And I still don't know your name.'

She blushes. A soft rosy glow rises from her chest and spreads up her neck and cheeks.

'Oh, I'm sorry,' she says. 'It's Christina.'

She's different from this morning, friendly. She didn't want to talk to him before.

'So how are you feeling?' he asks.

She looks down at the table and flicks a corner of her napkin over. 'I'm grand now. That was embarrassing. Thank you for helping me.'

'What were you doing up there? Do you have friends, family?' Why was she at Bill's house?

'I'm trying to find someone,' she says.

'Any luck?'

'I don't know. I think now, yes, now maybe I might find them.'

'That's good.' He finishes his pie, sits back and, raising his mug to his lips, looks at her.

'Do I know you?' she asks suddenly, then quickly laughs. 'But that's ridiculous, of course I don't.'

'Where are you from?'

'Ireland. I've never been in America before.'

'What do you think?'

She looks straight back at him now, for the first time. Her eyes are the same colour as the sky outside. 'I like it. It's not as flashy or fast as I thought it might be. It's not so different from home.'

She plays with her spoon and he looks at her fingers. She has a wedding band. She catches him looking and glances at his hand.

'Are you married?' she asks.

'Separated.'

'Right, sorry.' Again she blushes. He plays with his shades, pushing them further back on his head.

'It's okay. And you?'

'Same,' she whispers shakily.

'Are you sure?'

She laughs. 'Yes, absolutely. It's just...' she glances at Cian.

'Mammy, can I go and look at the books?' Cian has clearly finished his pie. He groans slightly and holds his tummy with sticky hands.

'Yes, but we can't buy anything, okay Cian?' She wipes his fingers with her napkin, wets it with her mouth and cleans his face.

'Okay,' he says dolefully.

'So, do you live around here?' she asks Luke, putting the damp napkin aside.

'Nope, Seattle. I was visiting people too.'

'Right. And are you going back to Seattle now?'

'No.'

Again their eyes lock. He feels like he knows what she's about to say.

'I wonder...' she swallows nervously. 'I wonder would you know the best way of getting to Vancouver Island from here?'

'Sure I do.'

She looks at him expectantly. This is strange, he thinks, this woman. Who is she?

219

'You can drive to the next town up, Anacortes, and take a ferry to Vancouver Island. It only takes a few hours and it's very scenic,' he adds, grinning.

'Right.' She looks crestfallen.

'You got a car?'

She shakes her head, picks up her coffee and sips it again. He watches her detach from the conversation, dip her chin down to her chest and finger the broken edge of the table. He could take her and the little boy to Canada. But that would mean he couldn't go and see Bill – he had wanted to go on his own. He looks out the door of the bookstore at the stores opposite, the legions of tourists gliding by, the white heat of the day glancing off the sidewalks.

'I can give you a ride,' he says quietly.

GRETA

She gazes east towards Ahous. The landscape is washed in a soft pink glow, the water lapping up onto the beach and gently folded further out. There's a slight breeze; it refreshes her.

Henry takes the pot of rice out from the sand where he buried it to keep it warm an hour before. They're back from the other side of the island and a swim by the rocks. Her skin still prickles from the excitement of the chilly water, and although her fingers are cold, she feels warm inside.

They hunker down by the fire and begin to eat. Henry has put avocados, red onions and olives in the rice. It's delicious, though she's so hungry anything would taste good.

'We should get an early night,' Henry says. 'We need to conserve our strength – we've got two long stretches of open water to cross tomorrow and they could be difficult. It depends on the weather.'

She nods, watching him as he eats. He looks the part – lean, hardy, a pioneer.

It was physical attraction that brought them together. That, and the fact that Bill drove her away.

She remembers the first time she laid eyes on Henry. It was impossible to miss him – he looked like he had walked straight out of a spaghetti western, he looked like Clint Eastwood. And he had the same silent presence about him. No need to say anything, he just exuded a quality that had every woman in the bookstore where she worked turning around.

At the time all she wanted to do was escape La Conner and Bill's probing. It had been fine when she had first married Bill. She had been attracted to his art and their romantic bohemian lifestyle and his wild ways, dancing naked in the moonlight, taking acid, planning trips to Tibet. It was so divorced from her previous life that it was easy to forget all that.

When Greta left Ireland, she headed straight for Boston and her sister Maureen. She'd been in an awful state.

Now when she looks back, Greta realises that Maureen was only trying to help her, but at the time she had felt that she was judging her. All those drugs they had pumped Greta with had her off balance. She began to hear voices. When Greta confided this to her sister, Maureen was keen for her to go to the doctor, but of course Greta was terrified of doing that. So one morning she just left, walked out of her sister's apartment without so much as a good-bye and caught a bus to New York. They hadn't seen each other since, though they had spoken occasionally by phone. Their relationship was still distant and stilted.

The day Greta arrived in New York, with no money and nowhere to stay, she ran into Bill. She was sitting on a bench in Central Park wondering what to do, and he had sat down next to her. He picked her up.

Bill took Greta to a three-day party, a hazy blur of nothingness, just what she needed at the time. They became a couple overnight, Greta immediately moving into his studio apartment in Brooklyn. It suited her to get lost in Bill's life, to focus with him on his obsession with his art. His career became the most important thing in their lives, which were hectic, chaotic days with little structure. Everything was part of the strive towards Bill's success.

After a couple of months Bill announced that he thought they should head west. He had heard of a place – La Conner – where lots of artists lived, inspired by nature and native mysticism. He needed to get out of the city and back to his roots. Apart from anything else, they owed back rent. So off they went on the longest bus journey of Greta's life.

It was when they got to La Conner that Bill started asking about her past. Said they should sober up and sort themselves out. She hadn't been able to handle that – Bill trying to get inside her head – so it had been easy falling for Henry.

He never asked questions.

They got together the first day she saw him. She had been walking home from the bookstore and Henry had driven past in an old pick-up truck and asked her if she wanted a ride. She had directed him the long way home and asked if he wanted to see a beautiful old cedar tree inside the woods. It was hard to remember who made the first move because they fused under the tree. They were kissing, just kissing, for more than an hour, until it got dark. Nothing else happened, but Greta knew that she could no longer stay with Bill. This tall stranger had mesmerised her. She had packed her things that night and left early the next day. She didn't even have the courage to tell Bill, she had just left him a note.

It was hard to believe she was still with Henry – over twenty years now. She'd never expected that.

They were growing old together.

'Do you remember when we met?' she says, using her fingers to eat some of the sticky rice.

'Sure,' he says, smiling. 'You were working in that bookstore, serving coffee. I went in to buy a book, but when I saw you behind the counter I just had to get a coffee.' He smirks, filling a small pot with water and placing it on the fire.

'What was it about me that you liked the most?'

'Your hair. No,' he says, 'it was your eyes, and the fact that you didn't smile.'

'Most people like it if you smile.'

'You just looked like a bit of an angel to me.'

'Henry, you old softy.' She goes over to his side of the fire and cuddles in next to him. He puts his arm around her.

'You couldn't wait to get away from crazy old Bill.'

'Poor Bill. I wonder if he ever made it as an artist.'

'I'd say so,' Henry says. 'He sure was serious about it.'

'It's odd to think that he's not that far away, really. All these years, we could have bumped into him. I still feel guilty about it all.' She takes Henry's hand and draws a circle in his hard palm with her finger.

'Well, Greta, I wouldn't feel too sorry for him.'

'What do you mean?' She stops playing with his hand and looks up at him.

'For a start, if he'd really loved you he should have come after you.'

'Is that what you would have done?'

'Well, you wouldn't just up and leave me, would you?' he grins.

'Don't be so sure of yourself.' She kisses his cheek.

'Anyway, I heard from a pal a few months after we left that Bill had already shacked up with someone else, that Martha woman who ran the bookstore where you worked.'

Greta pulled back from Henry. 'You're joking!'

'Yep. Didn't take him long to find someone to console him and she was pregnant as well, so it could have been going on while you were still there. You see, Greta, there's always two sides to every story. Strictly speaking, he wasn't the innocent party.'

'Why have you never told me this before, Henry?'

'Didn't seem to be much point. I know the way you hate talking about the past. Any time I ask you about your childhood or Ireland you clam up, but I can understand why you don't want to talk about it, the way your parents died like that…no wonder you left.'

'I'm sorry, Henry.'

224

'It's not important who you were then, I know who you are now. I know exactly what you like and what you don't like. I know your moods and when you want to be alone and when you want to make love. I know your scent and the little sounds you make when you sleep. You're my life partner now. We don't need to delve into what happened before.'

'But that's only a small part of me,' Greta says quietly. 'I've always felt that I haven't been completely honest with you.'

It's nearly dark now. Henry turns and looks into her face. She can see the whites of his eyes, bright in the darkness, and the outline of his long chin, like a chisel.

'Okay, tell me then,' he says. 'It won't make any difference. Tell me what you've been hiding all these years. It won't change who you are, Greta.'

Greta hesitates. Where can she start? How can she tell him without him despising her? She pushes her fingers under the sand, then brings them up so that the sand trickles off the back of her hand. A small spider scurries up her wrist. She blows it away.

'I was married before, in Ireland,' she says.

He smiles benignly at her. 'I'd guessed as much,' he says 'I knew you were on the run.'

'Why did you never ask me more?'

He shakes his head. 'I reckoned you were going to tell me when you were good and ready. Though I never thought it was going to take this long.' He laughs and gets out his tobacco pouch and papers and begins to roll up.

'What about you? What are your secrets?' Greta asks.

'I don't have anything to hide, Greta. You know I grew up in Vancouver, in the suburbs. I just had a regular childhood – a mother and a father, two sisters, one brother. You know all this, how I dropped out of college and drifted for a while, until I met you. It wasn't until I met someone more rootless than myself that I felt the

225

need to put down roots!'

He slides his tongue along the edge of the paper, twists the end and lights up, immediately passing it to Greta. She inhales deeply and closes her eyes, letting her nostrils fill with the aroma of grass. They sit in silence for a while, smoking.

Henry leans over and pushes the hair out of Greta's eyes. 'You okay, honey?' he says.

'Aren't you going to ask me who he was? Don't you want to know?'

'If you want to tell me,' he says, getting up and tying the food up in a bag. 'I'll just hang the food up,' he says and disappears in the dark.

Greta collects together the dirty pot and plates and goes down to the edge of the ocean. As she cleans them, by touch rather than sight, she decides not to say any more. Everything is so simple here, why complicate things?

Maybe that's the best way to live, she thinks. Maybe it's better to keep your secrets close to your chest and not tell anyone. But there were things that had never been explained.

Like why Greta had never wanted children. She'd been so adamant about it that the subject became a no-go area. Then there was the time Henry had picked up a second-hand sewing machine and brought it home for her, only to find it in the trash the next day. There were the days when Greta hardly spoke, just sat out front staring at the sea, questioning her own sanity. There would be no food on the table for dinner, no conversation, but Henry had learned never to interfere. Only once did he suggest she go to the doctor because she seemed a little depressed. Greta had exploded, storming out of the house, and at the time she had wondered whether she would actually return. But when she did he never asked her why she had got so angry, and now too many years had passed.

She goes back up to the camp and Henry is already inside the tent. She climbs inside.

'Okay?' he asks.

'Yep.' She snuggles in next to him. 'I love you, Henry Kittle.'

He chuckles and pulls her close to him. 'You do, do you?'

She shimmies down the sleeping bag and kisses around his belly button. Then she strokes him with her hand. Her tongue finds its target and she gently licks each ridge of skin before she opens her mouth. Henry moans and touches her hair, pulling it back from her face and gripping it with one hand in a tight ponytail.

'I love you too, Greta Kittle,' he sighs.

CHRISTINA

This is okay, she thinks. I'm not so unlucky. Luke has the window wound down on both sides of the truck. The air blows through, making it hard to speak. It's easier just to look out at the landscape and feel her hair lift up from her face. For the first time in days she has a moment to relax. Cian sits between them with Walter placed firmly on his lap. He's quiet too. Out of the corner of her eye she can see his eyelids droop and his head nod forward. She looks over at Luke.

Why does she think she knows him?

She smiles to herself. Declan would go spare if he saw them now, riding along in a truck with a complete stranger, heading off into the unknown. Declan had been so busy wrapping them all up in cotton wool that he hadn't realised he was suffocating her.

She can think about that time now. Here, where she's dislocated, where there's nothing to remind her of that pain. It had been summer then too, last year, and she remembered her sense of desolation as she wandered through the little laneways and boreens behind her house. All that activity around her, the flies buzzing, wood-pigeons cooing, the leaves whispering and people driving by, waving cheerily. Life went on around her and she couldn't find the will to be in it. She would walk for hours and when she finally got home it would be lunchtime and she'd tell herself that it would be okay to have a drink then – a glass of white wine sitting in the garden, that always made her feel better.

It was the boys who suffered. Cian spent the long, lonely summer all on his own, spending each day talking to his teddies, making up elaborate play games that she chose to ignore. She would leave him on his own in his room for hours, running around, talking to himself. She convinced herself he was happy enough, that it was good to learn to play on your own.

And Johnny – his shame, aware that she was drinking, embarrassed to bring friends home. He would disappear for days on end in the summer, hanging out at his pals' houses so that he seemed to have better relationships with their mothers than her.

It wasn't until she crashed the car outside Johnny's school that Declan had finally taken notice of her. It was only then, just a few months ago, that he had asked her what was wrong.

With Angeline's help she had tried to fix it. She stopped drinking, she stopped seeing Paddy and she went to the doctor and got some anti-depressants. Angeline would remind her, call her up.

But the pills didn't make her feel any better. Her soul was in pain, and all the Prozac did was get her moving on the outside but not inside herself. Angeline told her to hang on, that she needn't take it forever, it was just to get her back on an equilibrium, she said, and then she could get some therapy.

What for?

She had no idea what was wrong with her. What could she say? She would just look a fool, like always.

So Christina kept taking the pills. It looked like she was better. The house was immaculate, the clothes washed, she went shopping and cooked food. It was all a veneer, because at the times when she wasn't busy she would catch herself looking into that black hole, and it still terrified her.

Christina looks out of the truck at the broad, flat road and the cars weaving in and out of the traffic. She looks over at Luke and he glances at her and smiles.

'We've got a couple of hours before the next ferry. Do you want to stop somewhere, go for a walk maybe?'

'Okay, but Cian's asleep.'

'All righty, I'll take you somewhere there's a nice view.'

He turns off the highway and heads down a smaller road framed by pine trees. They drive for a while, twisting and turning until they reach a bridge. Christina looks at the ocean as they drive over it. The water looks so clean and pure. Luke turns off the road and drives into a small car park. There are cedar trees all around them and camper vans and tents sprinkled about. At the edge of the car park is a view down to a stony beach and the ocean. A few children run up and down it. There's a chilly breeze.

'It's nice to be by the sea,' Christina says.

'What's it like, Ireland?'

'Wet. Cold.'

'Like Seattle then,' he grins. 'What kind of place do you live in?'

'In the countryside. It's rural.'

'That must be nice.' When he smiles she can see that one of his front teeth is chipped.

'Yeah, it can be, but it's not as beautiful as this. The sky feels bigger here. I like the sea. I'd like to live by it.'

'Me too. I've been to the prairies, worked in South Dakota for a while, and man, is it flat there, just stretches on forever. You drive along these straight roads and you could be driving all day and all you see are fields, sheared dry, with not one tree or dip or hill, nothing. I don't know how people live there.'

'I suppose it's what they're used to, and it's home.'

'Yep, home is different for everyone.' He pulls his sunglasses off his face and she can finally see his eyes, amber brown, flecked with black. He has thick, heavy brows, but his face is open. He doesn't frighten her.

'So, are you from Seattle?'

'No. I grew up in Canada.'

She looks at him again. 'I thought you were different.'

'Different from what?'

She sees a hint of something in his eyes – is it pride? 'I don't know…just something.'

'Yeah, well, I've been living in Seattle a long time now.'

He's dark and earthy. His skin shimmers, his body is lean and muscular.

'And where are you from in Canada?' she asks, watching the shapes the light makes on his face.

'You really want to know, don't you?'

She feels foolish now. 'Sorry, it's just that back home that's the first thing you ask anyone – where are you from? Who's your family? And if they're from the same place as you you're bound to be related somewhere along the line.'

'It's not that different where I'm from then.' He's fingering a red ball on the end of his key ring. His hair is long – Declan would say too long – and strands of it fall across his face. The rest is tied up in a loose ponytail. He takes the key out of the ignition and back in again.

'I'm from a small island off the western coast of Vancouver Island, although I left there when I was really little. I've only gone back once since.'

'Is that where you're going?'

'I guess I am.'

'You don't sound very sure.'

'I suppose that would be because I'm *not* too sure. It's been a long time since I was there.' He sighs. She looks out of the truck at the soothing lap of the ocean on the beach below.

'How long?' She turns and smiles at him, and he smiles back.

'Twenty years long enough for you?'

'God, yes. You must be a little nervous,' she says cautiously,

231

watching for his reaction.

'Yep, that would be about right.' He pulls the hair out of his face, and then turning to her, so familiar again, he asks, 'And you, where are you going?'

'A place called Tofino. Do you know it?'

He's laughing now. 'This is crazy. That's exactly where I'm heading.'

'You're joking!'

'Nope, that's my way home, I grew up there.' He shakes his head. His hair comes loose again and he pushes it away.

'I don't suppose you could give us a lift?' She fingers the edge of her shirt. Is she being sensible? Is this wise?

'I sure can.'

He gets out of the truck and stands beside it, hands in his pockets. She glances over at Cian. He's still asleep. His head flops onto the seat as she gets out of the truck.

'Thanks,' she says. 'You don't know how much this means to me.'

'Obviously a lot.'

They stare at each other. Now his eyes do frighten her. They're so dark, and she feels like he's looking right into her, as if he knows all about her and what she's done.

'I'll be back in a minute,' she says and trots over to the toilets.

She takes her time, tries to sort out her head. Her proposition is still crazy. She now has only twenty dollars to her name. Even if Luke takes them all the way to Tofino, where are they going to stay tonight? And what about the ferry, how much is that? She takes her money out of her purse, empties her pockets and counts it again, hoping for a miracle. Twenty-three dollars and sixty-two cents. She shoves it back in again, then splashes her face with cold water from the tap.

It'll be all right, she tells herself. I'm doing the right thing.

Outside she blinks and walks through the dappled sunlight,

232

weaving in and out of the cedars. She stops and looks around her.

Where's the truck?

This was the place where they parked, she was sure of it. There's the beach, the litter bin, the map of the trail. Christina twirls around and her heart begins to freeze.

'Cian!' she croaks, and then beginning to run, she cries out, 'Cian!'

THE OCEAN

Luke was not allowed to see the coffin as it was carried out of the window, his mother in it.

He was in his grandfather's house and told to stay there. But still he managed to slide the door open quietly, peer around it and watch. The box looked too small for his mother. Was she really inside? It seemed impossible. His cold fingers gripped the damp door handle and he swung his head around as far as he could manage. His hair kept blowing in his eyes; he would not allow it to be braided.

All the others were there. But he had been told he was too young. He saw his brothers and sisters, his grandfather and father, and everyone from the village as they became a dark snake, walking the muddy track to the cemetery. No one was allowed to use or say her name.

Ok-yu-pa.

He could not say it. And after four years they would remove her name from the grave, and there would be nothing then. Just a bare wooden post like all the others.

Four years. That was half his life. His grandfather told him that his mother had gone away and was never coming back. His father had been unable to say anything. But it was okay, because Luke already knew.

He saw her before she died, and she did look very sick. She had turned yellow, and her eyes looked so large in her head that at first he had been a little afraid. But when she smiled at him he saw who she was. He knew she was not coming back. It made sense to him that her soul would peel away from her body, like the skin off a fish.

When the family turned the corner, with the coffin swinging to and fro, on the waves of their heads, Luke stepped outside. It was cold and the wind glanced against him, but he was not going inside. He ran down to the sea, and the rain pelted him all the way to the shore.

Luke stood on the rim of his world, staring out at eternity. He couldn't see a spot of anything but the grey churning ocean. The waves seemed angry, jumping up into the air. There was going to be a storm. He screwed his eyes up. If only he could see land, some other place to go to. He desired it now. He didn't want to stay here, now his mother was gone. He wanted to go with her.

He prayed to the unseen spirit, he prayed to God, and while the ocean danced in front of him and the sky opened up, he felt no fear in his heart. Now the worst thing that could ever happen had. He would never be afraid.

He could taste the salt in the air, feel it course through his veins. He was a creature from the wilderness, and he would always be free.

LUKE

'Bears aren't what most people ought to be afraid of, it's cougars and mountain lions that are more dangerous,' Luke says to Cian. 'But you have to know how to read bears. Sometimes they want to be left alone and sometimes you can stick around, but you keep your distance, right? And sometimes you get the hell out of there!'

Cian looks worried. 'Are there bears in this wood?'

'I don't think so. This place is too small, but there were bears up where I was camping last week.'

The child is mesmerised by him. 'Did you see any?'

'No, they're real shy, but I saw some prints all right.'

'What did they look like?'

Luke picks up a stick and then draws in the dirt. It's surprisingly easy to remember the shape, and it pleases him when he looks down at it.

'I'll tell you something,' Luke says, taking Cian's hand and walking on. 'My grandfather told me that he used to go trapping for bears with his grandfather when he was only a little bit older than you.'

'How did they catch the bears?'

'His grandfather made traps that would crash down on the animal. They were made out of heavy poles with a weight of rocks on top and baited with salmon.'

'What's bait?'

'Have you ever been fishing?'

'Yes, with Daddy and Johnny.'

236

'Well, do you put a bait on the end of the line to catch the fish?'

'Oh yes, it's a maggot.'

'Well, it's the same thing with setting a trap. You bait it with something the bear will want to eat so that he'll dislodge the trap and it'll fall on him and kill him. My grandfather told me that he was very frightened when he saw his first dead bear. He said he was sure it was going to jump up and eat him.' Luke laughs and chews on a stalk of grass.

'What did they do with the bear once it was dead?'

'Well, after taking the heavy rocks off the animal, his grandfather would drag it down to the river and load it onto the canoe, and then they'd head back towards camp. I remember he told me that as soon as they reached the mouth of the river his grandfather would shout "Hooooo-Naay!" four times and that was a signal that someone was bringing in a black bear. And do you know what they did then?'

Cian shakes his head.

'They'd have a dinner for the dead bear, and the bear was the guest of honour. He was put in a sitting position with a couple of feathers stuck up behind his head, and strings were attached to his paws so that when they were pulled the paws moved in time to bear songs sung by the people.'

'Like a puppet?' Cian says, fascinated.

'I guess.'

'Do you know the bear songs? Can you sing me one?'

'No, I never learned those songs. They're nearly all forgotten now.'

'That's sad,' Cian says. 'Will we make our own one up?' And skipping along the path, he begins to sing, 'Bear, big black bear, here we come to get you…'

Luke pauses, chews the grass and spits it out. He can hear the ocean lapping the beach below. If he had been born a hundred years ago his life would be so different. He tells Cian this story, but it's like it's about another person's family. He feels little connection to it.

'Cian!'

Christina comes tearing around the corner. She slams into him and lands on the ground.

'What's wrong?'

She's panting, trying to get her breath. 'Oh thank God, I thought you'd gone.'

'But we were just here.'

'The truck…'

'I had to move it, I was in the way there. I should've told you.' He kneels down and looks at her. Her forehead is white, her cheeks red. Sweat slides down her face so that it looks like tears. Cian turns and trots back. 'Mammy, what's wrong?'

'I thought…' She's gasping and looks at Luke. A blue circle burns in her belly. He steps back, astonished. He can see this quite distinctly, the blue of her, spinning around and around, churning inside her.

'Christina,' he says gently, 'I'm real sorry.'

She ignores him, focusing instead on the child, and calls him over. Cian lets her hug him and twists around to look at Luke. A minute ago he was okay, now he looks like he's going cry too. This isn't good.

'Come on, you guys,' Luke says. 'Let's get up, we don't want to miss the ferry.'

GRETA

She's back in the hospital again, waiting for Tomás's visit. But this week, for the first time, he doesn't come. He doesn't come the next week, nor the next. He never comes back.

This is the nightmare, to be so completely forgotten that the doctor no longer sees her and the nurses look through her and the other ones locked in with her are lost in their own dark worlds.

Weeks later they told her that she had gone into a catatonic state when Tomás didn't show. She had curled up on the floor and moaned and beat it and they'd had to take her away and put her all on her own because she was upsetting the others.

When she came back to the ward she was wobbly with drugs. Not once did anyone ask her what the matter was. Didn't they know that she had had a miscarriage? Didn't they know she had a daughter, outside, waiting for her?

The doctor had diagnosed her as bipolar, or in those days what they called manic depressive. If she closed her eyes she saw the words like a big sign hanging over her. He told her that she needed to stay in the hospital for her own safety, that she wasn't well enough to go home.

She remembered at the time that everything was jumbled up. She would hear snatches of things inside her head — Christina's tinkling laugh, Tomás yelling at the cattle to get into the wagon, Angeline chanting *Nam Myoho Renge Kyo* and the cotton reel song, over and over the *whiz, whir, whiz, whir*…and then she would think, They're right, I am going mad.

She learned to obey the rules. If she stayed quiet, if she took the drugs, they would let her have a bath and maybe wear clothes rather than a nightdress. If she was really good they would let her out of the lock-up ward and allow her to walk around the hospital, albeit accompanied by a nun.

The hospital was a cavern. She could lose herself walking along its corridors. Sometimes she thought she was back at boarding school because of the smell of the place and the colour of the paint on the walls and the linoleum floors.

Time passed. She watched the leaves turn brown and then drop. She watched it snow and rain and the wind howl around her grey prison. And the hole inside her got bigger and bigger, and the cotton reel song grew louder and louder.

When the buds started showing again she made a friend. Her name was Maggie and she was in the bed next to her. Maggie was older than her. She told Greta that she had been in the hospital seven times already, that she was manic depressive too and that because her parents were so elderly, they found it hard to cope with her at home.

'I'm all right most of the time,' Maggie said. 'In the summer I'm fine. It's the winters I spend here, like a holiday!' she laughed. 'But it's not too bad, is it? They're kind to us, aren't they?'

Greta nodded.

'Don't worry,' Maggie said. 'You'll be out soon.'

'I miss my daughter.'

'But you wouldn't want her to see you sick, would you?' Maggie said. Greta shook her head. 'At least we haven't been here all our lives, like poor old Brigit.' Maggie indicated a small, dumpy grey-haired woman sitting on her bed and pulling her socks on and off. 'She's been in since she was a young one. Schizophrenic,' she whispered.

Greta looked at Brigit, lost in her actions, completely forgotten about. That could be me, she had thought, and it was in that moment that she knew she would get out of St Finian's somehow, with or without her husband's help.

These memories play through Greta's head as she lies quite still in the tent, listening to Henry's breathing. She wonders where Maggie is now and whether Brigit is still locked up in St Finian's.

She's hardly slept, her night punctuated by disturbing dreams, reminders of how her mind felt when she was inside. This always happened when she smoked.

She crawls outside and sniffs the air. It's cold still and there's a sharp wind coming from the north. She starts to sort out breakfast as she hears Henry stir in the tent. She's nervous about today, as they have two big crossings to make. She knows the risks of paddling across large expanses of open water, how the wind can build up and create powerful currents. She hopes she has the strength to deal with this today. She feels exhausted.

Henry appears. His chin is grizzly and it makes him look even more rugged than usual. He yawns and stretches, then immediately goes over to the radio to check the forecast.

Greta looks at the sky. The clouds are moving fast, bands of fluffy wisps with the sun breaking through behind.

'We should be okay,' Henry says. 'The winds are changeable today, but nothing we can't deal with.' He picks up a piece of dried mango and chews it.

They eat and then pack up camp swiftly, hauling the boats and gear down the beach. They launch easily. The sun sparkles off the water and Greta can see the clouds reflected in it. She begins paddling and concentrates on the swing of her body and the feeling of the water swirling against her paddle. Once she's started moving, her trepidation about the day begins to dissipate. She trains her mind to focus in the present and drinks in all the sensations around her. The surf roars in her ears and she can feel the swell of the ocean beneath, propelling her forwards. This is why she likes kayaking, why she yearns for these trips into the wilderness. It's because they bring her beyond herself and she can see how tiny she is in the scheme of life.

Henry is silent and the couple slide across the water as if in a dream. Suddenly he raises his arm, pointing at a darting shadow under the water. Greta sees a shiny dark fin break the surface. It's a porpoise. A second later, she sees his companions. They curve gracefully in front of her and then speed off into the distance.

She inhales deeply, her heart racing from the excitement of seeing her favourite sea creatures. The weather has turned almost balmy and she feels like she's moving along in a golden light. Memories of the night float away.

They pause briefly for lunch on a small island. It's a barren, rocky outcrop with little shade, the only respite patches of lush dune grass, which are like razors on her legs. All around them are tiny little red flowers, now beginning to fade away.

'Indian paintbrush,' Henry says as he fingers them.

They talk little, conserving their strength for the long crossing that lies ahead. Henry plays with her hair, braiding it and unbraiding it while she closes her eyes and drifts in and out of consciousness.

The Pacific is home now. Greta could never imagine feeling this sense of belonging anywhere else. She wonders how she came to be here. Was it chance that she had come so far west? Or fate? Was this her destiny?

Conditions are perfect as they push out towards Flores Island. Greta relaxes and stares over the side of her kayak into the glassy green ocean. Aware of Henry's splashes ahead of her, she moves forward intuitively, watching the ocean life twirling beneath her as she does so. A tiny red crab spins into the dark depths and she watches until its red light goes out. When she looks up again she's surprised to find that the clouds have thickened in the sky and the sun is sliding behind them. Henry is a long way ahead. She quickens her pace. As she moves forward, focusing on the form of her husband in his kayak, she can see a dark band of fog hurtling towards her to her left, blotting everything in its path.

'Henry!' she calls.

He twists around and looks shocked to see her so far behind. Then he sees the fog.

'Take out your compass,' he yells. 'Go north-easterly. I'll keep in that direction, but very slowly. Don't worry.'

He's blanked out. The fog has come between them and she can see nothing but swirling white vapour. Her heart pounds as she pulls out her compass and examines it. Now the wilderness is no longer beautiful but dangerous. She's heard of kayakers lost in fog, never seen again.

'Henry!' Her voice echoes across the white sky.

'I'm here.' She can hear him calling back, but it's impossible to know where his voice is coming from. She knows well the tricks fog can play with sound.

She looks at her compass and focuses, beginning to paddle confidently in the direction Henry has told her to.

In the fog time passes slowly. These moments feel eternal. Greta keeps on moving, because to pause could put her at risk of drifting further out to sea.

'Henry! Henry!' she calls, but her voice is muffled and she can hear no one calling back. She feels chilled to her bones and begins to shake. Just keep paddling, she chants, just keep paddling.

And now, all sorts of ghostly apparitions assail her out of the fog. A tiny little islet is illuminated, a drop of green and blue, in the vast expanse of white. Then, just as suddenly, it has vanished. There seems to be some kind of glow breaking through the fog. She hopes it's Henry and a torch, but as she squints at it, the glow turns into a golden ball that drops into the ocean and spins out of sight.

She cries and gulps with fear. The fog has left her completely exposed. She can deny it no longer, put off her reckoning no more. Tears leave trails on her cheeks and drop onto her hands. Memories which she had managed to suppress that morning resonate through her. She can see figures floating above the waterline and pulling at her – her mother and father, Christina, Angeline, Tomás and Bill, and then the *click, lock, click* of the lock-in ward and the *whiz, whir, whiz, whir* of the cotton reel song.

She looks down at the compass she's gripping with white fists and wipes condensation off its surface. She's on course. And now, as she passes through the water, she can see the tentacles of fog, contracting as fast as they arrived, and in an instant, above a grey broad band, she can see the island.

On the shore is Henry, waving to her.

CHRISTINA

All the shapes of the islands look like a stationary herd, arrested in the slipstreams. A family. And the driftwood floating looks so odd to her. She imagines these logs of redundant timber, bleached and bony, piling up, divergent diagonals hemming the boat in until they stop moving.

And what is left?

The white. Blue sea bleached into off-white sky, not creamed but icy shades. And she's sitting on the white, hard metal lifejacket chests. There are white rails there for your safety, but to her they look like grills, too much like a prison.

She surveys this scene. It seems untouchable. When she lived at home, at The Mill, she used to love walking through the fields. Her daddy owned close to forty acres. Once you left civilisation – the house, the river and the garden – you could roam from field to field. And when she looked about her there, what she could see all seemed tactile. The hills rolled up and down in front of her eyes, partitioned into tiny fields, marked by the odd wobbly tree. It was like a soft blanket of green rolled out on top of a sleeping giant. She had always felt she could reach out and touch it because it was so much a part of her.

Here, in this western land, she has no sense of ownership. The sea, the sky, all these rocky islands command her respect. The ocean looks brittle, like a sheet of blue glass, and the ferry cuts through it, taking her closer to her mother, further from all she's ever known.

A bird casts a long shadow on the deck, but when she looks up she can't see what it is, the sun is in her eyes. She draws Cian closer to her, puts her arm around his shoulders. She thinks about Angeline, and how safe she always made her feel when she was little. It has taken her this many years to begin to wonder about her stepmother. Her childhood is a puzzle. Where exactly did Angeline fit in? Christina found it hard to distinguish between the time when she was just the housekeeper and when she actually moved into her father's bedroom. It had all seemed so natural at the time, seamless. Christina had been grateful for her Angeline. She never wanted her to go.

Did she even wish for her mother to come back? She must have. Her mother had been the biggest part of her life for six years. She had just forgotten to recognise it.

GRETA

The fire flickers and Greta watches the glowing embers. She feels calmer now. Henry had told her that she had only been lost in the fog for a matter of minutes, but to her it had felt so much longer and the experience has now put images inside her head that she can't shake.

When she had first landed she had lain on the beach trying to rest while Henry had gone back out to catch a fish for their supper. She had been afraid to close her eyes, and instead she had gone for a walk on the beach, following the lone tracks of a wolf. This had helped her to still her mind, and now she feels a quiet resolve.

They have just finished feasting on the wild salmon Henry caught and a handful of succulent gooseneck barnacles Greta collected on her walk. Henry is lighting his small pipe. He passes it to her, but she shakes her head.

'I don't think I will, honey, not tonight.'

He looks mildly surprised. 'Okay,' he says, puffing away. 'Are you feeling better now?'

'Yes, I think so,' she says, taking a sip of her orange tea. 'When I was in the fog I kept seeing the faces of people from the past.'

Henry's eyes look curious. 'Like who?'

'Bill...' she pauses, 'and my parents. And Tomás, my first husband.'

'Why did you leave him, Greta?'

'It's a very long story,' she sighs.

'It's okay, you don't have to tell me,' he says, tapping the dead ash out of his pipe.

'No, I want to. I think it's about time I did.' She continues, 'Tomás and I were very young when we married. Looking back, I think I was lonely because my parents were dead, and my sister, Maureen, was away in America and I was stuck with this dotty old aunt called Shirley.' She laughs softly. 'Oh, she was awful, Henry. I couldn't wait to get away from her, so when I began courting Tomás, I had one objective – to get married as soon as possible.'

She pauses, takes another sip of tea and stares at the small, neat flames of their fire. 'We lived in the middle of nowhere, in an old house that belonged to his family. It used to be a mill, and the wheel still went around. We lived on the water. Tomás was a farmer. We had a lot of land. It was hard work.'

Henry refills his pipe and lights up again. 'So what happened to you and Tomás?' he asks hesitantly.

'I never stopped loving him,' Greta says wistfully, remembering the churning river, the roll of the land around her old home and Tomás, standing in front of it as if posing for a photograph, his damp curly hair, tall heavy frame and a dog at his feet. She sighs. 'But things happened…and I could never go back.'

'What things?'

'I'm afraid to tell you,' Greta's voice cracks. 'But I feel like I can't carry the weight of it any more.'

'If you need to tell someone, then tell me,' Henry says. 'I'm your husband.'

Greta takes a deep breath. 'I suppose the beginning of the end was when Angeline came to work for us. Although at the time I thought it was great because I couldn't cook, and she was fantastic. She was an old school friend. I trusted her, but she betrayed me. She stole Tomás.'

Henry comes over to her side of the fire and wraps a blanket around both their shoulders so that they sit huddled together.

'Your husband betrayed you as well, Greta. He couldn't have been completely innocent.'

'And there's something else.' Greta speaks fast, afraid that if she slows down she'll never be able to tell Henry. 'I was pregnant and I lost the baby, and then I lost my mind. They locked me up, Henry. I was put inside a mental hospital for months.'

Henry looks horrified. 'Oh my God, could they do that to you? Against your will?'

'Yes. Tomás did that to me, Henry, and worse, he never came and got me. They put me there and left me to rot.' The tears are rolling down her cheeks and Henry holds her.

'Why did you bottle this up for so long, Greta? Why have you never told me?'

She shakes her head and is unable to speak, her mouth full of sorrow. Henry wipes her cheeks and kisses her forehead gently.

'My poor, sweet Greta. I'm so sorry.'

'My baby was called Matthew…after my father,' she whispers.

They sit in silence for a while by the fire. Tiny sparks shoot up into the starless sky. They sit on the white sand, the noise of the surf at their feet, with the dark green forest behind them. She sits between two worlds, between exposure and concealment, between silence and sound.

'But if your husband never came to get you,' Henry says, slowly gathering his thoughts, 'how did you get out of the hospital?'

'I escaped.'

Henry smiles. 'That's my girl.'

'I went back to The Mill to try to get Christina, but when I got there she was out, with Tomás. I came face to face with Angeline. I don't know how she managed it, but she persuaded me to leave. She told me that if Tomás found me he would drive me straight back to St Finian's. I couldn't take that risk. She gave me some money and my passport and told me to go to America, to Maureen. She said that

249

I would be safe there. So I went, Henry, I ran away. And that's how I came to be here. And I still don't know whether Angeline was trying to help me or not that day. I'll never know whether she's good or bad.'

She's been talking for a long time. The fire is almost out and Greta shivers, getting up and pouring a large mug of water from the water bag.

Henry sits behind her. 'Who's Christina?' he asks softly.

Greta's heart lurches. Her voice is so sore it sounds like gravel. 'My daughter. I had a six-year-old girl.'

'And you left her?'

'Yes, Henry, I ran away from my daughter as well.' She can see the shock register in his eyes as he tries to compose his face.

'But why did you never go back?'

'At first I was too sick. It took me ages to get off the medication, to get back to who I was, and then too much time had passed and I was afraid that if I went back they would still say I was manic depressive and put me back in the hospital.' She turns to look at her husband. She can see him struggling with all that she has told him.

'I wrote to Christina every week, but she never wrote back. I wonder if she even got the letters.'

Henry takes her hands and grips them.

'Do you think I'm terrible, Henry, for leaving her behind?'

'You had no choice,' he says tightly. 'How can I judge you?'

She bends her head into his chest, feels his hand on her hair and smells him, his wood smell of smoke and man. She has always felt safe in his arms, even from the beginning. Maybe that's why she never left Henry.

She feels him shift his weight. His hand moves to stroke her forehead. What does Henry really think? She knows he won't tell her.

Greta loved Henry's self-belief in what was right and what was

250

wrong, and how he would stand up for these things no matter how difficult it could be. But more than anything, she loved him for giving her shelter, protecting her and never asking her for a single thing. He was her tree.

What she has told him will probably change the way he feels about her forever. But she had no choice. No matter how hard she tried, over all these years her past just wouldn't go away. She had to tell him.

She closes her eyes and listens to the comforting swish of the waves. She feels like she's being rocked gently in rhythm with the sea. She's calling her daughter, praying that she'll look for her one day, because she'll never go back, even now.

LUKE

It's late afternoon by the time they disembark from the ferry. Christina spent the whole time sitting outside on top of the lifejackets, Cian pressed in close to her, the two of them sharing a secret, silent dialogue.

Luke had found a phone on the boat and called Sam. Being with Cian made him miss his own son. He envied Christina and the freedom she had to be with her child all the time.

Sam sounded good. He told his dad that he had been fine the very next day after Luke had left.

'Did you see any wolves, Dad?'

'No, not this time.'

'And Big Foot, any sign of him?'

'Nope, I guess he was on vacation someplace else.'

'Mom said she's going to take me to California in a couple of weeks with Larry and his son, Gene.'

'Who's Larry?'

'He's mom's friend, they go out drinking together.'

Luke winced. His son saw it all. 'Well, we'll try and do that camping thing again, right?'

'Sure, Dad,' Sam said, but Luke could tell he didn't believe it.

They spoke for a little longer. He could have talked to Teri and asked her about Larry and California, but it depressed him too much.

Luke drives out of Sidney and heads towards Victoria. It's getting dark by the time they drive through the city centre and back out along the coast road.

'I think we should find somewhere to stay tonight,' he says, breaking the silence. 'It's getting dark.'

He can sense her shift in her seat. 'Okay,' she says quietly. 'It's just…God, this is so embarrassing.'

'What's up?'

'I don't really have much cash.'

'That's okay, most places take Visa.'

'Well, I don't have a credit card either. Jesus, I know that you hardly know me, but would you mind lending me some money? I'll pay you back when I get to Tofino, I'll be able to get some money then.'

'It's cool,' he says. 'Not a problem.'

What was she doing halfway across the world with no money?

There was something wrong, definitely. He had seen it back there in the woods. He wasn't sure what it meant, but he had seen something coming out of Christina, an emotion that manifested into a blue light. That sounded crazy. He shook his head.

'I'm hungry,' Cian says.

'We'll find a place to stay and then get something to eat, okay?'

'Okay,' Cian says and squeezes his arm. Luke reaches down with his left hand and flips the cap off Cian's head. The child giggles. Sam hated him doing that now.

They find a quiet bed and breakfast with a secret path leading from its backyard down to a beach. The garden is pulsating with colour and the sweet aroma of dozens of different flowers and plants. It immediately seduces them, and Christina books the double room for her and Cian while he takes a single. The house is modern but full of beautiful old things. Christina tells him that most of the furniture is antique. She picks out pieces – Victorian, Edwardian. The words mean little to him, but he can appreciate their weight, the age of the wood, their resonance with history.

253

'You know all about that sort of thing then?' he asks.

'Not really,' she blushes. 'I mean, I never studied it or anything, but I used to enjoy buying things for my house. We had an auction in our town every month and I loved going. I just picked up the information there.'

She has changed now and is wearing a dress. It's black, like a long straight pinafore. It drops straight down to the ground. Her feet peek out at the bottom in a pair of black sandals. Nothing about her is contrived. Her arms are bare, pale and freckled. She's wearing no jewellery, just her wedding band, and no cosmetics. He can see that she has tried to tie her hair back, but it's already coming loose. He fights an impulse to pull it free. Cian is in the same clothes as earlier, though his face and hands are clean.

'I've got to wash some of his clothes,' she says as she sees Luke looking at him. 'Does he look really dreadful?'

'No, he's a kid, isn't he?'

They've been told about a nice place to eat. Luke drives down to a large pub, open and airy, with windows facing out onto the harbour.

'Cool,' Cian says, running down to the main window to look at the view. The sea is dark and the lights from the marina twinkle across it.

'So listen,' Luke says as he sits down. 'Don't worry about money, this is on me.'

'No, really, I have to pay you back.'

'It's okay, I've got extra. I was away last week and I didn't spend as much as I reckoned I would.'

'Where did you go?'

'Up to the mountains, the North Cascades, very near La Conner.'

'Was that the mountain I could see from the inn?'

'Yep, that's one of them, Mount Baker.'

'Did you go on your own?'

254

'Yep,' he says, then adds, 'I wasn't supposed to. I should have brought my son.'

She looks up, surprised. 'You've got a son?'

'Sam. He's a couple of years older than Cian.'

He takes out his wallet and shows Christina the photograph. She smiles at it. 'Oh, he's gorgeous. You've just one?'

'Yep.' He looks down at the menu and Cian comes over to the table.

'Who's that, Mammy?' he says, picking up the photo.

'Its Luke's son,' she says. 'He's called Sam.'

'Where is he now?'

'He's at home, with his mom,' Luke says. 'He was sick, that's why he couldn't come with me.'

'Will I get to meet him?'

'Afraid not. He lives in Seattle and we're going the other way, to Tofino.'

'Can we go to see him after we've been to Toffee-no?' Cian asks. 'Please, Mammy?'

'I don't think we can,' she says hesitantly. Cian moans and slumps onto the chair. 'Come on,' she says, flicking through the menu. 'What would you like?'

Christina doesn't eat much. Luke asked her if she wanted a drink and she ordered a bottle of wine. She was embarrassed when it arrived and he explained that he didn't drink. Now the bottle was nearly empty and her eyes were glittering.

'This is amazing,' she says. 'You know, I've never been anywhere like this before. My husband didn't like flying, so we used to holiday at home. I always wanted to travel.'

'I've never been to Europe,' Luke says.

'So that makes us similar, really, except that I never left home. I stayed living in exactly same town all my life and you left twenty years ago, didn't you? How old were you then?'

'Is that a crafty way of trying to find out how old I am?'

'Yes, of course it is,' she laughs.

'Well then, I'd have to be honest with you. I was sixteen, but I really left when I was even younger, around eight. I grew up in Tofino and only went back to visit the island when I was sixteen. After that I took off for Seattle.'

'That's very young. My eldest son is older than that, and he's still at school.'

'Is that Johnny?' he asks. She looks surprised. 'Cian told me about him.' She takes another sip of her wine. 'You don't look old enough to have a son that age,' he says.

'Now you're trying to find out how old I am! Keep guessing.' She takes another sip.

'How's the fish?' he asks.

'It's delicious,' she says, looking at it lamely. 'It's just that I'm not so hungry.'

'I am,' Cian says, finishing his last slice of pizza. 'Can I have a dessert?'

'You'd better ask Luke first,' she says, picking up the bottle and draining it into her glass.

'Sure you can, Cian,' he says.

'So, Luke,' she says, leaning forward across the table, 'are you visiting your parents?'

'No.' He stiffens.

'But I thought you were going home.'

'They're not there any more,' he adds.

'Oh.'

'Are you going to see your grandfather, the one who collects the songs?' Cian asks.

'Yeah, I hope so.'

'Will you ask him to sing you the bear song, and then you can sing it to me?'

'Okay.'

Christina looks confused. 'What's that all about?'

'It's a tradition where I'm from,' Luke explains. 'There are songs for everything. Each family has songs for different rituals. They all mean something. You can own a song. That is, the song belongs to you – it's yours. My grandfather is a singer of songs. He's collecting all the old songs so that they'll be saved because when someone dies the song goes with them. That's what he does.'

'That's wonderful,' Christina says. Her eyes are wide and bright.

'That's what I believe he's doing. He writes to me sometimes.'

'Luke, how does your grandfather collect the songs?' Cian asks.

'He goes around with a tape recorder and lets people sing the songs, then he marks the tapes with their names. Sometimes it can be difficult because people are afraid that he'll steal their songs. They're very precious.'

'I wish we had something like that,' Christina says wistfully. 'A song that belonged to our family, so that no matter where you were, you knew you were connected by the song, by the thread of it.'

THE QUILT

Two months after Luke's mother died, his father went out to sea and never returned. They said there was a storm and he drowned. His cousin told him that Thunderbird took him, brought him up to the mountain and he was happy there. But Luke knew what had really happened.

He saw it in his father, the light going out. He saw it weeks before he disappeared, so he wasn't surprised when he didn't come back. His father had let the sea take him because he couldn't bear to be without her, Luke's mother. He left them all behind.

Luke's grandfather wanted Luke to stay on the island with him, but Luke's sister, Gail, insisted that he go with her to live on the mainland. She said that he was too young to be raised by an old man. She promised Grandfather that they would visit often and he would be able to teach him the old ways.

Luke wanted to go.

He loved his grandfather and the stories he told him about the battles the Indians had fought a long time ago in the Clayoquot Sound. Afterwards Luke would spend hours drawing the characters in the sand on the beach, jumping up and down and re-enacting the drama. But he did all this on his own.

He was the youngest in the family. All of his brothers and sisters were grown up, and Gail, the eldest, was living just outside Tofino with her Canadian husband, Jeff.

Luke didn't want to be on his own any more. He didn't want to look out the front door of his grandfather's house and see the track to the cemetery. He didn't want to have to visit his parents' graves, see them take away their names. He couldn't bear that. Luke wanted to go somewhere new now. He wanted adventure.

Gail and Jeff ran a guesthouse just outside Tofino. They were planning a large family, but for now there was only Luke. He had his own bedroom, with a view of the ocean, and he liked to look out the window sometimes and imagine he could see Japan. He was just a regular kid now. He went to the school in the town and he had friends from Canadian families. He was different, but the same. Everyone was kind to him.

When he left the island Luke brought just one thing – a quilt. It was the one his mother had been making before she got sick. It wasn't finished, but he had all the pieces in a little basketry box she had made as well. He could have asked Gail to finish it, but he wanted it just as it was, incomplete, a fragment of his mother. The pieces of the quilt were the colours of the ocean – that's what he liked about it – and his mother had sewn whaling motifs on it in black. He always kept it at the end of his bed. When Gail asked him again and again if he would like her to finish it, he shook his head. He couldn't bear the thought of another hand on the needle, threading the thread, putting their touch upon his mother's creation.

In his little basketry box Luke possessed a secret – three strands of his mother's hair. Three black strands which remained strong while the rest of her faded away. The day after she died he had found them stuck to a sweater she wore and he had hid them in his box. He had this little part of her, and he would always have it.

GRETA

After all that time of thinking she was trapped for good, it turned out not to be so hard after all.

Over the last couple of weeks Greta had begun to notice that there was always a gap of a few minutes between the nurses coming off duty and the nurses coming on. This would be at visitors' time as well, so even though the door automatically locked every time it was closed, there would be people coming in and out. There could possibly be an opportunity to slip out.

Greta waited until it was a day when she was allowed to wear her own clothes. She was nervous but determined. Her opportunity came as a number of people left the lock-up ward. She looked about her, then quickly slipped out. The easy part was going down the stairs and out past reception because she attached herself to a large group of people who were leaving and walked behind them until they got to their car. It was then she had to make a dash for the gates, praying all along that no one was watching. Once she was out on the street she was completely disorientated. She just went towards the spires.

Greta ran nearly all the way into town, past the cathedral, and when she had put a little distance between herself and the hospital, she found the road to Oldcastle. She got a lift.

Greta went back to The Mill.

She believed she could pick up where she had left off. If Tomás would only look at her, he would know that he had made a mistake. She had stopped taking her medication the day before. It took her motivation away. She still had the pills in her pocket, in case, but she was feeling quite high then and had no intention of coming down.

When she arrived, Tomás was out. It was Angeline Greta saw, in the garden. She was planting dahlias. She had never wanted dahlias in her garden.

Angeline looked up, and her body tensed. She looked shocked.

Greta, how did you get here? she asked.

I escaped, Greta said.

Oh my God! But Greta, what are you doing here?

Greta's face burned. How can you ask me that question when you've stolen my life from me?

Angeline put down her shovel. We're all responsible for our own destinies, she said.

Greta turned white. She wanted to kill her, and she just might have if she'd had a weapon in her hand. Angeline became nervous.

I never meant to hurt you, Angeline said quickly. I've always tried to help you. I went to the hospital again and again, Greta, but they never let me see you. It's Tomás, not me, who wants you locked up.

Greta shook her head. She couldn't believe her.

Angeline continued, What do you think Tomás is going to do when he gets home? Did you think that he'll welcome you with open arms? Or will he just put you straight back in the car and drive you to St Finians?

Greta hadn't thought of that, and the possibility terrified her. She could never go back.

Angeline, where's Christina? Greta's voice broke. I need to see her.

She's not here, she's out with Tomás.

It was too much to bear. Greta began to feel herself fold in, her high spirits swept from under her. She was falling, falling, and she would never get up.

Angeline took her arm and brought her into the house. She gave her a drink and told her to stay calm. She said that she would help her, and that she would make sure that they never sent her back to that terrible place.

Greta was back in her house and nothing had changed, but it all felt different. The green hall was darker and the red carpet bloodthirsty. Angeline took down a small jar from the dresser and opened it. She took out a bunch of notes. She shoved the money into Greta's hand and told her to take it.

Where do I go? Greta asked in a daze.

Angeline thought for a second. Go to Maureen, go to America, she said. You should be safe there.

She ran upstairs, and when she came back she had Greta's passport and a few of her things in a bag. Greta looked inside – there was a picture of Christina. Her hands shook as she closed the bag again.

When you feel better, Angeline said, you can write, and we'll sort something out. But for now, you're better off running away. Tomás will only take you back to the hospital. Imagine what it would do to Christina if she saw you like this.

Don't let her forget me, Greta begged. Promise me that.

Angeline took her hands. Her fingers were cold, but her brown eyes were warm. I promise, Greta, she said.

At the door Angeline ran after her, hugged her, and said, But it won't be for too long, will it? You'll write soon, when you're better? You'll see Christina then, and Tomás.

Angeline moved away from her, looking uncomfortable, and Greta tried to search her eyes to find the truth. She still couldn't be sure of her.

Are you in love with my husband? she asked her.

No, Angeline said, not Tomás.

And it was as if she meant to say someone else.

CHRISTINA

She feels better now. The wine has warmed her, made her more confident. They walk back into the night. The air feels balmy and Cian's hand is warm inside her own.

'Will we walk for a while?' she asks.

'It's late,' Luke says, glancing at Cian.

'It's okay, he can sleep in tomorrow.'

They walk down a path in front of the pub, which eventually takes them onto the beach. The energy from the ocean vibrates around her and she can see huge piles of driftwood on the beach. She thinks they're beautiful. They look like prehistoric white bones in the moonlight. Cian lets go of her hand and runs ahead. She looks over at Luke. He follows his own path across the sand. His head leans forward and his hair falls across his face. She wishes she could express how alone she feels right now, how at this moment she's tiny and frightened, buoyed up by the wine, yes, but aware all the time of the edge, how she could tip off in a second, everything gone.

He says something.

'What? Sorry, I didn't hear you.'

'I was wondering why you're heading for Tofino.'

'I have to see someone there.'

'Who?'

She sits down on a pile of driftwood, pulls her feet out of the sandals and fingers her toes.

'It's my mother,' she says. 'When I'm thinking about it now, this

263

all seems pretty crazy, ridiculous. I really can't believe that I'll actually find her.'

He sits down next to her. She can feel his body close to her. She moves her legs over so that the material from her dress brushes his jeans. She continues, 'I haven't seen her since I was Cian's age. She walked out on me and my father and it's taken me this long to get around to finding her.'

'I can understand that,' he says quietly. 'You must be very angry.'

She's about to yes, she is, but when she thinks about it she knows it's not true.

'I don't know now,' she says hesitantly. 'How can you be angry with someone you don't know?' He says nothing and she continues. 'I've been bitter though, for a long time, because why should I be marked by rejection? Why me?' She shivers, feeling the familiar quickening of her heart, pins and needles spreading throughout her arms and legs.

'It happens to most people, you know,' Luke says steadily. 'You're not the only one.'

She thinks of Johnny and it makes her feel worse. The awful realisation of what she has done to her son hits her and she bangs her hand against a large rock behind the driftwood, saying breathily, 'Yes, but I was so little, and I needed her, and now I'm so furious because I gave all that love away to the one person I shouldn't have.'

Luke looks puzzled, but she just shakes her head, unable to speak any more. She stands up, panting. She can feel her heart surging into her mouth. She waves her hand at him, go away, go away.

But he doesn't move. She turns to look at him and he stares calmly back at her.

'What is it, Christina?'

She gasps, reaches out to him, but is unable to speak. Luke puts his arms on her shoulders, forces her to sit, then swivels her so that her whole body is facing him. She's breathing fast. 'I can't breathe,' she manages to whisper.

'Look at me,' he says.

Her head is swaying. She looks over towards Cian.

'He's okay, just look at me,' Luke repeats.

She looks at him then, and it's like she never looked at him before. His face is so wide it seems to take up the whole space of her vision. His lips are parted slightly and she can feel his breath on her face. She looks at his eyes and they suck her in, and again she has that feeling that she knows him, and from that feeling is a sense that he can see her, really see her.

'Okay,' he says, 'now close your eyes and listen to my breath.'

She closes her eyes, her nostrils dilate and all she can hear is the rush of sound within her — heart, mouth, breath, head — but behind that she detects his voice again. 'Listen to me breathe,' he says, and this time she can hear him. She listens to the breath enter him, as if it's coming from above both of them, and leave him, somewhere close to his belly because she can feel it bruise her as it exits.

'Try to breathe with me,' he says softly.

Images are propelled into her mind — running around the airport with Cian, jumping off the bus to get into the hotel, driving away from Johnny...

'Push all those thoughts away,' Luke's voice breaks through, 'and just breathe with me.'

She follows his lead, breathing in like a child and exhaling noisily through her mouth. Gradually she feels herself come down. The fear subsides, her fingers cool. She opens her eyes and shivers. His eyes are still closed and she's gripping onto his shoulders; she can see marks there. She leans forward and kisses him. He opens his eyes.

'Thank you,' she whispers.

He smiles, and before he has a chance to say anything, Cian comes bounding over.

'What are you two doing?'

265

'Luke was helping me,' she says.

'Why? What's wrong?' Cian's voice sounds tired.

'Nothing now.' She gets up. 'Come on, let's go.'

WHALES

We believe in God now Luke, Gail said to him.

But what's the difference between the unseen spirit and God?

His sister would shake her head in exasperation. Luke, would you just listen to me? You don't want to be different from everyone else, do you?

No.

We're Catholics now, like Jeff, and we're Christians like everyone around here. We believe in the baby Jesus and the Virgin Mary and God, okay?

Okay.

It's not so different from the island. Some of the people there are Catholics too.

I remember.

But Grandfather wasn't, nor was his mother and father.

Luke didn't want to make Gail angry, something he did often, and his sister could hit swift and hard. One look at the old wooden stick on the back porch was enough to bring him to heel.

Now go and dig up some potatoes, she said, pulling her dark hair back from her face, trying to look businesslike. We've got guests coming, they're already on their way from Port Alberni, and I need something to go with the salmon.

She went back into the house then and Luke stayed standing on the front porch for a few minutes. This summer he hadn't been back to the island once, and it didn't look like he would get the chance at all now. They were so busy. Gail and Jeff's guesthouse was booked solid for the whole of July and August and then he would be back to school. He had a feeling his sister didn't want to go back. He didn't care either way, but he would have liked to see his grandfather. He wanted to tell him all about his school.

Luke hopped off the porch, kicked a stone down the slope of the garden and picked up the spade. He hated digging up potatoes.

He knew why Gail was in such a bad mood. She and Jeff had been trying to have a baby for ages now. He had been there three years and still no sign. He knew it irked Jeff to have to look at him all the time, the only child in the house, not his. So Luke tried to stay outside as much as possible. He prayed that they would have a baby soon.

Luke hadn't meant to have a row with Gail. He had just got confused, because when he remembered the old stories his grandfather had told him he remembered this energy, the unseen spirit, and it was united with nature. It could transform into many different animals and creatures. It could take away your life and give it back in the breath of a hair. The Christian God wasn't half as exciting. It was a man, and to Luke, just a man seemed far too ordinary to have all that power.

Luke walked a ways down the garden. It was early still and the sun wasn't too hot yet. He wiped his forehead and looked out at the blue band of sea, the perfectly clear horizon. This was why his sister's guesthouse was so popular. The views of the Pacific were spectacular. They even had visitors in the winter, strange people, Luke thought, who wanted to stay inside and watch the storms for days on end.

Suddenly Luke dropped the spade. His heart leapt into his mouth as he saw the familiar shape of an orca whale rise and fall through the ocean. He scanned around. There had to be more. Sure enough, he saw another one behind it, then another, and another. The whales rose and fell like a long, wavy black line, the rhythm of their

268

movements hypnotising. Luke stood absolutely still. He could see not just one but two pods of whales out there, and not a boat in sight. He was the only person seeing this as far as he could tell.

Luke ran down the garden to get a closer look. He was up on a rise, at the edge of their land, right above the sea. The whales performed for him. One leapt out of the water, spinning and twisting her glistening body. They were playing. He would have liked to be out on the water with them, to be so close he could see their teeth, pink jaws and tiny hidden eyes. His heart surged with the excitement of this vision. Suddenly the day didn't seem so boring after all.

The whales passed by quickly, but Luke stayed watching until they were tiny black dots on the horizon.

When he lay in bed that night he could still see the waves of whales in his head. They moved as one. All the different parts of one pod were a single beautiful movement that passed through the ocean. He sat up, turned on his light and lifted up his mother's quilt. He looked at her killer whales, the strong black outlines with their round snouts, large mouths, perfectly symmetrical tail flukes and long dorsal fins. This was his family.

GRETA

The terror is real.

She wakes and it's still dark. Her throat is dry. Her mind is hurtling away from the images that persist in haunting her. She crawls out of the tent and sits on the sand. There's a quarter moon and a slight breeze. Shadows creep softly along the shoreline. She puts her head in her hands.

Brigit being restrained – that's the first face she sees. It's a scream, like the famous painting. Brigit's mouth is open wide, howling, her teeth half gone, her skin like thick white plaster, her hair functionally short. Where did they take her then? Greta never saw her again.

And Maggie. In a way her face is worse because she's smiling, yet her eyes are glazed over and she looks through her. Maggie sitting on the bed next to her, with the pillow propped up behind and clicking her needles together, knitting a hat for the man she'll meet one day and the booties for the baby she'll have one day. Maggie is chatting away, waiting on the trolley to come around with the drugs. Then she's silent for hours, staring at the wall, tears rolling down her cheeks.

She sees herself now. Greta with the long orange hair, frightened eyes and wet pleading lips being escorted to the special room – ECT, electroconvulsive shock treatment – three words that fragmented her forever.

She asked the nurse, 'What is my crime?' and the girl had turned away.

Afterwards, when she woke up she had been terrified. She hadn't known who or where she was. Nothing was familiar; everything was strange. And she had no identity. She had felt barely human. She felt feral, like a tiny animal. She was afraid to move out of the bed, afraid to speak or breathe. She had sat in her bed, rocking for days. They called her Greta and talked to her like she was a baby. They were so, so kind. And she kept rocking, and when they said, How are you feeling, Greta? Would you like a cup of tea, Greta? Look, isn't it a beautiful day, Greta? she moaned and said, Bad, bad, bad.

If Henry could see all that he would understand.

She reaches into the tent and pulls out her sleeping bag. She can hear her husband snoring softly. She slides inside her padded cocoon and lies back, staring at the sky above.

She wishes for a miracle to transform her past.

LUKE

What comes to him now, as he lies in bed with the sound of the sea sheltering him, is a story his grandfather told him.

When his grandfather told stories, they weren't fairytales or make believe like the books he had read to Sam when he was little. No. These were truth tales, legends with nuances added by each generation.

Luke had made him tell this story so many times because it fascinated him. It was about something his grandfather had seen with his own eyes. It was proof.

In his grandfather's time, people would see balls of snakes hanging from trees. These black writhing globes had the power to turn ordinary people into shamans. When he was a little boy, Luke's grandfather had met such a person. She was an old Indian woman, the grandmother of a friend of his. One day, as she was walking in the woods she came across one of these balls of snakes. She stripped herself naked and stood beneath the hissing mass. The snakes broke out of their ball and slithered down her body to the ground. This is what had turned her into a shaman, and from that day she was able to heal any broken bone or sore. With his own eyes Luke's grandfather described how he saw the old woman pick up fourteen live snakes and put one of them into her mouth, right down her throat. Gradually she pulled the snake back out and it had turned from green to grey.

Luke had never told Sam this story. Teri became angry when he tried to, saying it was impossible, there was no way the old woman could have done that and survived. He flared up then, saying his grandfather was no liar. But she made him feel ashamed and he began to doubt his own heritage so that he didn't have the heart to pass on anything to Sam.

He coughs, suddenly uncomfortable in the bed. He had turned his back on it all. In one moment he had made a choice to live life on the surface. He wonders whether it's too late now to go back, to try to unearth what was left of his childhood.

He turns on the lamp and leans over the side of the bed, picking up his notebook and pencils. He thinks for a minute, then taking out a black pencil he draws a tree with one branch hanging low. Taking up red, he starts to draw wavy lines curving in and out of each other. Growing in weight and density, he gradually adds to his ball of snakes.

There's a soft knock on the door. He gets out of bed, wraps the sheet around his waist and opens it. Christina stands there, her paleness shimmering in the dark corridor.

'Are you okay?' he says.

'Yes,' she whispers. 'Can I come in?'

'Sure.' He steps back.

She notices the light, the papers on the bed. 'You're still up?'

'I couldn't sleep.'

'Me neither,' she smiles awkwardly. 'Luke,' she says, going over to the bed and sitting on it, 'I never got to thank you properly, for tonight, the meal…and on the beach…'

'That's okay.'

'How did you learn to do that?'

'What do you mean?'

'Calm someone down like that? It was amazing.'

He laughs. 'I've never been in that situation before. I just used my instincts.'

273

'They were good.' She pauses and shifts awkwardly on the bed. He can see her right breast fall against the inside of her T-shirt, the outline of her nipple, its open tenderness.

'Do you draw?' she asks, picking up his notebook.

'No, I just started.' She turns the pages. He goes over. 'Don't, I—' But it's too late.

'Is this me?' she smiles, looking at him.

'I'm just practising...'

'Do I really look that sad?' She stares at him and he feels such a weight cast out from her eyes.

'Tell me,' he hears himself saying. 'Tell me what it is.'

'I can't,' she whispers, and then she puts her hand to her breast like it hurts. 'It's too much.'

She takes his hand and pulls him towards her, then she stands up on her tip-toes and kisses him. He finds himself kissing her back. He can taste the alcohol on her lips, is repulsed by it, yet he can't stop kissing her. He closes his eyes and he feels her hands on his face, pushing back his hair. Then she stops. He opens his eyes again, watches as she leans back and switches off the light, then pulls her T-shirt up over her head. Her hair swings back off her face and she's completely naked, her lips parted slightly, her eyes glittering. She fingers his sheet and it falls from his waist to the ground.

'Christina,' he says softly, 'you're drunk.'

She says nothing, but hugs him. He wraps his arms around her. It's been so long since he's been able to embrace another person.

CHRISTINA

She wants to have sex. That's all Christina wants. She came to his room because she wanted that feeling again, a sense of purpose like she used to have at the beginning with Paddy, like she counted. She's shocked by her desire. The wine has brought it out in her, and now she wants this man, Luke, to be inside her. That's all she needs. But something is happening, something else. Luke pulls back from her and his eyes are wet.

'Are you okay?' she asks.

'Look at you,' he says. 'Christina, I can see your pain.' He's crying. He goes to hold her again.

'No.' She pushes him away, confused, afraid.

'Let me hold you,' he says huskily.

She begins to shake, ashamed of her forwardness. She doesn't want him to see her, that's the point. She just wants him to fuck her because that's all she deserves. She grabs her T-shirt and tears out of the room.

THE LITTLE WHITE BOAT

The radio is on. Angeline hums as she works. Christina spins around the table, trying to dance. In the music there are giant ogres coming out of the woods and she's with the elves, running away, skipping this way and that.

Her father comes in.

Jim gave me these, he says, dumping a basket of runner beans on the table. Shall we have them for lunch?

Oh yes, how wonderful, Angeline says, wiping her hands with a dishcloth.

Christina stops spinning. She steps back by the dresser, fingering the sleeve of her cardigan, watching the adults. Her father has hooked his arm around Angeline's waist while she examines the crop. She glances behind her shoulder, catches Christina's eye, and whispers something to Tomás.

But sure, she saw us the other night, he says, turning around and looking over at Christina.

He comes over to her then.

Come on out to the garden with me, Christina, he says. I want to show you something.

Can I stay here, Daddy, and help Angeline?

Looks to me like you're more in her way. Besides, I've something for you. Come on. He holds out his hand. It's big and rough and dirty.

Go on, darling, Angeline says, smiling. Get some fresh air.

Reluctantly she leaves the sanctity of the kitchen and goes out the back door to the river with her father. It's bright out here, and breezy. They lean over the railings, looking at the water race by. On the other side of the river is a tiny landing. Tied to it is a little white boat, bobbing up and down.

See that little boat? says her daddy.

Yes.

That's for you.

She turns to him, wide eyed. But Daddy, isn't that dangerous?

He chuckles, Well, you're not to go out in it on your own, not until you're older and you can swim well. No, it's for us, together, he says.

He leads her by the hand and they cross the bridge, down the garden on the other side and past the big old apple tree. Daddy climbs down the ladder onto the landing and holds his arms up for her. She lets him lift her down.

Now, he says, once I get us some fishing rods, we can take this little boat down the river and catch some trout.

Fishing?

Wouldn't you like to go fishing with me? he asks. Don't you think it would be fun?

She doesn't, but she knows not to say so. Fishing would be smelly and dirty, and then there were those horrible maggot things that you put on the hooks for bait.

Come on, says her daddy, let's go for a little trip.

Isn't it time for lunch?

No, not yet.

He gets into the boat, moves the oars around and holds out his hand for her. Christina looks at the space between the landing and the boat. It looks wide and it keeps moving. What if she steps out, the boat drifts backwards and she falls into the river?

She shakes her head. No, thank you, Daddy.

He frowns and the colour of his cheeks deepen. This is a present for you, he says emphatically.

The little boat shifts around on the water. Nothing looks solid or safe at all.

I want to go back inside, she says eventually, looking down at her feet.

Ah Christina, he says, don't be such a baby. Come on, look, take my hand.

She shakes her head and the tears begin to well.

But he won't take no for an answer and he reaches out and grabs her hand, pulling her towards the boat.

No! she cries.

Come on, he growls. Don't be such a silly girl.

He pulls her off the edge of the landing and she stumbles onto the boat, her feet slipping around on the damp wood so that she slides into the corner and lands on her bottom with a bump. She cries now, hard, not caring what he thinks.

Christina, get up, he says sternly. Come on, sit up in the boat and help me row.

But she refuses to move. She sits huddled with her arms around her knees, sullenly looking at her toes as he takes them down the river.

Moments pass. She hears her father sigh and the splash of the oars in the water. She smells the river, its brown, and as she feels the light change around her, she looks up and sees the trees drip down above them.

Look, Christina!

A large dragonfly spins past. She can see a thousand little flies buzzing above the surface of the water. They make her itch.

Her father rows them downriver but she stays where she was, rooted to the spot on the bank, watching her fear in the boat – a sad little thing, a child who is afraid of life.

GRETA

It's hot. They walk up the dirt road, a gang of three small children tagging behind them. Greta can feel the heat off the sun beating down on her head. She takes off her hat and wipes the back of her neck with a handkerchief before putting the hat back on. She glances across at Henry, but he looks cool and collected in his khaki shirt. His eyes are hidden behind shades and his lips are pressed into a straight line. He has said nothing. Not since he came back from his walk this morning, not even while they ate and set off.

She wants him to speak, but she knows that she'll have to begin and she doesn't know how to. His silence irritates her because she feels that now he's judging her.

A truck goes by. It kicks up dust in its wake, and for a couple of seconds they're in a cloud. When it clears she can see the store ahead, a small ramshackle building with peeling white paint and a little brown dog panting outside, trying to keep cool behind an old water barrel.

Inside it's dark. Greta heads for the chocolate while Henry buys some tobacco and papers. A large man sits behind the counter, reading a book. A fan whirs behind him and she can see a circle of tiny flies flying in a circle above his shiny black hair.

'Hot day,' he says, putting the book down on the counter.

'Sure is,' Henry says as the man takes his money, throwing it into a metal dish.

He stares at them both then, picking up a piece of liquorice and chewing it. His eyes remind Greta suddenly of a cow's, deeply inquisitive and at the same time sure. Sure of what he is. 'You two take care now,' he says.

Back outside the sun feels even harsher.

'It's melting,' Henry says, indicating her chocolate as she walks back down the road.

She tries to wrap it up in her knapsack, but the chocolate is already soft and misshapen.

'That's okay, I'll eat it now,' she says, peeling off the foil wrapper.

He raises his eyebrows. 'All of it?'

'Sure, want some?'

He shakes his head.

Greta fills her mouth with chocolate. She had wanted to save it, but now she feels she has to eat it all. The children are still there, accompanying them back down to the boats. They eye her stash greedily.

'You guys may as well have this stuff.' She hands the rest of her load over to the delighted children, who run off to share it down by the water.

She's annoyed with him now. 'Why won't you talk to me?' she blurts out.

He stops stock still then and turns to her. 'But I am talking to you.'

'You know what I mean. You've said nothing about last night. I want to know what you're thinking.'

'Why?' His voice is suddenly bitter. 'Why is my opinion so important now, when it's obvious you never thought so before?'

'Of course I care what you think.'

'Then why have you based our marriage on a pack of lies? How do you think it makes me feel that you never trusted me enough to tell me that you had a daughter?'

What happened to the man who held her in his arms last night, who had stroked her forehead and told her it wasn't her fault?

280

'I thought you might despise me.'

He has taken his glasses off and his eyes are blazing. 'You know that's not who I am,' he says.

She wilts under his gaze. 'I'm sorry, Henry. I was frightened.'

'It's not the fact that you left your daughter behind that bothers me,' Henry continues. 'I think I can understand why. It's the fact that you never told me. Jesus! How can you think our relationship is real if you're unable to tell me something as important as that?'

She's unable to answer him. Beads of sweat mix with tears. She holds her sides and cries, 'I was afraid of losing you!'

A stray child stares at her, then scampers off down the dusty road.

'No, Greta,' Henry says calmly, unmoved by her tears. 'You know I would never have judged you. I think you were just afraid to acknowledge your daughter in our life. It's a shame, a goddamned shame.' He sighs and walks on. She stands on the road, shattered, sticky with chocolate and guilt.

He's right.

She tries to smile at the children playing in the icy water as they launch the boats, but she feels weak and withdrawn. Nevertheless, the kids wave them off, and one little girl even gives her a small red bloom. Greta tucks it inside her jacket.

They travel up the east coast of Flores, staying close to the shore and out of the tide. She gazes at the plump sea stars clinging to the rocks and smells the fresh coolness of the air as they drift into a narrow passageway. Henry paddles alongside her in his familiar steady rhythm. She's afraid to look over at him. The noise of the splash from their paddles sounds suddenly loud now that they're out of the wind. They push silently forwards, emerging into open water. What they see is a stark reminder of the real world. Far away in the distance are the scars of clear cuts on the hills, a few broken stumps of trees remaining. Greta can sense Henry's body stiffen. She knows this place means a lot to him.

The trees are Henry's cause, maybe even his priority in life. When the anti-logging campaigns started he would go missing for weeks. He even got arrested over it. She had gone on a couple of protests, but most of the time she had stayed at home, feeling out of place among Henry's environmentalist friends. Henry always said that they had won the battle but not the war.

The sight of all this destruction stirs him to speak. 'Would you just look at that?' He slams his paddle into the water. 'You'd think it was all for nothing,' he growls.

Greta wonders how long it took them to destroy this forest — three, four years? — something that had taken thousands of years to form and now can never be replaced.

As they gradually move away from the depressing view, they head towards one of their favourite spots — Shark Creek. Today, though, Greta finds it hard to enjoy the sight of the waterfall cascading over the rocks, shielded on either side by high mossy walls and falling into a small icy pool. Usually it thrills her and she can't wait to immerse herself in its freezing froth.

They tie up the boats and Henry gets out the camera, taking pictures of the giant firs surrounding them. Greta fiddles with her laces; she's not sure whether she wants to swim now.

'You're not going in?' Henry asks, surprised.

'I don't know. I'm not sure I feel like it.'

'But you look forward to this every year. You always say it's the highlight of the trip.'

'I can't just switch off and forget what you said to me back at the store,' she snaps.

'What did you expect, Greta? How could you think that I would be okay with what you told me?'

'But you said it wouldn't change anything. You said that you loved who I was now, that you didn't care about my past.'

Henry picks up a stick and rubs it between his hands. 'I know I said that, but I never guessed that you would have hidden something so huge from me. It hurts me that you kept it from me.'

She huddles on a rock and the waterfall crashes behind her. 'I know' She bows her head. 'It was stupid.' Then she looks up and stares into his sharp blue eyes. 'But what do we do now?'

He shakes his head. 'I don't know. I can't get my head around it. And then when I look at all this I think, does it really matter at all?' His arms swing wide and take in their surroundings – the cascading water and stately trees.

'Can you forgive me?' she asks.

'It's not about that,' he says. 'I don't have to forgive you for anything. It's just that you're not my Greta any more. You're not my girl.'

'But I am,' she pleads.

'Look, I don't want to talk about this right now. We'll talk when we get home tomorrow. I just feel really tired.'

He walks off into the forest and Greta grips her knees. Why is it so hard for him to see her point of view?

She thinks of the story behind Shark Creek. Pregnant basking sharks would come into the grotto to give birth. To her eyes, it seems incredible that these huge creatures would have been able to fit in here. But Greta likes the story and the idea of a safe place for mothers and their young. She's always felt something here – a presence that's comforting, yet at the same time removes her from her body. She curls up like a cat on the rock, closes her eyes and listens to the rush of the water. She imagines it running through her, cleansing her.

It's dusk when Henry returns. He taps her on the shoulder.

'Greta, come on, we'd better get going. We don't want to get stuck in the dark.'

They paddle through the sunset. Greta watches the colours of the sky reflected in the water as she's licked by the sun. Maybe Henry's right, she thinks. All her troubles are insignificant compared to these natural transformations. It puts her in her place.

CHRISTINA

Christina stands on the beach and looks at the ridge, a road running along the glacier-topped mountains. There is a white band of mist between its base and the sea, which stretches between here and the opposing peninsula in America. She imagines taking that road – following a trail, seemingly at the top of the world, wandering off into oblivion.

She sighs and drifts along the deserted beach. The sky is sparkling, open and wide, casting bright shadows all about her. Cian is in his element, climbing all over the driftwood, collecting pebbles and seaweed. Huge piles of discarded bleached pillars mark her way. Some are smooth and polished, others scaled with soft honeycomb.

She sits down on the stony beach and shifts her weight on the smooth broad rocks. She shades her eyes with her hands and watches Cian dancing at the edge of the water, making a tower out of his seaweed. His face loses its distinction and now he is just a child, dancing in the light.

Christina picks some dried seaweed off a stone. Not long now. Today she'll be in Tofino and tomorrow her mother, and this man, Henry, will be back. She feels a tight knot in her stomach when she thinks about it.

Is she brave enough to go on? But maybe this is the easier option, maybe it would take more courage to turn around and go back home?

She sees Luke's truck park on the road above the beach and

watches him get out. He sees her and waves; she raises her hand limply. He had already gone out when she and Cian had got up this morning. He had paid for the B&B and left a message that he would meet her down on the beach in about an hour.

He comes swinging towards her now, carrying a small package in one hand, a smile on his face. How could he be so relaxed?

She feels her mouth go dry and looks down. Cian runs over to him and jumps up and down. She looks at Luke out of the corner of one eye. He seems pleased.

'I have something for you,' he says to Cian and hands him the package. Cian opens it. A small red and white kite falls out. It's the Canadian flag.

'Cool!' He rips open the packaging.

'What do you say, Cian?' she says.

'Thank you, thank you!'

'Do you want to fly it?'

'Oh, yes please.'

Luke turns to her. 'How you doing?'

She can't look at him. 'Fine. Actually, I'm a little cold. I think I'll go and sit in the truck until you guys are finished.'

'Don't you want to play with us?' Cian asks.

'No, you two carry on.'

'Come on,' Luke says, holding out his hand. 'It'll be fun.'

She hesitates and looks up; her cheeks are burning. He smiles at her. His eyes are open and inviting, there's no hint of retribution. Cian runs away down the beach, unravelling the string.

'Luke,' she says, 'about last night...I...'

'It's okay, Christina.' There's nothing patronising about his tone.

'I was drunk,' she says.

'Alcohol makes you do things you wouldn't do normally, for sure,' he says.

'Is that why you don't drink?'

'Yep. Teri and I, we drank heavily, and you know, it never suited me. It makes me very sick.' He taps his head. 'That's no good for anybody.'

'Sometimes I feel depressed for days on end, and it's only when I drink that I feel a little bit better,' she says quietly.

'But you know that's a false sensation. There's no truth in that,' he says, 'because it's the booze making you feel down. You think you're sober, but the stuff's still in you, dragging at you.'

'But when I'm drinking it's the only time I feel good, vital, as if I can face anything.'

'You can feel like that without alcohol or drugs. And that sure is a whole lot better.'

'Is that how you feel then?'

He laughs. 'No, not all the time,' he says, then runs off towards Cian, who's waving the kite in front of him. She follows, starting off at a jog, then chasing them.

The sea crashes to her right and the white light bounces off the rocks on the other side of her. They race like chariots up and down the beach, catching each other, laughing and falling in a tumble. At one point Cian climbs on top of her as she lies on the beach. 'This is the best fun ever,' he declares, then he bends down and hugs her tight, smacking a wet kiss on her cheek.

LUKE

Luke leans back and watches Christina and Cian as they dip their toes in the icy Pacific. Cian screams and kicks a spray at his mother, who moves neatly out of his way. Everything Cian says and does reminds him of Sam, of only last summer when they were hanging out on a beach in Oregon. That was their last summer holiday as a family. That was all Sam knew about family, yet there was a whole other side to it he knew nothing about.

Luke had been sent to the white man's school, like his son, and at that point the link to his past was severed. He had been unaware of it at the time, just a vague sadness that he never got to see his grandfather any more. But he wanted to fit in and he had been popular at school, among his white friends and the white teachers. Yet he always knew there was a difference between them, something he could never shake off.

For a start, he was an orphan. None of his friends were without a father and a mother. His sister Gail was good to him, though strict, but as the years passed by she wholeheartedly adopted the customs of her white husband, Jeff. He wouldn't allow them to talk about the old stories of the island, and it became harder and harder to remember them. They never went home and his grandfather came to visit them only once. It was a tense occasion and ended with words between the old man and his sister so that he never saw him again, not until he grew up.

If Luke saw a Nuu-chah-nulth image of a whale or a thunderbird there would be a sense of recognition, and his friends at school would ask him about being First Nation (as they called it), questioning him on the legends so that he began to feel ashamed that he couldn't remember them properly. As a teenager he tried to hide his face under baseball caps. He was painfully aware that none of the white girls would date him, so he hid his embarrassment with alcohol. If anyone needed booze, it was Luke who could sort it out. He was always the joker at the party and usually ended up in a ditch, being picked up by Jeff in a rage.

On the surface Luke was accepted by all the other kids, but deep down there were age-old divisions. Couples like Gail and Jeff were rare.

Gail had warned him, whispering late at night, sitting on the end of his bed. Luke, just don't marry a white woman, it's too damn hard. She shook her head and stared at their mother's quilt, so worn and old now the whales were peeling off it. Thank God we never had kids, she said.

But she didn't sound like she was grateful. It was what split her and Jeff up in the end. Long after Luke had grown up and gone to live in Seattle, he had heard from his other brother, Pete, that Jeff had got a young girl from Tofino pregnant. She must have been half his age. Gail had finally gone home to the reservation, branded by the knowledge that she had always been to blame.

Luke returned to the island when he was sixteen. He was full of dreams of getting back with his real family and of learning the old ways from his grandfather, of finally living the life his father and mother had. When he got off Jimmy Star's boat he was shocked to see all the new houses and the motorboats down at the harbour, the cars and the trucks. Now the reservation didn't seem so different from Tofino at all.

He meant to go and see his grandfather first, but he felt so uneasy that he went and sat on the beach most of the day, getting drunk. He had two bottles of liquor in his bag, which he had brought with him.

He felt like a stranger in his own village. He felt completely dislocated.

When it got too cold on the beach, he had stumbled up to the cemetery and had desperately tried to find his parents' graves, but all he saw were lots of little wooden posts, no names, and he cried with frustration and fury at himself for not knowing where they were.

It was too late. He swayed back down the track, past his grandfather's house. He was too ashamed to speak to him now, and instead made his way to the harbour. The sun was beginning to set as Luke spoke to Jimmy Star, asked him to take him back to the mainland. He said nothing. He didn't tell him he was drunk or nothing, didn't try to tell him what to do, just nodded his head and said he'd be off in a while.

His grandfather found him just before he got on the boat. Luke hardly recognised him, he was so old and frail. He took his hand lightly, the way Indians do, stroked his fingers and sighed.

So you're going, Luke? he said.

Yeah.

And will you come back to us one day?

I will, but I have to go now. He couldn't say anything. He was unable to explain how it was, but he felt that his grandfather knew anyhow. He watched him board the boat without emotion. He raised his hand once and let him go.

At the time, Luke believed he would never go back. He was going to take on the skin of the white man, follow their laws and play at living their way.

Teri had never wanted to meet his family. She had married an Indian, yet she didn't like Indians. She said that they were dirty and messy, ruining the look of the place where her parents lived, not to be trusted. She said that Indians were drunks. He had let her say all these things about his people; he had forsaken them.

289

He feels the pulse of the earth beneath his hands, the impact of the ocean against the land. He's melded to the landscape, and as he inhales he takes with him the scent of the sea, the taste of salt in his mouth, the blue plains of the sky. He realises that this is what the last week has given him – a sense of connectedness with his environment, which he had lost driving buses, living in Seattle.

And with this realisation comes a sense of stillness and peace because he knows now he no longer has to make a decision. His task is to bring Christina and Cian back, and if that takes him to his village, then so it will be.

Christina comes bounding over, breathless, and squats down beside him. She no longer seems tense. He's glad. He doesn't want her to run away from him too.

GRETA

She had agreed to go to the hospital because she was in so much pain and she thought it would help. Even Angeline had thought it was a good idea. But when they actually arrived she changed her mind. She remembered the sight of the huge grey prison. It sent a shiver down her spine and she knew she didn't want to go in. She had asked Tomás to turn the car and go back home. But he wouldn't.

When he parked he tried to get her out of the car and she started to cry and told him she didn't want to go in. So he had said, 'Just see what it's like inside. It'll probably be better than you think. Please, Greta.' He had pleaded with her and told her she was so sick. Didn't she want to get better for Christina?

Eventually she had got out of the car and let him lead her in.

But the fear was worse when she walked through the door, and she started to pull away from Tomás and cried out, 'Let me go! Let me go!'

But he held her by the wrist. He was squeezing the blood out of her and she had never seen him so rough. Now he didn't look or speak to her, but began shouting out to the people in the place. She heard the words ring out across the tiled hall, 'Can I have some help here!'

She tried to tell them that she was all right, but they wouldn't listen to her properly and her words got all jumbled up and she was crying and laughing at the same time because it was all so stupid. And she tried to keep her feet on the ground, keep her feet on the

291

ground, keep her feet on the ground…

Then Tomás was gone and she was lying in bed. There was a nurse standing by her and she picked up her wrist and pressed a finger on her pulse.

'I want to go home,' she whispered.

'And you will, dear,' the nurse said, 'but not today. Let's get better first, shall we?'

'I'm not sick,' she said.

'Oh, but you are,' the nurse said confidently. 'Otherwise you wouldn't be here, would you?'

The nurse had given her some pills. 'Now pop them in,' she said encouragingly and stood over her until she did as she was told.

The first few weeks became one large lake of sorrow. She was right in the centre on a tiny crannog and there were no boats about. Her mind was so confused that the water became the sky and the rain the reeds and she was wet and hot at the same time.

The times she saw Tomás it was as if he was standing behind ten glass plates. She would reach out to him and beg him to take her home. He could say nothing to her.

She decided to stop taking the pills because she believed they were the cause of all her trouble. She hid them in the cuff of the sleeve of her nightie and flushed them down the toilet when she could. She thought, Now they'll see that I'm better. But no one noticed.

Still, her lake dried up and she began to see her little girl clearly in her mind's eye.

'There I am now,' she would say to herself, 'sewing away, and look at Christina, up she gets! She's dancing to the cotton reel song. Aha! Let's dance then.' And she would begin to spin with her daughter, their eyes locked onto each other, the world a whirling blur behind her.

Then the nurses stopped her and held her down. The doctor said

292

she was elated, and they put her in a white room all by herself, a place where the sanest person would go mad.

When Tomás stopped coming to visit her, she gave up on love. He broke her heart. And even though the drugs had her duped, she still woke in the night, heaving with pain. She could have loved him forever.

It was out of that dark hole she had crawled. She had fought with every last fibre of her being to find her bearings again. She thought that she would never trust another living soul ever again.

CHRISTINA

'How about we head into downtown Victoria for a while, check out the harbour?' Luke asks her. Christina nods – she'll do anything to postpone tomorrow.

Luke drives along the coast road, parking as soon as they hit the centre of the city. They walk along the wall of the inner harbour, then take a little boat-bus around it.

They can hop on and off the boat, so they disembark by a café and eat fish and chips, then they walk along the gangways looking at sweet little houseboats that look like they belong in fairytales. At one point a fat seal pushes his head out of the water and Cian squeals with excitement. Luke buys a large white fish from a nearby stall, and she watches as Cian leans over the water and gives it to the seal. Clumsy and awkward above water, the seal glides away under the surface. It pushes up beneath her, and it looks like a white sea-ghost rising out of the depths, with dark weeping eyes and elongated grey limbs. She turns away.

'You don't like the seal?' asks Luke.

'It looks spooky under the water, like a phantom mermaid,' she replies.

It's mid-afternoon by the time they leave the city and follow the signs for Nanaimo. Christina spreads the map out on her lap.

'It looks like we're going the wrong way around,' she says.

'It's the only way around,' Luke replies, grinning.

She raises her eyebrows. 'Christ!' She traces her finger along the thick green line, following it up to Nanaimo and further until it breaks off and becomes red. At this point it turns inland, and she traces it all the way across the island until it takes a right angle turn and ends up on the west coast in Tofino.

'It's a long way,' she says.

'It's not too bad,' he replies. 'But yeah, we could stop off on the way, stay the night somewhere. It's a long ride for Cian.'

'All right, I don't have to be there until tomorrow…it's just money,' she says nervously.

'I told you, it's okay.'

'As soon as I get to my mother, I'll make sure she pays you back, every cent.'

'Sure,' he says. 'It's fine.'

'Luke?' Cian pipes up. 'What's your job?'

'I'm a bus driver.'

'Really?'

Christina watches the way Luke glances at Cian. He's so easy with her son, as if they've known each other all their lives.

'Sure, I drive that big shuttle bus you got from Seattle airport to La Conner.'

'Why weren't you driving it that day?'

'I'm on my vacation right now.'

'Did you always want to be a bus driver?'

Luke chuckles. 'No, not really. That wasn't the way I was raised, to be something.'

She wonders about his childhood, how different their worlds have been.

'What do you mean? Everybody wants to be something.' Cian kneels up on his seat, leaning over towards Luke.

'What do you want to do when you grow up, Cian?'

Cian answers instantly. 'I want to be a clown or a horse dealer, like my daddy.'

295

Christina laughs and Luke smiles at her. 'Well, that sounds real exciting,' he says.

Cian sits down again and curls up, bringing his knees to his chest as he stares out the windscreen. 'I'm going to build my house right next to Mammy's cottage, so then I can see her every day and not just the weekends.'

The easy mood is shattered. Luke says nothing, but she can sense him thinking. Christina stares out the window, her back turned to Luke, willing Cian to stop talking.

'Do you think judges are always right?' Cian asks Luke.

'That's enough now, Cian,' she says. 'Luke's trying to concentrate on driving.'

'But he can drive and talk,' Cian says cheerfully, and then turning to Luke he continues, 'I'm not so sure. How can a judge know if my mammy is good or not? He doesn't know her.'

'I guess you're right,' Luke says quietly.

'He's just talking nonsense,' Christina says hastily, fiddling with the zip on her jacket.

'No I'm not,' Cian says indignantly. 'I asked Granny why you had to live somewhere else and she said the judge said so because you're not able to look after me properly.'

Several seconds of silence crawl like dead weights and she feels fear creeping towards her. But Luke says nothing, just carries on driving, and Cian instantly forgets what he has said, instead picking a scab on his knee.

'Hey, I could do with a coffee,' Luke speaks up, pulling into a garage. 'Either of you want something?'

'Yeah!' Cian says. 'Can I have a double chocolate muffin?'

'The boy sure knows what he wants. Christina?' Luke looks over at her, but she tries not to catch his eye. 'Just a coffee, thanks.'

Once Luke is in the store, Christina takes Cian's arm and pulls him towards her.

'Ow! You're hurting, Mammy!'

'Cian, you're not to talk about all that stuff,' she hisses.

'What stuff?'

'About me not living with you, and what the judge said.'

'Why?' He looks at her with innocent blue eyes and her heart melts.

'Because…because it's a secret, okay?' Her voice softens. 'Just between you and me.'

'Can we not tell Luke about the secret?'

'No. It's just between us, all right?'

He nods back at her, his face suddenly serious. 'All right.'

They head off again. Christina sips her coffee while Luke turns on the radio. He flicks through the channels and pushes a CD into the player.

'Have you heard of Damien Rice?' he asks.

She shakes her head. 'No.' She watches the road unfold in front of her. It's wide and grey and empty. The surface is unblemished, the bends not too tight and the hard shoulder is ample. Nobody drives towards them; nobody hugs their tail. They're alone, gliding to the west, so very far, far away from all that she was.

She closes her eyes and listens to the singer and his poetry. It makes her tip forward, her chin touching her chest. She imagines herself singing now, feeling free.

'I like the music,' she says.

'It's good,' Luke replies, glancing over at her.

He turns it down a little as she says, 'Did you study art?'

He laughs. 'God, no! I never went to college. No, I only started drawing the other day.'

'I like your pictures.'

'They're just doodles you saw.'

'But they were…I don't know, strong. All the lines were really deep, powerful, as if nothing got in the way between your eye and

297

your hand.'

'What do you mean?' He looks at her curiously.

'I mean that you look like you're drawing instinctively rather than worrying how something should look.'

'That's a nice thing to say.'

'It is?' She pauses then, staring at the white lines on the road. 'I always think that if I hadn't got married I would have gone to art college. I would have liked that.'

'Well, you sound as if you have an eye for it. There's lots of folks out there with talents they never get the chance to use.'

'Is that what you think? Everyone has their own thing they're good at?'

'Sure.'

'And you're discovering it now, through drawing?' she continues.

'Well, no...' He looks a little embarrassed now. 'I'm just messing about, but you know, I always thought about making pictures. Sometimes I think visually. When I have a feeling, like anger or joy or sadness, I see it in colours and shapes. I even see it as figures and places. It's like the art has a secret language. I don't need to explain anything with words, I can just say what I want with the picture.'

'I like that,' she says, and as he speaks Luke begins to fill out for her. He's not just another man, he's something else.

'These last few days,' he continues, 'I can't stop drawing. It's like a therapy.'

'Therapy for what?' she asks hesitantly.

But he doesn't answer her. Instead he pauses, glances over at Cian looking out the window, then quickly into her eyes before he turns back to the road.

'And what are you running from?' Luke asks quietly, changing the subject.

'Too much.' She cuts him dead, leaning forward and turning up the music. 'Too much to say.'

298

THE COTTON REEL SONG

What's a metaphor? Christina asks.

Angeline leans towards her and brushes her hair out of her eyes.

It's a comparison between two things. For instance, that cotton reel with our hair could be a metaphor for life. The thread represents us as we spin around the reel, which is our destiny.

Christina closes her eyes and imagines herself, Mammy and Angeline dancing around the cotton reel, attached by coloured threads. They fly in and out of each other and make a pretty plait — blue, red and green — so that the wooden tube of the spool is completely hidden.

She hums to herself. The adults are talking, then laughing, but all she can hear is the sound of the cotton reel song, on and on inside her head. She opens her eyes, humming still, and looks at the large wooden spool wrapped with their hair still lying on her mother's sewing table. She decides that her mammy has made a tiny piece of magic and she fingers her hair where her mammy cut a strand, but of course she can't feel where the small piece is missing.

Christina looks into the fire and sips her sweet cocoa. She can see a little city in the grate with flame red walls and tiny blue hearths. She imagines the little people living there and their busy little lives. The fire couldn't burn them. They would be made of something other than flesh, they could survive intense heat.

Christina!

It's her father.

Christina, are you not listening to me?

Sorry, Daddy.

I've two tickets for the circus. There's one coming to Navan.

She jumps up immediately and runs over to him on the sofa.

When? When? When? She pulls at him excitedly.

Well, that's the problem. It's tomorrow and I can't take you because I've some new stock arriving.

She slumps her shoulders and looks down at the ground.

But, her daddy continues, picking up her hand again, either your Mammy or Angeline can take you. Who would you like to bring?

She looks up and without hesitation says, Angeline!

They would look so pretty together, especially if Angeline dresses up as well. But as she thinks this she sees her mother's face. She looks upset.

I don't think I should, Tomás. Greta ought to bring her, Angeline says.

No, it's fine, her mother says stiffly, collecting up her sewing things and opening the little drawers of her box, putting it all away.

Christina is torn. She doesn't know what to say, but it's too late to change her mind, she's made her choice.

It's probably best, considering your condition, Greta. You don't want to be worn out, her father says.

What does he mean?

But before Christina has a chance to ask, Greta gets up and takes her hand.

Come on to bed, she says briskly.

They go out into the chilly hall and Christina feels as if she has done something wrong, but her mammy says nothing.

Mammy?

Yes?

What's your condition?

Her mother pauses, bends down to pick up one of Christina's

dolls, and hands it to her. She smiles. Don't worry about what Daddy said, it's nothing to do with you.

Christina hugs her doll. But what does it mean?

Your condition means how you're feeling.

Christina frowns. Are you sick, Mammy? She had noticed that sometimes her mammy had been unable to eat, and some mornings she stayed in bed. But her mammy laughs softly.

No, not at all. She takes her hand, and they go up the staircase two at a time. My condition is a little secret and soon I'll tell you what it means.

Promise?

Promise.

Her mother bends down and they embrace. The familiar scent of her mother comforts her, and she doesn't want her to go back downstairs now. She clings tightly to her.

Mammy? She mumbles into her mammy's shoulder. Will you sit with me until I go to sleep?

Of course I will, sweetheart.

Her mother's shadow is cast long. It is above her on the ceiling, like a big bird hovering. Christina pushes herself down further into the bed and watches it as her eyelids slowly drop. She wakes with a jerk and the shadow is still there. She closes her eyes, secure in the knowledge that her mammy will not go. She will sit through the night, until only daylight can snuff out her shadow. Then it is safe to leave.

LUKE

The sun is shining as Luke drives along the edge of Sproat Lake. Framed by tall trees along its shores, the lake is a small O of blue, nestled inland.

He feels so far away from the city now, and the closer he gets to the western edge, the more he feels the itch to be free.

They stop at a couple of guesthouses but they're all fully booked, so he heads back into the town, pulling into the car park of the first hotel. They clamber out of the truck, stretching their legs.

'I'll go see if they've got rooms,' Luke says, jogging into the front of the building.

There's a strong smell of wet paint in the foyer, but the hotel clerk cheerfully informs him that they have vacancies. He goes back outside, catching sight of Christina and her son. She's spinning Cian around in her arms and the child's face is wide with joy, screaming with pleasure. Luke can hear Christina's deep laugh. It tugs at him. Why does he feel suddenly responsible for this strange woman?

And then it dawns on him. Today he has felt part of a family for the first time since he was a small child. A wave of intense sadness washes over him. He was married for nearly ten years, and yet never felt this symbiosis with another adult before. He just wishes that Sam were with them because then it would be perfect.

'Okay,' he says as he strides towards Christina. 'They've got rooms.'

'Great,' she says, gently dropping Cian on the ground. She looks worn out.

'We'll dump our gear and get some food,' Luke says.

It had been years since Luke had been to Port Alberni. He had come here first after he left the island that day, practically running through Tofino in his haste to get away. He had worked in the pulp mill for a while before moving on to Victoria and trying to get work unloading fishing boats down the harbour. It was late summer then, he remembered, because when he arrived in Victoria it had been October, the season of fog. Some mornings he would wake up hearing the moan of the fog horns, which he found comforting, not frightening, and then in his mind's eye he could see the fog rolling in from the channel over the trees, gardens and houses and he'd turn over in bed and go back to sleep, secure in the knowledge that there'd be no work that day. He could hide in the white, blank fog.

They walk down the broad streets of Port Alberni. Nothing has changed that much. The town still has the air of somewhere no one wants to stop. There are a few deserted restaurants and eventually they pick a small diner with neon lights called The Paradise Café, which somehow looks a little more cheerful than the rest. Inside three televisions blare from different corners of the room. They slide into a booth.

Luke looks at Christina. She's been very quiet since he asked her what she was running away from. He recognises her introspection and doesn't intrude, focusing his attention on Cian instead and making paper planes out of the napkins.

She plays with her food again, but tonight she orders a Coke and sips slowly at the brown fizzy liquid, staring past him at the door as if she expects someone to walk in any minute.

The roads are quiet as they stroll back to the hotel. The dark night sinks in around their shoulders and he feels them blend into each other as they walk. They say goodnight. Cian hugs him tightly outside their room and Christina glides past him. Now the door is closed.

Luke goes into his own room, turns on the TV and lies down on the bed. He fingers the leather bracelet around his wrist and then goes into the bathroom and stares at the mirror, in the dark. He looks like an intruder, tall, shadowy, with long hair.

He picks up his notebook and pencils and leaves the room. It's early still and he can hear music on in the bar downstairs.

CHRISTINA

Christina has only been asleep for an hour, but she fell into a deep, terrifying dream. She turns on the beside lamp and looks over at Cian. He's curled around Walter, lost in sleep. She gets up and pulls the covers over him and thinks for a second. She knows that once Cian is asleep he never wakes up until five or six in the morning. Without hesitating she gets into her jeans and top and slips out of the room. She needs a drink.

Her nightmare was this: she was dressed in a long white nightie and was in a building up high, like she was a princess in a turret waiting to be rescued. But the place she was in was no castle. It was a prison. It was a madhouse. When she looked around her, she saw a mass of people, so many she found it hard to move through them, and as she pushed forward the tops of their heads, the whites of their faces, turned into the crests of waves and she was trying to walk through water. Logic told her to swim, but she persisted on walking, going deeper and deeper so that the salty sea was going into her mouth, making her cough, and now it was touching the bottom of her nose and suddenly she was completely immersed. She looked around her in the water and everything was crystal clear. Silver fish flickered past her and purple urchins marked her path. In the distance, swimming towards her, was a seal. She looped around her – she had to be a she by the way she moved, by the look in her eyes and her long, strong whiskers and mottled, waxy skin.

Christina reached out to touch the seal, this ghost queen of the sea, and the animal fled. It turned back once more, stopped short of her and looked at Christina which such intensity that she could read what she was saying with her eyes.

And Christina replied, 'It's okay, I forgive you.' The seal turned then and swam off. At this point Christina's feet started slipping on the soft, liquid sand and she knew she had gone too far. How was she going to get back to Cian now? In this moment she knew she was drowning, and that was when she woke.

She walks straight up to the bar and orders a whiskey. She feels cold, and she hopes the drink will warm her. She counts out her last few dollars, then turns around looking for a space to sit. Her eyes hit Luke's. She colours.

What's he doing here, in a bar? He doesn't drink.

He smiles at her. She has no choice but to go over.

'Hi,' she says awkwardly, sitting down. 'What are you doing here?'

'Just having a soda,' he says, 'and drawing some more.' He doesn't even look at her whiskey, says nothing as she sips it.

'Now that I've started, I can't stop,' he smiles. 'I must have a compulsive nature.'

Luke leans over his notebook and continues his work. She gazes across the table at his long brown fingers.

'So what about Cian? Is he okay on his own?' Luke asks, head still bent down to drawing.

'Yeah. He never wakes, not till the morning, and anyway, I'm only going to be a minute.'

'Right,' he says, but she thinks he's judging her.

'I'm not a bad mother,' she says defensively.

'I never said you were.' Luke looks up, surprised.

'No, but you implied it.'

'Hey,' he says, 'it's none of my business.'

'That's right.' Stupidly she can feel tears prick her eyelids. 'It is none of your business.'

He looks up and stops drawing. 'I'm sorry, Christina,' he says. 'The last thing I want you to think is that I'm judging you.'

'You're making me feel like I've done something wrong. You're making me feel how all the others do.'

'Who are the others?' he asks, his eyes suddenly dark.

'My father and my stepmother and even my husband. They all think I'm pathetic.'

'Well, that's not true.'

'You've no idea what it's been like for me, none at all.'

'You know,' he says smartly, 'there's no use dwelling on that.'

She feels hot now, angry with him. 'How dare you say that? You know nothing about me, or my life.'

He stays calm. 'I can guess,' he says.

She feels like he's winding her up, but his face is deadly serious, his wide, high cheekbones slanting into his glittering eyes. He watches her and she feels like she's his prey. Who is this man anyway? Why does she think she can trust him?

'You're doubting me now?' he says, reading her thoughts.

'No, its just...,' she starts, confused. 'You're making me angry because...because...no one ever listens to me.'

'I am,' he says. She shakes her head. 'Why are you on the run, Christina?' he asks her.

She's horrified. 'What do you mean?'

'Come on. After what Cian said today, I kinda worked it out.'

'I had to do it,' she says tightly.

'Do what?'

'Take him, take Cian. It was killing me, Luke. That's all I've done all my life – be a mother – and then they took that away from me, told me I wasn't fit to mind my own children. But it's not true, you have to believe me, it was all a terrible mistake.' She's shaking now, and in her upset state she can feel her heartbeat quicken, her breath come short. She's losing control again.

'Hey,' Luke says, taking her hands. 'It's okay. Just look at your son.'

She stares at Luke. 'What do you mean?' she says shakily, gasping for breath.

'Just look at your beautiful boy. You made him, you're rearing him and I think you're doing a pretty neat job. Nothing is black and white,' he continues. 'All these laws and regulations, they just make things messy, destroy lives. Soon they'll make us have licences to be parents!'

She laughs weakly, feeling her panic subside through his reassurance. She takes another sip of her whiskey. It burns her mouth but makes her feel more solid.

'It's going to be okay,' he says firmly.

'How do you know?' she asks.

'Because I know you.'

Their eyes lock and as she stares at him she can hear a sound, like the rush of falling water around her, and then strangely, behind it, another sound – *whiz, whir, whiz, whir.*

'But we're strangers.'

'We were never strangers, Christina.'

She knits her brow, confused. What does he mean?

He takes up another pencil and bends down over his work. She can see that it's an abstract drawing, a tight knot of curves and waves and that he's using blue, grey and white in the picture.

'Luke, why did you and your wife break up?'

'Because we were fighting too much and we didn't love each other any more. The usual.'

'Declan and I hardly ever rowed, but when we did it was bad,' she says. 'But we separated because of me, because of what I did.'

'Do you still love him?' Luke asks.

'No, not for a long time. I suppose not for years,' she says wistfully.

'So why did you stay together for so long?'

'Because of the children, and the house, and because he was my

308

husband…and, well, that was it. Where I live everyone's married and no one gets divorced.'

'Even now?'

'The community is like a family and you just become part of this one big thing, and if you leave your husband, well, you're on your own then, an outcast. I'm not saying every single couple stays married forever, but most do. It's just the way it is.'

'It sure is different in America,' Luke says, closing his notebook and slipping the pencils into his shirt pocket. He stretches. 'Well, I guess I'd better get to bed. Are you coming with me?'

She nearly knocks over her drink. 'I…'

He laughs then, a rich bass tone. 'Oh no, I didn't mean *with me*. I meant up to your room with me.'

'Right,' she says, feeling foolish, reminded of her behaviour the night before. 'Yes, I'd better.' She knocks back the whiskey, nearly choking, and follows him out of the bar.

Outside her room, she pauses. He stands behind her and she can sense the height of him. It feels nice, like she's protected.

'Would you like a coffee or tea? We have a pot in the room…' Her voice peters out.

'What about Cian? Will we wake him?'

'No, once he's out, he's out.'

'Okay, sure.'

They go into the dusky room. The lamp is still on and casts a golden glow about the space. She walks over to the coffeepot and switches it on.

LUKE

He watches her moving. She flits about the room, light and quick. He wants to ground her. Her top rides up her torso as she pulls her hair back from her face and he catches sight of her belly, a few tiny stretch marks worming their way across her skin. He wants to touch her there.

'Coffee? Tea?' she asks.

'Coffee, thanks.' He sits on the end of her bed and looks over at Cian. He used to love watching Sam sleep. It was when he could feel all the hurt of his marriage subside.

Christina comes over with a small white cup and hands it to him.

'I would've done the same thing,' he says.

She looks surprised. 'What do you mean?'

'If they hadn't let me see Sam, I would have taken him as well.'

'Well, I was allowed to see Cian, but not a lot. And it was like Declan had all the power. I couldn't put one toe out of line or he'd be down on me like a ton of bricks.'

'What about your other son? Johnny?'

She looks down at the floor and speaks almost in a whisper. 'I asked him, but he wouldn't come with me. He's doing his Leaving Cert – his final exams. They're very important.'

'I nearly didn't get any visitation rights at all,' Luke says.

'Why?'

He sighs. He can feel the burden of this weighing him down. He has to tell her.

'Because I hit my wife.'

She looks shocked. 'I don't believe it!' she says instantly.

He bows his head, the shame of it still hurting him. 'I did. I could tell you why and I could give you a thousand explanations and tell you that she was a bitch, and that I was drinking, and that she had been abusing me for years and I never, never beat her, but Christina, I can think of no excuse. I hit someone smaller than me. I hit a woman. It makes me sick.'

'Is that why you stopped drinking?'

'Yep. I had stopped before that but it had been a bad day, a bad week and I just thought I'd have one beer...once I started I couldn't stop, it was like I felt diseased, you know, insane. I just went crazy.'

'We all make mistakes,' she says simply.

'I guess we do,' he says, 'but in that one moment when I made that choice, when I raised my hand and slapped her face, well, I may as well have done it to my kid. I've destroyed his life by splitting the family.'

'No,' she says firmly. 'I always used to think that you should stay together for the children no matter what, but I don't think that's right now. It's better to be who you really are than someone you're pretending to be.'

'I could go with that,' he says. She's made him feel better; she hasn't judged him.

Cian stirs in the bed.

'It's late,' she says. 'We'd better go to sleep.'

'Yeah, sure,' he says, putting his cup down on the dresser. 'Thanks, Christina.'

They stand awkwardly at the door, then she reaches over and hugs him. 'No, thank you,' she whispers in his ear.

GRETA

Now when she wakes, alone in her tent, she realises that she wants the love back. Like the way she had felt about Tomás, she wants that for Henry. She wants to give him everything because now she's no longer afraid. She doesn't know how it happened, but overnight the beast has faded away. It's no longer snapping at her heels.

She lies still for a moment, feeling her breath on her cheeks and the beat of her heart. She can hear the click of the camera. Henry's already up, busy taking pictures of the scenery. She decides to make pancakes. Surely that will please him?

Little white clouds dart across the sky as she mixes her batter. She takes out a bottle of maple syrup while the pan heats up. Henry is walking back up the beach, his camera slung over his shoulder.

He smiles when he sees her cooking. 'Pancakes! That's a treat.'

'I thought so,' she says evenly. 'For our last morning.'

He squats down by the fire. 'Want some tea?' he asks.

'Sure.'

He puts a pan of water on the fire while she takes off the golden pancakes and slides them onto two plates, liberally dribbling syrup over them.

'Thanks,' Henry says shyly.

They eat without speaking. Henry makes liquorice tea and hands her a steaming mug.

'Henry,' Greta begins, 'I've been thinking...'

He looks at her, his eyes guarded.

312

'I've been a fool,' she continues. 'But you see, what happened to me…the fact that my husband signed me into an asylum…well, that's made it hard for me to ever trust again.'

Henry sips his tea and looks away at the horizon.

'That hurts me for you,' he says quietly. He turns and looks at her. Yesterday's anger has gone. 'I'm sorry, honey. I was just so shocked. I felt like an idiot because I always knew there was something. I should have asked you years ago.'

'No, I should have told you.'

'It just makes me feel so bad that you've suffered alone for all this time. It hurts to think that you could never fully trust me.'

Greta gets up and walks over to her husband. She sits down next to him and takes his long, bony hand. 'I do now.'

He turns to her. 'And it's not too late, is it?'

'Of course not.'

They kiss and Henry wraps his arms around her. She falls back onto the sand. His large palms frame her cheeks and they both close their eyes. Silently, working from sense rather than thought, she undresses him, and he her. The ocean crawls up the beach and tickles her ankles. The sand dips beneath her and cradles her, the bright sky strokes her head and Henry makes love to her. She feels him inside her more intensely than ever before.

This is it. Their love is complete; she feels it like a ring around her. It has taken twenty years to come to this, and yet it holds her in awe, surprised. She swims in her husband's eyes and he picks her up, casting the sad Greta of her dreams aside.

313

CHRISTINA

'The last time I took this road, I saw five bears,' Luke says. She looks at the fine dark hairs on his arm as he rests his hand against the wheel.

'Really?' says Cian, incredulous.

'It's not so unusual,' he says. 'You see, it was late summer, and they're out looking for berries.'

'Do you think we'll see some bears today?'

'We might. You just don't know.'

Her son is glued to the passenger side window, and she sits in between. Christina scans the roadside, hoping to see a large dark shape.

She would like to see a bear too. It looks like bear country. The road is empty and wide, winding, and hilly with thick spruce forests on either side. Every so often the trees clear and they come across a small creek, its banks littered with rocks, its shores full of shadows.

'Look, Walter,' Cian says, holding his teddy up to the window. 'You might find your mammy or daddy.'

'What are you like?' Christina laughs, tickling her son as he wriggles in his seat.

'It's a beautiful day,' says Luke.

It is, she thinks as she looks at the sky, clear and unblemished, and watches the heat haze shimmer above the road. Everything is bigger here, wider. She feels like she has more space to breathe. I could live here, she thinks, and then smiles to herself. Who knows what might happen after today? She feels ridiculously calm. It's insane, she knows, but Luke makes her feel better and she likes being with him. She sneaks a look at him now. His profile is strange. His nose is large and he has thick lips. Studying the side of his face you would think he was an ugly man, but if you looked at him straight on, took in the force of his eyes, their depth and compassion, he became the most attractive man she had ever met. She squirmed in her seat. She was thinking like a schoolgirl.

It didn't matter that he had hit his wife. He had chosen to tell her this terrible information about himself, and she had seen his shame. She could identify with that. They weren't so different. She knew she could trust him.

Christina digs her fingernails into her right palm.

'Not long now,' Luke says, looking at her. 'Are you okay?'

She nods, suddenly nervous.

Now the straight grey tarmac cuts right through the rainforest and she feels like they're blazing a trail. They're moving too fast and she desperately wants to back pedal.

'Do you mind if we stop somewhere?' she asks Luke, her voice cracking, her throat dry as dust. 'Just for a little walk? I need to get my head together,' she continues, her earlier calm prickled by nerves.

'Sure,' he says.

A few moments later he pulls in off the road and follows a track into a gravel car park.

'Where are we?' Cian asks, pushing himself up by the elbows and peering out the window.

'Long Beach,' Christina says, reading the sign.

They get out of the truck and follow a small sandy path through the undergrowth until they come out onto the sand. What she sees takes Christina's breath away. She has never laid eyes on such a place in her whole life, even in her dreams.

'The sea!' Cian cheers and bounds across the sand towards it.

The ocean sparkles before her. She feels like she's standing beneath it. Big waves rear to crash down on their knees in front of her. The water is the purest shade of blue. There are only a couple of surfers around, and a lone stranger walking a dog. The mist rises off the beach, like vapour lifting off her fears.

She takes Luke's hand. It seems the most natural thing to do.

'It looks preternatural,' she whispers.

He plays lightly with her fingers and turns to her. His eyes are as wide as hers.

'I had forgotten,' he says. 'It's like seeing it for the first time again.'

Cian has already kicked off his runners. Luke and Christina take their shoes off, tie the laces together and sling them around their shoulders. Cian skips in front of them, delighted by the imprints his feet are making.

They walk barefoot. Fine white sand is scattered on top of packed, moist golden sand. It looks like sugar frosting. Each step they take pillows out on its damp surface.

Christina glances behind her. The deep, dark viridian shades of the rainforest hang behind like a backdrop, a cool mist steaming off it. In front of the trees lie stacks of driftwood, like giant slabs of white ivory. The beach itself is clear, apart from the odd fossilised urchin or purple mussel shell. They turn to the left and she can see a lean, flat band of white beach all the way to two hulks of dark rock, lapped by the sea. The dense, damp world of the rainforest mixes with the sharp, crystal air by the ocean. Bands of mist streak the air between it and them.

Everything here is pared down to its essentials – big sky, crashing waves and white sand. Here nature is truly awesome and it humbles her.

316

LUKE

Luke remembered sitting crouched at the prow of Jimmy Star's boat watching the red orb of the setting sun sink into the choppy sea. The world that was spread before him didn't look easy. Almost immediately he felt sober again.

When he got to Tofino he started walking. He didn't think twice about going back to Gail and Jeff. He was young and strong and full of determination, and his legs took him right out of that town, as fast as they could away from everything that caused him pain.

When he was sixteen he thought that he could make it on his own. He could do better in the new world, make money. He didn't need his family. Now he realised it hadn't just been a matter of walking away. His heritage was inside him, in his veins, in his blood. He couldn't ignore it any longer.

The last time Luke had seen Long Beach it was almost dark. He had turned off the road that fateful night and wandered down the beach, sure he would find shelter behind a stack of driftwood, somewhere to sleep. As he was walking he saw a big glass ball, about the size of a grapefruit. It looked magenta, like the red sun he had seen sink out of the sky a while before. He knelt down and picked it up, recognising it as one of the Japanese glass fishing floats that would get washed into shore. In his grandfather's day these had been a dime a dozen but he had never seen one in his entire life, not in all the years he had been down on the beach at the guesthouse. He took it, wrapped it in his shirt and put it in his bag. He believed it to be

317

an omen.

The next day, when he looked at the float again he was surprised to see that it was amber, not red. It was the colour of a beer bottle. It made him want to drink.

He gave it to Teri the day they got engaged. She was confused by it, saying it was a very unusual engagement ring, and he had immediately regretted giving it to her. She still had it though. It was on the windowsill in her kitchen, gathering dust, and he could see it from the road every time he went to collect Sam. It blinked at him in the dappled light.

The float was a thorn in his side, a reminder of what he became. So many times he had wanted to charge past Teri, grab the damn thing and fling it out the window. He could see it now, shattering into shards of deep, dark orange, splintering all over her immaculate backyard, looking like just another smashed beer bottle.

GRETA

Afterwards they lie still in each others' arms listening to the ocean and the wind. Not until the sun is high in the sky does Henry slowly gather himself up.

'When we get back,' he says, 'we'll find your daughter.'

Greta sits bolt upright. 'We will?' she asks hesitantly.

'Sure we will,' he says. 'We'll go to Ireland and find her.'

'You'll come with me?'

'Greta,' Henry says sternly, 'I don't want you to ever be on your own again.'

'But do you think she'll want to know me?' Greta asks nervously.

'That I don't know, but you have to give it a shot, for everyone's sake. By the way,' he adds cheekily, 'if you were married in Ireland, does that make you a bigamist? Am I shacked up with a felon?'

'Oh no. Tomás managed to wangle an annulment. We had limited contact when I first moved to La Conner.'

'I think I'd like to meet that man,' Henry says with an edge to his voice. He pulls on his hat and walks over to the old radio, switching it on. 'I'd better check the forecast before we set off,' he says.

Greta starts to pack up. The morning's events have left them short of time now, but she feels so relaxed that she's unable to hurry.

'Darn, the batteries are gone.'

'Have we spares?'

'You know what?' He comes over smiling, ruffling her hair. 'That's the one thing I forgot to pack.' He sniffs the air then.

'It'll be okay,' he says. 'The conditions have been perfect all week.'

Greta looks at the water, smooth as a mirror. 'Remember, Henry,' she says, 'it can be deceptive here. Once we get out of the passage it could be really choppy.'

'We can manage that, can't we?' he says, packing up. 'It'll be good to have to put a little bit of elbow grease in. Tomorrow we'll be back to our old soft lives.' He chuckles.

A short while later they're spinning through the passage, hushed by the awesome shadows of the mountains on either side. They paddle side by side and Henry takes her hand as they lift up their paddles and float through a narrow channel between a little island and a rock.

As they emerge out of their sanctuary into the inlet, Greta suddenly feels anxious. The water is incredibly rough, dark grey with the wind, and the sky is almost the same colour. They bend over their kayaks, pushing their bodies forward and frantically paddling. The noise of the wind fills her ears and Greta ploughs the water with forceful strokes, bracing her legs to stay steady. She can feel the chop from the ebbing tide, its force pulling her along. Breakers wash over their laps and she's keenly aware that they don't belong here. She imagines the sea spurning them, angry at their presumption to want to cross it, to think that it would remain tame for them.

There's a noise. She hears it over the sound of the wind. At first she thinks it's a gunshot and she looks wildly about, but there are no boats, no ghastly day-trippers here to try to shoot bears. It's when the rain starts pelting her that she realises with horror that the noise is thunder. The sky is black now and the sea unrepentant. They're jostled up and down on the waves, like two flimsy sticks. How could this have happened so suddenly?

She looks over at Henry. He's shouting something at her. It's hard to hear him above the rain and the ocean but she sees him pointing his arm towards where they have come from. In the passage they could take shelter.

She fights against the sea, coming as close to him as she can.

'Can we make it?' Greta gasps.

'Course we can,' he says, smiling at her, leaning towards her and trying to take her hand. But she can sense his doubt.

Now as they paddle she can feel the swell increasing and hear the rumbling roar of the wind and the thunder. The rain is stinging her face and she feels terrified and exhilarated all at the same time. All her life force is concentrated in this one effort and she takes the lead as she paddles against the tide back towards the still lagoon of their earlier idyll. In this moment Greta feels something else around her, an energy or a force propelling her, helping her to stay afloat and move back across the angry water. Her heart rises in her chest as she nears the rocky entrance to the passage, its opening like a necklace of bony teeth, and with relief she glides through it into sudden calm. Euphoric with her achievement, Greta laughs out loud. It's still raining here, the water dancing on water, hard and keen, but at least they're out of the wind. They can go back to where they camped last night, dry out, wait until the storm passes.

'We made it,' she says triumphantly, turning around to Henry.

But he isn't there.

Her blood freezes. She looks through the lashing lines of grey, back out to sea, the violent water.

'Henry!' she yells.

Then she sees it. His upturned kayak. A slither of yellow bobbing up and down with the swell.

CHRISTINA

The water inches towards Christina and makes contact with her toes. She winces. 'It's cold!' Her teeth chatter and she looks like a little girl, hopping on her tiny blue feet.

'This water comes all the way down from Alaska,' Luke says. 'It's like melted glaciers.'

'Is that why it looks so clean?'

'It's pure liquid ice,' he replies.

'Tell me about your family, Luke,' Christina says, lacing her fingers through his. 'Who will be in your village when you return?'

He waits a while to answer. 'My grandfather, I hope. My parents are dead, but there's all my aunts and uncles, three of my sisters and their children. And then there's the cousins.'

'You've a large family.'

'It's part of our culture.'

'It's part of ours as well. It was always hard being an only child. All my friends had at least one brother or sister. They always had someone to play with.'

'Being on your own breeds self-sufficiency.'

'Didn't work for me. I was very needy. I probably still am.'

'There's no woman I know who would have done what you've done, come all the way to Canada with your little boy so you can find your mother.'

'And there's not many women who lose custody of their own children either,' she adds bitterly.

322

He says nothing and she silently curses herself for bringing that up again. She doesn't want self-pity.

They walk on and she closes her eyes, smelling the sharp tang of the ocean, feeling a sense of freedom course through her veins. If only she could feel this all the time. When she opens them again Cian has already reached the rocks and is clambering over them.

They approach the large wet boulders, which look almost black against the white sand. She can see sea urchins in the water and several fat starfish sucking onto the rock, alive and full-blown. She starts climbing up towards Cian, who's sitting on the top, bellowing, 'I'm the king of the castle!'

They sit on either side of Cian and he shimmies down between them. The three of them look out at the sea, the endless horizon.

'Luke?' Cian asks. 'Will you tell me a story?'

She looks over at Luke, his body a powerful silhouette against the midday sun.

She watches him as he leans back and looks up at the sky. 'My mother was from a place called Bear River and these people have a story about the thunderbird and the whale. Would you like to hear it?'

'Yes, yes, yes!' Cian says, jigging up and down on the rocks.

'Okay then. The people of Bear River used to walk over the mountains looking for medicines and lucky charms, so on their return there would be many strange stories of things they had seen. One time, one such group was walking in the mountains and they saw smoke in the distance. As they came closer they realised that the smoke was coming from a house. One of the men from the group crept up closer to the house and looked through a crack in the walls. Inside he saw a woman weaving mats from strips of bark. Suddenly he heard her say, "Come in, don't stay outside where it's cold, come into the house where it's warm." The man accepted her invitation and the woman asked him to wait until her husband came home

323

with a whale. The man was mystified how a mere mortal could bring a whale all this way up the mountain. Before long the sky darkened and hail began to fall, with thunder booming. He looked up at the sky and saw a massive bird. He had a large curved beak and a horn on top of its head, with eyes like an eagle, though many times larger. He could see lightning flashing from the eyes of the great bird and knew it to be a thunderbird. The man watched the great bird as it came closer, a whale in its talons. It dropped the whale and landed, and then, to the man's astonishment, its body opened and out stepped a young man! From that time the people from Bear River, or O-in-mi-tis, my mother's people, used the thunderbird as their crest.'

'Have you ever seen a thunderbird?' Cian asks excitedly.

'No, I don't know anyone who has. I think it's just a legend.' Luke folds his arms and looks out to the ocean. Christina can see sorrow in the way he sits. She wonders about his mother. He hadn't told her when or how she died.

Cian is up on his knees, peering out to sea as well. 'Luke, where are the whales?'

'Oh, they're way out,' he says, spreading his hand.

'Mammy, can we go in a boat and find the whales?' Cian pulls on her arm and she looks down at his charming blue eyes.

'It's not that easy.'

'Please?'

'Sure,' Luke says, looking at her enquiringly. 'Maybe once you've settled into Tofino, and if your mom wants to, you can come to my village on the island and I'll take you out.'

'Do you have a boat?'

'Nope, but I've got plenty of cousins who do. We'll find someone to take us. What do you think, Christina?'

'I think that would be nice.'

He grins, but still his eyes look sad. 'Good. That's a date.'

Unable to sit still any more, Cian starts sliding back down the rocks. She watches him as he goes down, his skinny arms and legs propelling him. On the beach he runs over to a pile of driftwood, his feet almost kicking his backside as he leaps across the sand. She sees him hunt for a stick. He pauses for a second, then starts frantically drawing lines in the sand. She looks back out to sea, the relentless fall of each wave, the reassurance of nature.

'That's the only story I remember my mother telling me,' Luke says softly.

Christina touches his arm, hesitantly. 'When did she die?'

'I was only eight,' he sighs. 'And then my father died a few months later. It sounds terrible now, if I tell someone, but at the time I was okay. I don't think I even cried. I left the island not long after,' he adds. 'I went to live with my big sister, Gail, in Tofino.'

Christina wants to ask him more, but he's completely still beside her and the sound of the ocean holds her tongue. She senses that he doesn't want to say any more. Moments pass and then she speaks.

'All this clarity.' She points at the horizon. 'The immensity of the ocean and the sky, the swell...all these things must inspire you.'

'You inspire me too.'

She laughs, embarrassed, looking down at her toes. 'How could I? I'm no portrait.'

'It's not how you look, it's who you are. You know, when I first met you I saw blue, this shade of blue,' he says, pointing at the ocean, 'with a white edge to it, brilliant and startling. It's the colour of your healing, your soul's search for relief.'

She knots her brows and looks at him. She's never heard anyone say such things before, yet she understands him perfectly.

He looks at the ocean again and says, 'In each moment we make a choice.'

'I know.' Her voice rises barely above a whisper. She pulls her knees up and hugs them. The ocean beckons to her, draws her in, and she feels impelled to speak.

'Cian could have died.' The words are wrenched from her gut. They feel like poison on her lips. 'He could have died because of me.' She's afraid to look at Luke, so she ploughs on. Maybe here on the edge of the world she can find redemption.

'I can make all sorts of excuses, say I was sick at the time or it was just an accident, but I knew what I was doing. I did. I had been okay. I had stopped drinking and I was taking anti-depressants. Myself and Declan were both really trying to make things work...'

'Then what was it? What made you want to start drinking again?'

She shivers and holds her sides. 'Johnny. It was something Johnny said. I wanted to go to a parents' association meeting at his school, I wanted to get involved, but he wasn't having it. Christ, I'll never forget the look on his face when I said I was going, the absolute horror.' She laughs bitterly. 'I suppose he couldn't think of anything worse than me mixing with his friends' parents. He said I was a disgrace. It sounded so funny, that old-fashioned, fuddy duddy word coming out of his mouth. His mother was a disgrace.'

Her throat has gone dry but she keeps on talking. She has to tell Luke now, before she meets her mother, before anything else happens. He has to know the whole of her.

'Because I hadn't been drinking for a few weeks the booze really hit me. Before I had been able to drink a bottle of wine and still drive no problem. But then, I only had three glasses and I was all over the place. I didn't know it, though. Of course I didn't.' She starts to cry, her tears hot with shame. Luke says nothing but she feels him take her hand and finger her ring.

'It's all a blur, really. I went to collect Cian from school as usual and they said I was driving practically in the ditch. It happened in a flash. One moment I was trying to put a CD into the CD player and the next we were off the road. It was strange. I was screaming but my voice was outside of myself.' She can feel the tears trailing down her cheeks. 'I was fine, not a scratch, but they weren't so sure about Cian. He was unconscious…'

She starts to shake. She turns and looks pleadingly at Luke. 'He was so still.'

She looks away and closes her eyes. 'He woke on the way to the hospital. He didn't even cry. They kept him in overnight, just in case. I know he was okay in the end, but it was so close. He could have died.'

She opens her eyes again and blinks in the bright Pacific light. 'That was the end of everything. Declan wanted me out, nowhere near the kids, and how could I blame him really? Cian, bless him, never talks about it. Sometimes I think he's forgotten about the whole thing. But I can never forget. I'll never forgive myself.'

'It's not so terrible,' Luke says gently. 'It was an accident, Christina.'

'But worse things happened,' she shouts suddenly, angry with Luke for being kind. Couldn't he see how bad she was? 'When we got home from the hospital and I saw Johnny, his teeth clenched, the hate spitting out of him, I just wanted out. I couldn't bear it, the pain of living. Each breath tore me. Johnny looked at me in a way…I don't know, it was a way that would make the toughest soul crumble. He despised me. I made a choice, and it took only a moment, to fill the glass with water and take all my anti-depressants, all of my medication.' She sighs. 'I had gone past any maternal instinct. Luke, can you understand this, how bad I was feeling?'

'I can see it,' he replies, his grip warm and strong.

'My stepmother, Angeline, found me. If it hadn't been for her I would have died.' Her face is wet and glistening, the tears dripping off her chin. 'And Johnny…Jesus, Johnny saw me. He came with Angeline into my room. He saw me lying there, he thought I was dead. No one else knew about it – not Declan, not my father. They both thought I was just drunk and mad, taking too much stuff by mistake. I've only told my stepmother what my intention was, and

327

then she betrayed me.'

'How?' asks Luke.

'It was her who swung the judge. She told him she believed I was a danger to my own children. I still can't believe she did that.'

There's no more she can say. She attempts to smother her sobs, but Luke leans over and places his hand on her back. He strokes her all the way down her spine from the nape of her neck to the tip of her backside. She opens her mouth and lets out a belt, like a howl from one of those lost wolves.

MAMMY

When Angeline brings her supper, she knows that something's wrong. She's allowed to eat it in her room, and she's allowed to eat two big pieces of chocolate cake.

She remembers then. Are Mammy and Daddy back?

No, not yet. Angeline looks away. Let's play a game, she says. Do you want to play snap?

So they go downstairs and play cards in the sitting room, and Angeline lets her win every game.

Time for bed, Angeline announces.

Christina looks out the window. It's nearly dark. The storm had cleared suddenly, and now the last rays from the sun shine weakly. Everything is still wet. Christina goes upstairs and changes into her pyjamas. She slips back downstairs again before Angeline comes up to her and goes into the sitting room.

Christina stands in the shadows and looks out the patio doors. It's just before night. Her mammy called it twilight and told her this was when the fairies came out. Christina stares hard, looking for fairies. She looks to where they might be – the small pond on the front lawn with the water lilies or the rockery stuffed with bright flowers. She can't see anything. And as she's standing there, she decides she doesn't want to go to bed, not until her mammy comes home.

These are the moments Christina had long since buried – looking at the shadows growing longer across the lawn, waiting and watching. She can still hear the clock on the mantelpiece ticking away; each second is a dead weight. It's like she can hear something growing, a stone in the pit of her stomach. She stands by the window until she sees car lights and her heart surges, only to drop when she sees just Daddy get out.

Her father comes in and she notices his cheeks are bright red. He huffs and puffs in the doorway.

Where's Mammy? she asks.

She had to go somewhere, he says awkwardly. She'll be back soon. Come on to bed, Christina. It's late.

No, I'm waiting for Mammy.

Daddy walks towards her, but Angeline stops him. Leave her be, she whispers.

Angeline brings her a blanket and a mug of cocoa. She sits next to her and waits too. Christina doesn't want to sit. She stands erect, to attention, her terror making her rigid. How can she live if her mammy doesn't come home?

Finally her legs buckle and Angeline catches her. She begins to cry.

Christina remembers the smell of Angeline as she holds her, the smell of lemons and garlic.

It's okay, she whispers, carrying her upstairs and tucking her into bed. I'll be your mammy for now.

GRETA

She was doing exactly what Henry had always told her never to do. She was going back out there. It was against all his rules, but she couldn't leave him. It was instinctive, her need to paddle towards him. She couldn't part with Henry, not now.

Greta takes a sharp intake of breath and spins her kayak back out through the opening of the passage, into the open water. It isn't as hard going out as coming in had been because the powerful tide is pulling her forward, like a giant's hand underneath her kayak, keeping her afloat, dragging her along. She tries to ignore the flashes of lightning to her right, illuminating patches of black water. It seems as if she's sailing into the waters of hell, somewhere so deathly and dangerous that nothing else matters now, just survival.

Henry's upturned kayak is just in front of her. She squints through the rain, and sees with relief his hand, almost blue with the cold, but clinging onto the outside of his boat.

'Henry!' She rounds his kayak, her own being practically lifted out of the water with the swell.

He's shocked to see her. His face is grey with the cold and she knows she has to get him out of the water.

'Here, take my hand!' she yells above the sound of the wind.

Maybe she can pull him up onto her kayak, then somehow get his righted? It seems an impossible mission.

He's shaking his head, but he reaches to her all the same, and she feels the tips of his icy fingers as they brush hers and then fall away again.

'Try again,' she urges.

This time she grips him, but as she smiles at him, trying to communicate that everything is going to be okay, he looks past her, his eyes opening wide in horror, and immediately he tries to pull away from her. She holds on tight and glances behind her. What she sees freezes her heart. It's a furious current of water, leaping and chopping, beginning to rock them.

Henry looks into her eyes. She can see the eternity of their love, she can see his blue lips mouthing, Let me go, but she's no longer afraid and she holds on tight. The water cups her and then spills her forth, and still holding Henry's hand they both go down.

The storm passes as quickly as it came. The sea calms down and the wind drops, gently ruffling the water's contours and picking up tiny white waves. This place is like a drop of heaven. The only sign of humans are two upturned kayaks nose to nose. And from above it makes a pattern – a yellow starflower spinning on a bright blue lawn.

LUKE

Luke cruises down the street past the large log house gallery, and taking a right, he pulls in on a hill The ocean is visible and the edge of Meares Island, across the bay. The town is busy, tourists ambling along the sidewalks, locals chatting outside the co-op.

Luke looks over at Christina. She's still pale and subdued from her confession, but there's a change about her. He can see the start of something.

'Would you like me to take you there, in the truck?' he asks.

She turns to him gratefully. 'Would you mind? It would be good to have an escape route, just in case.'

The road clings close to the coast. He stops to ask for directions and they head off again, eventually arriving at a group of three houses in a row, low down by the water, each one with a stretch of green lawn before it.

'Okay,' Christina says. He can see her hand shaking as she goes to open the door.

'Do you want to go down on your own?' he asks.

'I think so,' she says. 'Cian, you wait here, darling, I won't be a minute.'

Luke watches her walk over to the mailboxes, read them, then continue down to the middle house. A large golden retriever comes out from behind the last house and starts barking at her, but it looks friendly.

Her long blue legs slowly move towards the door. He watches her shake her head so that her hair falls down, escaping from her earlier attempt at an arrangement. He watches her knock. No one comes to the door. It's obvious that the place is still empty. Luke has the feeling that they haven't returned yet. Christina knocks again, then he sees her walking around the side of the house and peering into the window. The dog continues to bark and comes bounding over, and a woman comes out of the third house and follows the dog towards Christina. She's wearing an apron and Luke can see her dusting flour off her hands.

Luke watches the two women talk. He can't see Christina's face, but she looks like she's standing to attention, like a soldier. Suddenly, he sees her running towards him. Her face is green, her eyes black. She pulls the door of the truck open and climbs in, and before he can ask her anything, she says, panting, 'Drive…just drive, please.'

He hesitates.

'Just get me the hell out of here!' she screams.

He jolts, turns the ignition on, puts the foot down and accelerates down the road, spraying gravel behind him. He can feel Cian move closer to him, sense his fear.

334

CHRISTINA

She feels the stones of dread — in her throat, making it hard to breathe, on her head so that she feels a dead weight above her, in the pit of her belly so that she feels sick and her feet, heavy, her limbs dragging. There's the stone in her heart, banging against her beat, knocking her, making her shake.

She reads the mailboxes — Greta and Henry Kittle — and below it she reads Sacred Stone Spa. The irony isn't lost on her. She sees a small business card stuck on the mailbox and reads it — *Sacred Stone Spa offers a range of body therapies and healing services to restore the balance between the mind, body and spirit* So her mother had become a healer.

Christina tells herself she shouldn't be afraid. If her mother does this sort of thing, surely she's gentle, surely she'll be kind? What worries Christina is that she doesn't know what to say. She hasn't planned any speeches because she just doesn't know how to put it. She's terrified that at the moment her mother opens the door, she'll be struck dumb. Will she know who she is? Will she recognise her without Christina having to say anything?

Now she's on the porch. She knocks, hesitantly at first, then when no one comes, more firmly. A dog is barking at her, but she ignores it and begins to creep around the side of the house. She can see a room. It must be her mother's therapy room. It looks nice, all wooden, with a long massage table and lots of candles and crystals on shelves. God, her mother had become a hippy! She walks a little way along the decking, noticing lots of little things, like smooth, flat, round shells and small tubs of herbs and plants. A hammock swings in the breeze, and as she peeks around the back of the house she can see a clean green lawn running all the way down to the blue ocean.

'Hi.'

Christina jumps and turns. The dog is leaping up at her and a small dark-haired woman with a round face and in an apron is staring at her. This isn't her mother.

'Are you okay?' she asks, peering at her.

'I'm looking for Greta Kittle,' Christina says.

The woman shakes her head. 'Oh dear,' she says. 'Oh dear, I really did think that I'd called all of her clients. Did you have an appointment with her today?'

Christina nods.

'Oh dear, oh dear…'

'What's wrong?'

'They're missing.'

'Missing?'

'Herself and her hubby, Henry. They were kayaking around the Sound, and apparently, Lord help them,' she does the sign of the cross, 'they got caught up in a freak storm.'

'A storm?' Christina repeats.

'No one's seen them and then their kayaks were found, so we have to presume…you know…' The woman continues, shaking her head. 'I'm still in shock. I can't believe it. I was just talking to Greta the day before she went and then Henry left Lofty round.' She indicates the dog. 'It's just crazy.'

The walls are closing in. All she can see is this woman's face, the lips moving, the words flowing like hot lava down her back.

'No, it's not true,' she pleads.

'I know, it's just not right, is it?' the woman continues. 'Had you been coming to Greta for a long time?'

Christina pauses. Should she tell her the truth?

'No, this was the first time.'

'Ah,' the woman nods. 'That's a shame, she was a wonderful person. You missed out there,' she says tearfully. 'I'm sorry,' she says.

Christina runs down the white tunnel. All life around her is dead, blanked out. Blindly she gets back in the truck. She can feel herself falling apart, coming away from her core, but not here, not here on her mother's pretty front lawn, among the gladiola bursting from their beds, with the sound of the birds chattering all around her.

LUKE

Something terrible has happened, he knows that. Luke drives back into town, glancing across at Christina. She's shaking so much she looks like she's going to have a convulsion. Cian is staring over at her. 'Mammy! What's wrong? Mammy!'

'Stop!' she orders suddenly, her voice raw and hard.

He pulls in off the road, the brakes squealing. She jumps out and runs over to a tree, where she bends down and vomits. He attempts to distract Cian, who's fidgeting nervously beside him.

As she gets back in, he leans across, touching her hand, and says softly, 'What happened?'

'Please, do you have any water?' she asks stiffly.

'Sure.' He hands her the bottle and she drinks half of it, wiping her mouth and pulling her cardigan around her shoulders as she pushes herself back against the seat. He waits for her to speak. She stares out of the windscreen, and says, flatly, 'She's dead.'

'Dead?' Luke repeats.

'Who's dead?' Cian asks.

'My mother, darling.'

'Angeline?' Cian asks.

'No, my real mother. She died yesterday. For fuck's sake, only yesterday...' Her voice peters out.

'So we don't get to meet her?'

'No.'

'Who was that woman you were talking to?' Luke asks.

338

'She was a neighbour. She told me.'

'Did you tell her who you were?'

'No!' Christina wails. 'How could I? What's the point any more?' She slams her hand down on the dashboard.

'Mammy, when are we going home?' Cian asks nervously. 'I want to see Daddy.'

She's unable to answer, just utters one desperate grunt, and then, closing her eyes, she brings her fists up to them. She looks as if she wishes to burrow them out.

'Okay,' Luke says, trying to think quickly, 'let's find somewhere we can rest and talk, okay?'

She nods, so he starts up the truck again and drives back into town, pulling into the first motel he sees.

They book a room up on the second floor. The building is bright blue, with pristine white doors and a wooden roof. It looks sunny and bright and cheerful. He follows her up the stairs and helps her open the door. She says nothing, going straight into the bathroom.

Luke puts down their bags and opens the balcony doors. Cian skips out and sits on one of the chairs, swinging his legs. Luke follows him. They look at the view of the inlet and the islands.

'Luke? Can we still go whale watching?'

'I'm not sure. We have to see what your mother thinks.' He glances over at the bathroom door; she's been in there a long time. They go back into the room and Cian climbs up onto one of the beds.

'Can I watch TV?'

'Sure.' Luke turns it on for him and switches to a cartoon channel. He ruffles his hair and the child smiles up at him. Then he goes over to the bathroom door and knocks. 'Christina? Christina, are you okay?'

He hears the click of the lock. He puts his hand on the knob, turns it and goes in.

Even her top is wet from the tears, so damp it's transparent. She pushes the door shut behind him. 'Cian can't see me like this,' she says hoarsely.

'Are you okay?' he asks.

She bends over double, shaking her head. 'It h-hurts,' she stutters.

He comes behind her and lifts her up straight. She looks right into him; they're so familiar now. He's never felt so close to anyone in his life.

'Luke,' she cries, 'what am I going to do?'

He starts to kiss her and she pushes her hands into his hair, pulling it loose out of the ponytail. She trails her fingers down the side of his face. He catches them and presses them to his mouth. Then it begins, slowly, irrevocably, neither of them unable to stop the motion of it. She's up close and he lifts her onto the bathroom counter, her damp shirt pressing into his chest. He closes his eyes, smells her, senses her, lets her whole being consume him. He looks at her again. Her eyes are luminous, speaking to him. They unbutton their jeans and he pulls hers off, so the blue lies crumbled on the ground. Then he closes his eyes again and he feels her wrap her legs about his waist. He lifts her off the counter and pushes up into her. She makes a tiny gasp. They're a perfect match.

340

THE STITCHES

When his mother was dying, Luke's father hadn't left the house, not for days. All the family came and went, but his mother continually had a ring around her, a golden circle of light. And it was his father who spun it, the children entering and leaving.

It was hard for Luke's mother to talk, and everyone took turns to sit beside her, hold her hand and whisper love words to her. Luke had a stool he liked to sit on at the end of the room, his mother's unfinished quilt wrapped around him as he watched his father attend to his mother. Each little task – helping her to drink, coaxing her to eat, changing the bed, helping her to the bathroom, ironing a fresh nightdress – was done with devotion. Luke watched his father in the sickroom and it was there he learned about love.

His parents belonged together. Not that life had been easy for them. His mother had been married before, when she was very young. Years later Gail had told him the story of how her first husband had beat her up and how she had lost a baby.

Luke's father had rescued her, and for that she stretched out the whole of her soul for him and stitched love into his life, thick, rich threads that would bind them forever. No wonder his father couldn't stay when she left this world. Maybe he had seen her there, out on the ocean where both their hearts belonged, and it had been just a matter of taking her hand and walking forwards. She had come back, just for a second, just for him.

Luke watched his parents and the secrets of their intimacy and

341

how, just hours before she passed away, his father was able to make his mother laugh.

The last words Luke's mother said to him were spoken as she let him hold her quilt up to her face so that she could rest her cheek against it and close her eyes.

The stitches are my days, she whispered, and some can be full of pain, some of joy. The quilt is my life, Luke, with all its pinpricks, broken threads and missed stitches, yet the whole of it is perfect, is it not?

It is, he whispered, hushed and still.

She opened her eyes and when he looked at her it was a gaze so powerful he felt it could transform him. Her brown eyes were deep wells. The love was all that was left as her body slowly became transparent. This was what she gave him.

CHRISTINA

They lie on the cold bathroom floor.

His hair is loose, falling over her face as he cradles her. She closes her eyes. She has travelled so far. So much has happened. And yet, for the first time in years she feels like she's retrieving herself.

Christina – the girl before her mother left, the girl who believed in life.

'Mammy!' Cian calls from the other room. They scramble up, but he stops her before she leaves the bathroom.

'Are you okay?' he says. 'Do you want to talk?'

'What is there to say?' she replies desperately, 'I came all this way to find my mother and now she's dead. It's over.'

'But what are you going to do now?'

She has her hand on the knob, but turns around and looks at him. 'I don't know, Luke. I just don't know.'

'You could come with me,' he says softly.

'I could? But what about Cian?'

'Him too. He'd like the island, there's lots of wildlife, and then...I could take you to Seattle...you could meet Sam.'

'But what about Declan?'

'How would he ever find you?'

'I don't know if it's right, taking Cian away from his father. And then there's Johnny. I'd be deserting him.'

'But what will happen if you go back, Christina?' Luke asks, his eyes penetrating her. She breathes in.

'I can't make a decision now,' she says hurriedly and leaves the room.

LUKE

Luke stays in the bathroom. He closes the door and stares at the mirror. She has rearranged him. He feels no anger now towards Teri and what she did to him. Not a trace. He turns on the shower and strips off again. Getting in and turning it full on and cold, he gasps, enjoying the rush of adrenalin. Everything is going to change.

He comes back out into the bedroom with a big fluffy towel around him. The TV is off and Christina is playing a card game with Cian.

'What are you playing?' he asks.

'Happy Families,' Christina sighs, and twists her head around to smile sadly up at him. He holds her gaze for a second, then walks over to the other side of the room, flicking on the coffeepot as he does so.

'Want a coffee?'

'That would be lovely,' she says, bending down over her cards. Luke watches them play. They speak almost in whispers, and as he turns, catching the afternoon shadows lengthening outside, everything seems completely still, as if the clock has stopped.

He gets dressed leisurely, savouring the peace in the room, the hushed voices of Christina and Cian as they play their game. Nothing is certain, he knows this, but despite their strange situation, Luke has faith in it. He knows that he and Christina were meant to meet. This is not fleeting.

'Let's go get something to eat,' he says.

Christina and Cian look up at the same time. Their eyes are identical.

'Okay,' she says. She's incredibly calm now. It surprises him, since she has just found out her mother is dead. Yet wasn't he calm too? All those years ago, when he was a little boy, everything had seemed crystal clear.

They walk into Tofino, Cian skipping ahead. He holds her hand and she says nothing, just squeezes his fingers. They go into Breakers' Deli and order giant burritos, sitting on stools, facing out onto the street, as they eat them. The place is busy with surfers and tourists. Cian is excited by the holiday atmosphere, jigging up and down, hardly able to eat.

Christina gets off her stool and leans towards him. He feels pulled to her. 'Thanks, Luke.' She puts her hands on his arm and he takes them, holds them tight, unable to reply.

From behind Luke senses movement, then Cian yells 'Granny Angel!' and shoots past him out onto the street.

Luke and Christina turn in unison. Cian is in the arms of a strange woman. She stares at them. She's not young, probably in her fifties. Streaks of grey run through her jet black hair. Her eyes widen as she looks at him. Christina pulls her hands away. He can hear her throat contract, her breath falling short.

The woman comes into the deli, Cian clinging to her side. Luke looks at Christina, but she won't look at him. She stands rigidly, staring at the dark woman.

'What are you doing here?' She speaks almost in a hiss.

The woman looks up, gives Christina a beautiful smile, then says, 'I came to find you, darling. I've been so worried.'

Then the woman looks at him again. Luke feels her taking him in, looking him up and down

'This is Luke,' Christina says tightly. 'He's my friend.'

'I see,' says the woman, managing to make him feel ashamed with

346

just two words.

'And this is Angeline, my stepmother,' Christina says, turning to Luke. He looks into Christina's eyes but she won't hold his gaze. He can feel her slipping away, retreating.

THE TEMPLE

She goes looking for Angeline. It's cold at the back of the house and Christina shivers as she walks away, turning just once to see her mother still sitting on the windowsill. Snow streaks behind her. Christina is desperate to get outside.

Angeline, she calls, knocking on her door. But there's no answer.

Angeline, she says again, quieter this time. She senses light and warmth so she pushes the door open. The curtains are closed but there are dozens of candles lit, their flames flickering. The room is full of a strange, powerful scent and smoke billows from a stick in a small golden pot.

Christina steps inside. She knows she isn't allowed to, but the smell entices her and the room is all golden and bright. It feels like the warmest place in the whole house. It feels welcoming.

Angeline, she whispers, but of course she knows that she isn't there.

There's a little table with an odd-looking picture on it. In fact, it isn't a picture at all but a piece of old yellow paper with black spidery writing on it. Christina knows what language it is – Japanese. Maybe it's *Nam Myoho Renge Kyo*, she thinks, the little poem Angeline has taught her. She likes singing it, it sounds nicer than the hymns she sings in church or the nursery rhymes in her books, and when she sings it it makes her see a picture of pretty little girls dancing all in a ring.

This room is magical. On the table is a little bell. Christina picks

348

it up and rings it. Beside it is a little red book full of the funny black writing, and lying on a pink silk scarf is a string of bright orange beads with white fluffy balls on the end of them. Christina picks them up and rubs them. The beads rub against her palms and tickle her.

Christina!

She whips around, and there is Angeline, standing in bare feet (are her toes not cold?), her black hair down, frowning.

I was looking for you, Christina mumbles.

You know that you're not allowed in my room, Angeline says, but when Christina looks up she can tell she isn't cross with her.

I like it in here, she says boldly. It feels like a temple.

Angeline laughs. And how do you know what a temple feels like? she asks.

I don't know, Christina blushes, feeling suddenly shy.

Come here, Angeline says, and Christina lets her mother's friend hug her. She sighs, breathes in her smell of lemon and garlic, different from her mammy but just as comforting. She squeezes Angeline tightly.

Hold on, she laughs again, you're sucking the life out of me!

Can we go outside and play in the snow? she asks.

Sure we can, Angeline says. I just need a minute to get changed. Why don't you go and put on another jumper and a scarf and I'll meet you outside in a minute?

Okay.

Christina leaves the room, turning to close the door silently behind her. She can still see the glowing aura through a chink, and then Angeline's back as she kneels down and picks up her orange beads.

Back down the landing she passes her mother again, but this time she doesn't look at her as she passes. She can see she's there, like a black stone, not moving, just her breath that she can hear, as steady as the spill of water from the mill outside. But Christina doesn't want to look at her now. She's more interested in the white falling sky and the icy splash of the river. She's yearning to make her mark on the garden, its spotless, clean surface as fresh as her open heart.

CHRISTINA

They stand outside the motel, with Angeline looking down from above, and say goodbye. He asked her if she would come with him, and now she has said no, she has to go home.

There's no more to say. She feels awkward, embarrassed with her stepmother staring at them. Luke is perplexed. But what can she do? He reaches out his hand, to touch her face, but she steps back. He shrugs then, shakes his head and slowly, tortuously, turns and walks away.

The last thing she sees of Luke is his arm — brown, strong, the elbow out the window on the driver's side. His truck goes around the corner and there's just silence echoing in her heart.

When she first saw Angeline standing outside the deli she'd been shocked, but then came the relief, an overwhelming sense of it, that now Angeline was here, she could take over and Christina wouldn't have to think for herself any more.

Wasn't that how it had always been? Hadn't she made such a mess of things when she tried otherwise?

Angeline comes down the stairs now, holding Cian by the hand. 'Let's go for a drive,' she suggests, watching Christina carefully.

Christina tosses her hair. 'Okay,' she says as casually as she can.

It's surreal to be sitting next to her stepmother in this huge American car, cruising down the street in the sun. They park and go into a small bookshop/café. It's late now and they're hungry again. They go out the back onto the deck, looking at the boats and seaplanes in the bay.

Was Luke down there, taking off, flying away from her, from everything he had started? She feels a surge of anger at him, at herself for letting it happen.

'What's wrong with you?' Angeline asks.

She picks up on everything, Christina thinks, looking at her sharp, fine nose, her endless eyes.

'What the hell do you think?' she snaps. 'How did you find me? How come you always have to ruin things?'

She's behaving like a surly teenager, but Christine can't control herself.

'I guessed you would come here,' she says, smiling her strange lopsided smile.

'But how did you know this was where my mother lived?'

'I've known for years, Christina,' Angeline says, running her tongue over her lips, then looking quickly down at her plate of spaghetti.

'What?'

All this time her stepmother has denied her this information. Christina wants to smack her, knock her on the ground, but she can't. Cian's here. She grips onto the sides of her chair, unable to eat, unable to speak.

'Granny?' Cian pipes up, chewing a large oatmeal cookie.

'Yes, darling?'

'Are you still my granny?'

'Of course I am.'

'Good.' He stuffs the rest of the cookie in his mouth.

Angeline glances over towards Christina, then continues, picking up Cian's sticky hands and flicking crumbs off them. 'And we're all going to go home together, tomorrow,' she says.

'Back to Ireland?' Cian asks slowly.

'Yes.'

'But we never went to Luke's island, we never went to see the

352

whales,' Cian whines.

'Another time, Cian,' Angeline says. He looks downcast for a moment and then, peering back inside the shop, he flits to a new subject. 'Mammy, can I go inside and look at the books?'

'Yes, sure. Just don't go out the front of the shop.' She gives him a squeeze and a peck on the cheek before he skips off, oblivious of the tension between the two women.

Angeline puts down her fork, pushes the unfinished food away and crosses her hands on her lap. Christina can't help studying her face, how familiar it is, each contour, every line. Yet Angeline looks different here, younger maybe, without the backdrop of The Mill and Daddy.

'Padraig Kennedy came round and told us everything.'

'Oh.'

'Yes, "oh".' She sounds like a schoolteacher, thinks Christina.

Angeline continues, 'I couldn't understand how you could have got hold of the money for the plane tickets. Well, then Padraig showed up explained it all. When he heard that you had snatched Cian and run off, his conscience obviously got the better of him.'

Christina gets up, walks over to the railings and looks down at the small sandy cove. Her stomach churns and she feels dizzy and confused.

Why is it that she's always defending herself to Angeline? It was Angeline who should be explaining herself; it was she who should be sorry.

'I know what you did.' Christina turns around sharply, spitting the words out, eyeing Angeline.

'What on earth do you mean?' Angeline asks wearily, staring back blankly.

'I know that you drove her away.'

For once Angeline looks shocked, lost for words. 'No, it wasn't like that,' she murmurs.

353

'What did you do? Cast a spell on my father to make him want you and turn him against my mother?'

'I never wanted her to go into that place,' Angeline says quietly.

'What place?'

'St Finian's. That wasn't my idea, it was your father's family. They put such pressure on him. In those days, people didn't know what to do when something like that happened. That's why they hid people away, because of the shame.'

Christina takes a step back and holds onto the railing. What is she talking about? 'What are you telling me?' she asks shakily.

'That your mother never actually walked out on you, Christina.' Angeline flicks her dark eyes towards her and then looks away. 'She was put into a hospital, initially for a few weeks, but she never got better…and so, well, during that time your father and I got together. It's no one's fault what happened in the end.'

Her mother had been committed. She had travelled all this way to accuse this poor woman of deserting her when it wasn't even true.

Her throat is dry and she's unable to speak. She shakes her head uselessly.

Angeline gets up and puts a cold hand on her arm. 'And then she came to me. Your mother escaped from St Finian's and arrived at the house one afternoon. I knew that Tomás's family would have him lock her up again, so I helped her escape.'

'I can't believe Daddy would do that.'

'Just because he's your father, Christina, it doesn't make him better than he is. Tomás honestly thought that Greta was unwell at that time. He brought her to the hospital because he believed it was the best thing to do. Your father is a simple man. He was completely overwhelmed by what happened to Greta. He tried to visit her at first, but he couldn't cope with what he saw. She changed so much. So he shut down. Your father was afraid of the truth. He's still afraid to look inside himself.'

354

'So why did you stay?' Christina turns viciously on her. 'Why did you stick around with him all these years?'

'For you,' she says simply, looking deep into her eyes so that Christina knows it's true.

Christina pulls away and looks out at the inlet, the azure sea and the small green mound of an island across the way. 'Why does she have to be dead?' She drags her hands through her hair. 'I've travelled all this way, so that…so that I could finally stand before her and say I forgive you. That's what I wanted to say.'

'You never had to forgive Greta,' Angeline says by her side. 'It's me you have to forgive'

They look at the ocean together in silence. A seaplane is preparing for take-off and they watch the passengers board before it slowly taxis across the water, gradually picking up speed and lifting up into the sky. The air smells different here, thinks Christina. At home you can smell the earth, hide somewhere, create an enclave, but here everything is as open as the big sky, bright and exposed. It's impossible to conceal her feelings.

She hears the patter of feet behind her on the deck. 'Mammy!'

'Yes, darling?' She turns round to Cian. He's hopping from foot to foot clutching another Dr Seuss book. This is just one big adventure for him, thinks Christina.

'Mammy, can I have this book?'

'No, sweetie.'

'I'll get it for him,' Angeline says, taking the book and going back into the shop.

'Thank you, Granny!' Cian spins on the spot, then hops over towards Christina. 'Mammy,' he says, reaching up towards her, and even though he's big now, she still picks him up. 'Are we going home?' He presses his cheek to her face.

'Do you want to go home?' she asks him.

'I don't know.' He pauses, then squeezing her arm with his fingers, says, 'Only if you can come and live with us again. I want to be with you.'

She sits down, still holding Cian. He wraps his legs around her waist and squeezes her tight. She can feel his skinny chest pushed against hers, the quick beat of his heart.

Christina gives in to the hug, inhales his breath on her skin and embraces his need. She could hide forever inside the love of her son.

Darling Christina,

Happy birthday! I hope you like the card. It's by a local artist and is called Salmonberries. *Of course you don't get those in Ireland, but when they come out every year it's the most wonderful aroma. They're delicious and they make me think of you as the berries come out, just before your birthday.*

And so you're eighteen! It's hard to believe that so much time has passed since I last saw you. I've been writing to you all these years, darling, because I want you to know that not a day has passed when I haven't thought of you. I'm sure that you've often wondered why I left in the first place, but it's such a terrible tale that I felt I couldn't write to you about this when you were a child. It's a story I feel your father should tell you. He was there and he knows what happened, and now that you're an adult it's up to him to tell you the truth.

I often wonder if you've ever received any of these letters. Am I writing to no one? Will these words be cast aside, burned, destroyed before they ever reach your eyes? I pray not. I would prefer to believe that you read every one of my letters and chose not to reply rather than you never saw them at all. At least you would know then that I love you still and that I'll always be here for you, Christina, whenever you need me.

You're a young woman now, and it excites me to think what possibilities there are for your life. Always follow your dreams. I know that sounds corny, but so few of us actually fulfil our calling in one lifetime, and you know we all have one. For me, I'm just beginning to discover what I should do. I've opened up a small healing spa here in our house in Tofino and at the moment I only have a couple of clients but I enjoy the work so much. For once I feel like I'm doing something worthwhile.

Henry's still fishing. Oh, it's an awful stink when he comes into my sweet-smelling house! Remember that whenever you feel ready to come and visit, just let me know. I don't have much, but I always have enough set aside to send you the fare. It will be a surprise for my husband that I have such a wonderful secret to share with him — you!

Oh Christina, I could write to you forever, ask you so many questions. What do you look like now? What do you like doing? Do you have a boyfriend? Are you going to college? Is your father with Angeline? Do you remember her? Is she still there with you and Tomás? I would love to know the answers to all these questions and more, so please, darling, find it in your heart to forgive me and write.

I think this will be the last letter I send you. If you decide not to contact me then I must accept your choice that you don't want to be a part of me. Just remember, darling, that as far as I'm concerned you always have a home, right here with me.

*   With lots of love,*
*   Your mother, Greta*

CHRISTINA

It's no longer blank, the canvas of her mother. Christina lies in bed listening to her son's breath. She has the cotton reel in her hands, some of the hair wound round one finger, and she moves it back and forth between finger and spool. She watches the reel on her belly spinning and glinting as first light creeps across the room. She sinks into the past. They are the halcyon days, when she was very little in The Mill.

What can she gather up?

Her mother trying to manage Christina's hair, their two faces side by side looking into the dusty mirror. She remembers her mother's long, pale oval face with straight orange hair and Christina's cherry-shaped face, still babyish, with the cute rings and curls that her mother always failed to plait.

They're in the local shop and her mother is wearing a pair of white trousers. Christina stands right by her, her arm wrapped around her leg, tight, and sucking her thumb. She's cleaving to her side; she remembers the feeling of never wanting to be separated.

Making daisy chains. It's summer and they're sitting on the front lawn at The Mill and her mother is wearing a red dress. They're barefoot. It's hot, unusual, and she remembers her mother putting a small blue and yellow hat on her head. They're talking, her mother telling her about when she was a little girl and going with her father to watch a foal being born. Her grandfather was a vet.

She remembers now that her mother was a lover of animals, wild

359

and tame. She had befriended a small sparrow and she only told Christina this. Not even her daddy knew. In the spare bedroom at the back of the house Christina's mother had made a little nest for the bird on the windowsill, and together, in secret, the two of them would creep into the room, watch the bird busy about its home and scatter a few crumbs on the ledge. Once or twice Christina had watched the bird step onto her mother's hand and cock its head at her.

Her mother never shared the view that foxes were pests. She remembers her gently explaining that when the fox killed the kittens it was the law of nature. She hated to see the men go after it with their guns.

And there she is, little girl Christina sitting on her mother's lap, her mother's arms wrapped about her, her cheek pressed close on hers. She can see her eyes sparkling, feel the beat of her heart. Her mother is patting her knees in a steady rhythm and Christina is singing, *Whiz, whir, whiz, whir.* They're making the cotton reel song.

Christina's mother loved her. There's no denying it.

She closes her eyes. In the pale dusk of her mind she sees another picture. Her mother now, older, the flare of her hair faded. She's smaller. She sees her in the water, her little boat tipping over, her body popping out and hands trying to grab each other, big man hands, and hers, Christina's hands. She can see her own hands trying to pull her mother up. Christina's wedding ring is a tiny drop of gold in all the blue swirling mass of the Pacific Ocean. It's the same colour as her mother's hair. She watches the last strand swirl away, like a piece of electric seaweed. And she's gone. Her hands failed to grasp her, and she has lost her mother all over again, this time forever.

Christina shudders. She's suddenly cold. She gets out of bed and puts on a sweater, then sits on the sheet, cross-legged, looking at Cian as he sleeps.

Luke is gone.

360

She can still feel the imprint of his hand on the small of her back. He has made a small opening, a tunnel back down inside her heart. She has such an urge to see him now, just talk, just be together.

The shadows shift outside her door. There's someone out there. She waits for the knock, then slides off the bed. Maybe it's Luke?

But she knows that isn't his way, and when she opens the door she isn't surprised to see Angeline standing there, still in her nightclothes, a large green cardigan hanging off her shoulders, holding a suitcase in one hand.

'What are you doing up at this hour?' Christina asks impatiently.

'I wanted to speak to you,' Angeline whispers, glancing over at Cian. 'Before Cian wakes up…before the day starts.'

She walks into the room, uninvited, dragging the case behind her.

'What if I don't want to talk to you?' Christina replies churlishly, pushing back her hair.

'Put the kettle on please,' her stepmother replies crisply, ignoring her last comment and leaving the bag on the floor beside Cian's bed. She goes over to the porch doors, slides them back and steps out onto the balcony.

Jesus! Christina thinks to herself, flicking on the coffeepot and pulling out two cups. Why can't she just leave me alone?

'It's cold,' Angeline says, shivering and pulling her cardigan tight across her breasts as Christina comes out with the tea. 'But very beautiful.'

The bustling bay still sleeps and a hypnotic fog hangs over the sea. Christina says nothing, just sips the hot bitter tea and stares past her stepmother at the still landscape, hoping to let it swallow her, leave her dispassionate, detached, uncaring.

'I had to talk to you,' Angeline says. 'I couldn't sleep. All night I was thinking about Greta. She was my best friend, you know.'

'You wouldn't have thought so!'

Angeline turns on her; her dark eyes are fierce. 'How could you

361

possibly understand the kind of relationship I had with Greta? You never had a sister.'

'But she wasn't your sister,' Christina counters weakly.

'As good as. I don't think you've ever shared the intimacy I had with Greta with another woman. Have you?'

Christina says nothing. She kicks a small blue stone off the balcony and watches it drop onto the grass below.

Angeline is right.

But who's fault is that? She was always so cosseted by her father and Angeline, then pushed into marriage as soon as she left school. She'd made friends with other mums, but nothing close. She had never confided in anyone – until she met Luke.

'We immediately hit it off. The first day of school, we were next to each other in the dorm.' Angeline smiles and her features soften. 'Your mother was such an innocent. That was why I loved her. You could tell her anything and she'd believe you. I could be rather wicked to her sometimes. I remember once we were walking from the church to the main school building and it was lashing rain, and your mother had an umbrella and I didn't have one, and I told her that if my hair got wet it would turn green, so she gave me her umbrella. She was worried I would be embarrassed of my green hair! I didn't think she'd really believe me, but she did, bless her! I felt bad when she got a cold.'

'You were always a bitch then, were you?' She can't help it. It makes her angry that Angeline knew her mother, that she could tell her things about her.

'Do you really enjoy saying such things, Christina?' Angeline pauses and looks at her closely. Christina shrugs her shoulders, says nothing. 'It was just a prank. There's no need to be so melodramatic, Christina. Greta always forgave me.'

'I'm sure she never forgave you for stealing her husband and her child.' Christina feels the cold hurt slide down her throat as she says the words. This is what it comes down to, doesn't it?

'It's not that simple, and you know it,' Angeline sighs 'I don't want to argue with you any more. What's the point of hurting each other?'

Christina shrugs again and tries to look nonchalant, but she can feel a lump in her throat, her eyes tight and wide.

'I was awake all night, trying to work out what your mother would want me to do.'

It's on the tip of Christina's tongue to pass another cutting remark, like 'It's too late for that now' or 'As if you'd really care', but she bites it back, suddenly feeling like a difficult teenager.

Her stepmother cradles her tea, sips it and then speaks again.

'And I've come to a decision,' she says, her voice steady and clear. 'I don't think you should come back.'

Christina gulps down the hot tea, opening her eyes to the early morning light. Surely she didn't hear right?

'I don't know what you mean.'

'I mean what I say. Stay.'

Christina stares at her stepmother. She seems smaller to her now, shorter and thinner, and with her dark hair and the green cardigan wrapped about her, she looks almost native. Christina notices she has no shoes on, just a pair of large woolly grey socks. She looks down at her feet and is almost afraid to speak.

'Here?'

How can she stay?

Angeline walks over to one of the sun loungers and sits down, pulling her cardigan even tighter about her. She shivers and gazes past Christina at the sea behind, its promise of eternity.

'Yes,' she says so softly that Christina can hardly hear. 'Greta and Henry had no other children. That house should be yours. Make your claim and stay, meet the people who knew Greta, learn about your mother's life.'

'I can't do that.' Christina's voice shrinks to a squeak.

'I think Greta would want it.' Angeline looks straight at her. She smiles. Christina looks away.

'How could you possibly know that?' she says tightly.

'Because she was my friend.'

Christina walks over to the balustrade and leans on it. Her head is spinning and the fear is still there, in her like a bitter taste in her mouth. 'But…didn't you come here to bring me back? What about the others? Daddy, and Declan, and Johnny…' She trails off.

'They don't know that I've found you, and I can tell them you weren't here. I can say Greta is gone.'

Christina turns around and looks at Angeline. She has folded her hands on her lap and still smiles at her. Christina can tell that she has made up her mind.

'But why?'

'Because now is my chance to make the right choice.'

The light is breaking through the fog. It illuminates the view behind Angeline's head, a stretch of blue sea and a gathering of cedar trees. Christina can sense the town stirring, boats starting up, her anxiety rising.

'I have something for you,' Angeline says. She takes a handkerchief from her sleeve and blows her nose, then walking over to the case, she pulls it down on the ground and, kneeling before it, clicks it open. Christina looks in. The case is full of paper, piles and piles of envelopes, some written in black pen, some in blue and red, and all written by the same hand. And all of them, every single one, addressed to Miss Christina Comyn, The Mill, Oldcastle, County Meath, Republic of Ireland.

There are hundreds of letters.

'These belong to you,' Angeline says, stepping back. 'They're from your mother. She wrote to you every week until you were eighteen, and then I suppose she just gave up. I could never find the right time to give them to you.'

Christina bends down as if in slow motion. Her knees feel incredibly stiff, her body like lead. She picks one of the letters up and turns it over. Her mother's address in Tofino is written on the back. The letter is unopened. She picks up another and another. They're all the same – sealed. Each sheaf of paper inside is a particle of her blood mother. Her hands shake. She's too frightened to open even one.

She looks up at Angeline, her dark skin strangely flushed, and feels a wave of compassion for her stepmother, that she would covet these letters and hide them from her. And every week another one would pop through the letterbox, reminding Angeline that her own motherhood was an illusion. Greta would never let go.

ALONE

Now the room is locked.

Christina knows where the key is. She takes off her shoes, climbs on the broad window ledge next to the door, and then, on her tippy toes, she reaches around for the key. It's slipped behind the lintel. She has seen Angeline put it there many times.

The handle is a little stiff, but then suddenly it snaps open. Even standing on the threshold is different. Christina immediately feels disappointed.

Where has the temple gone?

Everything is missing. The bed is made up tightly with brown blankets and the little bedside table is bare apart from an old lamp. Even the crucifix is back up on the wall.

Christina walks around, opening the drawers of the dresser and the doors of the wardrobe, but they're all empty. She goes over to the window. It's jammed shut, the thick white paint peeling off the woodwork, the corners of the panes thick with cobwebs. She looks at the river below. How green it is. She can see thick emerald reeds running through it, pushed forwards by the current. They make the water look like soup.

She peels some paint off the wood. What will she do now? She's so bored.

And then, in the window, she can see a reflection of herself, and behind her, the bed and something else.

She turns and runs across the room, bending down and looking under the bed. There's a case.

Christina pulls it out. She sees a brown cardboard label and she reads it.

Angeline Mahony, 64a Station Road, Harrow, Middlesex, England

She tries to open it. It's heavy and stiff, but she doesn't give up.

Inside is her treasure – all the colour she has desired since her mother left.

There is Angeline's pink scarf and her scarlet dress and all the little gold pots. There's even a packet of the smelly sticks. Christina takes one out and smells it. It reminds her of last year, and the snow.

Right at the bottom of the case is the paper with the Japanese writing tied up in a roll and the little red book and orange beads. Why has Angeline put all these things away?

And suddenly it comes to her. Maybe she's leaving too. And the thought of that is so terrible that Christina feels like being sick.

She has to stop her.

CHRISTINA

'Christina, it's important that you understand something.' Angeline stops and looks up at the canopy of green that hangs above them. They're in the rainforest, walking back in time, sheltered by heavy damp swathes of trees, cut off from the open sea. Cian is ahead of them on the boardwalk. They follow him as he skips along the trail's languorous curve, a large figure of eight, which crosses over the highway and plunges straight back into the rainforest on the other side. Angeline is wearing a large straw hat. Light filters through its weave, freckling her face, reflecting soft olive shadows onto her skin.

'Do you remember what you said to me when we first met, when you were very little?'

Christina shakes her head. 'No,' she says, placing her hand on a stump of damp moss, then bending down to finger a large flat fern.

'You were in your bedroom, playing with that beautiful dollhouse your father made you. I came and said hello, and do you know what you did?' Christina watches her smile at the memory. 'You turned right around and looked me up and down, then you skipped towards me and took my hand, just like that, and you said, "You're my mother." It wasn't a game. You chose me, Christina, and that was why I vowed I would always look after you.'

'But I loved my own mother. When she went, I wanted her. I didn't want you, you never replaced her.' It's the truth. Christina can't spare her.

'Of course I didn't, though at the time I thought I could.'

Angeline walks on. Christina looks at Cian up ahead, twisting and jumping. She moves forward. She doesn't want to lose sight of him. 'I can see now how wrong I was,' Angeline says. 'You've always had the two of us. We were all connected. That's why you should stay here. You should discover her again.'

'But it's too late now.'

'Of course it isn't, your life is only just beginning.' To her surprise, Angeline picks up her hand and squeezes it. She doesn't let go.

'But how will I survive? What about money?'

'I'll help you out, and you'll find a job, a way of making a living. It will be good for you.' She smiles at Christina.

'But why have you always made me feel like I was useless then?'

Angeline looks shocked. Her dark eyes open wide. 'I've always believed in you, Christina, and here you look different to me...you *are* different.' She puts her hands on Christina's shoulders and a band of panic moves across Christina's chest.

'But what about Johnny? I can't desert him. And what about Declan?'

'Johnny needs time, and when you've done what you need to do here, contact him. He'll forgive you. You of all people should know that.'

'I don't know...' What is it she's really afraid of?

'Whatever you choose will be hard. It's the risk you have to take. But if you come home now, Declan will take Cian away. He's very angry.'

Christina imagines this – the supervised access, the biting loneliness she had endured the past couple of months, just waiting for it to change and the change never coming.

'But Johnny...he'll hate me, blame me for everything that goes wrong in his life, like I hated my mother...'

'Like you had begun to hate me.' The grief in her stepmother's voice resonates through her.

Christina looks at Angeline. She's small and dark, but her force is like an arrowhead. In her life, and in her mother's, Angeline has had the ability to propel them forwards into the unknown. Christina fingers the cotton reel in her pocket. She can feel the fine threads of hair unravelling.

It's true; they're connected. This feeling floods Christina, that she always had a mother, and that she was Angeline.

'No,' she says meekly. 'I loved you too much.' The force of her revelation knocks her back and she squats on the boardwalk, shaking, unbelievably sad. 'I thought my mother left because she believed I preferred you to her.'

Angeline squats down opposite her and looks deep in her eyes. Christina can see her love, unconditional, constant.

'I always thought it was my fault,' Christina mutters.

'Oh, Christina!' Angeline's voice breaks, and for the first time in her life Christina sees her stepmother cry. She's never seen such a thing. It's like the shattering of glass.

HOME

Luke always lost the kelp game. But when he ran home crying to his mother, she would tell him not to cry. 'Go out and cut more spears and get back in the game,' she always said.

It had happened so fast, her illness. No one had told him until right at the end, and he found it hard to believe how quickly the life could drain out of someone. His mother had always been so strong. He remembered her hands, quick, light, but muscular, and how they would always be busy, cooking or sewing. That was her favourite occupation. Her sewing machine was her most prized possession.

There were times in Gail's house when he thought he was in a dream and soon he would wake up. He would be back at home, sitting on a stool, watching his mother make quilts and his father make the tiny dug-out canoes he would sell for forty dollars apiece to the tourists. Of course they couldn't be dead.

Luke remembered the day his father told him they would make a proper dug-out canoe, the real thing. It was just before his mother got sick. There had been lots of talk then in the village of reviving the old traditions, and his parents and grandfather had all been part of it.

Luke loved to play with the tiny tourist canoes. His father was able to paint intricate little designs on them. Luke liked to try to identify the different animals and which tribe they belonged to – deer, whale, thunderbird, bear.

Both his parents lived on in him; Luke knew the truth of this. But little Luke still needed to grieve and he knew that this could only be so when he went back to the island. When his feet hit the soil of his homeland he would at last be free.

CHRISTINA

It's afternoon now and Christina is in the sky. They're flying so close to the ground, she feels as if she could jump it. The noise of the small plane and their headphones makes it impossible to speak. She grabs Cian's arm as the plane circles a gathering of sea lions sunbathing on a small crop of rocks.

They skim over the islands, the forest verdant and dense, then out to open sea. The water is a mixture of shades of red and green. It takes on a quality she's never experienced before, so vibrant you would hardly believe it could be real. Suddenly the pilot points his finger and she follows the direction, looking out to her right.

A whale.

Cian has already seen it. He bounces up and down in his seat, rubbing his hands with glee and flashing his bright eyes at her. They're right above it now. It's splendid, seamlessly flowing through the ocean, every now and again water shooting out of its blowhole. It has a rhythm of its own, a majestic, indifferent pace.

It was Cian who wanted to take the seaplane to Luke's island. She had been unsure but was finally swayed by the fact that it took only fifteen minutes, compared to nearly two hours by boat. Now that she's made her decision, she doesn't want any time to reflect. She just wants to get there and see Luke again.

She should be frightened. The plane is tiny and they're so fragile – a molecule of metal above the vast Pacific. But this isn't how she feels. She looks out the cabin window at the iridescent stretch of the horizon, its limitless possibilities. She surrenders herself to the moment and sees an eagle swoop down to the sea's surface, plucking from it its silver prey, water sprinkling the air, reflecting a thousand parts of herself.

ACKNOWLEDGMENTS

I'm deeply grateful for those of my friends and family who read early drafts of this book, gave me great support and feedback and also helped me with elements of the research: Kate Pengelly, Fintan Blake Kelly, Thérèse Dalton, Donna Ansley, Stephen Sibley, Monica McInerney, Eileen Blishen and Bernie McGrath. Many thanks to Anabel Lyon and Anakana Scofield, who helped me immensely with the Pacific side of the book, to my wonderful editors Alison Walsh, Imogen Taylor and Kristin Jensen and all at Tivoli in Ireland and Pan Macmillan in England, especially Michael Gill and Trisha Jackson. Thank you to my agent Marianne Gunn O'Connor for her unerring support and dynamic vision.

The book has been very much inspired by the writings of Peter Webster, a First Nation Canadian, and from reading his book, *As Far As I Know: Reminiscences of an Ahousat Elder,* I was able to write about native traditions and stories particular to the Nuu-chah-nulth. I hope that I have written about these traditions with the appropriate sensitivity and respect. Joanne Streetly's book *Paddling Through Time* was hugely influential in helping me plan Greta and Henry's journey and gave me a wonderful inspiration for that part of the book. *Salt in Our Blood: An Anthology of Westcoast Moments,* edited by Joanne Streetly, was another fascinating resource, as was the Museum of Northwest Art in La Conner and the work of the artist Morris Graves. Thanks also to Dale Irvine for house swapping with me and providing me with the chance to explore the Pacific North-West.

The gorgeous B&B is based on Seacroft B&B By-the-Sea in Victoria, run by my good friend, Ginny Youens. There is also a mention of Kraft Kaffee in Oldcastle, run by Kathleen O'Reilly, who has provided a tiny haven for me lately.

Áine Tubridy's books *When Panic Attacks* and *Going Mad?* provided me with great insight into exploring both Christina's and Greta's situations. *Buddhism of the Sun*, compiled by Jim Cowan, was a helpful source for Angeline's Buddhism. The music of Damien Rice was a prime inspiration for the mood of the book. I'm extremely grateful for his permission to use lyrics from the track 'Cold Water' from his album O. Irish artist Kathy Prenderghast's piece *The End and the Beginning II* was the inspiration for the cotton reel metaphor, and the passage 'The Stitches' was inspired by concepts explored by Oldcastle artist Aoife Curran. What Luke sees and imagines as pictures is very much inspired by the soulful work of American artist Ashley O'Neal.

This book is dedicated to my mother, Claire, who died during the time I was working on it. I'm forever grateful for all the gifts she has given me in this life and I'm constantly inspired by her spirit. My humble thanks to Barry Ansley, who has been my 'tree' during this difficult time, and to his patience and support while I disappeared for hours, writing. Thank you to all my friends and family – my stepfather Roger, my stepsisters Liz and Carolyn, their children and my aunts, uncles and cousins as well as Barry's family and of course my brother Fintan – for their love and support. Last but certainly not least, thank you to my stepdaughter Helena, who helped me to see through the eyes of the young Christina, and to Corey, my son, for his wonderful insight into Cian's world.